BRIDES
OF ROME

A NOVEL OF
⊹THE VESTAL VIRGINS⊹

BRIDES
OF ROME

DEBRA MAY MACLEOD

**BLACK
STONE**
PUBLISHING

Printed in the United States of America

First edition: 2020
ISBN 978-1-09-400024-4
Fiction / Historical / Ancient

1 3 5 7 9 10 8 6 4 2

CIP data for this book is available
from the Library of Congress

Blackstone Publishing
31 Mistletoe Rd.
Ashland, OR 97520

www.BlackstonePublishing.com

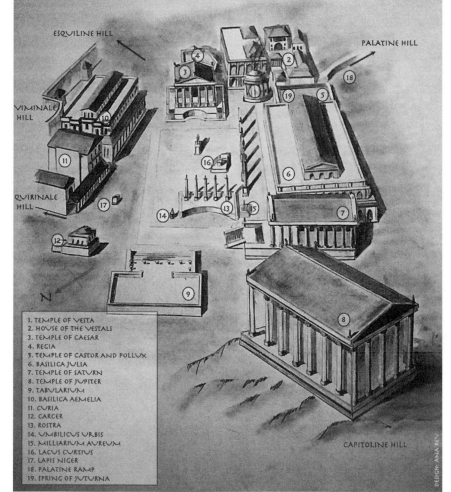

FORVM ROMANVM
-AREA SACRA OF VESTA-

ESQVILINE HILL

PALATINE HILL

VIMINALE HILL

QVIRINALE HILL

N

CAPITOLINE HILL

DESIGN: ANA REY

1. TEMPLE OF VESTA
2. HOVSE OF THE VESTALS
3. TEMPLE OF CAESAR
4. REGIA
5. TEMPLE OF CASTOR AND POLLVX
6. BASILICA JVLIA
7. TEMPLE OF SATVRN
8. TEMPLE OF JVPITER
9. TABVLARIVM
10. BASILICA AEMELIA
11. CVRIA
12. CARCER
13. ROSTRA
14. VMBILICVS VRBIS
15. MILLIARIVM AVREVM
16. LACVS CVRTIVS
17. LAPIS NIGER
18. PALATINE RAMP
19. SPRING OF JVTVRNA

AUTHOR'S NOTE

At the front of this book, you'll find a simplified illustration of the Roman Forum and the structures mentioned in the story.

At the back, I have included a dramatis personae, or cast of characters. You'll also find other reader-friendly resources there, including the names of the gods and mythical figures mentioned in the book, a glossary of Latin and other important terms, and several illustrations that tie into the story line and that I think you'll find fascinating.

Thank you for reading.

PROLOGUE

The Campus Sceleratus
The "Evil Field" just inside the city walls of Rome

113 BCE

Licinia tasted sour vomit threatening to rise in her throat. The green cypress trees that dotted the landscape and the blue sky overhead swam in and out of her field of vision as she struggled to maintain her balance. She swallowed hard, but her mouth was dry with the thick summer heat and her own stark terror. It felt like a blade was piercing the back of her throat.

A blade. She had prayed to the goddess for a blade. Even criminals and gladiators met death by the quick work of a sword or dagger, yet she, a revered priestess of Vesta, was denied that mercy. Her guards had been as kind to her as their station permitted, yet not one of them had dared to smuggle a blade into her room, no matter how much she begged.

Not one of them had risked providing her with what she needed to end her suffering at once, even when in her most panic-stricken moments she had offered to dishonor herself and her virginal service to the goddess by pleasuring them, however they wanted her to do it, in exchange for even the dullest of kitchen knives.

No doubt they had seen her supposed lover flayed alive in the Forum.

Red spots of blood soaked through the white linen of the *stola* that clung to her body, the scourge gashes on her back once again opening. The *Pontifex Maximus* took her arm and pulled her toward a gaping black hole in the ground.

Around it stood several somber priests and two of her fellow Vestals, the docile Flavia and the duteous chief Vestal Tullia, their eyes moist and their palms up in supplication to the goddess.

The black hole was at her feet now. Licinia looked down into the void and felt a rancid mist of cold, dank air rise from its depths and cling to her face. At once gripped by terror and filled with a macabre fascination, she blinked at the blackness. She could just barely make out the first rung of a ladder that extended down, all the way down, to the pitch-black end of her life.

"*Protege me, Dea!*" she heard herself cry out. Goddess, protect me!

"Mother Vesta goes with you."

It was Tullia who had spoken. It was against custom for her to speak to a Vestal condemned to death for *incestum*—breaking her vow of chastity—but the Pontifex Maximus was in no mood to remind the austere *Vestalis Maxima* of decorum. This ugly business would be finished soon, but he still had to work with her. No point making matters worse.

The chief priest stepped back and nodded gravely to the executioner, a war-torn Hercules of a man whose body took up the space of two men. He hesitated for a moment—this was a *priestess of Vesta* after all—and then extended an uncertain hand toward her, urging her to descend the ladder and praying to Mars that she would go willingly.

She rounded on him suddenly. "Do not touch me," she spat. "I serve the immaculate goddess."

He pulled back his hand.

"You have served the goddess well," said the Vestalis Maxima. "May you continue to do so."

Licinia felt her throat tighten, but she inhaled sharply to stop the tears. She looked at Tullia's face, expressionless in the glaring sunshine, and then gathered the bottom of her stola in one arm, holding the drapery aside so that she could descend the ladder without tripping on it.

She slipped one sandaled foot into the black void and felt the cool, clammy air envelop the bare skin of her foot and shin. A chill ran up her spine as her foot found the top rung in the blackness. Her other foot followed. She stepped down to the second rung, feeling the raw wounds on her lashed back tug and bleed anew. She stepped down again. The black dirt was at eye level now, and her fingers were stained with soil as she clung to the earth. To life.

It was so strange to be at this angle: staring at the sandaled feet of people who, when this duty was done, would ride back to Rome in their litters, with fresh air still in their lungs, to continue with their day— talking, eating, sleeping, and waking in the morning to the light of dawn. How foreign and impossible those things seemed to her at this moment.

Her body immersed to the neck in Hades, Licinia turned her eyes away. She didn't want her last image to be the crookedly tied sandals of a priest. What idiot slaves he must have. Either that or they secretly despised their master.

She peeled her eyes open wide, hungry for light as she descended the ladder, rung after rung, into the ever-blackening pit until her feet landed on solid ground. She looked up. The opening to the world above looked like the disk of a full moon shimmering white against the black sky.

Licinia's heart pounded so hard that her chest and back ached from the pressure. She couldn't take a deep breath: it was as though a tight band had been wrapped around her upper body. She stood like a statue in the dark, feeling the spindly legs of an unseen insect scurry over her foot, and terrified to look around her. That would make it all too real. And she wasn't ready for that yet.

The ladder moved upward quickly—too quickly for her to grab onto it. She watched it rise and then disappear into the glaring lightness above and, a moment later, saw a basket descending to her on a long rope. She reached up to catch it in her arms and then removed the items before those above could remove the basket as quickly as they had the ladder.

A round loaf of bread. A small amphora of water. An oil lamp that burned with a small but steady flame.

As she stared into the flame, she heard a grating sound from above and felt soft earth fall onto her veiled head. Her tomb was being sealed.

She looked up. The full moon above gave way to a half-moon, and then to a crescent as the last sliver of light disappeared and she was left with only her pounding fear and the flickering flame. Tullia was right.

Vesta was with her. The Vestalis Maxima would have undoubtedly lit the oil lamp with the sacred flame from the temple.

She cradled the small oil lamp in her palm and turned around slowly, as if sensing a ghost standing behind her, to look around the silent, black pit.

The pit was larger than she had expected and more or less rectangular, with smooth dirt walls. A few steps to her left stood a small couch and on the ground in front of it—Licinia cried out—a *body*!

It was dressed in a fine stola similar to her own, but that lay disheveled and rotten against decayed flesh and exposed bone. The arms and legs were splayed, and the skull was visible, as was a patch of straggly, long hair. The mouth was open.

Feeling the blood leave her head, Licinia slowly lowered herself to her knees. If she fainted—and she was close to it—she would drop the oil lamp and her only source of light would be lost.

She inhaled a few breaths of the stagnant air and felt it stick in her nostrils like a foul film.

Something caught her eye, and she glanced to her right. Lying against the dirt wall were two more bodies. These were arranged in a more dignified state, their decaying stolas wrapped carefully, respectfully, around them and their veils covering their faces. Dry bone was visible through the fabric.

The chief Vestal's words echoed in Licinia's head. *You have served the goddess well. May you continue to do so.*

Setting the oil lamp gently on the dirt floor, she crept toward the splayed body of the Vestal. She gently put her hands around the bony arms and folded them across the torso and then drew in the decomposed legs.

Gingerly she pulled the old, delicate fabric around the body, doing her best in the dim light to wrap the Vestal with dignity. Once done, she rolled the body until it lay restfully against the other priestesses. Lastly, she covered the dead Vestal's face with the age-yellowed linen of her veil.

Licinia moved with purpose back to where she had set the water and bread, carrying them to the oil lamp and sitting cross-legged in front of it. She tore a small piece of bread from the fresh loaf and held it above the oil lamp, sprinkling crumbs into the flame.

"Mother Vesta, your humble priestess, who has served you these fifteen years with purity and reverent duty, honors you with this offering. Please light my way to the afterlife."

The heat of the summer day was a distant memory now as the skin on her bare arms prickled in the cold air of the black pit. The deafening silence of her deep tomb throbbed in her head, yet through it she heard the words of Anaxilaus, her Greek physician.

Do not prolong your suffering by drinking the water they give you. Show Hades you are ready, and he will take you sooner. Even he can have mercy . . . in his way.

She tipped the amphora over and watched the water seep into the dirt, trickling into the underworld.

Forgive me, Goddess, she thought, *but my last offering must be to Hades.*

CHAPTER I

Veni, Vidi, Vici
I came, I saw, I conquered.

−JULIUS CAESAR

ROME, 45 BCE

Sixty-eight years later

A red-cloaked legionary soldier stood under the Aquila, the golden Eagle of Rome that was perched loftily atop a tall military staff. He blew his horn and shouted, "All make way for General Gaius Julius Caesar!"

The Forum Romanum was the central hub of Rome's political, economic, and religious life. Even on a slow day it could be crowded and hectic as everyone from senators in their best white togas to slaves in battered sandals carried on whatever business concerned them.

Today was not a slow day. It was a historic day. It was the day that the masses could finally get their first really good look at their new dictator as he began to make his way along the Via Sacra from the Curia, Rome's Senate house, to the Temple of Vesta, all against the backdrop of towering, multicolored marble temples and a massive two-story basilica, the long shop-filled arcade of which stretched down the street.

People had come out in droves to watch Caesar stroll down the cobblestone streets of the Forum, under the Eagle, like he owned the world. In fact, he *did* own it. The powers invested in him as dictator said as much.

Preceded by his bodyguard *lictors* and surrounded by what looked to be a small army of legionary soldiers in full armor, Caesar waved to those in the crowd who threw flowers at his feet and ignored those who didn't.

Some loved him. Some hated him. Most couldn't care either way. As long as their bellies were full and there was wine to be had, as long as those damn unshaven Gauls weren't shouting war cries at the gates of the city, life was good.

As Caesar's robust procession made its way past the Basilica Aemilia, several well-placed soldiers unfurled scarlet banners from the arches and columns of its long arcade. The banners dropped down like a series of theater curtains, each one boasting a gold medallion of Venus in its center. Venus, the goddess from whom Caesar claimed to be descended.

"Caesar's sure putting on a show," an impressed woman said to her friend.

Her friend leaned in. "Have you heard the song that his soldiers sing about him?"

"No, but I can imagine . . ."

"It goes like this: *Home we bring our balding womanizer! Romans, hide your wives away! All the gold you gave him bought him ten more tarts to lay.*"

The women laughed in unison, winding their way through the chattering crowds, bumping into bodies and lifting their stolas to avoid dirtying them on the cobblestone until they reached the front of the round, white-marble Temple of Vesta. Green laurel wreaths hung from each of the twenty fluted columns that encircled it.

Inside the temple's sanctum, where no one but the Vestal Virgins were allowed to go, burned the sacred flame of Vesta, goddess of the home and hearth. Hers was the Eternal Flame that protected the Eternal City. As long as the fire burned, Rome lived, and so the priestesses of Vesta tended the fire day and night.

Intricately carved marble pedestals stood along the winding Via Sacra and around the sacred area of the well-guarded temple. On top of each pedestal was a gleaming bronze bowl that contained a fire lit from the eternal flame inside the sanctum.

The women shouldered through the crowd until they reached one of the firebowls. It was a pleasant February day, but it grew cool when the clouds covered the sun. Surely the goddess wouldn't mind if they warmed their mortal hands over her immortal flame.

The one who had sung began to sing again, "*Julius Caesar, knows how to please her—*" but stopped in midsong as one of the embossed bronze doors of the temple opened and a stately woman dressed in a white stola, head veiled, descended the steps. Both women knew her. Everyone knew her. She was the High Priestess Fabiana who had served as Vestalis Maxima, the head of the Vestal order, for decades. The two women and everyone around them lowered themselves to their knees.

As the chief Vestal stood on the bottom marble step, she was immediately joined by two armed centurions, their scarlet cloaks framing her white stola.

The more senior soldier removed his red-plumed helmet and bowed his head. "Great Lady," he said, "shall we accompany you now?"

"Yes," said the Vestal. Her voice was lighter than her seventy-six years. "Thank you."

The splendid trio moved toward the columned portico of the adjacent House of the Vestals, the large, luxurious home only steps away from the temple, where the priestesses lived during their years of service to Rome.

As the Vestal passed by, men and women dropped to their knees before her on the cobblestone, their palms held upward. A chorus of murmurs went up.

Please ask Mother Vesta to protect my son who serves in Gaul . . .

Preserve my family, High Priestess . . .

Bless my daughter's marriage . . .

My child is sick. Please ask the goddess to save him . . .

The Vestal pulled back the linen *palla* wrapped around her shoulders to reveal a handful of sacred wafers, the traditional salted-flour offering to the goddess. As she glided past the kneeling suppliants, still accompanied by her gleaming centurions, she placed these wafers into the palms held up to her.

"Offer to the *viva flamma*," she instructed. To the living flame.

The suppliants rose and moved off to the firebowls to make their offerings.

A horn blew again as Caesar's impressive procession arrived at the portico to the House of the Vestals at the same time as the priestess.

"All make way for General Gaius Julius Caesar!" shouted a soldier, although the Vestal only rolled her eyes at him as if to say, *Yes, we can all see him.*

More soldiers pushed back the crowd as Caesar, draped in a white toga with a wide purple border that displayed his status and power, held out his arms to the elderly Vestal. Her eye roll softened to a smile and she embraced him.

To her, he was no dictator. He was family.

The ornate wooden doors of the House of the Vestals—deep red, with white and blue rosettes—opened and the centurions stood guard as Caesar and the Vestal passed through into the vestibule.

As they did, one of the soldiers turned to wink at the two gawking women, who were back on their feet and vying for position in the crowded street. His fitted iron breastplate caught the sun, and he puffed out his chest.

"*Mea Dea*," one of the women exhaled. "Forget those sweat-stained gladiators clambering in the sand." She elbowed her friend. "I'll be picturing that shiny pair of centurions when my husband rolls on top of me tonight."

* * *

Julius Caesar rested on a cushioned marble bench inside the lush open-sky rectangular courtyard of the multistory House of the Vestals. He grinned inwardly at the impressive gathering of senators, high-ranking priests and other patrician guests who had accepted his invitation to meet here, in the Vestals' large garden, to celebrate his powerful new status.

"So tell me, Julius," said Fabiana, "shall I now call you king?"

Caesar smirked. "Are you trying to get me killed, Great Aunt?"

"If I wanted you dead, you'd be dead. Now pass me a cup of wine."

Caesar took a gold cup from a slave's tray and handed it to the Vestalis Maxima, who sat next to him. "Priestess Fabiana, I need your help."

"I know," Fabiana said matter-of-factly. "You have been appointed, or rather managed to appoint yourself, *dictator in perpetuum*. Dictator for life. Congratulations, Imperator." She looked at him over the rim of her cup as she drank, her black eyes showing a spark of the temerity she was known for. It was always that way with the high priestess. She was kind yet imbued with an edge of impatience and candor that came from decades of managing too many people and personalities.

"It's for the good of Rome," said Caesar. "You've dealt with the Senate." He spoke under his breath. "A bunch of rich old men waxing poetic about the virtues of the Republic, and for no other reason than to put more coin in their purses and squander more land. Under my command, Rome will be more of a republic than it has been in decades."

"Some aren't so sure. Some say you are King Tarquin reborn."

The centurion who stood at Caesar's side widened his eyes and tightened his lips. Had anyone else said those words to the dictator, their head would be topping a spike by now.

"Tarquin, with all his arrogance, would have made a better senator than king. You will see, High Priestess . . ." He looked distractedly over the Vestal's shoulder as a flourish of whispers and muted excitement swept through the gathering. "Ah, but now enough talk of kings. I see a queen has arrived."

Cleopatra VII Philopator. The notorious queen of Egypt had already been in Rome for a year, living in Caesar's country house with their young son, Caesarion, and providing a well-spring of scandalous gossip the likes of which Rome's upper class hadn't enjoyed in generations.

Caesar had not—would not—publicly acknowledge the boy as his own; the child's sharp nose and small, close-set eyes, however, were an acknowledgment in themselves. They were a mirror image of the Roman general's own.

As she did everywhere she went, Cleopatra strolled into the courtyard as if it belonged to her, cutting a swath of superiority and style through the chattering cliques of patrician Roman matrons and men. Her long golden gown clung to her slight waist, curving over her hips and extending down her legs to feather the ground. Her arms were bare except for the gold bracelets that snaked around both upper arms.

Her dark hair was pulled back into a tight bun, and on her head was a gold diadem with the symbol of her monarchy, a ruby-eyed cobra, in the center. Like her, the cobra gazed down at the world, regal and ready to strike at any moment. Polished white pearls and dazzling gemstones were nestled into her black hair to create the type of striking contrast the queen was known for.

With her hook nose and large eyes, she was no exotic beauty. Pretty at best. Yet her slaves knew precisely how to accentuate her allure and shroud her flaws. She moved with the grace of a cat and purred when she spoke.

Caesar and Fabiana rose. Caesar took the queen's hand as she floated toward them.

"Majesty," he greeted. "I'm delighted you could join us."

"It is your great day, my love," she said. "I am honored to share it with you." She turned to Fabiana, her smoky eyes lined with black kohl and her red-ocher-painted lips narrowing into a smile. "And in the company of Vesta's high priestess, no less."

"It is good to see you again, Queen Cleopatra," said Fabiana, not bothering to sound convincing. She was getting too old for that.

"Has Caesar told you of his plans to build a great library here in the Forum?" Cleopatra queried her. "It is to be modeled after the Library of Alexandria: thousands of scrolls for study, a museum, public gardens . . ."

"And, of course, a special building for the Vestal order," finished Caesar.

The old priestess laughed out loud. "The priest Lucius tells me you have promised to build a massive temple to Mars as well. Where will you get all this marble?"

"Well, if you refuse to ask Vesta for it on my behalf, I shall ask my ancestor, Venus. Or I shall ask Cleopatra to petition Isis for me."

"Immortal women love you as much as mortal ones," smiled Fabiana. "You shall have your marble, no doubt. And I will be glad for it, Julius. Learning belongs among the temples."

"We can agree on that much, Great Lady," said Cleopatra. "Priestess Fabiana, tell me truly—what do you think of Caesar's dictatorship? You are his kin so you must know his heart. Is it not for the good of Rome? I have been in your city for a year now, and even in that time, I have seen things improve. Caesar's policing forces have made the streets safe. His accounting has lowered taxes for the common people. The friendship between Egypt and Rome has filled Roman stomachs with Egyptian grain. You have even adopted our calendar . . ."

"Queen Cleopatra has given us much," said Fabiana. "Perhaps Her Majesty should be dictator of Rome as well as pharaoh of Egypt?"

Caesar slapped his leg at his aunt's gibe. "She could do it too." He picked a stuffed olive off the tray of a passing slave and pushed it into his mouth, his eyes widening as he spotted a familiar young priestess.

Like all the Vestals at the party, she wore a white stola and a veil that covered her head. Her personal slave, an auburn-haired Greek beauty five or six years older than her and dressed in a fine green dress, stood dutifully behind her mistress.

"Ah, Priestess Pomponia," said Caesar. "Come closer. You are also celebrating a great day, are you not?"

"Yes, Caesar, I am surprised that you would remember such a thing."

"How could I forget?" He gestured for a servant to hand Pomponia a cup of wine. "Cleopatra, young Priestess Pomponia is today celebrating ten years as a Vestal."

"That is significant?" asked the queen.

"Vestals serve the goddess for thirty years, Majesty," said Pomponia. "We study for our first ten years as novices. After that, we are dedicated full Vestals who tend the sacred flame and perform public rituals." Despite the fact that she was a few years younger than Cleopatra and was speaking to a queen, the Vestal had not a trace of subordination in her voice.

Caesar swallowed a mouthful of wine from his gold cup. "Lady Pomponia and I have a history," he said casually to Cleopatra. "As Pontifex Maximus, I recommended her to the order when she was only a child of seven." He turned to Pomponia. "I remember the day you took your vows," he said. "After Priestess Fabiana cut your hair to wear the veil, I took the locks to the Capillata tree and hung them on the branches. I can still see them blowing in the breeze."

"It's a tradition that's better for the birds than young girls," smiled Pomponia. "No doubt some sparrow made a fine nest of my hair. It's grown back, though. It's long again." She pulled back her veil to show her chestnut hair and then, too informally and without thinking—"Caesar, where is Lady Calpurnia?"

She realized her error immediately. Everyone knew that Caesar's wife Calpurnia avoided public functions if there was a chance her husband's Egyptian mistress might attend.

Pomponia swallowed so hard that Quintus, a young priest of Mars who was standing an arm's length away, raised his eyebrows and looked at her, scolding her with his eyes.

"I'm afraid Calpurnia is ill," said Caesar.

"I will offer to the goddess for her health," said Fabiana.

"Thank you," said Caesar. "How kind." His glance shifted to Pomponia's slave, who stood quietly behind her mistress, head down and hands clasped together. She was taller than Pomponia, with a beautifully angular face and naturally sharp features that impressed even without a touch of cosmetics. "And how are you, Medousa?"

"Imperator, I am well."

Cleopatra's smile tightened even more. "I have not known you to be so familiar with slaves, Caesar."

"This one is special. I purchased her myself in the Graecostadium on the morning that Priestess Pomponia took her vows. She seemed a fine slave for a Vestal: physically flawless and well educated." Caesar reached out to touch the pendant of Medusa, the snaked-haired Gorgon, which hung around the slave's neck. "I named her Medousa for the charm she wore," he said. "Medusa, to ward off evil." His fingers traced a circle around the pendant.

Pomponia wasn't sure, but it seemed as though Cleopatra's entire body had tensed.

Caesar turned to Fabiana with a sad sigh. "*Tempus fugit,*" he said. Times flies. "What I wouldn't give to have those ten years back. I was in battle, but my armor was not so tight."

"Ten years ago I could still walk up the temple's steps without my knees cracking louder than the sacred fire," said Fabiana.

They all laughed.

Pomponia exhaled and looked over her shoulder, trying to avoid eye contact with her companions. She noticed Rome's great lawyer and senator Marcus Tullius Cicero talking to some men by one of the courtyard's decorative pools. He waved politely at her. She smiled and waved back, her bright hazel eyes and soft features relaxing.

She liked Cicero. He had successfully defended a Vestal's brother years earlier, and he had spoken in favor of giving even more privileges and protections to the order. She had once sat next to him in the arena during a particularly spectacular animal-hunt performance when she was a young girl. The games had been in celebration of an important military victory of Pompey the Great and had included the slaughter of over twenty elephants.

Pomponia could still hear their cries. Screams, really. It had taken the giant beasts so long to die. They had clambered together, the older ones trying to protect the younger ones.

When Pomponia had looked away, Cicero had patted her hand. *We are of one mind, Lady Pomponia,* he had whispered. *The games have their purpose, but I derive no pleasure from this either. In fact, I have often suspected that animals have much in common with mankind. Surely such butchery does not please the gods.*

A political animal through and through, Cicero was one of the senators who had accepted Caesar's invitation to attend this gathering. Like most senators, he revered the Roman Republic and looked down his nose at Caesar's grab for power. Unlike some senators, however, he was willing to wine and dine Rome's dictator to stay in the game.

Pomponia tensed as Marc Antony, Caesar's brilliant but boorish general, swaggered up to the senator and threw his arm around him. Antony was an unusually muscular man with a thick neck, a head of curly, dark brown hair and a face leathered by years marching under the sun on military campaigns.

"So, Cicero," Antony bellowed. "What's this I hear about Cleopatra refusing to send some promised books your way? It's all anyone can talk about! Gods, you'd think this town would have bigger problems, eh? What with our new dictator and all . . ." He poked a finger into Cicero's shoulder and then looked across the courtyard to see whether Cleopatra had overheard.

"A misunderstanding," said Cicero. He pulled his head back, avoiding the wine stench of Antony's breath and sidestepping the general's efforts to stoke open conflict.

"That's a good man," barked Antony. "Forgive and forget, eh?"

"The choice of the wise," said Cicero, knowing Antony neither forgave nor forgot. "*Mea sententia,* General."

Pomponia turned back to her companions. With Fabiana, Caesar, and Queen Cleopatra now immersed in conversation that fluttered between politics, wine, and astronomy, she decided it was a good time to discreetly make her retreat. Politics were exhausting.

Moving across the gardens with Medousa in tow, she took refuge in the columned peristyle that surrounded the courtyard. She stood in a slant of shade cast by a tall statue of a long-dead Vestal priestess.

And although she didn't give him the satisfaction of returning his chastising gaze, she still felt the critical eyes of the young priest Quintus watching her.

* * *

The last of the gathering's guests had departed. The Vestal priestesses Fabiana and Pomponia sat languidly in the courtyard as slaves noiselessly cleaned around them, returning tables and couches to their proper places and fishing litter out of the garden pools.

"It's getting cool," Fabiana said tiredly. "I think I shall retire for the evening."

"Caesar will never forgive me," said Pomponia. "He thinks I was trying to be clever."

Fabiana smoothed the veil around the younger Vestal's soft face. "Caesar has known you since you were a child," she reassured. "He knows your heart. And he is worldly enough to tell the difference between youth and malice."

"Why did he choose to meet here today? Why not celebrate at his home?"

The old priestess sighed. "He was sending a message to the people and the Senate. He wants them to know that he has the support of the Vestals. You must remember, Pomponia, Vesta's eternal flame sustains Rome itself, and we are tasked with sustaining it. Regardless of what changes come and go, regardless of what dictators rise and fall, regardless of what disease or devastation sweeps our streets, the sacred fire burns on. It comforts the people. It reassures them that the goddess still protects them and Rome. It is the one constant in a changing world. That is why he sought my help. He wants the people to know that their world will not change under his dictatorship."

"What did he want you to do?" asked Pomponia.

"To stand on the Rostra with him during his speech tomorrow," Fabiana replied.

"Are you going to do it?"

"No."

"Why not? If the people need us, what harm can it do? Is Caesar not family to you? He has always supported our order."

"Our duty is to the goddess, not to Caesar," said Fabiana. "You must always remember that." She pulled off her veil with a sigh, revealing the short gray hair beneath. It was not something the conservative Vestalis Maxima would have done ten years ago, but the courtyard was private enough, and her age had loosened her stern adherence to tradition.

"The Vestal order is the oldest and most revered priesthood in Rome's history," said Fabiana, "but that hasn't stopped a few people from using it for their own purposes." She folded her veil in her lap. "We must never allow others to exploit us. We must protect the sacred flame . . . and each other." She paused and then continued. "Someday I will tell you the story of the Vestal Licinia and you will understand." Fabiana arose slowly. "I'm taking my old bones to bed now. *Bonam noctem*, my dear."

"*Bonam noctem*, High Priestess."

Pomponia pulled her palla more tightly around her. It was cooling off quickly now. She cast a glance around for Medousa, but the slave was nowhere to be seen. She was likely cleaning up in the kitchen or, much more likely, supervising other slaves while they cleaned. The Vestal stood up tiredly, pulled off her veil, and thanked the goddess that she wasn't on watch in the temple until morning.

She left the greenery of the beautiful garden to slip through the peristyle and enter the grandeur of the Vestals' home, a residence that rivaled the affluence of any *domus* in Rome.

She bent over to unfasten her sandals and then strode barefoot across the white-and-orange floor mosaics and up the stairs, finally shuffling into her private well-furnished chambers to feel the warmth of the hypocaust heating embrace her. Two slaves entered after her, carrying basins and fresh bedclothes, and began to undress and wash their mistress.

Outside the House of the Vestals, on the cobblestone street of the now quiet and darkening Forum, Julius Caesar's large, gilded *lectica* sat idle with several centurions standing guard around it and eight litter-bearers waiting patiently. The heavy curtains were tightly drawn.

Inside the lectica, Medousa lay naked on a smooth cushion. Her eyes were fixed on the rich red tapestry that covered the ceiling and the gold medallion of Venus that stared down at her.

The back of her neck burned as the chain of her Medusa necklace dug into her skin. Caesar was clutching the pendant in his hands, twisting it around his fingers ever tighter. But then that pain was replaced by a sharper pain between her legs.

Caesar prompted the Vestal's slave to open her legs further and she obeyed, squeezing her eyes closed to stop herself from crying out as Rome's dictator thrust into her, finding yet another way to enjoy the pleasures of sole power.

CHAPTER II

Ut Sementem Feceris, Ita Metes
As you sow, so shall you reap.

−CICERO

ROME, 44 BCE

One year later

The morning of March 15, 44 BCE—the ides of March—began as any other. Dressing. Breakfast. Prayers. Washing the marble pedestal altar in the temple with pure springwater and offering into the sacred fire that burned atop it. Taking inventory of documents in the Vestal offices and the temple's vaults.

By midmorning, Pomponia's stola was damp from a sudden fearful sweat. A line of perspiration formed along her veil, dripping into her eyes. She blinked the stinging away.

The dictator Julius Caesar was dead.

A temple messenger had banged on the door of the House of the Vestals so hard that it sounded like Jupiter himself had thrown a thunderbolt at it.

"Caesar is assassinated!" he said from the street, bending over with his hands on his knees and gasping for breath. He had run nonstop from Pompey's Curia, the building that was being used to hold senate while the old Curia in the Forum was being fitted with new marble and mosaics.

Pomponia pulled him into the atrium of the House of the Vestals and, impatient with his attempts to catch his breath, slapped him across the face. "Speak sense, you fool."

"Priestess," said the messenger, "I saw it with my own eyes. He was stabbed just inside Pompey's Curia. Senator Cimber grabbed his toga and tried to pull him down. Caesar was shocked. He cried out '*Ista quidem vis est!*' at the violence. But then Senator Casca tried to stab him in the throat." The messenger gulped for air.

Pomponia struck him on the face again. "And then?"

"Caesar grabbed Casca's arm, but Casca rallied the other senators and they all attacked him. They all stabbed him, even Senators Cassius and Brutus. Caesar stumbled out of the chamber and then fell down the steps outside."

"Are you sure he is dead?" asked Pomponia. "Where was General Antony?"

"Caesar is dead, Priestess. It is certain. I saw Antony run toward Caesar's body, but he fled when he saw the assassins."

Pomponia waved the messenger away and then slipped out the doors of the House of the Vestals. Her two guards, Caeso and Publius, instantly appeared at her side to escort her to the temple. Their eyes darted here and there as the cries went up in the Forum: "Caesar is dead! Caesar is dead!"

And then silence fell like a stone. The streets emptied as people fled home to their families and locked their doors.

Who was in control of Rome?

Pomponia joined four other Vestals within the sanctum of the circular Temple of Vesta. They stood around the sacred fire that burned in its hearth, palms up in prayer to the goddess. "Mother Vesta, your faithful priestesses ask you to protect Rome."

The crackle of the fire answered their low prayers and echoed off the pristine white marble walls. Pomponia closed her eyes and felt the heat of the eternal flame lick the back of her hands.

High Priestess Fabiana burst into the temple. "Get Caesar's will," she said breathlessly. "Bury it in the courtyard near the statue of High Priestess Tullia. Put some flowers on top of it." She shoved a scroll into Pomponia's hands. "Put this in the vault in its place."

Her chest pounding, Pomponia rushed to the *penus*, the secret chamber hidden in a section of the temple's interior wall.

With trembling hands, she opened a thick marble door seamlessly disguised in the architecture of the wall and pulled out Julius Caesar's last will and testament, encased in a cylindrical scroll box. She replaced it with the decoy copy, an empty but official-looking scroll that had Caesar's seal on it.

There's no way the assassins will break into the temple, she thought. *It would be an outrageous sacrilege. They would lose the support of the people.*

It was customary for Rome's most important men—generals, dictators, certain senators and consuls—to keep their wills secure in either the vault within the House of the Vestals or, for the most important men, within the temple itself. Treaties and other vital political documents were also kept there, as were Rome's most sacred objects, including an ancient statue of Pallas Athena that Aeneas had saved during the fall of Troy. There was no safer or more sacred space in the Roman world. In the many centuries that the Aedes Vestae had stood in the Forum, there had not been a single violation of the tradition or of the temple's sanctity.

And considering Rome's violent past, that was saying something.

Pomponia wrapped Caesar's official will in her palla. She moved hurriedly through the temple, hearing Fabiana whispering hushed instructions to the other Vestals around the sacred fire. She looked back. Fabiana nodded curtly to her. *Do it. Hurry.*

She pushed open one of the bronze doors of the temple and raced down the marble steps—directly into the solid chest of the priest Quintus.

"Do not touch me," she scowled. Of all people. The last thing she needed right now was to deal with his predictable disapproval. Every public ritual, every ceremony or festival, it was the same thing: Quintus, priest of Mars, finding a reason to scold Pomponia, priestess of Vesta. She was in no mood for his finger-wagging. "Move," she said. "I am tasked by the Vestalis Maxima."

"Priestess Pomponia," said Quintus. His face was pale and tense, but his demeanor was as high-handed as ever. "For your own safety, I shall accompany you."

"I have my own guards," she chided. "I don't need you."

"I have the permission of your guards," he countered. "There is no time to argue. Do what I say."

Pomponia looked up. In addition to its usual watch of well-armed Roman soldiers plus the personal bodyguards of each Vestal—two soldiers per priestess—the temple was being guarded by some twenty or more priests of differing ranks from a number of religious collegia.

Quintus's superior, the *Flamen Martialis*, High Priest of Mars, was present. So too was the *Flamen Dialis*, High Priest of Jupiter, as well as the *Rex Sacrorum*, King of the Sacred Rites. All held daggers.

A number of additional Roman legionary soldiers also stood guard— these were Caesar's men. For the moment, they had no master. Caesar was dead. Yet their duty had led them to the Temple of Vesta to watch over their general's will. His estate had to be protected. His true heir had to be named. His final wishes had to be honored. If his assassins got their hands on it, none of those things would happen.

Clutching the scroll box in her palla, Pomponia scurried toward the adjacent House of the Vestals as Quintus stayed at her shoulder, matching her pace with long strides.

She noticed for the first time that he wasn't in his priestly attire or a toga, but rather wore a simple knee-length belted *tunica*. He had come in a hurry.

His hand rested on the dagger at his left hip as he strode alongside her, his eyes making quick assessment of the Forum. A dirty child ran by, with a barking dog in pursuit. Fruit rolled out of a basket that had been dropped on the ground. A few shifty-looking men slunk behind columns, either waiting for news or waiting for an opportunity to profit from the anarchy.

Rome was a beast with its head cut off, a beast that would destructively convulse until, like the Hydra, a head grew back.

Pomponia and Quintus darted through the House of the Vestals and burst into the courtyard where—shockingly—an unkempt slave had somehow managed to enter. He was drinking from one of the pools, his cupped hands draining water into his mouth and splashing water on his face.

Quintus drew his dagger. He rushed toward the man and raised the blade, about to strike, when the slave turned around. It was Marc Antony.

Quintus quickly lowered his blade. "General Antony," he breathed. "What is happening?"

Antony sat down heavily on a marble bench beside the pool. He wore the face of someone who was thinking a thousand thoughts at once.

"*Futuo*," he swore. "He's still lying there like a sacrificed goat," he muttered and then sneered in disgust. "It's a sacrilege." He looked up at Pomponia with bloodshot eyes. "Send some temple slaves to get his body. It's on the steps of Pompey's Curia." Again, that image—Caesar's body, his friend's body, Rome's great general lying in a bloody heap on the bottom step—inflamed him and his face reddened. "Tell the slaves to take him to his house. Calpurnia will be waiting."

"I will send Medousa," said Pomponia. At the whisper of her name, Medousa emerged from behind a column in the peristyle. She nodded at her mistress before darting off to find help. Pomponia watched her leave. *Was that a smile on her face? No, just fear.*

Antony squinted and shook his head in disbelief. "I laughed at Calpurnia this morning," he said. "I *laughed* at her. She's a superstitious old bird, I'll give you that, but she was so damn sure of herself. She warned him not to go today . . . said she had a dream that he would die." He looked squarely at Quintus. "A *dream*! Gods, it's absurd, is it not?"

"It doesn't matter anymore," said Quintus. "His body will be taken to her. She will care for it. You must hide."

Antony stood up so fast that Quintus jumped, his hand instinctively touching his dagger. The Roman general held his hand out to Pomponia. His eyes were on the cylindrical object wrapped in her palla. "Priestess Pomponia, give me Caesar's will."

She hesitated, but then Quintus nodded at her, his eyes commanding her to do it. She suppressed a scowl. Even now the young priest of Mars didn't seem to know his place and was giving her orders. And although she hated to do it, she obeyed.

* * *

Charmion, Cleopatra's adviser and servant, swept into the queen's luxurious bedchamber in Julius Caesar's country house, dispensing with protocol and gracelessly dragging the three-year-old Caesarion behind her. He was in the middle of a royal temper tantrum, but she paid him no heed.

She tossed a pile of dirty clothes onto the queen's bed. "Majesty will put these on at once," she said. "The prince must also wear them."

"What is wrong?" the queen asked, holding her breath.

"Caesar is dead," said Charmion. "Assassinated."

Cleopatra dropped the glass perfume bottle in her hand. It shattered into pieces on top of a golden Roman Eagle mosaic that stretched across the floor. She pulled her silk dress over her head and stepped naked toward the pile of clothes on the bed as Charmion outfitted the squirming prince. Two rough woolen tunicas, stained and stinking like manure.

"Majesty will leave on horseback," said Charmion. "A horse-drawn litter is waiting a few miles away. We must all make our way back to Egypt without delay." Charmion wrapped a frayed rope around the prince's waist to fasten the tunica.

Cleopatra gripped a bedpost. "When did it happen?" she asked. "How long do we have?"

"It happened this morning, perhaps two hours ago. We have minutes. The assassins will be coming for you."

The door to the bedchamber opened. Both women tensed, but it was only Apollonius, another of the queen's trusted advisers.

"You and the prince will go with Apollonius on horseback," said Charmion. "I will go with your decoy in the royal litter."

Finally, a trace of emotion. Fear. "No," said the queen, "you will come with us."

But for the first time in her twenty-five years of service to the pharaoh of Egypt, the slave known as Charmion did not obey her queen.

* * *

The throngs of people in the Roman Forum parted to make way for the Vestal lectica. A portable enclosed couch that was carried on the shoulders of four, eight, or even more slaves—depending on its size and number of occupants—a lectica was a privileged way for the Vestals and other important people to move through the streets of the Forum in comfort and privacy.

Moving aside for a Vestal wasn't just respectful; it was the law. Anyone who refused to make way for a priestess's litter, whether she was being carried in her lectica or pulled in a horse-drawn carriage, could be publicly whipped and executed. The same punishment applied if a person laid hands on a Vestal without her permission.

The Vestal lectica traveled along the Via Sacra, the sacred central street that wound through the Forum, to set down beside the great marble Rostra, the high speaker's platform near the Senate house. It was from this large and decorated platform that Rome's most historic speeches and announcements had been delivered.

Medousa pulled back the curtain of Pomponia's lectica to allow the Vestal to gracefully step out first. "We could have walked for all the trouble," the slave said under her breath. "It would have been faster."

Flanked by her two guards, Pomponia stood on the cobblestone and brushed a stray strand of her warm brown hair off her softly rounded face, tucking it behind her white veil. "The Vestalis Maxima wants a show of ceremony today," she said to Medousa, and then added with a bite, "but if you think it wise, I can ask her to consult with my slave next time."

"As you wish, Domina." Despite using the deferential *Domina*, the name a slave always called a female owner, Medousa braved a slightly insolent expression.

Pomponia studied her. "Medousa, we're here for Caesar's funeral rites. It is a dark time, nay? Yet all day, you've been grinning as if Apollo himself just secretly granted you your freedom and asked for your hand in marriage."

"I am stricken with grief, Domina. Forgive my behavior."

An official-looking slave bowed to Pomponia and led her to a raised platform alongside the Rostra, upon which High Priestess Fabiana and two other Vestals, Nona and Tuccia, sat upon red-cushioned chairs.

The elder Nona sat rigidly but Tuccia, Pomponia's closest friend in the order, reached out to clasp her hand in warm greeting. Pomponia once again gave silent thanks to Vesta that she was chosen to attend the ceremony while two other Vestals remained in the temple to tend the sacred fire.

The Vestal order comprised a minimum of six full priestesses, as well as a number of novices. It was the long-standing rule that at least two full

Vestals had to be in the temple at all times, day and night, to maintain the fire, perform rites to Vesta over the flames, and teach the novices how to do the same. That left four Vestals free to perform their many other religious and official duties.

Pomponia settled in beside Fabiana and was about to say something to her, when she noticed the high priestess's red eyes. To Fabiana, this wasn't just a state funeral for a dictator. To Fabiana, it was the funeral of a family member—her great-nephew. Caesar had always been something of a pet to her, and everyone knew the affection the general had for the Vestalis Maxima. Pomponia squeezed Fabiana's hand and felt the older priestess squeeze hers in return.

Pomponia looked around. She couldn't remember the last time she had seen such a crowd packed into the square in the Forum. Men and women—dressed in the finest of togas and stolas to the most threadbare of tunicas—stood shoulder to shoulder, peering over each other's heads to stare up at the Rostra. A few of the more ambitious, if misguided, in the crowd had even tried to scale the high monuments around the Senate house in the hopes of getting a bird's-eye view, only to be yanked down by the ankles by testy soldiers tasked with keeping order.

Above the expansive marble Rostra, red banners hung down, those great letters—*SPQR*—emblazoned in gold in their center: *Senatus Populusque Romanus*. The Senate and People of Rome. It was the phrase that expressed Rome's philosophy: a great city, a great power, ruled by the people and for the people.

On top of the Rostra, the body of Julius Caesar lay on a carved ivory couch, covered by a deep-purple cloak that moved noiselessly in the slight breeze. Near the head of Caesar, a larger-than-life wax effigy of the dictator stood on a wide pedestal. No less than twenty stab wounds had been carved into the wax statue. Blood oozed out of every one.

Antony commissioned that in a hurry, thought Pomponia.

Yet despite the dramatic imagery and the occasion, the multitude in the Forum was strangely silent. Uncertainty and expectation hung in the cool March air. Rome was less in a state of violent turmoil and more in a state of noncommittal wait-and-see.

But then a horn blared and Caesar's second in command, the fearless General Marc Antony, appeared. He strode across the platform of the Rostra as if it were the world's stage and he its star actor, wrapped in a dark toga with wide gold cuffs encircling his wrists.

To Pomponia, he was a different man than he had been only the day before in the Vestal courtyard, disguised in a foul slave's tunica and slurping water from the pool like a stray dog.

On the Rostra, the black-robed priests of Pluto, god of the underworld and divine brother of Vesta, solemnly moved aside for Antony. Fragrant smoke from their incense burners rose up to the gods, creating the sense that the marble platform was a large sacrificial altar. Antony's political message was clear: Caesar was an innocent. A victim.

As he approached Caesar's body with slow, severe strides, Antony suddenly extended his arms and dropped to his knees, wringing the purple death cloak in his hands and looking up to the sky with moist eyes. "Gods on high," he cried out, "Mighty Father Mars, forgive us for the death of your blessed soldier, Rome's great avenger! We could not protect him as he protected us!"

Like waves on water, gasps of emotion moved through the mass of people. They had never seen the great general like this, and his burst of grief seemed to rouse their own. Eyes moistened and heads nodded. Shouts of *Caesar! Caesar!* began to ring out.

"*Mea Dea*," Fabiana whispered under her breath. "The song has only begun and already he plays the people like a lyre."

Pomponia checked herself. Antony's performance was making tears form in her own eyes. She had so much to learn from the high priestess. She sighed and glanced around, noticing for the first time that Quintus stood on the far end of the Rostra, holding the Aquila on a high staff.

Normally, an enlisted legionary soldier of high rank would hold the Eagle as a military standard; Quintus, however, had a somewhat unique standing. Not only was he a priest of Mars, but he had also served in Caesar's army in Gaul and discharged only after being seriously wounded in battle. He was conscious of every step now, careful to conceal a slight residual limp at all times. No doubt he saw it as a sign of weakness. Pomponia had noticed it, though.

Antony collected himself and stood tall on the Rostra. "It is not proper, my fellow Romans, that only a single voice sing of Caesar's life." He held his hands out to the people. "I will speak for all of us. When you hear my voice, you hear your own."

As Antony began to list out Caesar's military victories, Pomponia took a rare opportunity to study Quintus unnoticed as he held his position.

He wore the red cloak and fitted iron armor of the soldier, but no helmet. His short black hair was neatly combed, and his face was clean-shaven, although even from her seat some distance away Pomponia could see the scar that extended from his right ear back into his hair and the slight roughness of his complexion. Even as a child, when they were first brought together to learn how to perform their joint religious duties, his complexion had seemed harder than would have been expected for his years.

Below the Rostra, at Quintus's feet, a pretty girl who was quite obviously pregnant looked up at him and braved a discreet but flirtatious grin. Pomponia had seen her before: Quintus's young wife, a girl by the name of Valeria. She carried on her hip a small child, their first daughter, who waved shyly up at her father.

They're proud of him, thought Pomponia. But then Quintus shot his family the same chastising glare that she had received so many times during their religious or social functions. In response to the glare, Valeria quickly grabbed the child's hand and moved away from the Rostra. Quintus seemed happier with that. *Why could the man not be more pleasant?* Pomponia wondered. *Why did he feel compelled to control and correct everyone?*

The priestess shook her head. It was no wonder that so many Vestal priestesses chose to remain with the order instead of getting married after completing their years of service to the goddess. If all husbands behaved so, it was a much better option.

And yet she would have expected better from Quintus. Although he was so changed that the memory was hard to summon, she recalled the day she was told her father had been killed in battle. As a novice of only nine years old, she withheld her tears—priestesses of Vesta did not cry—and ran off into the Forum to hide. Fabiana, the other priestesses, the guards, and a number of priests and senators had spent hours searching for her.

It was a young Quintus who found her crouched between two large piles of bricks and building material that had been stacked up alongside a section of the Forum's encompassing wall. He had crawled over the broken brick and stone until his knees bled to sit beside her. Ashamed of her tears, Pomponia covered her face, but Quintus did not chastise her. That part of him was not yet formed. Instead, he gave her a handful of purple flowers he had stolen from the sacred garden behind Juno's temple. *My mother calls these flowers Juno's tears*, he told her. *Maybe you will feel better if you know the goddess cries with you.*

But Pomponia knew the tenderness of a young boy could not last long in the world, and Quintus was no exception. His demeanor had grown harder with each passing year. His military service had also changed him, and although marriage managed to soften the hearts of many Roman men, it seemed to have done the opposite to Quintus.

As Antony neared the end of his funeral oration, he approached the very front of the Rostra. Now that he had reminded the thousands of mourners present of how many military campaigns Caesar had won, of how many barbarians he had slain for Rome, and how many times he had filled Rome's coffers with the spoils of war, he was getting set for a strong ending.

There was no doubt in Pomponia's mind that he had a purpose in all of this, one that went beyond eulogizing Caesar. She was proud of herself for thinking like this; Fabiana would be pleased. A Vestal had to think for herself.

"My fellow citizens," Antony cried out. "Hear me now. You were loved by the man who lies dead on this altar. A great man who many of you knew only as the great name you now call out—Caesar! Sacrosanct Caesar, who served as Pontifex Maximus, High Priest of Rome! A merciful man in peace but a fiery monster in wartime, a soldier who defended Rome's honor in barbaric lands, who spent years in gory battle for the glory of our Eternal City."

In one swift movement, Antony lifted the purple cloak that was draped over Caesar's body and grabbed the bloodied toga underneath. He took the Aquila out of Quintus's hands and used it to thrust the toga high in the air. The white folds were drenched in Caesar's blood, the fabric in shreds from the assassins' daggers.

The sight had the effect of a lightning bolt striking the crowd: they jumped where they stood, startled and shocked, and a chorus of cries and shouts went up.

"*Homo homini lupus est!*" cried Antony. Man is a wolf to his fellow man! "This soldier, this son of Rome, survived the swords of a thousand enemies, only to be ripped apart by the fangs of those he called friends!"

The muscled arms of the robust general held the bloodied toga even higher. He looked up at the wax effigy of Caesar as if he were gazing at the face of a god.

"Even Jupiter's heart of stone must crack—" Antony's voice broke.

Many in the crowd began to openly weep.

Lowering the Eagle and then holding the torn toga close to his chest, Antony ran his fingers over the dried blood. "Caesar's blood, so often spilled on foreign soil, now stains his toga on the Rostra!" He choked back a sob and then bored his eyes into the crowd. "The assassins say they murdered Caesar to protect Rome. But I say that Caesar was Rome's protector! Hear me, Father Jupiter,"—Antony shifted his eyes to the Capitoline Hill, which overlooked the Forum, the colossal red marble columns of the Temple of Jupiter standing bold against the blue sky—"I will avenge Caesar and the city he lived and died for."

Antony narrowed his eyes. Pomponia and the thousands of other mourners present followed his spear-like gaze as he pulled it away from the Capitoline and aimed it down at a number of senators, including Brutus and Cassius, who sat rigidly alongside the Rostra. Their faces had blanched with disbelief.

This was *not* the diplomatic, unifying funeral speech that Antony had promised to deliver.

But then, just as quickly, the general cast his piercing eyes upward again, this time to the heavens. He outstretched his arm, gesturing to the strange star that had mysteriously appeared in the sky shortly after Caesar's assassination.

"We have all been amazed at the brilliant star that hangs in the heavenly canopy above, that shines with equal light both day and night. The finest Roman, Greek, and Egyptian astronomers cannot explain this star—but we the people know what it is!"

Pomponia glanced up. It was a strange sight: a star with a tail, one that hung suspended in the sky night and day. The priests had been beside themselves with speculation and study, and augurs had been taken on the hour since it first appeared. No one could explain it, but Antony seemed to have an explanation in mind.

"It is *Caesaris astrum*!" he shouted. The star of Caesar! "Nay, the very soul of Caesar!"

A mad cheer of wonder and jubilation swept through the Forum. Rome's dispassionate state of wait-and-see had come to an end. It was all passion now.

Antony didn't let up. "Gaius Julius Caesar, *Divus Julius*! Once a son and father of Rome, now a god of Rome. Today, his place among the gods can be seen above us." He placed his hands on his chest as if to stop his heart from breaking. "We must pay tribute to such celestial rebirth. The gods demand it. I therefore decree that the month of Quintilius, the month of Caesar's mortal birth, be renamed in his honor—July!"

A second cheer—this one pulsating with a volatile mixture of grief, anger, and awe—surged through the crowd of onlookers. History was being made on the Rostra before them, and they were witness to it. They were a part of it. They loved it.

Antony pressed on. He could never have hoped it would go this well.

Taking in a great breath through his nose, one that inflated his sizable chest even more, General Antony extended his arm and a soldier slapped a scroll into his palm. Pomponia recognized it instantly—she had hidden it in her palla, after all.

"I have in my faithful hands the last will and testament of our great father," said Antony, "kept unmolested and true by the Vestal priestesses in the temple." He unrolled it before a starving crowd that was hungry for more. "It was the last wish of the divine Caesar that the Roman people, whom he loved as kin, take pleasure in the life that was denied him."

Antony nodded to a group of soldiers alongside the Rostra, and with some effort they hauled a gilded chest onto the platform. Antony plunged his hand into it and then held up a handful of coin, letting some of it slip through his fingers to land on the marble platform of the Rostra. "To each and every male Roman citizen, the divine Caesar bequeaths seventy-five drachmas."

Another wave of gasps—shock, joy, despair—moved through the mass of people.

"To the people of Rome, the divine Caesar also leaves his private walks and orchards, which they may use for their pleasure. May they bring you as much peace as they brought our great father!"

A shout went up from the crowd, and then another. Jostling. Pushing. Shoving. A forward thrust of thousands of bodies, all moving toward the Rostra.

Antony's rapier gaze settled once again on Brutus and Cassius, two of Caesar's assassins. It was clear from their ashen complexions that they knew it was all about to come apart. Roman riots formed faster than storm clouds. The two men stood up slowly, cautiously inching toward their litters.

That's right you bastard dogs, thought Antony. *Now it's your turn to run.*

Suddenly, Pomponia felt a firm hand on her shoulder. Quintus. "A priest can be flayed as well as any other man," she said. "Do not touch me."

"Priestess Pomponia, it is time to leave," he said. To Pomponia, it sounded too much like an order.

"Perhaps you need a lesson in religious protocol," said Pomponia. "A Vestal answers only to the Pontifex Maximus. And unless you have been promoted . . ."

A deafening crash. A rush of people moving past her, knocking over chairs, climbing up onto the Rostra and heading toward the body of Caesar.

Marc Antony gave a silent order to his soldiers—stand down. Let it happen.

The impassioned mob swarmed Caesar's body, and more cries went up at the sight of his pierced corpse. Blood spotted through the fabric of his death toga, mapping the blade wounds. His eyes were closed. In his mouth was a coin to pay the ferryman Charon for passage across the River Styx to the afterlife.

Pomponia stood and watched in bewilderment as the mob lifted the body of Caesar onto their shoulders and carried him off the Rostra and into the mayhem of the Forum.

She heard more chairs fall around her and noticed that she had been pushed away from her seat. The high priestess and the priestesses Nona and Tuccia were nowhere to be seen. No doubt their guards had swept them back to the safety of their lecticas and they were already being escorted back to the temple by soldiers.

She spotted her guards, Caeso and Publius, calling out her name and trying to reach her. They held their daggers in the air as they pushed through the throngs of people, but in the madness they couldn't get to her.

Pomponia didn't know what frightened her more: the idea of being at the mercy of the mob in the street or having to face Fabiana when and if she made it back to the temple. The Vestalis Maxima would be furious with her for not paying attention. The guards who had taken their eyes off her, probably distracted by Antony's dramatics on the Rostra, would be lucky to escape with a lashing. Medousa would definitely get one.

Quintus gripped her shoulder. "Come with me, Priestess," he said. "Now."

Pomponia hated to do it, but she obeyed.

They weaved for a long time through the riotous street and the frenzied crowd in the Forum, back toward the Temple of Vesta. It was the same direction in which the crowd was headed, still carrying Caesar's body on their shoulders. Pomponia's heart pounded as she watched the dead general's limp arms and legs flail as his body moved ever closer to a makeshift funeral pyre the mob had started to build only steps away from Vesta's temple.

An endless flow of men and women came from all directions, and threw any kind of kindling they could find—baskets, wood benches, shopkeepers' stands—under the body.

A woman held up a torch lit by one of the firebowls near the temple. "Send him to Pluto in Vesta's fire," she shouted.

And then the flames went up, strong and loud and hot, crackling sparks into the air and licking Caesar's flesh with devouring heat. Women tore the jewelry off their necks and arms and threw it into the bonfire—the bone fire—of the funeral pyre. More gold to pay the greedy ferryman.

At last, Pomponia and Quintus reached the steps of the round temple. As before, soldiers, priests, and centurions stood guard to protect those who protected the sacred flame. Breathless, Pomponia put her foot on the first step and then turned around to say something to Quintus.

He stood several feet away, arguing with his frightened, disheveled young wife. "I knew you would be here!" she shrieked. He grabbed her by the arm and dragged her away.

Pomponia climbed the white marble steps of the temple, pulled opened a bronze door, and shuffled toward the roaring red hearth within the temple's inner sanctum. Fabiana embraced her. The other Vestals wiped their tears and made an offering of gratitude to the goddess.

Pomponia lowered herself and sat cross-legged on the white-and-black mosaic floor, leaning her back against the cool marble of a column to catch her breath. She smoothed down her white veil and let the sacred space calm her.

All six Vestals, her sisters, were together. The high priestess Fabiana and the elder Nona with their wise, age-worn, motherly faces. The lovely, softhearted Tuccia with her bright amber eyes and skin that Venus would envy. The studious and reliable Lucretia and Caecilia, always quick to smile and do their duty.

The divine fire of Vesta burned in its hearth—a wide bronze firebowl set into a round marble pedestal that stood near the center of the sanctum. The fire had burned here, in this very spot, for centuries, surrounded and loved by priestesses no different from the ones who surrounded and loved it now.

Pomponia watched Tuccia gently place kindling on the sacred fire as Fabiana poured a few drops of oil into it from a shallow *patera*. The flames roared and crackled, and the smoke floated upward, slipping through the hole in the middle of the domed bronze ceiling to rise over the Forum and reassure the people—even this mob—that all would be well. Dictators lived and died, but Vesta and Rome were eternal.

Pomponia pushed herself to her feet and approached the hearth, staring into the moving red flames of the eternal fire and feeling its heat on her face.

How strange. The dictator Julius Caesar was dead, now made *Divus Julius*, the divine Julius, a god. The maniacal mob was burning his body just steps away from the temple doors. A fearful omen hung in the sky. Antony had turned like a mad dog on those who thought they could leash him. Rome continued to convulse like a beast with no head.

And yet all she could think about was Quintus's hand on her shoulder.

CHAPTER III

Timeo Danaos et Dona Ferentes
Beware of Greeks bearing gifts.

−VIRGIL

GREECE, 43 BCE

One year later

The only thing the young Livia Drusilla hated more than a fat old Roman man was a fat old Greek man.

She reclined on the couch and swallowed the largest gulp of wine she could hold in her cheeks, not caring that it dribbled out the sides of her mouth and down her neck or that her midwife had warned her against excessive drink while pregnant.

An arm's length away, her husband Tiberius—middle-aged, round, and idiotic—chortled at a dirty joke told by his Greek friend Diodorus, owner of the villa they were visiting in Athens.

Livia drained her cup. What further damage could she do to her baby? With a father like Tiberius, the child was destined to be a fat, vapid *stultus* anyway. Not only was Tiberius an idiot, he was her cousin. Apollo often cursed the infants of such coupling with both dullness and deformity.

The baby kicked, and Livia shifted uncomfortably on the couch, suddenly suffering an unwelcome flashback of her first night with Tiberius. His weight had pushed the breath out of her, and when she turned her head to avoid his sloppy lips, she had caught a glimpse of his wide ass in the polished-bronze mirror beside the bed.

She winced at the memory. The wine burned in her throat, and she tossed her cup onto the floor. She knew what would happen next. A female slave bent down to pick it up, and when she did, Tiberius slid his hand between her legs and squeezed his fingers into her body. "There's room in here for both of us," he chortled at Diodorus. Another stupid, stinking joke from a stupid, stinking fool.

"I have to take a piss." Diodorus stumbled to his feet and shuffled past Livia, glancing down at her reclining form on the couch and mischievously raising his eyebrows as he stole a look down her dress at her breasts.

Feigning good sportsmanship, Livia grinned. She hated that she had to be nice to this hairy Greek pig, but she and Tiberius were dependent on his hospitality. In fact, thanks to her husband's unbridled stupidity, their very lives depended on this Athenian refuge. She uttered a silent curse to Juno, goddess of marriage. Why had she been saddled with such a husband?

Wrapping her palla around her chest, Livia wondered what was happening back in Rome. It had all gone to Hades after Marc Antony's rousing speech on the Rostra during Caesar's funeral.

Rome had split in half as influential men and families were forced to pick a side. You were either a supporter of Caesar's assassins, led by Brutus and Cassius, or you were a supporter of Caesar's allies, led by the general Marc Antony and some upstart nephew of Caesar's named Octavian.

The latter man—barely twenty years old—was Julius Caesar's sole heir and posthumously adopted son. Octavian had been a nameless nobody a year earlier. Now he was the new Caesar.

Between the two factions, there really was no contest when it came to strength. Antony and Octavian had all the muscle. They had the loyal support of the Roman army, commanding those mighty legions that had served Julius Caesar for years and that now regarded him as a god.

On the other side, Caesar's assassins—a bunch of lily-handed senators—were friendly with some of the wealthiest patrician families in Rome. Brutus and Cassius had money and connections, but no muscle.

Livia had known from the beginning which side wielded the bigger sword. She was not surprised when her idiot husband chose the wrong side. He had openly supported Caesar's assassins and given them coin.

Shortly after that, Antony and Octavian had begun to hunt down anyone who had contributed to the assassins' purse. Their brutality had prompted many of their opponents to tuck and run for their lives, fleeing Rome as if it were the burning city of Troy.

And so here she was, hiding out in Greece, eating bad fish, and slumming in a villa that boasted all the style of a slave's latrine, all to avoid Antony's sword on their necks.

"Husband," she said to Tiberius, "any word from Rome?"

"Only that Antony's thugs have moved from slaying to stealing," he slurred. "Every day they add new names to their death list—men that are to be arrested and either executed or exiled, and whose fortunes are to be confiscated to fund their hunt for Caesar's killers."

"What about our names? Are our names on the list? And our estate, is it protected?"

Tiberius burped and laid his head back on the couch. "*Solum tempus monstrabit.*" Only time will tell.

In other words, the drunken idiot had no idea.

As Livia heard Diodorus's familiar shuffling behind her, she rested her face on her hands and closed her eyes. The ruse didn't work, however, since he stopped in front of her couch and reached down to tug at her hair.

"Tiberius," he said, "your wife knows how to go through the wine. I think she should start earning her keep around here, don't you?"

A snore from Tiberius's couch.

Swaying on unsteady legs, Diodorus lifted his tunica. The stench made Livia cough and she opened her eyes to stare at the patch of coarse black hair between his legs, his sweaty manhood hanging limp at her forehead.

"Laocoön knew better than to trust the Greeks," he said, as he clutched a handful of Livia's hair and pulled her head between his legs. "Especially those bearing gifts."

CHAPTER IV

Adversae Res Admonuerunt Religionum
Adversity reminds people of religion.

–LIVY

Later the same year

"Pomponia, this water doesn't smell right." High Priestess Fabiana stood tiredly by a fountain in the courtyard in the House of the Vestals, sniffing the contents of a clay amphora. "It's from the spring, so it should be fine. Maybe it's my imagination. Put some in a glass jug and smell it. Have a couple of the slaves drink it. Let me know if they get sick."

"Yes, Fabiana."

The year following Caesar's assassination had taken its toll on Fabiana. The political maneuverings of Rome's most ambitious and ruthless men, and their constant petitioning for favor from her as Vestalis Maxima, had made the lines around her eyes deepen and her normally light temperament grow heavy.

More and more duties, especially the political or ceremonial ones performed during public festivals or rituals, were falling on the younger Vestal Pomponia. The elder Vestal Nona Fonteia was more senior than Pomponia and should have been the natural choice, but it seemed to be Fabiana's wish that Pomponia take on more responsibilities, and the high priestess had come to rely on her for duties small and large.

Nona didn't seem to mind. A deeply devout priestess of Vesta, she had always preferred the more private, even secret, aspects of a Vestal's duties to those that involved public ritual or political ceremony.

Even when it wasn't her watch, Nona spent much of her time in the temple's sanctum offering prayers to the goddess of the home and hearth on behalf of Rome. If she wasn't there, she was either in the mill overseeing the preparation of the sacred *mola salsa* mixture and ritual wafers, or in the study instructing the novices.

Nonetheless, even Nona was required to perform more public functions these days. In the aftermath of Caesar's assassination and the bloody power struggles that followed, the Vestal priestesses worked, by daylight and candlelight, to fulfill their duties and do what they could to maintain calm in the city.

Pomponia arranged for the water to be tested and then headed out of the house wearing a sleeveless stola and light veil. Her guards escorted her to the front of the Temple of Vesta, where Nona was supervising a group of novices. They were taking flames from the sacred hearth within and placing them in the bronze firebowls around the temple.

Except for a few days during the Vestalia festival in June, the public was not allowed to enter the temple or see Vesta's fire. Yet these firebowls, each secured to the top of a white pedestal, allowed people to take embers of the sacred fire home to burn in their own hearths. Even before the first temple to the goddess had been built in the Forum by the second king of Rome, Vesta had been honored this way: privately, by families who heard her laughter in the crackling of their home fires and were comforted by it.

Pomponia saw Nona ascending the steps of the temple. As Pomponia walked toward her, she noticed a loose cobblestone on the street and pointed it out to the guard. "Fix that."

"Yes, Priestess."

Pomponia caught herself. "Please."

"Of course, my lady."

"Sister Nona," Pomponia called out.

Nona stopped midstep. "Yes, Pomponia?"

"I've messaged the brickmen as you requested. They will be here at daybreak tomorrow to repair the oven in the mill and start building another one."

Nona brushed some ash off her stola. "Good. I can't keep up. Every morning there are more people waiting outside the temple for the sacred wafers. I'll need more for public functions too. Our new Caesar is planning extra sacrifices next month. Rome will run out of bulls at this rate." She sighed. "I'll have to double production at least. I may as well have my bed moved into the mill."

"I know something that will make you feel better."

"What is that?"

Pomponia grinned. "I've ordered fifty amphorae of Pompeian wine, just for you. They can keep you company in the mill."

Nona laughed as she pulled open a bronze door to the temple. "You hit the mark, sister. That does make me feel better."

As the older priestess returned to her duties in the temple, Pomponia walked back to the house, pointing to one loose cobblestone and then another as the guard nodded and assured her he would have them secured immediately.

Back in the House of the Vestals, she headed to her office and sat at her desk. She blinked at the sprawl of documents and began to organize them—what needed her urgent attention and what could be delegated or ignored altogether—and then procrastinated even more by tidying a few things up.

She had just started tackling urgent matters when a temple slave appeared in her office doorway. "Domina," she said, "there is a Lady Valeria here. She says she is the wife of a priest of Mars and humbly requests an audience with you."

Lady Valeria—that was Quintus's wife. Pomponia frowned. As if Quintus weren't self-important enough, his wife clearly had no problem assuming she could command an audience with a Vestal priestess. Still, as the wife of a priest she did have standing to do so.

"Shall I put her in the *tablinum*?" asked the slave.

"No, I will meet with her in the courtyard," said Pomponia, rising from her desk. For some reason, she preferred an open space to meet with Quintus's wife.

Pomponia had no sooner arrived in the courtyard and sat down on a cushioned couch near some white rosebushes than a distraught Lady

Valeria burst into the garden, running ahead of the temple slave to collapse in an undignified heap at Pomponia's feet.

"Help us, Lady Pomponia. They've arrested him!"

"They've arrested whom?" asked Pomponia, quickly standing.

"Quintus!" Valeria put her hands on her face. "His father too! They came into our home yesterday . . . They dragged them both from the house! No one will tell me anything, Priestess. I don't know where he is."

"Who dragged them from the house?"

"A soldier," cried Valeria. "One of Octavian's men." She kissed Pomponia's sandaled foot—a serious breach in protocol—and then placed her forehead on the ground. "I beg you, Priestess Pomponia, on the affection my husband has for you . . ." Her voice trailed off and then she began again. "On the *respect* my husband has for you as a fellow member of the religious collegia, I beg you to intercede."

Pomponia felt the blood drain from her face. She knew exactly where Quintus and his elderly father would be: in the Carcer, Rome's infamous prison, which was located not far from the Senate house.

"Go home," said Pomponia. "Let me think . . ."

Valeria looked up. "You are a priestess of Mother Vesta," she pleaded. "You have the authority to pardon the condemned, do you not?"

"Yes, but Vestals rarely invoke that power. We serve the goddess, not the accused."

"Quintus is innocent. He is a priest of Mars. He served Julius Caesar and was injured in battle. He does not support the assassins, he does not sympathize with them, he has never given them a single denarius! What proof do they have of any wrongdoing? Why do they want his head?"

They don't want his head, thought Pomponia. *They want his money. They need to pay their soldiers somehow.*

Pomponia sat down again with Valeria still at her feet. It was the first time that Pomponia had seen Quintus's wife up close. The young woman truly was lovely, with raven hair that fell in soft curls around her smooth shoulders. Pomponia felt something—jealousy? No, that wasn't it. Not quite. Rather, it was a sense of satisfaction that she, Pomponia, had a power over Quintus's life that Valeria could never have.

"Please, Priestess Pomponia," Valeria's voice was even louder now, and heads turned in the normally serene garden.

Medousa appeared suddenly in the peristyle and marched across the courtyard, her anger barely contained, and put her hand on Valeria's shoulder.

"Shall I see Lady Valeria out, Priestess?" asked the slave, although it wasn't really a question at all. It was more of an adamant suggestion.

"Yes."

Valeria kissed Pomponia's sandal again and then allowed herself to be escorted out. She had done everything she could. It was in the shining hands of the goddess now.

A moment later, Medousa was back standing before Pomponia. She cast a warning eye at her mistress. "I have heard the news," she said. "Whatever you are thinking of doing, you should consult the high priestess first."

"Fabiana had Julius Caesar spared during Sulla's proscriptions," said Pomponia. "She even gave him sanctuary here in our house until the danger to him had passed. And that was before she was made Vestalis Maxima. I have standing."

"Don't do anything impulsive."

"The high priestess is resting and should not be disturbed. Anyway, Medousa, there is a saying: *Melius est veniam quam licentiam petere.*" It is better to ask for forgiveness than permission. "Prepare my lectica."

"Yes, Domina," said Medousa. "But it may not be wise to travel through the Forum right now." She lowered her voice. "My lady, I know you were fond of Senator Cicero . . ."

"What of it?"

"I have just received word from a temple messenger that he was killed yesterday, executed by Antony's forces while traveling on the Appian Way." Medousa assessed her mistress's blanched face and then continued. "I am told that Antony ordered the senator's head and hands be brought back to Rome and put on spikes on the Rostra. A crowd is gathering to look as we speak."

"My lectica," the Vestal repeated. "At once."

"Yes, Domina."

A brief wave of dizziness passed over Pomponia. If what Medousa said was true, Rome was convulsing out of control. Cicero had been one of the most respected and influential men in Rome for decades, yet it was no secret that he and Marc Antony had been at each other's throats for years. The only thing they had in common was ego.

Cicero had often spoken against Antony in the Senate. His criticisms had been open and caustic, and although he had not played a part in Caesar's assassination, he had nonetheless expressed the fanciful wish that Antony had been stabbed alongside the dictator.

Yet Cicero's ultimate desire was for peace and order to be restored to Rome. He had calculated that the new Caesar was the man most likely to make that happen and so had begrudgingly thrown his support behind Octavian; however, that clearly hadn't protected him from Antony's wrath.

Pomponia's thoughts turned to Quintus. If the untouchable Cicero could be executed with impunity, no one was safe. Especially not someone like Quintus, a man whose family possessed great wealth but little political importance.

As her lectica was being prepared, Pomponia had Medousa and two other slaves dress her in a finer white stola, cinching it under her breasts with a knotted rope belt and then draping a linen palla over a shoulder. They arranged her hair into the *seni crines*, the traditional braided hairstyle of Roman brides. As brides of Rome, Vestal Virgins wore the style with particular pride. Next, Medousa secured an *infula*—the Vestals' red-and-white woolen headband—onto her mistress's head, attaching the ribbon-like *vittae* and then placing a white veil over her head.

"Such dress is for public rituals and sacrifices," muttered Medousa.

"Such dress is for commanding reverence," Pomponia corrected. "No matter the occasion."

Medousa smoothed the veil on her mistress's head and then placed her hands on either side of Pomponia's face, staring into her eyes with sudden severity. "Valeria is his wife."

Medousa felt the sting of Pomponia's hand on her cheek.

They exited the House of the Vestals and stepped without speaking into the lectica waiting near the portico. They sat opposite each other as the *lecticarii*—eight muscular temple slaves, four in the front and four in the rear—lifted the lectica off the ground by its long poles. Carrying its weight on their shoulders, they began to make their way over the cobblestone, toward the Carcer, escorted by the guards Caeso and Publius.

Medousa leaned forward to pull the heavy red curtains of the lectica closed.

"Leave them open," said Pomponia. Medousa leaned back. *I should discipline her more often*, thought the Vestal. Still, they had known each other since they were both children, bound together as more than mistress and slave, as friends. "I am just concerned about my colleague," she said, softening.

"And I am concerned about my mistress," replied Medousa. Her voice was still harder than Pomponia would have expected. "You push the limits of your privileges, Domina."

"What Vestal hasn't?"

"You know what will happen if people misinterpret your concern for him as something else."

"I have done nothing that could be taken as impropriety."

"No, but these are unpredictable times," said Medousa.

"It would be expected that a priestess of Vesta would speak for a priest of Mars," said Pomponia. "It would look strange if I did *not* try to spare him."

The slave slumped back. "Perhaps." She crossed her arms and fumed under her breath in Greek. "*Hēra, eléēson.*" Hera, have mercy.

"Medousa, *siōpā!*" Pomponia snapped back, chastising Medousa in the slave's native Greek.

The Vestal and her slave proceeded along the Via Sacra, soon passing by the massive and bustling Basilica Aemilia, its long expanse of two-tiered arches filling Pomponia's field of vision.

The haggling of shoppers on the street, the gossiping of various officials, and the loud, grumbling negotiations of merchants and bankers in the basilica's colonnade died down a bit as those who saw the Vestal litter lowered their voices and their heads in respect to the priestess who passed.

The procession paused momentarily as a matted little dog nipped at the heel of one of the litter-bearers. It took a slave in a torn tunica and two politicians in expensive snow-white togas to free the man's sandal strap from the dog's mouth so the lectica could move on.

"*Mehercule!*" swore one of the politicians as he put a bloody finger to his lips. "That's the hellhound Cerberus, escaped from the underworld."

The lectica hadn't cleared half the basilica when Pomponia saw the chattering, ruminating crowd gathered in the open space in front of the Rostra. They were pointing up, shaking their heads and trying to decide what it all meant.

This crowd had seen much in the last year. They had seen the body of the dictator Julius Caesar lying on the Rostra until Marc Antony's speech had incited them to rise up, claim it as their own, and burn it to ashes in the Forum, near the Temple of Vesta.

But this was different. Cicero was no dictator, no soldier. He was a politician. A civilian. And despite the stature and wealth he had acquired for himself, many still saw him as a man of the people. The sight of his head— tongue pulled out to mock his famous oratory—and swollen purple hands suspended above the Rostra was something they hadn't seen before.

It wasn't the gore that upset them. They were fine with that. They had seen far worse during the wild-beast hunts and gladiatorial fights of the games. Even a chariot race in the Circus Maximus couldn't be considered a success without a few severed limbs rolling onto the track or some broken bodies, whether charioteers or spectators, being tossed around.

The frightening thing about the sight of Cicero's body parts on the Rostra was that it represented a total breakdown of Republican order. If Cicero could be murdered, and his murder so blatantly waved before Rome's collective face, there was no telling how far Antony and Octavian would go.

As the lectica passed by the Rostra, Pomponia turned her head away. She would not dishonor Cicero's life by gawking. *Surely this butchery does not please the gods.*

She thought of him that day so long ago, that day when the elephants were slaughtered at the games and she was still a child who knew so little about the power and purpose of Vesta's sacred fire. She said a silent prayer to the goddess. *Please Mother Vesta, let this not be a mistake. I will offer into your divine flame when I return to the temple.*

Yet instead of feeling comforted, instead of feeling reassured, Pomponia felt a sudden flare of shame spread throughout her body. All of

Rome was in turmoil, and yet her only concern at this moment was for Quintus. That was not right.

She was a Vestal priestess, and her duty was to Rome. She promised herself, and the goddess, that once Quintus was safe, she would put him out of her mind. Whatever feelings she had for him, she would indulge them no further.

For everyone's sake.

* * *

The Carcer loomed in front of Pomponia. Its unadorned stone face and utilitarian columns were a sharp contrast to the fluted Corinthian and Ionic columns and brightly colored ornamentation of the temples and monuments around it. It was the most unfriendly, austere building on the Capitoline or in the Forum. Then again, a pretty prison wouldn't have the same impact.

Medousa stuck her head out of the lectica and spoke to one of the litter-bearers. "Set down near the entrance."

Once the lectica was on the ground, Medousa stepped out and then turned to help Pomponia exit gracefully. A throng of onlookers had already gathered. A Vestal priestess coming to the prison? Why? Could she be pardoning someone? Murmurs of speculation and excitement filled the air.

Without a moment's pause, without stopping to think about what she would say or do, Pomponia pulled her palla tightly around her body and, as if she were Vesta herself come to earth, strode past the dumbfounded guards who stood at the front entrance of the prison.

"My lady," she heard one stupefied guard attempt, but he was quickly hushed by his colleagues. *Leave it to the prefect*, seemed to be the general consensus. *That's why he makes more money than us.*

Pomponia stood just inside the Carcer's portico as the prison's prefect—a tall, angular man caught with a mouth full of bread—stood up quickly from his desk, knocking over a cup of wine and trying to swallow his food whole.

"Priestess," he choked. And then more clearly, "Priestess, how may I be of service?"

"You may show me to the prisoner Quintus Vedius Tacitus without delay."

It was the *without delay* part that troubled the prefect. Shouldn't he check with someone? "Priestess," he stammered. "Perhaps I could just send a messenger to get General Antony or Caesar . . . They are just in the Tabularium, so it would only take a moment . . ."

Caesar, mulled Pomponia. She would have to remember to call him that. Julius Caesar hadn't just left his great-nephew Octavian his fortune; he had also left him the powerful Caesar name. Knowing the weight this name gave him, Octavian now insisted on being called Caesar at all times and by all people. And why not? His name made him *divi filius*—son of a god.

Apparently the only one who wouldn't do it was Marc Antony. It was bad enough that Julius Caesar hadn't left him so much as a dirty toga in his will. There was no way in Hades he would call the suckling Octavian by Caesar's name.

"You can get Caesar and the general if you wish," said Pomponia, "but I will see the prisoner now."

Exploiting the prefect's uncertainty, Pomponia strode past him. She didn't want to give him time to think or stall or come up with another option.

The prefect rubbed his head. What were his options? He certainly couldn't restrain her. If he laid a hand on her, he would quickly find himself a tenant inside the very prison he guarded.

Sending a silent message with his eyes to an open-mouthed guard— *Go get Caesar! Go get General Antony!*—he fell into step beside the Vestal.

"My lady, it's this way."

"Thank you, Prefect."

Within four or five steps, the light of the world disappeared and Pomponia found herself swallowed by dank darkness. Cold radiated out from the square blocks of stone that confined her like a tomb, and she pulled her palla around herself more tightly.

With each cautious step into the black, airless space, she felt more disconnected from the living world. Her elbows brushed the hard rock walls. Instinctively, she began to take shallow breaths and lowered her head.

The heavy stone roof hung impossibly in the air above her. It felt as though it could collapse at any moment and crush her. Tiny shafts of light managed to snake through the small chinks between the thick blocks of stone, but other than that, there was no light.

Why had the prefect not brought a torch along? A dry, hacking cough emanated from somewhere within the stony gloom. *He doesn't want me to see what's in here*, she realized.

And then a few feet ahead, the underworld appeared.

It was a small hole in the stone floor, no larger than a man's body, from the depths of which flickered a faint orange flame. A low murmur reverberated from the hole. The voice of Hades.

No. She knew the voice. It was Quintus, in prayer.

Pomponia felt lightheaded. She had heard about this hole. Prisoners who were to be executed were thrown down it—literally *thrown* down it—to squat twelve feet underground in filth and fear until the day of their death.

It wasn't that long ago that Julius Caesar had defeated the mighty Gaul warlord Vercingetorix, chieftain of the Arverni tribe, and then had him thrown down this very hole, where he had rotted for five whole years. The next time Vercingetorix saw the light of day was when he was pulled out for Caesar's triumph. He was paraded in the Forum before a jeering Roman mob, ultimately needing to be dragged along the cobblestone by a horse when his legs gave out. Men and women swore and spat at him. Children threw food and feces at him. Two executioners lugged him onto the Rostra, tore off his clothes, and strangled him to death.

Pomponia remembered watching the whole thing. It had been a great day. The warrior king of the Gauls—Rome's greatest enemy—was dead. Hail, Caesar.

Swallowing her dread, the Vestal lowered herself with as much dignity as possible onto her knees. The cold instantly sank into her bones. The sewer-like stench from the pit was unimaginable.

"Quintus Vedius Tacitus," she called down.

The murmuring stopped. Shuffling. Pomponia leaned forward, straining her eyes to peer into the dimly lit tunnel to the underworld.

A voice rose up from below. "Priestess Pomponia?"

No pretense, no conceit. Just fear and desperation.

"Yes, are you—"

"My father," his voice was hoarse. "Have you seen my father?"

"*In dea confide*," said Pomponia. Trust in the goddess.

"I trust you," he replied.

Pomponia had no idea why, but her heart sank just a little. Just then, she sensed someone else in the space around her. Still kneeling, she turned around to look behind her.

"Lady Pomponia," said Marc Antony. "To what do we owe the honor of a Vestal's presence in such a hateful place?" An edge of impertinence.

Pomponia stood up and faced him squarely. "In the sacred name of Vesta, I ask for the release of this prisoner, Quintus Vedius Tacitus, citizen of Rome, priest of Mars, *causarius* soldier of Julius Caesar." She paused and then met his impertinence with her own. "And his father."

"I see . . ."

Another voice. This one younger and sharper. "Free the prisoners immediately."

Pomponia looked past Antony. Even in the faint light she could see the glimmer in Octavian's cool gray eyes.

"Caesar," said Pomponia. "Thank you."

"Not at all," said Octavian. "I must thank you for bringing the innocence of this man and his father to our attention. They will be released at once and any claims against their estates shall be removed. Chaos reigns in Rome right now, and such mistakes are lamentable." He took a step back. "Now please, Lady Pomponia, let me escort you out. This is no place for a priestess of Vesta."

"Of course, Caesar. How kind."

The daylight bored painful holes into Pomponia's eyes, and she squinted as Octavian led her back outside toward her lectica and an astonished Medousa, who stood beside it. Pomponia had the inopportune urge to laugh at her slave. With her expression—eyes wide, mouth hanging open—Medousa looked a little like the wild-eyed Gorgon depicted on her pendant. The slave had not expected to see her mistress exit the prison all but hand in hand with Caesar.

"I shall send some extra guards to accompany you back to the temple," said Octavian. "You have my word that all I have said will be done." He smiled. "My divine father had great respect for the Vestal order. As Caesar, I intend to build upon that friendship."

"I am happy to hear you say so," said Pomponia. She made a quick study of him: he was taller and much younger than Antony, who stood behind him, but not nearly as muscular. A model of diplomacy and shrewdness, she knew that she was not as much studying him as they were studying each other.

"Priestess Pomponia," he said. "I have been told the Vestalis Maxima has charged you with many duties. I expect we will be working together more. We should get to know each other better, nay? I will have my clerk arrange a meeting."

"I would like that, Caesar."

Over Octavian's shoulder, Antony spat on the ground near the entrance to the Carcer. A look of restrained irritation crossed Octavian's face. As allies, he and Antony were united in their hunt for Caesar's assassins. As men, however, they were oil and water.

Pomponia stepped into the lectica, followed by Medousa. The lecticarii lifted it off the ground and turned back the way they had come, with the crowd of enthralled onlookers tripping over each other to clear a path for them.

"Perhaps this Caesar is not all bad," Pomponia said to Medousa.

But her slave only huffed. The memory of the rich red tapestry that had covered the ceiling of Julius Caesar's gilded lectica and of the gold medallion of Venus that had stared down at her while the dictator had taken her innocence filled Medousa's mind.

"If you've seen one Caesar, you've seen them all," she said.

CHAPTER V

Πῦρ Γυνὴ καὶ Θάλασσα, Δυνατὰ Τρία
Fire, woman, and the sea are the three mighty things.

−AESOP

EGYPT, 42 BCE

One year later

"Apollonius, if you give me one more papyrus to sign, I shall have you ripped apart by crocodiles in the bathhouse."

Queen Cleopatra slouched back into the carved wooden chair that sat in the middle of her large study within the Royal Palace in Alexandria. She threw the stylus at Apollonius, making a half-hearted attempt to hit him as a sleek brown cat leapt lithely onto her lap.

"Majesty," said the slave, bowing. He collected the scrolls that were scattered across the queen's ornate desk, the surface and legs of which were inlaid with gold and lapis lazuli. "I will speak to the vizier about this. I believe there is much here that he can handle."

"I'm hungry." Cleopatra snapped her fingers, and a female slave knelt before her. "Iras, bring me some wine cake."

"Yes, Majesty."

As Apollonius leaned over the desk to gather the last of the papyrus scrolls and pile them neatly into a basket, Cleopatra's languid gaze settled on him. "Any news?"

"The Roman civil war continues," said Apollonius. "Although things may change soon. Only this morning I heard that General Antony and Caesar"—Cleopatra struck him on the head and the cat jumped off her lap—"General Antony and *Octavian* are in Macedonia. All sources say that Brutus and Cassius have fled there. Perhaps Antony and Octavian have finally hunted them down."

"One pair of Roman wolves hunting another pair of Roman wolves." She snorted. "Typical."

Iras returned with a platter of wine cake and set it before the queen. Cleopatra picked at it without taking a bite. An oil lamp on her desk sputtered, and she passed her hand back and forth over the flame, lost in thought.

"Majesty," said Apollonius, "will you be attending the Royal Library today? The curator humbly requests your approval on a new wing dedicated to Majesty's writings. I have seen it myself, and it is quite splendid. There is a central reading area with your works on mathematics and astronomy, and then another for philosophy."

"Yes, Apollonius." She pushed the wine cake aside and took a sip of cool honey water. "It's just a matter of time until a Roman wolf is at our door. The Royal Library needs to be protected. Certain works must be hidden."

"Romans are not accustomed to educated women, Majesty. Nor to queens. Regardless of which wolf wins, they will try to destroy your books. A strong woman makes them look weak. And you did make enemies during your time in Rome."

Cleopatra rubbed her temples. "I did my best Apollonius, but they were such vapid oafs!" She winced at the memory. "During supper, they would gorge themselves on baked dormice and ostrich brains and birds baked in feathers, all of it washed down with a drink made of fish innards. The worst of them were skillful enough to ingest all of this while tonguing the breast of someone else's wife and calling for more wine. It was unbearable. And forget trying to elevate the conversation to something above the groin! Oh, there were some bright lights. I did enjoy Senator Cicero's company in the beginning. He was fascinated by Ptolemaic Egypt." She tapped a finger on her desk, thinking back. "That buffoon Marc Antony was always creating trouble between us, though."

The brown cat lifted a paw to claw at the queen's dress, but she brushed it aside, standing. "Are the prisoners ready?" she asked.

"Of course, Majesty. They have been brought to the courtyard and all is prepared."

Cleopatra strolled regally across the large brown and green tiles of the palace floor, past a colonnade of thick columns painted to look like towering palm trees, and then past a long row of larger-than-life statues of Egyptian gods and goddesses.

Isis, all-powerful goddess of marriage and wisdom, wearing a scarlet dress and holding a cobra. Osiris, god of the underworld and husband to Isis, his skin painted a fertile green to symbolize the cycle of death and rebirth. Horus, the sun god and son of Isis and Osiris, his falcon head painted brilliant blue with a red-and-white crown atop it.

Cleopatra felt a pang of nostalgia. She had walked this corridor many times with Caesar. Once, he had stopped in his tracks directly in front of the statue of Tawaret, goddess of pregnancy and childbirth. With the head of a hippopotamus, limbs of a lion, tail of a crocodile, and belly of a pregnant woman, it had made him laugh out loud.

Cleopatra, he had said, *when I am dead, I fear my Egyptian statue will have the limbs of a tortoise, the tail of a camel, and the head of an ass.*

Ah yes, my love, she had replied, *but I will make sure it is dressed in full Roman armor. How better to outfit an ass-headed god?*

As the brown cat trailed behind her, playfully pawing the back of her dress and catching his claws in the fabric, she strode past the chamber room in which she had first met Caesar. She had been so desperate then.

Her brother Ptolemy—that mouth-breathing, backstabbing little bastard—and his push for sole power had forced her into the desert, on the run for her life and struggling to raise an army, while he ingratiated himself to Caesar in her palace.

But she had always been smarter than him. She had arranged to have herself rolled into a carpet—oh the stifling heat in there!—and carried into the palace as a gift to Caesar, and all of it right under Ptolemy's ugly, upturned nose.

Cleopatra smiled at the memory. The guards had unrolled the carpet at Caesar's feet and, to his astonishment, out she had tumbled. The exiled queen of Egypt herself, her gold bangles jingling, and her royal diadem perched in her messy hair.

Caesar had jumped to his feet in surprise and amusement. They had talked all night in the flickering light, the scent of the castor oil in the lamps perfuming the air. When his eyes fell on her breasts, she had pulled him down onto the carpet, on top of her, and they had made love until morning. The virgin queen of Egypt lying under the Roman general Julius Caesar. It was the way he wanted it. It was the way it always had to be.

A while after that royal coming together, her brother Ptolemy's body had been found floating facedown in the Nile, his flesh so green with rot that even the vultures hadn't touched it. Julius was a man of his word.

For the most part, it had been a good personal and political arrangement for both of them. Caesar was a reasonable lord, and he trusted her judgment. She showed him Egypt's mysteries, including the great pyramids, and they sailed along the Nile, not just as lovers and allies, but as true friends.

She took him to the tomb of his hero, Alexander the Great, where he stood with bated breath while she pulled back the drapery of Alexander's sarcophagus to reveal the warrior's mummified body. Caesar was moved to tears by the sight of the great general's soft wisps of hair, and she had kissed his face dry.

They had so many plans. If a Roman general and an Egyptian queen could be lovers, could not Rome and Egypt be true friends? She thought of the great library they were to build together in the Roman Forum. Even the Romans had welcomed the idea. Senator Cicero and many others had expressed their support. And then there was Caesar's influential great-aunt, the chief Vestal, who had paid for a beautiful shrine to Isis to be built in Rome.

Ah, but Caesar was gone. So too were the certainty of Cleopatra's reign and the stability of Egypt. Most frighteningly, also gone was the safety of Caesarion's life. When it came to Caesarion, it didn't matter which Roman wolf won. Both would tear out his throat.

Caesar's assassins would never let a son of Caesar rule Egypt. One day he would seek to avenge his father's death—they knew that—and he was too much of a risk. And Antony and Octavian? Perhaps Antony would not care. But Octavian, that opportunistic little runt who had the gall to call himself Caesar, he would definitely want Caesarion's head on a spike. Two Caesars was one Caesar too many.

As Cleopatra approached the courtyard, two slaves pushed open the heavy doors and an explosion of hot sunlight burst into the palace. She squinted but kept walking until the smooth tile under her sandaled feet turned sand-covered and the courtyard surrounded her on all sides.

Five wooden chairs sat in a semicircle on the sandy tile of the court-yard floor. Four men in loin cloths and one woman in a short dress were tied to the chairs. Two of the men were writhing in pain, mouths bubbling sputum and eyes rolling in their sockets.

The queen sat on a long couch that faced the chairs, tucking her feet under her body and casually scooping up a spoonful of cool pomegranate seeds from a large silver bowl on a nearby table.

"Proceed," she ordered to no one in particular as she crushed the seeds between her teeth.

A man with a bright orange scarf around his head bowed before the queen. "Thank you, Majesty." His voice was as gravelly as the sand under his feet.

He gestured showily toward the semicircle of chairs. "The first prisoner is experiencing arsenic poisoning, while the second is demonstrating the effects of a hemlock tincture. Both were administered thirty minutes ago."

The first prisoner emitted a guttural groan of agony and vomited on his loincloth. The second jerked and then began to convulse so violently that his chair fell over. Two male palace slaves rushed over to prop it back up only to have it topple over again a moment later.

The slaves looked uncertainly at each other and then shrugged at the queen before leaving the prisoner to jerk and writhe on the ground, still tethered to the chair. A pool of urine spread out across the sand as the pris-oner lost control of his bladder.

Cleopatra's handmaiden Charmion arrived to stand at the queen's shoulder. She turned up her nose at the twitching, drooling prisoners.

"An undignified way to meet Osiris," she said. "Bloated, retching, and contorted in pain. Majesty will not give her enemies the satisfaction of seeing her like this."

"If it comes to that," qualified the queen.

"If it comes to that," agreed Charmion. "If Majesty must take her own life, there are ways that are more becoming a queen." She snapped her fingers at the man with the bright orange scarf. "The snakes now."

Obligingly, the man knelt before the queen, and Charmion, as his assistant placed a long rectangular tray, upon which sat two round covered baskets, on the ground in front of him. The man opened one basket and expertly pulled out a yellowish-brown snake with a horned head and prominent brown crossbands down its length.

Still clutching the snake, he rose to his feet and approached the third male prisoner, who shrieked in wide-eyed panic, desperately struggling against his restraints and pleading to the queen and the gods for mercy. Cleopatra crushed another mouthful of pomegranate seeds between her teeth.

The two slaves who had tried unsuccessfully to right the convulsing prisoner's chair each grabbed hold of his head and tilted it back to expose his neck. The snake handler clamped the snake's jaw on the prisoner's neck and a trickle of blood ran down it.

They all stood back to give the queen a clear line of sight.

Cleopatra stopped chewing and looked at the prisoner with interest. Almost immediately, the prisoner cried out in pain and the area around the snake bite swelled into a hard ball the size of a man's fist. The skin around it bruised into an ugly purplish hue.

The prisoner tensed and then fell into a paralytic state. His bowels emptied. The orange-scarfed man's assistant quickly covered the foulness with a large embroidered silk blanket, silently cursing himself for not bringing a cheaper papyrus one.

I'll take a beating for this later, he thought.

Cleopatra cast a sideways glance at Charmion. "That won't do," she said.

"This one may be more suitable for her Majesty," said the snake handler. He lifted the cover off the second basket and diligently grasped the snake inside, holding it up for the queen's inspection. "Cobra."

The snake handler carried the ribbon-like animal to the last male prisoner, who opened his eyes and mouth wide, pleading for mercy. He cast his frantic eyes at the queen and Charmion, and then at his fellow prisoners.

The three other men were dead—and unpleasantly so. The female prisoner was staring straight ahead and muttering a prayer in a language that he didn't know.

Again, the two palace slaves jerked the prisoner's head back and the snake handler clamped the cobra's jaw on the exposed neck. They all moved aside and stared expectantly at the prisoner who, like them, also waited to see what the effects of the snake venom would be.

At first, nothing. And then the prisoner inhaled deeply, as if caught off-guard by a sudden shortness of breath. His breathing became shallow, labored, and his head fell back.

And that was it.

"A fitting death for a queen," said Charmion. She nodded approvingly to the orange-scarfed snake handler. "Bring me two or three of your best specimens in the morning," she ordered. "And a handler as well. We shall keep them at the palace."

"Yes, Lady," he said. "I am honored to be of service to Her Majesty."

As the queen began to stand, the female prisoner felt a swell of relief in her body. Tears ran down her cheeks and she silently praised the gods.

"Majesty," said the snake handler. "If I may be so bold, may I suggest that you witness the effect on the female body? I have selected a woman of a similar size and weight to your Majesty." He waved his hand toward the female prisoner.

"Oh," said the queen. "I suppose that's wise. Carry on." She took another spoonful of pomegranate seeds from the silver bowl.

* * *

"My Queen," her royal astrologer had said, "the signs are clear. General Antony and Octavian will defeat the assassins. They will avenge the father of your son. Then Antony will come to you."

And so it had come to pass.

Brutus and Cassius were dead, defeated at Philippi. Caesar was once again a powerful name in Rome. The unstoppable General Marc Antony was on his way to Egypt to meet with its queen.

Cleopatra descended the six marble steps into a giant oval bath and sank to her neck in the hot goat's milk. Iras poured a pot of melted honey into the bath, and Cleopatra swam leisurely to stir the luxurious mixture. Still, she couldn't quite relax.

Antony's messenger had stated the official purpose of his master's imminent visit to Egypt: an administrative meeting to ensure that Queen Cleopatra would continue to pay her taxes and send grain shipments to Rome.

But Cleopatra knew there was more to it. Antony would want to know why she had delayed so long in sending coin or reinforcements to help him in the hunt for Julius Caesar's assassins.

What could she tell him? The truth was, she could not risk taking sides in the Roman conflict. What if the side she chose ultimately lost? She would be seen as a conspirator by the victors, and any chance she had of keeping her throne would be gone.

A large oil lamp fastened to the aqua-and-brown mosaic wall sputtered and then ran dry, and the room dimmed. Iras quietly scolded a slave who, just as quietly, poured more olive oil into the basin. The lamp flickered back to life.

Submerged in the hot milk-and-honey bath, Cleopatra absently fiddled with the garnet gems in her gold bracelet and then slipped it off and tossed it onto the steamy tile floor at Iras's feet.

She chewed her lip and thought back to the Marc Antony she had known during her time in Rome. He was loud and fleshy, antagonistic and carnal. A buffoon. But a brilliant general.

Cleopatra knew little about his personal habits or vices. Now, she had to rely on her spies who still resided in Rome, those who had continued to move in Antony's circles.

Even as she bathed in Alexandria, they gathered the information she needed to know in Rome. What were his interests? What wine did he like best? What did he prefer to eat? What entertainment did he take? What did he find amusing? What were his weaknesses? Most important of all, what kind of woman was he attracted to?

Antony would be difficult to manage when he arrived in Alexandria.

He would be indignant and eager to exert his authority over her and Rome's authority over Egypt. She had to find a way to lower his guard. She had to slip through his defenses and get in close enough to make sure that she and her people were safe.

Cleopatra sighed. Yet another artless Roman man to seduce.

CHAPTER VI

Aeterna Flamma Vestae
The eternal flame of Vesta

ROME, 40 BCE
Two years later

It was the kalends of March, the first day of the month and the date upon which the most sacred ritual in the Roman world took place: the annual renewal of Vesta's eternal fire within the temple.

The ceremony was an old one. Traditionally, it was performed in secret within the sanctum of the temple, but Fabiana had allowed some transparency after a priest, himself inclined to laziness, had questioned whether the Vestals really went through all the trouble of renewing it. Nonetheless, Nona and Pomponia had persuaded the chief Vestal to return to the old ways. This would be the last renewal performed outside the temple.

Accordingly, throngs of people had come out to witness what might be their only chance to see the ritual extinguishment and renewal of the sacred fire. Thousands of men and women—patricians, soldiers, plebeians, freedmen and freedwomen, slaves—now filled the Forum Romanum and surrounded the area around the Temple of Vesta.

While most gatherings of this size would be loud and unruly, this one was quiet and reverent. Mother Vesta had sustained the people of Rome in the tumultuous years following the assassination of Julius Caesar. Sober gratitude had to be shown.

The Vestals, Rome's only full-time, state-funded priesthood, had kept the living flame burning and performed the ancient rites without error, thus ensuring that the Pax Deorum—the peaceful agreement between the gods and mankind—would continue. It was they who had secured the goddess's protection for the city. The crowd's reverence was for them too.

Scarlet banners embroidered with the gold letters *SPQR* hung from the high basilicas and monuments of the Forum. The statuary, fountains, colonnades, and splendid facades of the other temples nearby had been scrubbed clean for the occasion, and the Via Sacra had been swept bare.

Yet by midmorning the cobblestone around the sacred area of Vesta was covered in wild-picked flowers, mementos, and plates of food—all humble offerings to the goddess.

In years past, Fabiana had instructed temple slaves to remove these offerings as quickly as they were placed, yet the Vestalis Maxima, whose health continued to deteriorate, was too fatigued to participate. As a result, Pomponia had inherited the sacred duties and rites. She left the offerings where they lay.

The Temple of Vesta itself had been adorned with long garlands of fresh laurel that hung from its high frieze and wound around each of its twenty columns—columns that rose up from the white marble podium of its round base to support its bronze roof with intricate Ionic capitals. The fine metal screen behind the columns had been polished, and the entire temple had been meticulously dressed in greenery and white flowers according to tradition and to High Priestess Fabiana's exacting specifications.

Through an opening at the apex of the temple's domed roof, smoke from Vesta's fire billowed out and then began to taper off as Pomponia and the other Vestal priestesses inside allowed the fire to weaken. Palms up to the goddess, they prayed and petitioned for her to send sunbeams strong enough to respark her sacred flame.

The temple's bronze doors, which faced east, toward the sun, were usually closed to protect the sanctity of the inner hearth. They were open now though, letting in the sunlight and prompting people to crane their necks to catch a glimpse inside.

With the sacred fire reduced to embers, Pomponia raised the handles on either side of the wide bronze firebowl and lifted it out of its cradle in the round marble pedestal of the hearth.

"*Vesta, permitte hanc actionem*," she said, securing the goddess's permission to perform the ritual.

Pomponia carried the firebowl across the mosaic floor, through the open doors, and down the temple's steps. The other Vestal priestesses followed her out in solemn procession. First was the elder Vestal Nona, who carried a small terracotta figurine of High Priestess Fabiana. Tuccia was next, followed by Caecilia Scantia and Lucretia Manlia.

As soon as the last Vestal had exited the temple, the novices slipped into it to clean the walls, floor, and marble hearth with pure, fresh spring water.

The sight of the Vestal Virgins dressed in their ceremonial white stolas and veils ignited a collective exclamation of awe from those gathered. The only flashes of color in the purity of their dress was the red of their woolen headbands, the crimson border of their formal *suffibulum* veils, and the gold rosettes of the fibula brooches that pinned the bottom edges of the ritual veil in place at the breastbone. People lowered themselves to their knees, many tossing fresh-picked flowers at the feet of the priestesses.

Pomponia led the Vestals to the laurel-draped marble dais that had been erected adjacent to the temple. Upon it stood the Pontifex Maximus, a serious looking man by the name of Marcus Aemilius Lepidus. Carefully, she climbed the flower-lined steps and strode across the platform to set the bronze bowl on an altar.

The two pontifices, the Pontifex Maximus and the de facto Vestalis Maxima, stood side by side as the other Vestals lined up behind them.

To the left of the dais, designed to be a smaller version of the Rostra, sat a who's who of Rome's religious collegia, including the *Rex Sacrorum* and the *Flamines Maiores*, the High Priests of Jupiter and Mars, along with a number of other priests, all seated in the proper order. Pomponia acknowledged them with a respectful nod.

She saw Quintus out of the corner of her eye but avoided looking directly at him. After his experience in the Carcer, she had thought his arrogant nature might soften. It hadn't. He hadn't even acknowledged what she had done for him or his father.

His wife had, though. The day after Pomponia had secured Quintus's release from the prison, Valeria had appeared at the House of the

Vestals with a beautiful gold bracelet and tearful expressions of gratitude.

The next time Pomponia saw her, her eyes were blackened from her husband's fists.

Regardless, Pomponia had kept her promise to the goddess. Once Quintus's safety had been assured, she had done her best to put him out of her mind.

In fact, the two of them seemed to have made a competition out of who could ignore the other more, regardless of whether they were at a public or religious function or simply passing in the street. Every now and then, though, Quintus still found occasion to cast a cold, scolding glance her way. She looked past him to acknowledge the public augurs.

To the right of the dais sat just about everyone else of importance in Rome, most notably Octavian with his sister Octavia, as well as the imposing figure of Marcus Agrippa, Octavian's brilliant general and closest friend, and Octavian's sharp-eyed political adviser Gaius Maecenas.

Pomponia smiled inwardly to notice that Marc Antony was still absent. He was still in Egypt talking money and grain with Queen Cleopatra. Although if the rumors were true, it wasn't all business.

As the Vestal stood before the altar on the dais, a swelling, affectionate cheer went up. "Bless us, Priestess Pomponia!"

"I bless you in the name of Mother Vesta," she said. She heard the authority, the commanding certainty, in her own voice. Fabiana was a meticulous teacher.

Pomponia had presided as acting Vestalis Maxima in several rituals over the past while: the Equus October, the rites of Bona Dea, the Lupercalia, last year's renewal ceremony, the Fordicidia, a number of *lustrationes*, and even the annual opening of the inner sanctum of the temple to Roman matrons during the Vestalia. With each ceremony, with each new responsibility, the natural ease with which she performed her duties increased.

The Pontifex Maximus bowed his head in respect to Pomponia and then put his hands up to begin. "Many generations ago," he said loudly, "our great ancestor, the Trojan prince Aeneas, fled the burning city of Troy with his family. From his royal bloodline sprang the kings of Alba Longa and King Numitor, father of the Vestal priestess Rhea Silvia. This priestess was beloved by the goddess Vesta, but another god loved her with an even greater passion: Mars, the god of war. One night, as the virgin slumbered, Mars could no longer resist. He came to her and coupled with her."

Countless people were watching the ceremony, yet Pomponia suddenly felt the weight of a single, hot gaze settle on her flesh. Her eyes moved straight to Quintus. He was staring at her.

The Pontifex spoke on. "The immaculate Vestal gave birth to the sons of the god, twins she named Romulus and Remus. But her father's enemy learned of the boys and, fearing the powerful men they would grow to be, had them ripped from their mother's arms. The infants were put in a basket and thrown into the River Tiber. But Mars heard the cries of the virgin and her infants. Despite his hard heart, he asked Father Tiber to bring their basket to shore."

A snap from the sacred embers called Pomponia's attention away from Quintus's unreadable stare and back to the bronze firebowl in front of her. She placed her hands on its edges as if protecting the last of the life within it.

"Mars sent a great she-wolf to rescue his sons on the banks of the river. The she-wolf took the infants to her cave on the Palatine Hill, where she nursed them, nourishing them with the spirit of their divine father. When the boys became men, they desired to build a city, the greatest city that ever was or would be. But the brothers had the spirit of the war god within them and fought over who should lead it. To end the conflict, Mars sent an augur who divined that Romulus would build a city, an Eternal City, a city that would rule the world. Remus resisted, but Romulus slew him and named the city in his own honor."

Pomponia steadied herself, willing the Pontifex to speak faster and fighting the urge to look at Quintus again. She gave in, disguising the glance as a respectful nod to the priests who sat next to him. Her pulse quickened. *Damn him to Hades. He's still looking at me.* She looked away yet again and locked her eyes on the fading embers in the bowl.

"In honor of his mother the Vestal, Romulus built a sacred fire on the ground. Around the fire, he built Rome itself. His successor, King

Numa, built a temple around the fire and appointed a priesthood of chaste women to care for it. It is that fire we renew today, upon the very ground our founding father first lit it."

The Pontifex pulled back a heavy red cloth on the altar and Pomponia picked up the earthenware cup of wine underneath. She called out the sacred rites. "Art thou on the watch, heaven-born Aeneas? Keep watch." She looked down into the bronze firebowl. Only a few red embers were left burning.

Pomponia doused the last embers in the bowl with the wine, extinguishing the old fire. It had to be done. It was the only way to truly renew the flame and Rome's devotion to the goddess. Death, then a pure rebirth. The eternal cycle.

Those present fell even more silent. Until the fire burned again, Rome was vulnerable.

The Vestals typically renewed the sacred fire using branches from the *arbor felix*, an oak tree blessed by Vesta and Jupiter themselves. While every priestess was skilled at this and additional wood-friction techniques, other ways to renew the fire were permissible, as long as the goddess was properly invoked and the new fire was not derived from the old.

Today, for this renewal, Fabiana had instructed Pomponia to take advantage of the unusually sunny kalends of March and renew the fire with nothing but the rays of the sun. Not only was it an unpolluted act, it was an impressive sight.

Pomponia lifted a tool of polished bronze off the altar. Its metal had been polished to a mirror shine by the novices so that it could reflect the sun's rays and ignite the new fire. It was a technique borrowed from the Greeks but refined by the Vestals. The Pontifex placed a new bronze bowl before her and she looked inside. The tinder was there, as she had arranged it: dried grasses from Vesta's grove in a round bird's-nest shape.

She looked up at the sun. As she arranged the tool to catch the sun's rays and direct them to the tinder, the Vestals behind her held their palms up to the goddess.

"Vesta Aeterna," called out Pomponia. "First and last, your inviolate priestess begs you to enter this flame so that we may renew your eternal fire."

Heated only by the sun, a black spot formed in the tinder. A moment later, red embers glowed. Wisps of smoke rose up, sunlight filtering through them, but still the fire struggled to be reborn.

Pomponia set down the bronze tool. She covered her mouth with her veil and bent over to recite the Precatio Vestae, the secret prayer that called upon the goddess, into the embers. Her whispered breath made the embers flare up and reach out, crackling to life and quickly consuming the tinder.

She lifted up her hands. *"Vestam laudo,"* she said, *"ignis inexstinctus."*

The Pontifex put his hands in the air. "It burns!" he called out and a thousand voices praised Vesta's name at once. Pomponia carefully added more tinder to the bronze bowl and the fire crackled louder. A loud fire was a good sign. The cracks and snaps were the voice of the goddess speaking to her faithful. But what was the goddess saying to her?

Pomponia smiled down at the new fire. And then, without thinking, she looked up directly into the face of Quintus. A hammer of emotion struck her in the stomach. He had not looked away. This time, she defiantly held his gaze. Would it soften? For a moment she thought it might, but it remained cool and critical, and she turned away.

With all reverence, Pomponia lifted the bronze firebowl and led the procession of priestesses back toward the temple. Inside, they would complete the ritual by placing the new firebowl in the hearth, laying sanctified kindling on it in the proper divine pattern, and performing the last of the secret rites to Vesta.

Pomponia ascended the top step of the temple and moved into the sanctum. Behind her, behind all the Vestals who now surrounded the hearth, the bronze doors of the temple closed tightly.

Moments later, plumes of smoke began to once again rise through the opening in the temple's domed roof. There was a collective cheer from the crowd.

The priests and politicians around the dais stood up, stretched their legs, and began to mix and mingle, strolling into the Forum and making plans for the rest of the day.

Similarly, the large crowd of spectators broke apart as groups of friends and family members started to make their way out of the Forum and into the livelier streets, shops, taverns, and even brothels of Rome.

But Quintus stayed in his seat and continued to stare at the closed bronze doors of the temple.

* * *

By midafternoon, the celebrations had spilled into the Campus Martius, the sprawling public land dedicated to Mars. That was for a good reason. The kalends of March wasn't just the annual date Vesta's fire was renewed; it was also the traditional birthdate of Mars himself. Such an auspicious day presented political opportunities that Octavian wasn't about to pass up.

Earlier that day, Pomponia had graciously accepted yet another of his massive donations to the Vestal order. Now, as he attended a public sacrifice to Mars in the Campus Martius, he was vowing to build two new temples in Rome.

Pomponia shifted on her feet as she stood next to him in front of a grand marble altar to Mars. It had been a long day. She wished she could have stayed in the temple to care for the new fire, but a Vestal was required at all religious functions. Her status, and the day's importance, meant that Vestal was her.

At least she had help. Tuccia and Medousa were with her. It would've been impossible to keep Tuccia away. The day's events were to end with a much-anticipated chariot race between the Greens and the Blues in the Circus Maximus, and Tuccia would have sulked openly if she couldn't attend.

"At this moment, the foundation of the Temple to the Divine Julius Caesar is being laid on the very spot of his funeral pyre in the Roman Forum," Octavian's clear, commanding voice boomed outward. "It will stand only steps away from Vesta's temple. In honor of the goddess's life-giving light, in honor of the star that shone over my divine father's funeral pyre, this temple shall be known as the Temple of the Comet Star."

A happy cheer rose up, but it wasn't just for the temple. To the delight of the Roman people, Octavian's generosity extended beyond temples to include large donations of bread, wine, and coin that were being distributed throughout the city. The more people ate, drank, and put into their purses, the more they liked their new Caesar.

"As Romans, we all share in the victory over my divine father's assassins. Thanks must be given to Mars Ultor, Mars the Avenger! That is why, out of my own purse, I also pledge to build the Temple of Mars Ultor in my new forum, where the priests of Mars shall make daily sacrifices to my victory at Philippi!"

Another happy, wine-fueled cheer.

But then Octavian raised his hands. The crowd fell silent, their cheers replaced by sudden reverence and the sound of pipes. The procession of the sacrificial animal had begun.

Shuffling and a loud bellow. Everyone turned their heads to see a great white bull being led toward the altar. Its mighty head was topped with laurel and its horns had been gilded. Its muscular body was draped in ribbons and strings of colorful flowers. Impressed murmurs ran through the crowd.

The Pontifex replaced Octavian at Pomponia's side and stood before the grand altar. "*Favete linguis*," he called out, signifying the start of the sacrifice. All fell silent again as the magnificent beast approached.

Pomponia's stomach dropped to see that Quintus was at the animal's head, gripping the gold nose ring in its flared nostrils and guiding it toward the altar. He was dressed in his priestly white woolen toga and, like all priests of Rome, he performed his duties *capite velato*, with his head covered by a fold of his toga.

He looked handsome.

She clutched the bowl of sacred wafers in her hands. *Why must he lead the beast?* But she knew it wasn't his choice. Like her, he was bound to the rites and rituals of his god. Like her, he performed the duties his high priest put upon him. And guessing from his position, he was being groomed as the next Flamen Martialis.

She met his eyes for a moment and then looked at the marble altar. On top, a bronze firebowl burned with Vesta's flame and incense pots sent fragrant smoke to Mars. A patera and a long-handled *simpulum* ladle held libations of oil and wine respectively.

As Quintus grew nearer—they would be uncomfortably close during this ritual—her eyes dipped down to study the colorful relief carvings of battles, horses, and legions that adorned the altar. Her eyes hesitated over one scene: the god Mars crouched over the sleeping Vestal Rhea Silvia.

In the carving, the priestess's white stola had fallen off her shoulders to reveal the outline of her bare breasts. The mighty god gazed down passionately at her, reaching out one hand to touch her while the other moved his red cloak aside to expose his arousal.

When Pomponia next looked up, Quintus was standing only an arm's length away. His eyes moved from the suggestive carving to her. She felt her cheeks warm with embarrassment, but he looked away indifferently, his attention focused on the bull he restrained. One hand clutched the gold ring in its nose and the other held a length of rope that attached to a loose halter around its giant white head. The animal was docile, having been hand-raised for this purpose, and contentedly chewed at whatever was in its mouth.

The Flamen Martialis approached the altar. "*O divine Jane, divina Vesta*," he said, beginning the ceremony with the traditional invocation to Janus and Vesta. He poured oil over the altar and sprinkled a few drops into the fire that burned on top. "O Father Mars, we pray that you strike down our enemies. We pray that you fill the hearts of our sons with courage and vengeance. We pray that you lend your fearsome strength to the people and the Senate and the soldiers of Rome. To you, Mars Pater, we offer this fine beast as testimony of our will and devotion, so that you may do these things."

Pomponia took two sacred wafers from the terracotta bowl in her hands and then set the bowl on the altar. Quintus pulled downward on the bull's nose ring, compelling it to lower its head, so that she could more easily lift the wafers over the tall beast's head.

As he did, Pomponia noticed his hands. They were large and strong, and she could see the muscles of his forearms tense under his toga as he clung to the nose ring and rope. Wide gold cuffs encircled his wrists, and he wore a single silver intaglio ring. She squinted at the image of the god on the ring's carnelian sealstone. Not Mars. Vesta.

"*Vesta te purificat*," she said. Vesta purifies you. She crumbled the wafers between the bull's golden horns, careful to avoid its eyes. It was important the animal remain unperturbed and willing.

"*Deis*," said the Flamen Martialis. To the gods. He took the wine-filled simpulum from the altar and offered it first to the Pontifex Maximus before taking a sip himself and then passing it to Pomponia, who did the same.

According to custom, she then offered the simpulum to Quintus . . . and then immediately realized that he could not let go of the animal. Instead, she held the vessel to his lips and watched his throat move as he swallowed the wine. Her skin flushed. She had performed this ritual many times with priests, but this time it felt strangely intimate. She poured a small amount of wine over the bull's head and then set the simpulum back on the altar.

"*Victimarii*," the Flamen Martialis called out. At that, two men, their upper bodies bare in preparation for the bloodbath that often attended the sacrifice of such large animals, replaced Quintus at the head of the bull. One of them gripped the handle of the silver dagger atop the altar.

"Step up, Priestess," Quintus commanded under his breath. The same brash, reproaching tone.

She cursed herself. Why was she so distracted? Lifting her stola, she stepped onto a marble elevation alongside the altar. As she did, one of the men raised the bull's head and the *victimarius*—the man in charge of performing the sacrifice itself—opened its neck in one deep, skillful stroke.

Without so much as a groan, the bull fell onto its front knees and then collapsed onto its side, its breath heaving for a moment before stopping altogether. Warm blood surged out of its neck to quickly fill the gold bowl Quintus was holding in place.

Quintus passed the full bowl to another priest in exchange for a new one. The animal was so voluminous, though, that blood still pooled under Pomponia's raised step. The worst of it was absorbed by the sand that covered the base of the altar, but rivers of red still ran across the marble floor to soil the priests' sandals and spill over the edge of the platform onto the soft earth.

Two haruspices knelt in the bloody sand at the animal's side as the man who had dispatched the bull skillfully opened it up and placed part of its entrails into a bronze bowl for the haruspices to read for signs. They muttered to each other, to themselves, and then to each other again before finally nodding in approval.

The signs were good.

Lepidus reached into the bowl and lifted out the animal's weighty innards, holding them up high and then lowering them into the fire on the altar. The pungent smell of the burning viscera was slightly masked by a sweeter fragrance as he sprinkled incense and then poured wine into the fire. The gods would be sated.

"*Gratias vobis ago, divine Jane, divina Vesta,*" said the Flamen Martialis. The ceremony was over.

Thank the goddess, thought Pomponia. She lifted her stola to her ankles and stepped down onto the sand- and blood-covered marble floor. The haruspices were still examining the animal's copious innards. She felt like her own insides had been exposed for the world to see, and she avoided looking at Quintus, who was now toweling the blood off his hands and arms. She was relieved that no one had noticed the tension between her and the priest of Mars.

But in fact, someone had: Quintus's wife.

As the smoke from the marble altar wisped into the air, several butchers approached the fallen sacrificial animal and began to do their work. The best cuts of meat would be given to the priests and senators. The rest would be distributed to the public.

Yet from the way the crowd dispersed, it seemed that most people were prioritizing sport over sustenance. There were still chariot races to be enjoyed at the Circus Maximus. Others were scattering into areas of the Campus Martius, where Caesar's bread, wine, and coin were calling.

Pomponia would have liked to leave as well, but she was delayed by Tuccia, who was busy laughing with a number of senators and priests, all of them arguing about the races, laying bets, and insulting each other's favorite horses and charioteers.

Distractedly, Pomponia clutched the heavy white woolen palla that Medousa—when had she appeared?—had wrapped around her shoulders.

"You're shivering, Domina."

"It's chilly."

"It's warm enough." Medousa's beautiful face was stone.

Pomponia pulled the palla tight around herself. Her slave didn't miss a thing. They stepped silently up into the Vestal's ornate horse-drawn carriage, the gold-and-red-colored curtains pulled back to await Tuccia, who finally dove in, glowing and grinning, to sit opposite Pomponia.

"I have fifty thousand sesterces riding on the Blues," she said. "I swear to the gods, I'll have Proserpina herself toss that twit charioteer Flavius's balls into the underworld if he wraps himself around the *spina* in the first lap again."

"Flavius has more curses on his head than a poxed whore," said Medousa. They laughed at their own flippant bawdiness. It was a release from the day's strict rituals and solemn religiousness.

Finally allowing herself to relax a little, Pomponia tiredly reached down to tug on a sandal strap. "My feet hurt. I should have worn my woolen shoes."

"Then you'd complain your feet were hot," said Tuccia. "Just be thankful it isn't raining. It's been good signs all day."

"Give me your foot, Domina," said Medousa. She began to loosen Pomponia's sandal straps, but Pomponia slapped her hands away.

"Leave it. It'll just hurt worse when you tie them back up." She leaned back on the cushions inside the carriage, wishing it were her own bed, and closed her eyes.

* * *

When Pomponia next opened her eyes, Tuccia was slipping out of the carriage with a determined look on her face. They had arrived at the Circus Maximus. The races had already been underway for hours, and she didn't want to miss another lap. Tuccia was halfway to the entrance of the stadium, her two guards rushing to keep up with her, before Pomponia had even straightened her veil.

Pomponia exhaled and wondered how Tuccia still had so much energy. They had been up since well before dawn. An energizing thought occurred to her: perhaps Quintus would be at the races as well. She felt a sudden longing to see him again. It was the way his throat moved when he swallowed . . . She swore at herself for succumbing to such thoughts. Yet she understood why she was having them.

Vesta's priestesses served the goddess during those years when natural desire was at its strongest. At twenty-two years old, Pomponia knew that her body's instincts would work against her sacred duty. Yet there were regimens that could help. Some Vestals applied camphor oil to their breasts twice daily, using the scent to quell desire. They also ate the berries from the chaste tree at every meal to resist the passions that Venus placed in their hearts. Pomponia decided that she would start such a regimen immediately. Caecilia had already been following one for a year or more.

While sexual indulgence was strictly forbidden—every Vestal knew the horrific punishment for incestum—Vestal priestesses nonetheless enjoyed the distraction of other physical indulgences. The House of the Vestals was as comfortable as any palace or upper-class estate in Rome, with private rooms and the finest of baths, studies, and gardens. Vestals ate the most sumptuous of foods, and their every need was tended to by slaves.

Still, the sight of Quintus's strong hands gripping the bull's rope lingered in Pomponia's thoughts. She heard his whisper, deep and masculine, in her ear. *Step up, Priestess.*

Pushing the memory from her mind, she stepped out of the carriage after Tuccia. Medousa followed on her heels.

Even before they entered the stadium, their eardrums throbbed from the sounds of the races. The thunderous sound of hooves pounding the sand. The loud roar of wooden chariot wheels shaking and straining under high-speed pressure. The slap of the charioteers' whips on the backs of the sweating horses. The constant, deafening din of the crowd as over one hundred thousand spectators cheered for their favorites and jeered at their foes.

Vendors lined the entrance to the Circus Maximus, selling wine and fresh sausage, and the smell made Pomponia's stomach rumble. She tried not to think about food as the guards escorted her, Tuccia, and Medousa to Caesar's private seats. Normally, they would sit in the area reserved for Vestals; however, with most of the priestesses busy at the temple, Octavian had invited them to watch from Caesar's private balcony.

"Ah, Priestess Pomponia," said Octavian, rising to greet her. "Welcome. And welcome to you, Priestess Tuccia."

"Thank you, Caesar," said Pomponia. "I hope we haven't missed the final race. Tuccia has a small fortune riding on it."

Octavian grinned at Tuccia. "As do I, Priestess. Greens or Blues?"

"The Blues," said Tuccia. "And I am certain that Caesar would never bet against a Vestal."

Octavian put his hand on his chest. "*Numquam!*" Never! "I would never cross Vesta Felix. Ladies, please sit." Graciously, he seated Pomponia and Tuccia on either side of his sister Octavia. She wore a white stola, not unlike a Vestal, although it was decorated with deep purple embroidery that complemented the purple border on her brother's toga.

Octavian returned to sit next to his general Agrippa and his adviser Maecenas as a line of well-armed soldiers stood behind them all, keeping vigilant watch over their master while their crested helmets and gleaming armor advertised Caesar's power to the citizens of Rome.

The massive oval of the Circus Maximus, the oldest and largest race-track in Rome, spread out in the long valley below Pomponia. Waving, shouting fans lined its mile-long circumference as four teams of four-horse chariots thundered down the track, shaking the ground and taking the turn around the spina at breakneck speed.

"Priestess Pomponia," said Octavia, "forget the chariot races. Let's bet on which one of us most wishes she were home right now sitting in a hot bath."

Pomponia laughed. She had always liked Octavia. Despite Octavian's obvious efforts to nourish a friendship between the two women—such an alliance could only benefit his position—their friendship needed no encouragement from him. It had deepened on its own over the past couple of years. Pomponia's friendship with Octavian had similarly grown. He had kept the promise he had made to her years earlier, when she had first met him at the Carcer.

"How is your son Marcellus?" asked Pomponia.

"He is happy," replied Octavia. "Such is the blessing of childhood. His father died only months ago, but all he cares about is his wooden toy horse and honey cakes."

"I was saddened to hear of Gaius's passing. He was a good husband to you."

Octavia leaned closer to her. "It hasn't been officially announced yet," she whispered to the Vestal, "but it looks as though I am to be married again."

"So soon? To whom?" asked Pomponia.

"To Marc Antony. It is no secret that he and my brother have had strained relations. Caesar believes such a marriage will strengthen their political alliance."

"Oh . . ."

"You don't approve, Priestess?"

"It's not that . . ."

"You're thinking of the rumors about him and Cleopatra," said Octavia. "Don't worry. I've also heard them."

"Are they only rumors?"

Octavia looked sideways at Pomponia. "Of course not. Everyone knows they've been having an affair since the moment he landed in Alexandria last year. Although I cannot blame Antony. He's only a man, and you remember what Cleopatra was like. Every man in Rome was fascinated by her."

"Men are always fascinated by novelty," said Pomponia. "Roman men are accustomed to Roman women. Cleopatra was something different. She wasn't ruled by a man. She ruled *over* men. At every party, while Roman women gossiped with each other in the garden, she was in the *triclinium* drawing magistrates into debate. I never once saw her wear a proper stola or palla. Her gowns clung to her breasts more tightly than a senator clings to his purse. I don't know how the fabric held." Pomponia shrugged. "Like you said, they're only men."

Octavia grinned. "Well, Antony will have to make do with a wife who wears looser-fitting clothing, I'm afraid. My brother believes that women should be virtuous in all things, including dress. He'd have me outfitted as a Vestal priestess if custom allowed it."

"This Caesar, even more than the one before, is a great friend to the Vestal order," said Pomponia. She smiled warmly at her friend. "Antony is a Roman man, Octavia. When it comes down to it, he will prefer your virtue. And I am certain the affection that he and Caesar have for you will become a bond between them, especially when a child comes. It will strengthen their alliance and maintain the peace. All of Rome will have you to thank for that." She tugged at Octavia's stola. "Loose-fitting clothing and all."

The crowd erupted into a sudden roar, and Pomponia and Octavia stood up, along with tens of thousands of other spectators, just in time to catch a glimpse of a green-and-silver chariot as it bounced into the air, flipped over, and landed hard on the track, flying apart into wooden splinters.

"Where's the charioteer?" asked Pomponia.

"There he is," said Octavia, pointing at a pair of legs, one of them bent at an impossible angle, lying under the pile of large wooden fragments. "Oh, and there's the rest of him." The charioteer's head and torso lay on the sand a few meters away. His body had been severed in half from the force of the impact and from the reins that he had wrapped tightly around his waist.

The crowd erupted into an even louder roar as another chariot approached the wreck at full speed. It was too late to maneuver, and the driver had no choice but to trample the body of his competitor, mashing what was left of him into the sand.

"Normally I prefer the races to the games," said Octavia, "but not today."

"I remember watching an elephant hunt once when I was a child, and Senator Cicero said—" Pomponia bit her lip. What a stupid thing to say.

"I am sorry, Priestess," said Octavia. "My brother deeply regrets the loss of Cicero. He was a shrewd politician and a true Roman, and would have been a valuable adviser to Caesar." She folded her hands in her lap and spoke more privately. "Octavian bartered tirelessly for Cicero's life. He even offered Antony a large sum of money. But Antony was immovable. He wanted Cicero dead. It threatened to undermine their alliance and their hunt for the assassins, so Octavian finally conceded."

"Let's hope a softer voice can temper Antony's nature," said Pomponia.

Octavia nodded. "Yes, let's hope." She parted her lips to say something else, thought twice, and smiled pleasantly instead. "Bad luck for that driver," she said airily. "I don't know if you follow the races, but he's driven as a slave for ten years and was just about to be manumitted."

"Tuccia is the race fanatic," said Pomponia. "I cheer for whomever she's cheering for. I've found she's easier to live with that way."

A female slave with a platter bowed before Octavia and the Vestals. "Mint water, Dominae?"

They all took a glass. Pomponia had to stop herself from draining the cool, refreshing liquid in one swallow. To her delight, the slave returned moments later with a selection of pears, oysters, and cold meats. Gold cups filled with good wine followed.

Pomponia's stomach had just settled, when a familiar deep voice made it flip. Quintus. *When had he arrived?*

". . . Yes, it took longer than expected, Caesar. The haruspices think the more time it takes them to study the entrails, the more impressed we are at their divinations. They mistake our relief at the end of their study for awe."

"Do you know the old haruspex Longinus?" Agrippa asked Quintus, and then without waiting for an answer, "May the gods either help you or slay you if you put a pig liver in front of that man! He'll poke it and interpret for hours and then say the signs are unclear and start over with a different pig. And all just to hear his own shrill voice prophesize. He could talk the ears off a donkey, and the donkey would be grateful for the silence."

"Thank merciful Fortuna he retired last year, General," said Quintus. "But there's always another. *Semper idem.* It's always the same thing with haruspices."

Pomponia willed herself to make small talk with Octavia, doing her best to ignore the sound of Quintus's voice and the looming presence of his body standing next to her. But it wasn't to be.

"Ah, Priestess Pomponia, your colleague Quintus has joined us," said Octavian. "What good fortune to have both of you here today. With Vesta and Mars on the side of Caesar, what need have we of haruspices? The signs can only be good."

Pomponia offered Quintus an obligatory formal smile. Her blood quickened in anger as he turned back to Caesar without so much as acknowledging her presence.

"Caesar, rumor has it that you are ready to be Pontifex Maximus. Has Lepidus tired of ceremony so soon?"

"Lepidus tires of anything that requires work," said Octavian. "But no, I am going to let him keep his office for now. He is a better priest than soldier. I look forward to the appointment, though. My divine father per-formed his solemn duty as chief pontiff, and I desire to do the same."

A clamor rose from the track, and Pomponia blinked to see fresh chariots charge out of the starting gate. She had been so distracted by Quintus's ar-rival that she hadn't even noticed that one race had ended and another begun.

As the horses charged down the track, their hooves kicking sand into the air, the chattering ceased, and everyone took their seats to watch. Pom-ponia's chest tightened as Quintus sat in the empty seat next to her.

She turned her head to busy herself by talking to Octavia, but Caesar's sister was now turned in her seat and in deep conversation with Terentia, the young wife of Maecenas, who sat behind her.

Pomponia watched Quintus out of the corner of her eye, careful to appear captivated by the race below. He sat rigidly in his chair, setting his hands on his lap and then awkwardly placing them on the armrests. He cleared his throat.

"There's a lot of money riding on the heads of these drivers," he said, making a clumsy attempt at small talk. "Which man do you favor, Priestess?"

"I favor no man in particular." The words had a more bitter edge than she had intended.

He said nothing. Then softly, intimately, "Pomponia . . ." But he caught himself and stopped.

The unexpected softness of his voice struck Pomponia harder than she could have imagined. She hadn't heard a man say her name plainly, without an honorific before it, since she was a small child. She felt a flut-ter deep in her stomach, and her throat tightened as if tears would follow.

Quintus had exposed himself simply by the way he had uttered her name. And in that one moment, he had shattered years of pretense be-tween them.

CHAPTER VII

The Altar of Juno

"The augurs are good for a wedding. Too bad the groom is already drunk as Bacchus on the Liberalia."

The Vestalis Maxima Fabiana laughed at her own joke with only slightly less discretion than she would have in days gone by. Pomponia smiled at her. It was a gift from the goddess to see the high priestess feeling well enough to leave her bed and return to public life. It was an even greater blessing to see glimmers of her usual audaciousness shine through the sickness that had plagued her for months.

The wedding of General Marc Antony, newly returned from Egypt, and Caesar's sister Octavia was a political match through and through. Everyone knew the marriage had been Caesar's idea. It was his way of building a bridge over the rough waters of his and Antony's alliance.

Yet Antony had not refused. He had left Alexandria and Queen Cleopatra for Rome the day after Caesar had proposed the union. That was a good sign.

The assembly of wedding guests reflected the political nature of the marriage: senators, army generals, high-ranking priests, Rome's wealthiest and noblest families, a few foreign dignitaries, and of course, the Vestal priestesses. The men were dressed in their ivory-colored togas, the women in their brilliantly colored stolas and jewels. Even Fabiana and Pomponia had accentuated their white stolas and veils with their best jewelry to mark the occasion.

Marc Antony and Octavia Minor stood under a sky-blue canopy before the Altar of Juno, goddess of marriage, as a robed and hooded priest said incantations to Jupiter.

Upon the altar was a bronze firebowl that burned with Vesta's fire. Pomponia had started it herself with a flame from the sacred hearth. Beside the bowl were a gold cup of wine, the wedding cake, and the marriage contract. Wedding torches burned on either side of the altar.

Octavia was a beautiful, perfect bride. She looked fresh and duteous, the living image of Roman tradition. That was her purpose, after all: to represent her family, specifically her powerful brother Caesar, as the embodiment of traditional Roman values. That, and to produce children. Preferably male children.

She wore a pretty white dress tied at the waist with the *nodus Herculaneus*, the knot of Hercules, a symbol of her fidelity to her husband. The knot was believed to be so strong that only the demigod Hercules or a loving husband could unfasten it to enjoy the pleasures it protected. A vivid orange veil covered her face, and upon her head was a wreath of flowers and fragrant herbs.

Her hair was arranged in the *seni crines* and, as was customary, her hair had been parted with the tip of a spear. Not only was the spear sacred to Juno, it honored the earliest marriages in Rome, when the first generation of Roman men abducted—at the point of their spears—women from the neighboring Sabine tribe.

The groom looked resigned. He wore a white toga with a red stripe. The wide gold cuffs around his forearms looked like manacles. He was blinking just a little too slowly, obviously feeling the effects of his premarital reveling.

Pomponia cringed. *It's like watching Europa and the bull. May Juno protect her*, she thought.

The priest said a final prayer to Juno as Octavia stood regally and Antony rocked on his heels. Octavian stood behind his sister with his palms up to the gods. He watched, like an all-powerful overseer, as the priest poured wine over the wedding cake on the altar as a libation to the gods and then placed the right hands of the bride and groom together.

The hooded priest wound a white band of cloth around the forearms of Antony and Octavia, binding them together as husband and wife. Stepping forward, Octavian lifted the corolla of flowers and herbs from Octavia's head and raised the veil off her face so that she and Antony could exchange the traditional Roman wedding vows.

"*Ubi tu Gaius, ego Gaia,*" said Octavia. As you are Gaius, I am Gaia.

"*Ubi tu Gaia, ego Gaius,*" said Antony. As you are Gaia, I am Gaius.

Two people becoming one person.

Or at least that's the idea, thought Pomponia. *There's no way in Hades that Antony really loves her. But then again, marriage is business, not pleasure.*

Antony took Octavia's left hand and slipped a gold ring onto the third finger, around the *vena amoris*—the vein of love—that traveled from the third finger directly to the heart. She tried to do the same, but the general's thick, battle-scarred fingers seemed to resist the shackle. He shoved the ring on.

Next, the priest held out his arm to Octavian, indicating it was time for him as the *pater familias*, the male head of the household, to give his sister to her husband's care. Bending over the altar, Octavian pressed the red wax seal of Caesar onto the marriage contract.

The priest uncovered his head to show that the ceremony was complete, and the wedding guests erupted into applause. If this marriage lasted, so too would the alliance between Caesar and Antony. And as long as that alliance lasted, Rome would be at peace. Many stood and threw grain onto the new couple to promote their fertility.

"If the grain sprouts, it will only be a burden to her," Fabiana whispered to Pomponia. "Take me to my lectica, my dear. I will rest on the way to Caesar's house, and we will offer our sympathies"—she winked playfully—"I mean our *congratulations*, there."

"It warms my heart to see you well," said Pomponia. She linked her arm through Fabiana's and escorted her toward the waiting Vestal lectica, noticing just how frail the chief Vestal had become in recent months.

A sudden crash made them both spin around just in time to see

Antony clutching the side of a table to regain his balance as two slaves hurriedly mopped up the shattered amphora of wine at his feet. Octavia was apologizing to those whose togas and gowns were splattered with wine.

Blessed Juno, thought Pomponia. *She hasn't been married long enough to boil an egg, and she's already making excuses for her husband.*

As she helped Fabiana into the lectica and stepped in after her, Pomponia thanked the goddess for making her a priestess and freeing her from the obligation to marry. As a Vestal, she would step down from the order, if she so wished, with wealth, property, and privilege.

As a Vestal, even a retired one, she would never be forced to marry a man she didn't want to, nor would she ever be subordinate to a husband's will or whims. She would never be forced to bear children for him, again and again, until her body wore out in the quest to give him the perfect son he could parade around as his legacy.

She had seen countless women endure the rigors and risks of pregnancy only to have Pluto drag them to the underworld in the midst of their fear and screaming agony, with or without the child inside them. And as often as not, the grieving husband had a new wife in his bed before his old wife's ashes had even cooled.

Talk about a thankless job.

Pomponia arranged her stola and glanced at Fabiana. The high priestess was resting her head against the cushioned side of the lectica, her eyelids already struggling to stay open.

"Sleep, Fabiana," said Pomponia.

Quietly, she instructed the lecticarii to not lift the lectica just yet. She wanted the high priestess to rest. There was plenty of time to make it home and freshen up before the reception. Judging by how freely the wine and conversation were flowing, it would be a while before the wedding guests all made their way to Caesar's house anyway. She sighed contentedly, sat back, and watched it all from the comfort of the lectica.

With a raucous laugh, Antony extinguished one of the wedding torches and passed it to Octavia, who jovially tossed it high into the air. Male and female guests scrambled at once to retrieve it. It was good luck to catch the wedding torch. And for those who were still single, it portended imminent marriage.

Pomponia wrinkled her nose. *Hercules couldn't force that wretched thing into my hands*, she thought, *even if it does burn with Vesta's flame.*

* * *

The first thing that always stood out to Pomponia about Octavian's estate was the fact that nothing stood out about it.

Located on the Palatine Hill, Caesar's private domus was strategically close to the ancient hut of Romulus, Rome's legendary founder. The hut had been damaged and restored more times than anyone could remember, but still it stood, as it had for centuries: a small, round, single-room peasant house that Romulus himself had once called home.

While Caesar's palatial home was definitely an improvement on the rough walls and thatched roof of the domus that belonged to Romulus, it was nonetheless far more modest than many of the homes owned by senators and families of patrician or even equestrian rank. His comparatively simple living arrangements reflected his personal desire for purity in all things.

Yet Pomponia knew that Octavian's penchant for modesty was as much about propaganda as it was personal preference. He led by example, promising the Roman people that his rule would usher in a return of Rome's most honored virtues such as *pietas*—the sacred loyalty to one's family, past and present, and to the gods—and *gravitas*, the development of a dignified, thoughtful, and strong character.

After the violent uncertainty that had infected Rome following the assassination of Julius Caesar and during the bloody years of the proscriptions—for a while, it had been every man for himself—Romans of all classes were once again aspiring to these traditions and holding them up as the virtues that first brought glory to the Eternal City. Rome had come out of the darkness and back into the light.

And Octavian was carrying the torch. He wore the traditional toga and insisted that all male citizens do the same. He required the female members of his family, especially his sister Octavia, to dress in the traditional stola and encouraged all Roman women to have more children. More Romans!

He sang the praises of the traditional Roman matron while simultane-ously proposing laws and policies that advanced the rights of respectable women, finding precedent in the old Republic and citing Cato the Elder, Cato the Wise, who said that a man who struck his wife profaned the ho-liest of holy things.

To Octavian, Rome was a mixture of piety, tradition, virtue, and family. And by the gods, he was determined to make sure his vision of Rome was realized. Not that anyone was offering a contrary vision. It had been a long time since Rome had been so united and hopeful. Octavian had been a merciless butcher during his rise to power. Once established as Caesar, however, he had become remarkably benevolent, even good-humored.

Like the two-faced god Janus, thought Pomponia. *Let's just hope his benign face isn't a mask.*

No doubt others had similar hopes. Despite the unified front and political alliance between Octavian and Antony, Octavian was clearly be-coming the lead wolf in the pack. Pomponia had always known that was inevitable. The name Caesar had a king-like ring to it. And most kings shared a similar character trait: a strong preference to rule alone.

Perhaps Octavia could temper that trait. Perhaps her devotion to Antony would moderate Caesar's ambition. Perhaps she would be the one to finally leash Antony and break the spell that senators and gossips alike believed Queen Cleopatra had put on him.

But even if she did, how long would the proud general be content to play second man to the upstart Octavian, who, brother-in-law or not, was twenty years his junior and had few battle scars? How long before one wolf lunged at the throat of the other and Rome once again convulsed like a beast with its head cut off?

The Vestal litter approached the portico of Caesar's house and stopped before the colonnade that adorned the entrance. Pomponia heard the buoyant festivities of the wedding party within. The mouthwatering smells of the banquet and the happy sounds of music wafted out of the open windows.

She instructed the lecticarii to go a little further and set down closer to the portico than would normally be proper. The high priestess, just now rousing from her nap, was easily winded.

Pomponia stepped out of the lectica to greet Medousa, who had gone ahead and was duteously waiting for them at Caesar's house. Her long auburn hair was blowing in the breeze and she was trying to brush it off her face.

"*Salve*, Domina," said Medousa. "Was the wedding ceremony a tear-jerker? Or was it only the bride who wept?"

"The bride didn't have time to weep," said Pomponia. "She was too busy mopping her drunken husband's wine off her sandals." She stepped out of the lectica and then held back the curtains for the high priestess, who also slipped out.

"You should beat your slave for that mouth of hers," said Fabiana, knowing that Pomponia would never do it. "Now mind yourselves. Here comes Lady Octavia."

Octavia glided out of the house to greet the Vestalis Maxima with all the grace expected of Caesar's sister. She had changed out of her wedding dress and now wore a light-orange stola made of linen rather than the more luxurious silk, widely belted around her waist, her only jewelry an understated set of gold earrings and a bracelet. Her makeup was equally subdued, with the shades of color that had brightened her cheeks and lips during the wedding ceremony largely wiped away.

"High Priestess Fabiana," said Octavia, bowing deeply to the chief Vestal. "I prayed to the goddess that you would be well enough to attend." Her words were utterly sincere. "I am so happy to see you."

"I am sorry we are late, my dear," Fabiana replied. "I would like to say it is out of fashion, but alas, I fell asleep in the lectica and Pomponia wouldn't wake me."

"She cares for you as a mother," said Octavia.

"And fusses over me as a child," Fabiana replied. She took Octavia's hands in her own. "Congratulations on your marriage and the success of your family, Lady Octavia. You have married one of Rome's great men, and your brother is Caesar. Fortuna smiles on you."

"May she continue to do so," said Octavia. "The gods can be fickle. Now let's go inside. It's a hot day for October, nay? And Priestess Fabiana,

I know there is someone special here who will be delighted to see you."

They strolled past the columns of the portico, through the vestibule, and into the atrium of the house, enjoying the coolness given off by the rainwater in the *impluvium*—the sunken pool in the marble floor—and the lush greenery that surrounded it.

A pair of sparrows quarreled noisily over some seeds that lay scattered under a rosebush until one of them flew up and out of the opening in the ceiling through which sunlight filtered into the home and rain fell into the impluvium below.

The *lararium*—the household shrine that graced every Roman home no matter how prosperous or poor—stood just inside the atrium as a symbol of pietas. Located here, near the entrance to the home, it served to bless the comings and goings of family members.

On top of the lararium stood statues of the household gods and Vesta, and beside those a white earthenware oil lamp burned with the sacred flame from the temple. Mementos of family members living and dead also adorned the shrine, as did a guardian snake made of ivory. The diamonds that lined the serpent's long back twinkled as they reflected the flame from the oil lamp.

On the scarlet wall behind the lararium hung several death masks of Octavian's great ancestors. Naturally, the most prominent of these was of Octavian's adopted father, *Divus Julius*, the divine Julius Caesar.

Although Caesar's face had suffered stab wounds during his assassination, the mask-maker had done a remarkable job of capturing the dictator's solemn facial characteristics in wax and then overlaying it with gold. His slender face with its sharp nose and strong chin, his piercing eyes and receding hairline—it was all there, no different in death than it was in life.

The effect was masterful. Visitors were greeted by the omnipotent, godlike face of the revered Julius Caesar, a man whose name had taken on an almost mythical quality in the few short years since his death. His great presence was palpable and sent an unmistakable message to all who entered the new Caesar's home: *You are now within the walls of the most important house in Rome.*

And those walls were something to see. As Pomponia and Medousa trailed respectfully behind Octavia and the Vestalis Maxima to join the wedding guests already mingling in the boisterous atmosphere of the triclinium, Pomponia gazed at the colorful frescoes that animated every wall and ceiling in Octavian's home with theater scenes, garden landscapes, exotic animals, birds, flowers, and dazzling geometric designs.

What Octavian's house lacked in size or marble statuary, it made up for in the grandeur of its frescoes. With every step, the eye was treated to a rich feast of blue, red, yellow, and turquoise images framed by ornate painted columns and brought to moving life by the flickering oil lamps that illuminated them and the lively sound of music that washed over them.

Octavian was a vocal patron of the arts and often boasted that he had hired the best artists in the Roman world. For a man who rarely boasted, that meant something. His love of art and his willingness to invest in it wasn't limited to his own property either. From temples and fountains to basilicas and bathhouses, Rome was slowly enjoying a much-needed facelift. And all of it on Octavian's denarius.

The new Caesar had already gifted a monumental sum to update and expand the House of the Vestals, adding new rooms, painting frescoes in both the triclinium and tablinum, and having elaborate mosaics laid on the floor of the atrium, all of which had been done at the speed of Mercury.

Once that was finished, he had privately commissioned five more marble statues of Vestal priestesses for the peristyle that surrounded the central courtyard and personally hired contractors to restore the temple itself with white marble from the mountains of Carrara. He had even proposed motions in the Senate that markedly increased the already generous pensions and land that Vestal priestesses received for their service to the goddess.

His generosity had its reasons. Partly, it was gratitude for the safety the House of the Vestals had offered Octavia when he and Antony were outside of Rome hunting down Julius Caesar's assassins. There had been rumors that supporters of the assassins had targeted his sister, so he had sent her to live with the Vestals as a precaution. But Pomponia suspected there was more to it, something beyond gratitude and religious piety. Someday, he would need something from her. She knew it. And despite their friendship, she dreaded it.

As she accepted a ruby-rimmed gold cup of red wine from a slave,

Pomponia had a sudden flashback to a conversation she had had with
Octavian years ago—a conversation in the black, dank depths of a stone
prison. *My divine father had great respect for the Vestal order. As Caesar, I
intend to build upon that friendship.*

She sipped the sweet wine and took inventory of the wedding cele-
brants in the dining room. As with all Octavian's functions, the guest list
was a social register of Rome's most influential people, all of whom were
well known to her. Octavian's closest friends and colleagues, Agrippa and
Maecenas, as well as his ally Lepidus, who currently served as Pontifex
Maximus, were in a heated discussion about a treasury matter.

Close by, three prominent senators, the Rex Sacrorum, and the chief
priests of the Mars and Jupiter collegia were laughing and draining their
wine as Marc Antony lifted the tunica of a very pretty slave woman,
pointing between her legs and nodding in approval. Pomponia could hear
Medousa's low groan of sympathy.

In the center of the dining room, lavishly dressed Roman matrons
mixed, mingled, and gossiped their way to a good time. To Pomponia,
they looked like a moving rainbow in their elegant gowns of blue, green,
saffron, gold, and violet. Even through their chatter, which increased with
each cup of wine consumed, she could hear the soft clinks and chimes of
the gold jewelry that hung like ornaments from their limbs and swayed
with every motion they made.

"Ah, here comes your special friend, Priestess Fabiana," said Octavia.
"He has missed you terribly."

Fabiana cried out in delight and Pomponia swallowed her irritation as a
small, white, fluffy dog came bounding around a column to scramble gracelessly toward the high priestess, its nails scratching the floor, and its tongue
lolling out of its mouth. It shoved its pointed nose into the folds of Fabiana's
stola and whimpered with joy as she reached down to tug gently on its ears.

"Perseus!" exclaimed Fabiana. "Oh, my little friend! Octavia, I have
not seen him since your mother died."

"I know, Lady Fabiana. He was my mother's favorite, but she knew his
heart belonged to you."

Fabiana laughed, and the sound of it dissolved Pomponia's annoyance at the little dog's ceaseless hopping and the sharp, high-strung whining that pierced her ears. She turned to Medousa. "Perseus, hey? The hero who slew the Gorgon Medusa. Better keep your distance."

"How clever, Domina," Medousa muttered, only loud enough for Pomponia to hear.

The wife of the high priest of Mars, a dignified woman by the name of Cornelia, noticed the arrival of the Vestalis Maxima, and before Pomponia knew it, Fabiana was surrounded by a throng of matrons asking about her health and giggling at the antics of the little dog.

Hungrily eyeing the several dining tables stacked end to end with cooked meat, cheese, dormice, and other delicacies—she had missed lunch thanks to Fabiana's extended nap in the litter—Pomponia discreetly excused herself to stack a plate with what she knew was more food than was becoming a lady, never mind a Vestal.

Medousa stood a few paces behind her. Pomponia would have liked to offer her something as well, but it was bad enough she was stuffing her face with all the decorum of a toothless peasant. She couldn't be seen letting her slave eat off Caesar's table on top of that.

"You can gorge yourself like the Cyclops when we get home," she whispered to Medousa, who raised her eyebrows as if to say, *Oh, I will.*

Pomponia had just pushed a piece of oil-soaked bread into her mouth—the whole thing at once—when she suddenly felt an uneasy presence beside her. Holding a cloth to her lips and praying that her cheeks didn't look stuffed, she turned around to find herself looking into the lovely young face of Lady Valeria. Quintus's wife.

She wore a pink sleeveless dress, richly embroidered with tiny flowers, and a long violet veil that was fastened to the back of her head to hang down her back. Gold bracelets wound around her bare upper arms and long gold earrings brushed her shoulders. Small pink flowers peeked out from between the black locks of her hair, and black kohl lined her eyes in the almond-shaped style that immediately reminded Pomponia of Queen Cleopatra.

Valeria caressed the soft mound of her belly in the exaggerated manner that too many pregnant women seemed to display when in the company of those believed to be barren.

"Priestess Pomponia," she said pleasantly. She raised her eyebrows at the oil on Pomponia's lips. "My, you're looking healthy."

Pomponia wiped the oil off her mouth, taken aback by Valeria's thinly veiled cattiness. Quintus's wife had clearly indulged in too much wine. Before she could think of what to say in response, Valeria let out a furtive sigh and rubbed her fruitful belly again.

"Oh, I wish I could eat like that," she said. "But I always lose my appetite in early pregnancy. I don't know what it is about Quintus's children. They are as hard on my body as their father is." She smiled widely, goadingly, at the Vestal.

Pomponia sensed Medousa's body tense in anger behind her.

The priestess smiled back. "Congratulations on being with child yet again," she said. "Perhaps this time Juno will bless your belly with the son your husband is no doubt praying for. Third time's a charm, nay?"

The smile melted off Valeria's face. She bowed to the Vestal. "I am feeling unwell. With your permission, Priestess, I shall take my leave of you and find some fresh air in the courtyard."

"Why, of course," Pomponia replied. "You always have my permission to leave, Lady Valeria."

Medousa watched Valeria slink away into the gardens and then turned to her mistress. "What a meager little trollop," she said through clenched teeth. "You could have her thrown off the Tarpeian Rock, Domina."

"Medousa, I can hear your teeth grinding in your skull. It is no matter."

"I could launch her off the edge with my own foot."

"You're a harpy when your stomach's empty, Medousa. Here—I don't care who sees it—eat this dormouse."

"Did you see the way she was rubbing her belly? Gods! She acts like she's carrying a demigod son of Zeus!" Medousa swallowed a mouthful of meat, and her shoulders relaxed. "If not the Tarpeian Rock, Priestess, at least order a public beating? I shall speak with the magistrate—"

"You will do no such thing," said Pomponia.

"Are you sparing her the punishment, or are you sparing her husband the embarrassment?"

"It would be a debasement to respond to the sad trilling of a common housewife, Medousa. Her life is punishment enough. Think of it! Always subordinate, always doing what you're told."

"Yes, how awful," quipped Medousa.

"You could have it worse. Now come help me find this new fresco Lady Octavia was telling me to look at . . . some garden scene with blue birds. She said I'd know it when I saw it. We aren't staying long. I told Tuccia and Caecilia I would be back in time for them to make the races."

Pomponia wandered through Octavian's house, easily greeting friends, engaging in snippets of small talk with senators and their wives, and accepting pious nods and smiles from those few people she didn't personally know.

As always, Medousa walked several paces behind, seeming to disappear when Pomponia was in conversation and then reappearing to once again trail duteously behind her mistress.

The Vestal liked occasions like this. She was free to socialize with friends old and new without the responsibility of ceremony or duty. It was pleasant to be a guest, rather than having to fret over every detail of a ritual while at the same time trying to ignore the itch of the woolen *infula* under her formal veil and the restrictiveness of her layered clothing. A simple white veil and dress, like the ones she now wore, were much more liberating.

"Ah, this must be it." Pomponia smiled as she found the fresco she sought. It was suitably situated in a serene, private alcove of Octavian's house. The fresco depicted the garden of the Vestal courtyard.

In the painting, white rosebushes surrounded one of the courtyard's rectangular pools, in the center of which stood a marble statue of Vesta. The goddess tipped a bowl of orange flames which cascaded down to magically transform into the turquoise water that filled the pool. Inside the pool, ten or twelve blue birds splashed happily and shook the water from their feathers.

Pomponia's nose almost touched the wall as she inspected the intricate details of the fresco. "It's beautiful," she said to Medousa, who stood at her shoulder.

"If such things please you." A man's voice. It wasn't Medousa who stood beside her, it was Quintus.

Her stomach dropped, and she quickly looked at him. As ever, his expression was impossible to read. Anger? Disapproval? Her brow furrowed in confusion and at the unease of his closeness.

His toga was ivory colored with an embroidered stripe: an expensive, upper-class touch. He was freshly shaven and smelled slightly of oil—no doubt having just come from the baths that morning—and Pomponia's eyes once again fell on the silver ring he wore, the one with the Vesta intaglio.

"You and I once saw another creature splashing in that pool," he said.

"What creature was that?"

"The groom."

Pomponia bit her lip to stifle a laugh. Quintus cocked his head and looked at her curiously, and it occurred to Pomponia for the first time that perhaps she was as much a mystery to him as he was to her.

She allowed herself an indulgent look at his face: his dark hair and eyes, hardened complexion, the scar on his ear that extended into his hairline. He seemed to be studying her the same way—her chestnut hair, hazel eyes, and soft features.

"I hear that Caesar has granted you the office of the quaestorship," she said, trying to sound mostly indifferent. "Congratulations, Magistrate."

"He did so when my father retired."

"Well, I'm sure you deserved the posting."

Quintus gazed at her coolly, eyebrows raised. "I never thought otherwise."

Pomponia stiffened. "Well, no man can think of everything."

An awkward silence.

"I've been watching your temple, Priestess," Quintus said cautiously. "The improvements that Caesar has made are . . . acceptable."

"Acceptable?" said Pomponia. "Yes, Magistrate, the improvements are acceptable. But tell me, what about the construction of the new Temple of Mars? I regret that my duties have kept me from visiting Caesar's new forum in the last while. Do you find the construction to be . . . acceptable?"

Quintus looked at her, and Pomponia held his gaze. *I cannot tell if he wants to smile at me or strike me*, she thought.

The priest of Mars and the priestess of Vesta stared at each other in the quiet alcove. Although they had known each other since they were children, this was the first time they had shared a truly private moment as adults, a moment where no other eyes were upon them.

Pomponia felt the familiar flutter in her stomach, the flutter she had started to feel whenever Quintus was near. In a nervous gesture, she raised a hand to smooth the side of her veil, and when she did, the sleeve of her dress fell to reveal the gold bracelet Quintus's wife had given her years earlier, when she had demanded his release from the Carcer.

Quintus's eyes fell on the bracelet, and before Pomponia could react, he reached out his hand and grasped her wrist tightly. Pomponia heard herself gasp and pulled her hand back, but Quintus held it firmly, his grip so tight that it hurt.

"You will let go of me at once," she spat. "Or I'll have you thrown down the same black hole I had you pulled out of."

His grip around her wrist loosened, but then his hand slipped up under her sleeve to clutch the bare skin of her upper arm. His face wore an angry, almost pained expression that betrayed the struggle he was having with his own restraint—wanting to hold her but knowing he should let go—and his nostrils flared with every deep, deliberate breath.

"Quintus, you're hurting me."

In an instant his face softened, and he pulled her toward him, his one hand still clutching her upper arm, his other moving up to hold the back of her neck. Pomponia felt the fullness of his warm lips press against hers. His fingers clutched the fabric of the veil behind her neck, and he brought her lips even closer to his. His tongue slipped into her mouth, his hot breath mixing with hers.

The wave of her body's reaction flooded over her, washing away the sense of outrage, of violent indignation, that she had felt only moments earlier. Instead, her heart pounded, and she surrendered herself to his mouth, his tongue, his force.

"Pomponia," he said breathily. "What do you think of me?"

She swallowed. "I think you're a savage in a good toga who has to control every situation and who delights in telling me what to do."

He smiled, and his face opened up as Pomponia had never seen it.

"You have me there," he said. "Tell me that I'm the only man you'll ever love. Swear it on the Altar of Juno."

Was this *love*? Pomponia opened her mouth but nothing came out.

Quintus moved his hand under her veil to feel her hair. His fingers slid up the back of her neck, caressing her scalp, and a shudder ran through her.

And then they were apart. From out of nowhere, Medousa stepped between them. She turned to Quintus and pushed him with both her hands, causing him to stumble backward. Her beautiful face showed none of its usual sarcasm or removed amusement. Rather, sheer terror filled her eyes.

At the same moment, a shout echoed off the frescoed walls of the alcove.

"Damn you to Hades!" Quintus's wife Valeria was standing at the entrance to the alcove, her lips quivering with rage, and her eyes wildly glaring with shock and spite. She pointed at her husband and the Vestal. "*Incestum!*"

* * *

Although they were in a private alcove of Octavian's expansive house, three or four wedding guests heard the shout and quickly came to investigate. An outburst like that could only mean one thing: some very good gossip was about to be had.

The first to arrive was Caesar himself. "Are you well, Lady Valeria?" he asked Quintus's wife. His eyes were cool, but his face had the faintest trace of a grimace. Octavian was not a man who approved of such unseemly behavior on the part of a well-bred Roman matron.

Valeria dropped her jaw open and shook her head, still pointing to her husband and the Vestal. Her whole body wobbled. "My husband," she slurred, "and that . . . that *woman* . . ."

She muttered something inaudible, pointed her chin at Pomponia, and then shouted directly at Quintus. "I knew it! You told me I was mad, but I knew it! Every time there is a crisis, where are you? Certainly not at home protecting your wife and daughters! Oh no, you're at the Temple of Vesta, rushing to *her* rescue. You have a sickness, Quintus, a sickness and a perversion in your heart. Every day you pass by the temple, every day you stand outside the House of the Vestals and stare at the portico as if Venus herself stood there naked for you!" She swallowed hard as the wine came up her throat. "I tell you, it's a sickness and a perversion! And you are a faithless husband!"

"Oh, let off, you drunken fool," said Marc Antony, himself slopping wine from his cup and slurring his words. The hypocrisy wasn't lost on those around him, and they burst into laughter, as did he. "Jupiter only knows what your dog of a husband has been sniffing after, but there's no way he's wolf enough to catch a Vestal."

"You are wrong. He—"

"It is *you* who are wrong," said Medousa. "*I'm* the one he loves and has loved for years." She bore her eyes into Valeria with the fury of a Gorgon. "And who can blame him, with a wife like you? It is no wonder he thinks of me first. It is no wonder he comes to me every day. What husband would want to come home to you?"

Valeria blinked stupidly. "No, you're not . . ." She shook her head feebly.

"Ah, the smoke clears," said Antony. He pursed his lips and looked at Medousa, nodding in approval. "Quintus, I commend you on your choice of mistresses. You are a true connoisseur, sir." He took a stumbling step toward Medousa, his hand outstretched to touch her auburn hair. "But how did such a creature escape my notice?" Suddenly, he turned to Octavian and slapped him hard on the chest. "*Attat!* Vulcan's red-hot cock, my boy, you're right! I do have to be more aware of things!"

At that, he let out a good-natured guffaw and turned on his heel, heading back toward the party in the music-filled triclinium. The few guests who had gathered to watch the scene unfold followed him. The gossip wasn't that good after all. Just a drunken wife driven mad with jealousy over the beauty of her husband's bed slave. Amusing. Not scandalous.

Only Octavian remained in the alcove. Medousa looked at him and then turned to the dumbstruck Pomponia. "I submit myself to your mercy, Domina," she said. "My indiscretion is unforgivable."

"Caesar, the fault is mine," said Quintus, "for allowing my wife to attend today. The physician says her humors are unbalanced and I should be keeping her confined. Her behavior will be punished. I apologize for the disruption."

"Not at all," Octavian replied. "It would not be a wedding party without some kind of scuffle. Send her home and stay, Quintus. There will be more dramatic tussles to come as the evening proceeds."

Quintus smiled graciously. "Thank you, Caesar. I will do that." He turned to Pomponia. "Priestess, I apologize to you as well. Please excuse me."

Without another word or glance at Pomponia or Medousa, Quintus placed his hand on his stricken wife's back and escorted her away.

Octavian stepped closer to Pomponia. "Shall I have Lady Valeria executed? It could be done quietly, if you prefer. We could dispense with the public scourging and just have her killed—"

"No," interrupted Pomponia, struggling to keep her composure and marveling that no one seemed to hear the thumping of her heart in her chest. "It is already forgotten, and Quintus and I have been colleagues for too long. His wife is unwell . . . and I am not blameless . . ."

"Forgive me, Domina," Medousa blurted out. Her eyes were moist with what Octavian took to be shame but what Pomponia knew was fear. "I should never have put you in this position. I begged you to let me see him, and you allowed it out of your love for me. I am sorry."

Pomponia took Medousa's hands in her own. There was so much she wanted to say. *It is I who am sorry, Medousa. I am sorry that my weakness and my foolishness forced you to do this. You are the best friend I have in the world.*

But there was nothing she could say. For the sake of her own life, the life of Quintus, and the esteem of the Vestal order itself, she had to go along with the fiction Medousa had created.

Octavian tugged absently at his toga, adjusting a fold. "Your slave has exploited the affection you have for her," he said to the Vestal. "It's always bad business to give them too long a chain. I have made the mistake myself, Priestess, especially with those slaves I've known since I was a child. However, I can always use educated Greek slaves in my household. You can leave her here. She will be treated well enough."

"Yes," said Pomponia. There was no other way. She was lucky enough to have dodged Valeria's arrow of accusation once. Suspicion was bound to follow if she, a priestess of Vesta, knowingly retained a slave who had engaged in indecorous behavior. The Temple of Vesta and the House of the Vestals were enduring symbols of purity. Medousa could no longer be associated with them. "Thank you for accommodating us, Caesar. I am certain she will serve you well."

"I have no doubt."

Before she could say goodbye to Medousa, before she could speak with her in private about what had just happened or how her life now belonged to Caesar, one of Octavian's house slaves quietly ushered Medousa away. Caesar was not known for his sentimentality. And slaves were not people. They were property.

Pomponia regained her poise. She had never felt such a flood of conflicting emotions before. The arousal from Quintus's closeness and her desire to be close to him again, the shock and terror of Valeria's accusation followed by the quick relief that no one had taken her seriously, the guilt over Medousa's sacrifice and the sadness of losing her lifelong friend and companion—all of these feelings swirled in the pit of her stomach. Yet she calmed them, calling upon the grace of Vesta and her years of Vestal training—years spent learning how to remain dignified and clear-headed in all situations, from banquets to barbarian invasions.

A familiar voice, although one she hadn't heard for a long time, filtered into her ears.

"Julius had a new slave girl in his bed every market day. You didn't see me making a scene of it on the Rostra, did you? I swear, Priestess Pomponia, the Roman matron just isn't what she used to be."

It was Lady Calpurnia, Julius Caesar's widow. She had watched the drama unfold from the safety of the shadows. Always seeing, but never being seen. Such was her talent. More than that, it was how she had survived life with the dictator.

"My divine father had his vices," Octavian said to her. "How fortunate for him that his wife conducted herself with decorum and dignity at all times. I wish my wife, Scribonia, would follow your example, Calpurnia."

Pomponia said nothing. Caesar had quietly wed the wealthy Scribonia years earlier. But like so many patrician marriages, it was loveless and held together by politics rather than passion. They rarely saw each other, with Scribonia choosing to live in the country and only visiting Rome on the most necessary of occasions. The only time Pomponia had met her was when she had briefly returned to Rome for the funeral of Octavian's mother.

"Scribonia is dutiful enough, Caesar," said Calpurnia. "And she serves her purpose, does she not? She had a large dowry and has given you a healthy daughter."

"Yes, I was able to get close enough to her for that, thank Juno," said Octavian, "but I would divorce her today if you would have me, Calpurnia."

Calpurnia laughed. "I have had enough Caesars. But wouldn't the scandal be divine?"

"And useful," grinned Octavian. "It would distract the people from blaming me for the grain shortage."

Pomponia compelled herself to join the conversation. "I have heard that Sextus Pompey's naval forces are blockading the shipments."

"That is so," Octavian replied. "He uses the empty stomachs of his countrymen to barter for power. His great father would be ashamed. Antony and I will offer him some token posting to keep him happy."

"What about Queen Cleopatra?" asked Pomponia. "Is she still sending grain from Egypt?"

"Yes, for now. But there is nothing reliable about that woman."

"You can rely on one thing," said Calpurnia. "Cleopatra will not be pleased to hear of Antony's marriage to Octavia. I pray to the gods the marriage will strengthen your alliance with Antony, but it may mean even less grain in Roman bellies until the general returns to Alexandria."

"Stability in Rome is a priority," said Octavian. "A hungry Roman is better than a dead Roman."

He was about to say something else, when the bulky form of General Agrippa approached, nodded politely at Calpurnia and Pomponia, and then discreetly whispered in Octavian's ear.

Octavian pressed his lips together, irritated. "Please excuse me, ladies. It appears that a couple of senators are coming to fisticuffs over some disbursements I made in the Subura."

"Of course, Caesar," said Pomponia.

"Fisticuffs," Calpurnia sniffed. "May blessed Concordia protect you, Caesar. Senators may show their fists, but they hide their daggers."

Octavian kissed her on the cheek. "You and I know that all too well," he said as he parted.

Now alone, Pomponia and Calpurnia fell into easy conversation, slowly making their way back to the crowd of wedding guests in the main part of the house.

In the large, frescoed triclinium, Antony lay on a couch chatting loudly but idly with Octavia and Maecenas. He openly eyed his new bride, looking up and down her body in obvious anticipation of the wedding night.

"Do you think there is any affection at all between them?" Pomponia asked Calpurnia.

"No," Calpurnia replied, "but in time, there may be. Antony has not had a wife like Octavia. His other wives were shrews, especially that Fulvia. Not one was a proper Roman matron. They were ambitious and wanton. One of Antony's house slaves once told me that Fulvia used to dress in a toga! Gods, can you imagine such a thing? Octavia is different. Modest, virtuous, subordinate to her husband—those are qualities Antony may grow to admire." She took a sip of wine. "If he can forget that painted whore-queen of the Nile, that is."

"May the gods make it so," said Pomponia. "Oh, Lady Calpurnia, look—there is Priestess Fabiana with that vicious little dog again. She will not part with it. It dirties her stola and causes the most foolish cooing sounds to come out of her mouth, yet she doesn't notice any of it, not even the smell that comes from its yellow teeth."

"*Amare et sapere vix deo conceditur*," Calpurnia replied with a forgiving smile. Even a god cannot love and be wise at the same time.

Pomponia felt a sudden heaviness in her heart. "Perhaps." She touched Calpurnia's shoulder. "You have been kind to accompany me, Lady Calpurnia. Now go visit High Priestess Fabiana and her little white Cerberus. She would like that. I have duties at the temple and must leave soon."

Once Calpurnia had taken her leave, Pomponia exhaled deeply for the first time since the episode in the alcove. She mingled duteously with friends and colleagues, relieved that Lady Valeria was nowhere to be seen. Her husband had sent her home.

But Quintus remained. He stood by a fountain, deep in animated conversation with Agrippa, two or three of Caesar's other advisers, and the high priest of Mars. He was smiling and drinking wine as if nothing had happened. Detached. Cold.

She glanced his way, and he met her eyes for a moment, but he only smirked with that all-too-familiar edge of superiority and indifference before ignoring her and laughing with his companions.

Pomponia put her hands on her stomach to quell the storm of confusion swirling inside her. Lady Valeria's words filled her mind. *You have a sickness, Quintus, a sickness and a perversion in your heart.*

Perhaps he did. Pomponia knew that many men found sport in the conquest of an unattainable woman. To these men, seducing such a woman was a roguish diversion that bolstered their ego.

And there was no doubt that Quintus had the ego of Hercules himself. She had seen it many times. Every scowl, every criticism, every chastening and condescending rebuke she had endured from him over the years, they all came back to her with renewed clarity.

Perhaps his wife was not as mad as she appeared. Pomponia thought back to Valeria's blackened eyes and submissive disposition, to the way she cowered and quickly retreated into obedience when her husband so much as looked at her.

Slowly, the confusion in Pomponia's stomach gave way to indignation, and she cursed her own weakness, her womanish imprudence. It hadn't just stripped her of her dignity. It had cost her the lifelong companionship of Medousa.

It was not proper for a priestess to weep over the loss of a mere slave, but Pomponia had a sudden memory of the day of her *captio* ritual. On that day, Julius Caesar as Pontifex Maximus had taken her to be a Vestal. It was the same day that he had taken, or rather purchased, Medousa from the slave market.

As Pomponia's hair was being cropped for the Vestal veil, she had started to cry at the sight of the long chestnut locks falling onto the white-and-black-mosaic floor. Medousa—herself just a child of twelve or thirteen years—had picked them up and held them to her face, making herself into a bearded man and shouting mock orders at those around her until Pomponia giggled. That night, the first night Pomponia had spent in the House of the Vestals, Medousa had climbed into the bed with her and hummed a song in her ear until she stopped sobbing and fell asleep.

The memory was too much. Knowing the tears would soon come, Pomponia said a brief round of goodbyes and ordered one of Caesar's litters to take her back to the temple. Fabiana was enjoying herself and could follow later in the Vestal litter.

Fabiana. Pomponia knew exactly what *she'd* say when she heard about Medousa: *Good riddance. That woman doesn't just look like Helen of Troy, she causes as much trouble too.*

The Vestalis Maxima had never liked Medousa. Fabiana showed little affection for any slave, but even less for her. If only she could know the truth.

Pomponia passed into the relative quiet and fresh air of the atrium. In the corner adjacent to Caesar's family lararium, the sacred flame burned in a bronze firebowl. The priestess took a sacred wafer from the earthenware tray beside it and crumbled it into the fire as an offering to the goddess.

Divina Vesta, protect Medousa in her new household.

And then the priestess walked out of Caesar's house and into the waiting lectica, feeling more foolish and alone than she had ever felt in her entire life.

* * *

Somewhere in the dimly lit room, an oil lamp sputtered noisily. Other oil lamps burned with more strength, their tall orange flames casting flickering shadows onto the frescoed walls.

In one painted scene, Cupid lay on top of his beautiful lover, Psyche, his wings caressing her bare skin and his hands exploring her body.

Another fresco brought to life the erotic myth of Leda and the Swan: Zeus, in the form of a swan, resting his long neck between the bare breasts of Leda and making love to her in her sleep. The child of their union would be Helen of Troy, the most beautiful woman in the world. Helen, the Greek queen whose love affair with the Trojan prince Paris sparked the Trojan War. Helen, the woman whose face launched a thousand warships.

But one fresco was more prominent than the others. It was painted on the wall opposite the large, luxurious bed. In it, the god Mars lay before a fiery hearth with the Vestal Virgin Rhea Silvia. One of his muscled hands held her down in the frenzy of his passion, while the other hand tore at the fabric of her white stola.

Medousa knew the story well.

Caesar's chief house slave, a middle-aged Greek woman named Despina who had served Octavian since he was a young boy, sat beside Medousa on the bed. "Are you a virgin?" she asked.

"No."

"Who has had you?"

"Julius Caesar took me for the first time. He had me several times. He was the only one."

"I see." She paused. "You will find this Caesar to be a less reciprocal lover. More aggressive too. You will remain still at all times. Say nothing. Do nothing. It will not last too long, and you will be cared for afterward." The slave's words were blunt but kind.

A beauty slave entered the bedchamber carrying a tray of grooming tools. She instructed Medousa to sit on a chair and then brought a pair of shears to her scalp. Long locks of auburn hair fell to the marble floor. Another slave quickly swept them up.

Medousa's head felt strangely light and airy without her mane of thick hair. She clenched her jaw. She would not cry. It was pointless to cry. It wouldn't change anything.

"Stand up and remove your clothing," said Despina.

Without a sound, Medousa stood up and stripped out of her fine tunica dress. As she stood naked in the room, the beauty slave brought the blade to her pubic hair and removed every trace of it. She instructed Medousa to raise her arms and then removed the hair from under them as well.

"Let's get you dressed." Despina snapped her fingers, and a young servant girl approached carrying a pure white stola. Medousa stood silently, holding out her arms as the slaves worked together to dress her in the stola. A white veil followed. It covered Medousa's short hair and fell to her midback.

"Caesar will treat you more favorably if he believes you are a virgin," said Despina. "He is Mars, you see, and you are Rhea Silvia. That is how it will happen." She held a hand out to Medousa. In her palm was a small sponge soaked in blood.

"Put this inside you," she said. "When he penetrates you, the blood will come out. When it does, you must pretend to feel pain. He will finish more quickly that way, and it will be over."

"Thank you for your kindness," said Medousa. She spread her legs and put the sponge inside her body. *Do not cry*, she reminded herself. Despina wiped away the blood on her fingers.

A creak of a door and a slant of light pierced the room. Octavian entered the bedchamber with the same stately presence with which he entered every room, strolling to the bed with confident purpose and natural supremacy. The slaves and servants scattered subserviently and disappeared.

Medousa lowered her head but said nothing and did not look at him. She heard Octavian's toga fall to the floor. He muttered something as he struggled with a sandal strap, but a moment later he was standing in front of her, naked and already fully erect. His eyes moved up and down her body.

He pushed her gently toward the bed and then roughly threw her onto her back, quickly mounting her and tearing at the stola and veil. He inhaled sharply at the sight of her close-cropped hair and smooth pubic area and entered her, fast and hard, all at once.

Medousa cried out in pain, not having to pretend at all.

CHAPTER VIII

Audentis Fortuna Iuvat
Fortune favors the bold.

—VIRGIL

ROME, 39 BCE

One year later

Livia Drusilla reached down to grab her young son's arm and yank him up into the carriage. The little brat was pissing on the slaves' sandals again. She'd be smelling urine until they reached the next milestone. What evil spirit had charged her with such a child? What debt to Dis, that unhappy god, was she fulfilling by enduring such an utterly horrible son?

His name was Tiberius, so-called after his father, but the similarities didn't stop there. He had the same dull-wittedness, the same brainless humor, and the same square block of a head.

A priest of Diana had once told her that a child's capacity was always superior to that of its parents. Livia vowed to herself that if her path ever crossed that charlatan priest again, she would strip him of his robes on the street and beat him to death with the first piss pot she could find.

Still, things were looking up. The proscriptions in Rome were over, and Caesar had announced a general amnesty for those Romans who had fled during them. For the time being at least, Rome was at peace, thanks to the marriage between Caesar's sister Octavia and the general Marc Antony.

Athens was behind her, and so was that stinking, sticky Greek pig Diodorus. No more would she have to suffer his ribald jokes or feign illness to avoid his vile fondling. The smell of his unwashed genitals still lingered in her nostrils. The taste of his bad wine and salty olives still stuck in her throat.

She glared at her dozing husband on the other side of the carriage. Tiberius, a dreadful husband at the best of times, had been an absolutely atrocious husband during their years of exile in Greece. He should have been outraged every time Diodorus stumbled into her bedchamber to pound into her with all the finesse of a battering ram.

Instead, he had turned a blind eye. The coward. Not only had he fled from Rome like a bawling catamite, he had been too chickenhearted to speak against his hairy beast of a benefactor.

Then again, life hadn't been as intolerable for him as it had been for her. The wine was wastewater and the food was excrement, but there were plenty of both. There were plenty of slave girls too. Livia, a woman not inclined to sympathy for anyone, never mind slaves, had nonetheless felt sorry for them.

She had seen them scramble out of Tiberius's bedchamber night after night, sometimes three or four of them at a time, and the expressions of disgust they wore on their faces were nothing new to her.

She had seen the same expression stare back at her from her own mirror. The gods only knew what he had made them do to him, to each other, and to themselves.

The carriage driver shouted an order, and the horses began to move again. Livia held back the curtain and looked out. She sighed contentedly at the sight of the tall cypress trees that lined the long cobblestone road. Little Tiberius kicked her shin as he clambered to sit beside his snoring father, but Livia took no notice. She was going home.

Home. Her brow furrowed. What condition would their home be in? After years of their absence, what valuables would remain? The letters from the house slave had stopped coming months ago. It was likely that at least some household treasures had been looted, perhaps by the slave himself. Either that or he had been killed or stolen trying to defend his master's house.

She offered a silent prayer to Vesta. *I don't give a fig for Tiberius's wretched marble statues and gold dinnerware, but my jewelry! My good dresses! May they still be where I hid them.*

She smiled as she remembered her favorite—a yellow stola with red and orange embroidered birds—but her smile quickly melted into a scowl of worry.

Her blood hadn't come for the past few months. It would be ages before she'd be able to slink into that dress. But her growing waistline wasn't the worst of her worries.

Would the child have Tiberius's blockhead or Diodorus's hairy back? Pray Juno it would be another boy. Pray the gods would be merciful and not burden a girl with the attributes of either man. It would take a dowry the size of Olympus to marry off such a creature.

The pace of the carriage slowed, and Livia cranked her head out to see the massive stone blocks of the Servian Wall ahead. It reached ten meters into the sky and surrounded Rome, protecting the Eternal City from the barbarians and invaders that always seemed to be at its door.

The Porta Collina, a major gate that led into the city of Rome, was visible in the distance, although a bottleneck of congestion forced the carriage driver to stop once again as a throng of people, animals, wagons, litters, and vendor carts of all kinds slowly filtered past the inspectors, through the gate, and into the great city.

Normally, such a delay would have angered Livia. But not today. She had waited years to return to Rome. Another hour or two to pass through the gate was nothing to be upset about.

A dirty child managed to slip past the slaves who guarded the carriage and stick his grimy hand inside, begging for coin. Livia was about to stab his hand with a hairpin, when she noticed the temple that stood not far from the Porta Collina—the Temple of Fortuna. It would be bad luck to stab a child, even a peasant one, so close to the temple. The goddess would not like it.

Instead, she reached for a small sack of coins on the floor of the carriage and sprinkled a couple of denarii into her palm. The peasant boy's eyes opened wide, and she tossed the coins outside, watching him dive to the muddy ground and roughly shoulder two other children aside to retrieve them.

A snort and a cough from Tiberius. "Juno's tight ass, woman! Are you throwing money away?"

"How remarkable," Livia said to her husband. "You manage to sleep through a brawl of drunken Dacians rushing the carriage and shouting war cries, but you awaken at the soft chink of coin."

Tiberius huffed and Livia curled up on her cushioned seat as the carriage driver shouted something and the horses slowly moved forward in stops and starts, making their way through the clattering, clamoring gridlock of congestion at the gate.

The journey is so much more pleasant when he's asleep, she thought.

Eventually, they passed through the Porta Collina. Just inside the walls of Rome, the booming voice of a public herald shouted out the latest news that would be relevant to returning citizens or visitors to the city: upcoming market and religious days, the latest laws passed by the Senate, current games and chariot races, Caesar's building projects, road closures, and so on.

Tiberius elbowed his son and pointed to the field beyond the road. "That is the Evil Field," he said. The blockheaded toddler squealed with excitement. "Do you know what they do there?" he asked the child, who blinked stupidly back at his father, opening and closing his mouth like a carp. "They bury Vestal priestesses alive!" Tiberius made a spooky look, and the child squealed again. The sound pierced Livia's ears.

"Well," she groaned to herself. "That's one way to get some peace."

* * *

"*Ave, Caesar!*" Hail, Caesar!

Octavian stood at the front balustrade of the large, ornate marble balcony that had been designed specifically for him and his guests. He looked down into the arena to acknowledge the two gladiators, who saluted up at him.

"*Avete*," he shouted to them. Fare you well.

Octavian sat back down next to his well-groomed friend, a man by the name of Titus Statilius Taurus. Taurus was the wealthy senator who had commissioned construction of the new amphitheater the games were being held in, and he was having a very good day.

The first permanent amphitheater of its kind in Rome, the arena was located in the Campus Martius. Its oval shape, massive size, and stone construction made it a spectacular improvement on the temporary wooden semicircular structures that had in the past been erected there to house the games.

Although construction in the sublevels wasn't quite complete, the amphitheater was nonetheless functional enough to comfortably seat and impress many thousands of spectators. Its arched walkways, fine sculptures, vibrantly painted walls, and gold-and-scarlet banners brought beauty to the bloodshed.

The oval fighting arena was covered in sand to prevent the gladiators from slipping on their own or their opponent's spilled blood. The sand also made clean-up easier by absorbing the blood of the brave, as well as the urine and feces of the less brave.

"The structure is remarkable, Taurus," said Octavian. "Rome rejoices in your generosity."

"I would have built a temple, but you've snatched up all of those," grinned Taurus. "With great speed, I might add. Perhaps you should build a temple to swift-footed Mercury? I think he's the only god you've missed."

"I shall think on it," replied Octavian. "I admit that I prefer religion to sport. You know I'm no lover of the games, but I am well aware how popular they are with the people. And when the people are entertained, they are easier to govern."

"Such has always been the purpose of sport, Caesar. And I know you are a pious man, but perhaps that is also the purpose of religion."

Caesar returned Taurus's grin. "For a man so blessed by the gods, that is an unwise philosophy."

Taurus laughed and held his hands up to the sky. "I take back the words, mighty Iuppiter!" He clapped his hands together excitedly and admired the stadium around them. "My architects modeled this building after the amphitheater in Capua. Of course, this one is much bigger and more modern. Rome is the Caput Mundi, and the capital of the world deserves only the best. You will see that the drainage is superior to any structure in Rome. If you look over there,"—he twisted his body and pointed—"you will also see that more private box seating is being constructed. Another box for your guests and one for the Vestal priestesses next to it. There will be all manner of hidden trapdoors for wild beasts and the reenactment of famous battles. And when it rains, a great canopy will stretch over the stands and . . . Ah, look, Caesar. They're finally finished tiptoeing around each other and are ready to fight."

The *summa rudis*, a retired gladiator who now officiated the fights, barked his final rules and warnings to the gladiators and then retreated quickly as the two warriors faced off.

The crowd erupted. Noblemen and freedmen, patricians and peasants, matrons and children—all cheered the name of one gladiator in fervent unison: "Flamma! Flamma! Flamma!"

Flamma. The Flame. A gladiator of celebrity proportions, he was idolized throughout the Roman world for having the longest winning streak in recent history. He had won over twenty matches in a row, each victory bloodier and more dramatic than the last. And Taurus was the man of the hour for having managed to snag him for today's headline match.

In response to the crowd's applause and cheers, Flamma thrust his *gladius*—the gladiator's sword—into the air and bellowed a deep, murderous roar. The crowd descended into unbridled frenzy.

"Gods, he sounds like the Nemean lion!" said Taurus.

"From what I hear, it will take Hercules to kill him," Octavian replied.

The great gladiator Flamma was a *secutor* fighter. Naked except for a loincloth, his body armor consisted of nothing more than a metal greave on his lower left leg, a leather guard over his right arm and a close-fitting helmet. He carried a heavy curved shield called a *scutum* along with his gladius.

As always, the secutor's opponent was a *retiarius*—a net-fighter. Agile and quick in comparison to his opponent, the retiarius carried a long three-pronged spear called a trident as well as a net.

The fight was as simple as it was brutal. The secutor was to chase the retiarius around the arena trying to kill him with his gladius. The retiarius was to evade his opponent while at the same time trying to cast a net over him. If the retiarius managed to entangle the secutor in the net, he would proceed to stab him to death with the trident.

The Flame charged at his opponent, bursting with sudden violence, like some kind of fiery Vulcan belched from the mouth of an erupting volcano. The net-fighter twisted his body to barely avoid the advancing gladius. He sprinted for a few steps, sand flying under his feet and the crowd screaming in his ears, before stumbling and falling to the ground. He landed painfully on his back.

The roar of the crowd was deafening. The scent of imminent death was in the air, and like wild animals, they fell back on brutal instinct—kill him! Make it gory! Let us see it!

A flare of rage ran through the net-fighter. To die this soon would be a disgrace. He saw the flash of Flamma's polished gladius descending upon him like a silver lightning strike from a black cloud. He gasped and turned his head at the last moment, but the point of the blade came down hard at his throat.

The retiarius scrambled to his feet, his hand instinctively going to the wound on his neck—no blood! Flamma's blade had missed its mark by a hair's breadth.

But Flamma didn't know that. After his lunge, he had leapt up, tossed his helmet aside and faced his adoring fans, strutting like a peacock toward a group of young women who were shouting his name and promising him favors after the fight. In a show of overconfident bravado, he hadn't bothered to look back at the fallen retiarius whom he believed to be lying dead in the sand.

The Flame held up his arms to Victory as the crowd jumped to its feet. Shouts echoed off the stone walls of the amphitheater, and thousands of arms waved in the air to celebrate his twenty-second consecutive win . . . But wait . . . what were they shouting? It didn't sound like a victory cheer.

The net fell over Flamma's head as if dropped from the heavens by Jupiter himself. The rope was heavier than it looked, and the weights fastened to the corners did a surprisingly effective job of securing it down. He struggled to find a loose spot, an opening, which he could pull over his head, but one of his feet became entangled in the mesh and he fell onto the sand of the arena floor.

Unlike Flamma, the net-fighter cared nothing for showmanship. Survival was all that mattered, and Fortuna had granted him a split second of opportunity.

In an act that seemed surreal even to him, he thrust the points of his trident into the net again and again. Blood spurted out of the net as the Roman world's most famous gladiator thrashed about inside. From the most distant seats in the amphitheater, it could have been a net full of fish flopping on the shore.

And then the thrashing stopped. The crowd fell silent for a moment. Had they really just witnessed a no-name retiarius defeat the Flame? They burst into a maniacal cheer. They had come to watch Flamma extend his winning streak. His victory had been certain. Instead, the Fates had cut a thread that no one imagined could be severed.

"Ah," said Octavian, more to himself than anyone else. "There's a lesson here."

Flowers and palm leaves littered the sand of the arena as the ecstatic spectators celebrated the underdog's victory. The retiarius's *lanista* burst into the arena and threw his arms around his star gladiator's shoulders, hugging him tightly and promising rewards of coin, food, drink, women, boys—whatever he wanted.

Meanwhile, several arena slaves busied themselves at the body of the Flame. They untangled him from the net and rolled his huge, bloody corpse onto a stretcher. A strange horn sounded loudly as the giant doors to the arena opened wide. The crowd fell silent, their interest piqued. What was happening now?

Slowly, a frightening figure strode onto the sand of the arena floor, moving toward the body of Flamma. It was dressed in torn black robes and held a long pole with a human skull on top. It was Charon, the lifeless ferryman who carried the souls of mortals to Hades by ferrying them across the River Styx, the river that separated the living world from the afterlife.

The ominous figure lifted his black arms up and shouted in a deep, raspy voice. "*Flamma est mortuus!*" The Flame is out.

The slaves lifted the stretcher and moved forward as the dark, sober figure of Charon escorted the celebrated gladiator out of the arena for the last time. In the silence of the amphitheater, a low death chant arose from the stands, and a few sobs echoed off the stone walls.

"I commend you, Taurus," said Octavian. "Your people certainly know how to put on a good show."

"Thank you, Caesar," Taurus replied. "You know that I am a lover of Greek theater. A touch of it adds even more drama to a good fight." He shook his finger at Flamma's corpse as it was carried from the arena. "Did you know that he was offered the *rudis* four times? Yet each time he turned it down and chose to fight again. Imagine that! He could have retired a rich man, could have been coupling with his wife right now, but instead, he's crossing the black river." He clucked his tongue. "Why would a man make such a choice?"

"It was not his choice to fight," said Octavian. "It was his nature to fight."

"But for such a magnificent fighter to be brought down by such a scrawny cipher! I've seen chickens with bigger bones than that retiarius. Then again, I once saw a . . ." He stopped speaking and followed Octavian's stare as it suddenly fixed on someone over Taurus's shoulder: an exceptionally beautiful young woman and an older man walking through the arched pathway alongside Caesar's balcony.

Taurus could take a hint. He stood and waved to the couple. "Join us," he said, at the same time motioning for the soldiers guarding Caesar's balcony to permit the couple to enter.

The older man looked stunned by the offer, but the young woman appeared unfazed. She strode onto Caesar's balcony like it had been built just for her.

"Caesar," said Taurus, "may I introduce you to Tiberius Claudius Nero and his lovely wife Livia. They are recently returned to Rome after an extended . . . *vacation* in Greece."

Octavian regarded Tiberius. "We are no strangers. I hope you are well, Tiberius. Welcome back to Rome. I trust you will find it a more peaceful place than when you departed."

"Thank you, Caesar." The name Caesar stuck in Tiberius's throat, but he forced himself to say it. He had no choice. Both men knew that Rome's peace and Tiberius's return to the city had come at a price.

As Octavian had done to so many nobles who had supported the assassins Brutus and Cassius, he had stripped Tiberius of much of his wealth and property. Tiberius had been allowed to return to Rome, but he was much poorer than when he had left it. He had also been forced to take an oath of allegiance to the new Caesar. Such was the cost of amnesty.

"What an exquisite creature you have on your arm, Tiberius," Octavian said as his eyes moved to Livia. "You are the daughter of Livius Drusus Claudianus, are you not?"

"I was while he was alive," said Livia. "My father killed himself in his tent at Philippi."

Octavian held her gaze. He knew that this young woman's father had fought alongside Julius Caesar's assassins. He also knew that the man had chosen to fall on his sword after their defeat rather than live to see a second Caesar rule Rome.

"Your father was a man of principle," he said. "If only all men were so."

"He was a wise father, but a foolish man," Livia replied. "You must forgive me, Caesar. I mean no disrespect to my great family, but my father had no mind for strategy. If in any given situation he had the choice of using his head or his heart, he would invariably choose to use the wrong one." She glanced sideways at her husband. "It runs in the family."

Tiberius clenched his jaw. His little trollop of a wife was ingratiating herself to Caesar by clawing over his own back. He managed to hold his temper only by imagining the ways he would beat her once they got home.

"Such sagacity in a woman is a rare thing," admired Octavian, "and of more value than the Golden Fleece." He looked at her pregnant belly. "Pray Juno your child will be as politic."

"Pray Juno," said Livia. She openly studied Octavian. So this was the *divi filius*? The son of the god Julius Caesar?

Because of his hunt not just for Julius Caesar's assassins but also for anyone who sided with them, she had been forced to flee to Greece and spread her legs for Diodorus. Because of his push for power, her father had committed suicide. Because of his royal ambitions, half of her fortune and all of her dowry were gone.

But Livia Drusilla had ambitions of her own. As Caesar took his leave of her and Tiberius to exit the amphitheater, she summoned her courage and let her eyes move over him. At the same time, she stroked her pregnant belly, letting the back of her hand caress the area under her full breasts.

Caesar was unreadable; Tiberius, however, was as conspicuous and inelegant as always. The moment Caesar was out of sight, he grabbed his wife's arm and dragged her unceremoniously out of the amphitheater and toward the litter that was waiting for them in the street.

"You're a backbiting little harlot," he said as she shoved her inside the lectica.

"Give me a reason to not be so," she shot back.

They didn't exchange so much as a look on the way home, but as soon as the portico of their house was in sight, Tiberius jumped out of the moving litter and stormed inside.

"Lock the doors," he shouted to his slaves. "Let the bitch sleep outside like the rest of Rome's she-wolves."

Livia reclined against the cushions in the lectica. She wouldn't give him the satisfaction of banging on the doors or begging entry to the house. She'd sleep outside all night long if it came to that.

But as it happened, it didn't come to that.

For when night fell and Tiberius finally opened the doors and shouted for his wife to come inside, he found that to his great surprise, she wasn't sleeping in the lectica after all.

"Where is she?" he asked a blanched-faced slave.

"Domine," the slave dropped to his knees. "A litter came for her. It was Caesar's litter. We were ordered to say nothing." The slave braced for his master's fist, but it never came.

Quietly, Tiberius turned and went back inside. Despite his aching rage and the heat of his humiliation, he couldn't stop himself from marveling at his young wife's audacity. *It is true what they say about Fortuna*, he thought to himself. *She always favors the bold.*

CHAPTER IX

Aut Viam Inveniam aut Faciam
I will either find a way or make one.

−HANNIBAL

ROME, 39 BCE

Later the same year

The Vestal Virgins were judging her. Livia Drusilla knew it. She could tell by the way their eyes moved from her belly, still distended from giving birth to Tiberius's child only days earlier, to her saffron wedding veil—the one she had donned to wed Caesar earlier that day.

She wished Caesar hadn't insisted on inviting them to their wedding reception at his home, but she was quickly realizing that there were few private or public functions where he didn't drag the Vestals along. She knew she'd have to find a way to deal with them.

She pretended to scan the room of guests looking for her sister, but really, she was studying the priestesses. They were standing in the center of the triclinium surrounded by some of the most important people in Rome. Caesar was relating some kind of amusing anecdote to them, waving his arms and looking up at the ceiling as he told it.

Livia rolled her eyes. It was probably some story about how his father had dreamed that a sunbeam had burst from Octavian's mother when she gave birth to him, or how a senator had dreamed about Jupiter giving the seal of Rome to a certain man, only to see Caesar years later and recognize him as that man.

My husband is the subject of more men's dreams than Helen of Troy, she thought. She found herself in a scowl as one of the Vestals—the one named Tuccia—caught her eye. The priestess smiled but didn't call her over. Livia forced herself to smile back.

They're just jealous, she told herself. *They're jealous that Caesar divorced his wife Scribonia to marry me. They know they're just a bunch of dried-up old crones that no man would want.*

The problem was that they didn't look old or dried-up. Well, not all of them. The Vestalis Maxima, Fabiana, and Priestess Nona were old as Rome itself, but the four priestesses who had attended their wedding and reception—Pomponia, Caecilia, Lucretia, and especially that amber-eyed Tuccia—were too attractive for Livia's liking.

She couldn't even mock their barrenness to feel better about herself. While Livia had given birth twice, both children were by her first husband, Tiberius, not her new husband, Caesar. And having children by an oaf like Tiberius was barely better than having no children at all.

Still, Fortuna had always fought on Livia's side. She thought back. Even her pregnant belly hadn't dissuaded Caesar from wanting her. Octavian had ordered Tiberius to divorce her and had continued to take her until the last days of her pregnancy.

The moment she had pushed the baby out of her, before the blood was even wiped from its wrinkled face, Caesar had had it whisked off to live with Tiberius and their first son, the blockhead. She had only learned later that the child was a boy. Tiberius had named him Drusus.

Of course, that was all fine by Livia. She was marrying up. Yet she had her share of problems. First, there was the irritating fact that Caesar's child by his ex-wife Scribonia was disgustingly cute. Caesar insisted that his daughter Julia live with him and Livia, and he doted on the girl as though she was born to be Empress of Rome. When he wasn't fussing over her, he was praising his young nephew Marcellus: *Look how he holds a sword! So capable for a child.*

Livia's second problem was that she could no longer claim the respected status of the *univira*, the virtuous woman who had married, coupled with, and borne children by only one man. As if a woman had any say over such matters.

Livia snubbed her nose at such ridiculous notions of modesty. Weren't a cunning mind and a beautiful face, especially when matched with a noble family name, to be more desired in a woman than some fabricated idea of virtue? If so, then why were so many men tripping over their togas to speak with the Vestals?

Her elder sister Claudia, who now always dressed in royal purple to assert her new status, seemed to read her thoughts as she approached.

"You forget yourself, Livia," she said under her breath. "You are now the wife of Caesar. We are standing in his house, *your* house. There is your grand husband, consulting with the greatest men in Rome—the generals Antony and Agrippa, the heads of the religious collegia, the noblest of senators and magistrates. Think on it! Only months ago you were squatting in a gruesome Greek villa and our family was forsaken. Whatever injustices you suffered there, you have redeemed your honor and our family name."

"Let's hope the redemption lasts," said Livia. "Caesar is a capricious lover, sister. He plays games but bores of them quickly."

"Then you must find a way to make the game last," Claudia replied, "or to at least come out the winner."

A chorus of shrill barks suddenly echoed off the lavishly frescoed walls, and both sisters jumped. Perseus the little white dog was yipping and squirming wildly in the arms of Caesar's sister Octavia while the Vestal Pomponia pulled her head back from it.

Octavia called out to her new sister-in-law. "Livia, come meet Perseus," she said. "You can say hello and goodbye at once."

"Why is that, dear sister?" Livia asked sweetly as she joined them.

"Because Perseus is moving out of my brother's house on the same day that you are moving in," she said. "I am sending him to live at the House of the Vestals. And look, Lady Pomponia, he is already dressed in white to serve the goddess." Octavia laughed at Pomponia's curled lip.

"He will lift the spirits of the high priestess," Pomponia said, "and for that I give thanks. But as you know, Octavia, a Vestal has her hair cropped when she enters service. We shall see how Perseus likes temple life when he is pink to the bone."

Tuccia took the little dog from Octavia's arms. "Oh, Pomponia," she said, "we all know your heart is as soft as a lamb. You will be cutting up Perseus's food for him by the Lupercalia."

Livia laughed along, all the while assessing the company she now found herself in.

Her sister-in-law, Octavia, was the quintessential Roman matron: well mannered, pious, and devoted to her husband, Marc Antony. In fact, she was already pregnant with their first child together. No surprises there. She knew what her powerful brother needed her to do, and she was doing it.

The Vestal Tuccia was also what one might expect. She looked to be the same age as Livia and was by far the prettiest of the priestesses, although she appeared guileless and oblivious to anything other than the ugly little dog that flopped around in her arms and talk of the chariot races.

The Vestal Pomponia was more interesting.

When Livia had left Rome for Greece some four years ago, the Lady Pomponia had been a subordinate Vestal, but it was clear that the priestess's status had grown while she was away. From Caesar to the house slaves, everyone seemed to regard her more highly than the others.

Pomponia scratched the little dog's head, strategically dodging its efforts to stuff its nose into her palm. "Excuse me, ladies," she said. "You know that my former slave Medousa now serves Caesar. I wish to speak with her before I leave."

As the Vestal walked away, Claudia whispered in her sister's ear. "You must befriend that priestess," she said. "You will gain a virtuous reputation merely by association. The people are easily swayed. They will see you with a Vestal and forget your past life."

Livia nodded and watched the Vestal cross the triclinium to speak privately with Medousa. The slave greeted her former master with more familiarity than Livia thought appropriate.

Then again, there was much about the slave named Medousa that Livia didn't approve of. That included Caesar's preference for her.

"Domina, you are looking well."

"Medousa," Pomponia began. She looked worriedly at the slave's dress—the white stola and the head-covering veil—and pursed her lips in concern. "Why are you . . . ?"

"All is well, Priestess." Medousa ran her fingers down the white veil on her head and spoke discreetly. "It is not as it seems. Do not worry about me. I made an oath to you as a child, remember? It was an oath to the goddess, as well. I can honor that oath still, even from Caesar's home."

"Now I know something is not right," Pomponia said flatly. "It's not like you to be so sacrificial."

"Then repay me for my sacrifice," Medousa said, her voice taking on a harder tone. "Stay away from Quintus Vedius Tacitus."

"I have petitioned the goddess to forgive me," said Pomponia. "He played me like a lyre, and I was too womanish to stop the music. Fear not, Medousa, I shall not let him play me again."

"It's not him I fear," said Medousa. "Have you seen the Lady Valeria lately? I can't tell if there's a child in that belly or she swallowed the Trojan Horse. She's huge. She's a wreck at the best of times, but this pregnancy has made her even madder. Gods, what does Juno do to a woman's mind when she's with child? Do not give Lady Valeria any reason to speak against you, Domina."

"I will not live in fear of a common woman, Medousa."

"It's not fear," replied the slave. "It's prudence."

"Enough, Medousa. Now tell me, how is life under Caesar?"

Medousa huffed. "You hit the mark. I live *under* Caesar. Life is very different than it is at the temple, but the food and wine are just as good, and he is not a vicious master." She pointed her chin at Livia. "It has been better since he took up with that one. He is tiring of me, but she is still new."

"I am sorry he has dishonored you, Medousa."

"A Caesar cannot dishonor a slave, Domina." Medousa laughed and Pomponia saw a flicker of her former impishness. "Anyway, Spes looks over me. Caesar says that I remain your property. Once your thirty years of service to the goddess are over, you can reclaim me. If you choose to stay with the Vestal order, I can live in one of your villas in the country."

"It will be so." Pomponia took Medousa's hands. "Only fourteen years to go until you and I walk through the green fields of Tivoli together."

The slave squeezed her mistress's hands. "Stay away from him, Domina," she repeated, "or we shall be walking through the green fields of Elysium together instead."

CHAPTER X

Plutoni Hoc Nomen Offero
This name I offer to Pluto

ROME, 39 BCE

Later the same year

Valeria felt the familiar cramp of pain deep in her belly. Blood trickled down the inside of her legs, but she didn't stop. She gripped the handle of the lash whip more tightly and struck the slave again on her back.

Good. Now she wasn't the only one bleeding.

Quintus walked into the room and casually bit into a pear. "Why are you beating her?" he asked his wife. "It wasn't her fault."

"The sheets look worse than they did before she washed them!" howled Valeria. "They're ruined. She didn't get any of the blood out!"

"Jupiter gives a shit about the sheets," Quintus replied. He turned to leave, but Valeria threw down the whip and scurried after him.

"Where are you going?"

"Not that it's any of your business, but I'm going to the Tabularium."

"Let me guess, husband. You're going to pass by the Temple of Vesta on your way."

Quintus threw his pear on the floor and the slave with the bleeding back crawled over to dispose of it. He wiped his mouth with the back of his hand and then pointed to a blanket-covered basket in the corner of the room.

"If that thing isn't gone when I get home, I'll throw it in the Tiber myself. And you with it, gods help me."

"Yes, throw it in the river, Father." Their seven-year-old daughter,

Quintina, shuffled into the room, half-carrying and half-dragging her little sister, Tacita, along the expensively tiled floor.

Valeria pointed at Quintus. "Do you see, daughters, how little your father cares for his children?" Her hand trembled as she wagged her finger at him. "We shall have to find you husbands soon so that you may leave his house."

"I don't want a husband," said Quintina. "I want to be a priestess like my great-aunt Tacita. I want to guard the sacred fire and go to parties at Caesar's house."

"Do not talk to me of the sacred fire!" Valeria stomped across the room and spat into the flame of an oil lamp.

Quintus turned to the slave. "Mind the children," he said. "Don't let her see them today."

"Yes, Domine." The slave ushered the girls away.

"You cannot keep me from my children, Quintus. You may not care whether they live or die, but I do!"

Quintus shook his head and walked away. Only the crash of the oil lamp breaking against the wall made him stop and turn around.

"I piss on the sacred flame," said Valeria.

A moment later, she found herself on the floor. Her jaw ached and her eyes streamed with tears. She blinked to clear the blurriness from her eyes and tried to get up, but the room was spinning so she sat back down and stared up at her husband.

"Get rid of that wretched thing today," he said, pointing angrily at the basket. "It's been dead for a week. The rats will be at it soon."

"That *thing* is your son!" screamed Valeria. "Come back here!"

But it was too late. His back was already to her, and he was gone from the house before she could get to her feet. She moved across the floor on her hands and knees until she reached the basket. Slowly, she pulled back the blanket.

The baby was gray now and his face was sunken, although his neck and body were bloated. The smell made her stomach rise. She touched his hair and recoiled as the soft skin of his scalp sloughed off under her fingers. She couldn't wait any longer. She had to send him to Pluto.

Gently, she placed the blanket back over his small body and tucked the corners into the edges of the basket. She looked at the broken oil lamp on the floor.

This was the fault of Priestess Pomponia. She knew it. The priestess had cursed her child. She had called upon Vesta to destroy Valeria's home because of the lust she had for Quintus.

She had sacrificed to the goddess, and Vesta had answered by keeping the child, the son Quintus so desperately wanted, too long inside Valeria's womb. When the child did not come at the right time, Quintus had grown suspicious. He claimed it was not his.

He also blamed Valeria for its death. The midwife had told him that excessive drink had caused the child to wither and weaken, and he foolishly believed her. Valeria had tried to tell him that it was Pomponia—she had killed their son by some black magic!—but her only answer from him had been yet another blackened eye.

His perversion for the priestess ruled his mind. Something had to be done.

She looked around the room. The slave, the one she knew Quintus regularly bedded and ordered to spy on her, was elsewhere in the house with the children.

Quickly, she wrapped herself in a palla, gathered the basket in her arms, and slipped unseen from the house. Quintus had left on foot for the Forum. He would be easy enough to follow.

Well, on a normal day he would be easy enough to follow. Today, however, her belly cramped and the dried blood on the inside of her legs pinched her skin as she trailed behind him along the cobblestone streets.

Valeria darted, unseen, in and out of porticos. She ducked behind the columns and stately trees that stood before the fine homes along her street, and then, as she followed him still further, she hid behind the laundry that hung down from *insulae* windows above, all while tightly clutching the death basket in her arms. She gritted her teeth through a cramp, pausing only a moment to let the pain subside and to catch her breath before hurrying after him again.

She was confused, though. Quintus didn't seem to be headed for the Roman Forum. That meant he wasn't going to the Temple of Vesta either.

Perhaps he was meeting his lover somewhere else. Somewhere secret, maybe a brothel or a rented apartment. Many men of class carried on illicit affairs in such places.

Eventually, she found herself tracking him through the newer streets of the Forum of Julius Caesar, the smaller forum that the dictator had started to build a few years before his assassination. The new Caesar was improving it, and construction was underway on a number of projects.

Quintus weaved through the scaffolding, dodged falling hammers, and stepped carefully to avoid the nails that littered the construction-filled streets.

Gritting her teeth through another cramp, Valeria hobbled behind at a safe distance and then retreated into a portico when Quintus stopped in front of the high steps to the Temple of Venus Genetrix.

He looked up thoughtfully at the statues that stood on either side of the temple's entrance. One was of Venus blessing a child. The other was of Julius Caesar.

Valeria's heart leapt up. Venus Genetrix, goddess of motherhood and domesticity: Quintus was there to pray for the health of his wife and the soul of his son.

Yet instead of climbing the steps to enter the temple, Quintus turned to walk down a side street where a number of shrines to Venus had been erected against the marble exterior of the massive temple.

He stopped before one of them. Valeria hid behind a shoddy scaffold from which some workers had hung their dusty cloaks. She was closer to Quintus than was probably prudent, but she needed to see what he was doing. She needed to hear what he was saying.

The shrine consisted of two marble pedestals supporting a thick, carved wooden altar, its surface inlaid with gold. Bunches of dried myrtle and roses had been fastened to the pedestals. A lifeless swan had been affixed to the wall in front of the shrine as a sacrifice to the goddess. The taxidermist had replaced its eyes with ocean-blue beads to symbolize Venus's birth from the sea. Several large scallop shells adorned the top of the altar and a tall candle burned within each one.

A man dressed in a white tunica with a blue cloak bowed deeply to

Quintus as he approached the shrine. They exchanged a few words before Quintus passed the man some coin.

Quintus knelt before the altar. He placed his hands upon it and looked into the ocean-blue eyes of the lifeless swan.

"*Venus Dea*," he said. "You will not have had occasion to know me, but I am Quintus Vedius Tacitus, former loyal soldier of your progeniture Julius Caesar and priest of mighty Father Mars. Hear me now, goddess. I offer this fine sacrifice to you in exchange for the heart of the priestess Pomponia."

Quintus took hold of a dagger that lay on top of the altar. As he did, the man in the blue cloak reached into a cage that sat on the ground and pulled out a plump white dove. With his head lowered in solemn respect to the ritual, he passed the dove to Quintus.

"Venus, I make this offering so that her affection for me will live as embers in the sacred fire until we can be together."

Quintus drew the blade across the dove's throat in one move, and the bird's tiny head collapsed between his fingers. Its blood trickled down his arm to form a small pool of red on the cobblestone.

Valeria gripped the scaffolding beside her. In all her years of marriage to Quintus, she had never seen him humble himself so. She had never known him to show any softness, and certainly never anything resembling love. Not to her. She took a final look at him—his head lowered in prayer and blood running down his arm—before she turned and walked away.

She walked for a long time. She walked until the cobblestone streets of the Forum Julius became the cobblestone streets of the Forum Romanum, and then she kept walking. She walked, drained of emotion but full of purpose, until she reached the Shrine of Pluto, god of the underworld.

A thin woman with blood painted on her cheeks and a black palla around her shoulders eyed Valeria and the basket she carried.

"Domina," she called out. "Come."

Valeria obediently followed the woman to a row of wooden shop fronts adjacent to the shrine and into one which was heavily draped in purple and black cloth.

As she entered it, the light of day faded into a space that was dimly lit with oil lamps and that smelled strongly of incense.

Without a word, the thin woman took the basket from Valeria's arms and set it on a table.

She lifted the blanket and looked at the dead baby underneath it without any discernable reaction—or rather, with the reaction of someone who was accustomed to looking at dead babies.

Valeria reached into the basket to remove a small purse of coins buried under the blanket. She pressed a few pieces of bronze into the woman's palm and then placed a shining gold coin—an aureus—into the baby's gummy mouth to pay the ferryman for his passage to Hades.

"It won't take long, Domina," said the thin woman as she gently removed the baby's body from the basket. "And, of course, all is done with the utmost respect."

She carried the baby away, waiting until she had safely passed behind a black curtain to remove the gold coin from the child's mouth and replace it with a bronze one. Surely Charon didn't charge that much for something so small.

Feeling detached from reality, Valeria sat down on a chair to wait for her child's ashes. As she stared into the flame of an oil lamp, her thoughts wandered to her life with Quintus Vedius Tacitus.

She had been given to him as a bride when still a teenager. It had taken him months to couple with her. Even then he had preferred his slaves to his wife, although she had never understood why. Everyone said she was the most beautiful woman to be born to her family in generations. She had performed her duties as his wife with devotion and diligence. She had given him two perfect daughters. Yet when she dared ask why he felt no love for her or for them, his answer had come in the form of his fist.

But now all was clear as glass. His obsession with the Vestal had taken hold of him before they had even married, when he and the priestess Pomponia were still children. He had fallen in love with her inside Rome's marble temples as they learned to perform their sacred duties to Mars and Vesta.

Yet Quintus, more than anyone, knew it was impossible. The priestess was bound to the Vestal order and a life of chastity for thirty years. They could never have a life together. And still, every time he saw her the fantasy of that life flickered before his eyes.

How could Valeria compete with that? How could the reality of his all-too-familiar wife, whose body was his to take or leave as he pleased, compete with the fantasy of a woman he could never know in that way? It was not fair.

It was not fair that his first thought in times of danger or public discord was of the priestess. It was not fair that he rushed off to protect her, leaving his wife and children at the mercy of whatever mob might surround them or break through their doors.

Spite tightened her chest. How she longed to see Priestess Pomponia climb down the ladder into the black pit in the Evil Field. How she longed to see her husband whipped in the Forum, not just for his sacrilege, but for the years of cruelty and indifference he had inflicted upon her.

Her chest ached with growing anger. She could not accuse the priestess of breaking her vows to the goddess. There was no proof the Vestal and Quintus had coupled—in fact, Valeria doubted they had—and the priestess had powerful friends. Caesar himself doted on her. Plus, most of Rome already thought Valeria was mad on account of her outburst at the Lady Octavia's wedding reception.

And although she hated to admit it, she did not want Quintus dead. She just wanted him to love her as his wife and to regard his children as blessings rather than burdens.

There was only one path left open to her.

"Bring me a lead sheet and a stylus," she said to no one in particular.

A boy, perhaps ten or eleven years old, quickly collected a tray and set it on the table before the distressed woman. Her request was nothing unusual. Those who found themselves drawn to the Shrine of Pluto often had reason to use a curse tablet.

Valeria flattened and smoothed the thin sheet of lead and clutched the stylus in her hand. She pressed the tip into the soft metal and drew a circle with vertical lines on top of it—a rough representation of the round Temple of Vesta with its encircling columns—and then wrote her curse below it.

"I call upon black and shaded Pluto," she whispered. "I call upon dark and hidden Proserpina. *Plutoni hoc nomen offero:* the *Virgo Vestalis* Pomponia, white-veiled harpy. I curse her food, her drink, her thoughts, her virginity." She drew a swirl of fire in the center of the circle and dragged the stylus over the lead sheet, creating deeper swirls that expanded outward, like flames engulfing the entire temple. "I curse her watch over the sacred fire and her service to the goddess. I divorce her as a bride of Rome and marry her to Pluto."

Quietly, the thin woman reappeared and placed a terracotta urn on the table beside the curse tablet. Valeria removed the lid and dipped her fingers inside, scooping out a wet pile of gray ashes. Her son's ashes. She smeared them over the lead tablet and then rolled it up as though it were a scroll.

She sat back in her chair as the young boy leaned over the table. He held a thin nail over the curse scroll and then tapped it with a small hammer, nailing it closed to seal the curse.

Valeria stood. She held the urn in one hand and clutched the lead scroll in the other.

"You can do what you like with the curse tablet," said the thin woman, "but I recommend throwing it in the Lacus Curtius if you can, or burying it in the grove of Pluto or by the Temple of Ceres. The dark gods will read it faster."

"*Gratias tibi ago*," said Valeria, "but I know precisely which temple to bury it by."

CHAPTER XI

Vestalis Maxima

ROME, 38-37 BCE

One year later

"*Salvete*, Caesar and Lady Octavia," Pomponia welcomed Octavian and his sister into the courtyard of the House of the Vestals. "I had not been informed you were coming. I will have some lemon water brought out."

"It's already on the way," said Fabiana, emerging from the peristyle. "Thank you both for coming." She gestured to the cushioned benches beside one of the pools. "Please sit."

As they did, Fabiana sat beside Pomponia. She put her hand on the younger Vestal's knee. "Pomponia Occia," she said, using the Vestal's full name to emphasize the significance of what she was about to say. "In the presence of Caesar, you will let me speak and not interrupt."

Pomponia was taken aback. "Of course, Fabiana."

"I am eighty-three years old," said the high priestess, "and I have served Vesta for seventy-seven of those years."

"No," Pomponia stood up. "It is not proper." She caught herself— Fabiana knew her too well—and sat back down.

Yet instead of chiding the Vestal, Fabiana's voice took a forgiving tone. "It is time, Pomponia. The goddess wants me to rest."

"It is not proper for the Vestalis Maxima to—"

"There is precedent in the archives for the chief Vestal to step down," said Fabiana. "You know that. I shall remain active within the order, but you shall lead it." She took Pomponia's hands. "That is no small duty. The Vestal order cannot be guided by a weak and frail priestess. It needs—it *deserves*—a strong and vibrant Vestalis Maxima. As the sacred fire is re-kindled, so must our order be rekindled."

Pomponia furrowed her brow. "I am too young. Priestess Nona is next in—"

"Priestess Nona would rather boil her hands in a pot of oil than be Vestalis Maxima. She has never enjoyed public worship or spectacle. If she could do it, I suspect she would close the temple and return to the days when Vesta was only honored in the home. Nona supports my decision and will be an invaluable resource to you. Priestess Arruntia would have been next, but alas, Charon's boat came for her too soon. I have spoken privately with Caesar and the Pontifex Maximus. Tuccia, Caecilia, and Lucretia as well. We are all agreed. You have served as the de facto chief Vestal for years and always with grace and diligence. Your sisters here and the priests of the other collegia respect you. The people love you and the Senate trusts you. It shall be you. That is the end of it."

Pomponia opened her mouth to protest again, but Octavian cleared his throat and faced the older Vestal.

"We are all indebted to your lifetime of service to the temple and to Rome," he said to Fabiana. "You've sustained the sacred flame for many years and helped to maintain the Pax Deorum, but you've always had a certain wit that has sustained the people's spirit too. I can see why my divine father cared for you so. In fact," Octavian cocked his head, "had you not offered Julius Caesar sanctuary all those years ago, he might have died an insignificant soldier instead of being made a god. And I might still be begging for the quaestorship instead of being Caesar."

"Nonsense," said Fabiana. "A determined man always finds his path. But I thank you for your kind words. It has been a good life, and I am priv-ileged to have served Rome. Now if you will excuse me, I am going to go sit in the shade." She squeezed Pomponia's knee. "Do you see? I have learned to shirk my duties already. I must read some letters that arrived for me this morning. My great-niece has married again—fourth time, *Mea Dea!*—and she is either asking for advice or money. I suspect I know which one."

As Fabiana rose to leave, a slave appeared with a tray of lemon water. "It's about time," Fabiana rebuked as she took a glass and walked off.

Octavia raised her eyebrows. "High Priestess Pomponia," she said, "you look like you've seen a basilisk under your bed."

"I feel that way," replied Pomponia. "She is not so old, is she?"

"Priestess Fabiana will be with us for many years," assured Octavia.

Octavian drained a cup of the cool water and set the empty glass back on the tray. "The woman would strike Charon with his own oar if he came for her. Everything is as it should be, Priestess. I knew you would be my Vestalis Maxima the day I met you."

His Vestalis Maxima, thought Pomponia. *Not Rome's.*

It was a revealing slip of the tongue, but Octavian did not correct it. He held out his hand, and a slave placed a scroll into it. "I have your first official task as head of the order. A list of twenty girls who I think have potential."

"Ah," said Pomponia, brightening as she focused on the task at hand. "We are of one mind. I have been thinking that we need at least one more novice."

"I have taken the names from the best families in Rome," Octavian continued, "and I have seen the girls myself. They are all of high intellect and free of defect." He handed Pomponia the scroll.

"I will start interviewing each girl and her family," said Pomponia. "You can expect my recommendation to the Pontifex and Senate by the kalends."

"Very good," Octavian replied.

"Brother," said Octavia, "if temple business is finished, I think I should like to visit a while longer. I will have a Vestal litter take me home."

"As you wish, sister." He looked back at Pomponia. "You and the other pontiffs will accompany me to the Senate tomorrow morning for the official announcement of your promotion. Following that, the news will be nailed to the Senate door, and the public herald will call it out from the Rostra." He made to go, then added in a slightly more personal tone, "It is well earned, Priestess."

"Thank you, Caesar."

Pomponia regarded Octavia. Her brother had no sooner exited the courtyard than she burst into tears.

"Oh, Lady Pomponia," she wept, "your appointment isn't the only thing the newsreader will be shouting from the Rostra."

"What else? What is the matter?"

Octavia sighed and wiped her eyes. "You know that Antony has been in Egypt. My brother sent him back to administer the province."

"Yes, I know."

Octavia's eyes watered again. "He promised me he would not take up with Cleopatra again. But he has. He has even claimed his children by her. Twins!" A sob caught in her throat. "A boy and a girl. Cleopatra Selene and Alexander Helios. Their names mean *moon* and *sun*." Her fingers tightened around the glass of water in her hands. "Isn't that sweet?"

"Sweet as poison, Octavia. What will Caesar do?"

"He will do nothing. There's nothing he *can* do right now." Octavia regained her composure. "Antony has proven a faithless husband to me, but for now he is honoring his agreement with Caesar. The taxes and the grain arrive. They aren't always on time, but at least they come. That is Caesar's main concern. Antony's infidelity is of little significance, even if it is humiliating to me."

"The Roman people will think no less of you because of Antony's carousing," said Pomponia. "They love you. It is only Antony who stands to lose their respect."

"That is what my brother said. If I am honest with you, I think the news pleases him. The worse Antony looks to the people and the Senate, the better he looks to them."

"He is a politician and a Caesar. That is to be expected." The Vestal rubbed her friend's shoulder affectionately. "Never doubt his love for you, though."

Octavia passed her glass to the slave and folded her hands on her lap. Pomponia noticed something—in the last several months, she had rarely seen Octavia wear anything other than a modest white stola with minimal jewelry. It seemed a curiously subdued choice for a woman with more gold than Midas. Perhaps Caesar's sister couldn't choose her own clothing any more than she could choose her own husband.

"I refuse to rain any more tears on your big day," said Octavia. She nudged Pomponia's shoulder with her own. "Let's see the names on that list. Who will be Rome's newest Vestal novice?"

Pomponia opened the scroll and tried not to react at the first name she saw: Quintina Vedia. Quintus's eldest daughter. Now eight years old and from a noble family—Pomponia should not have been surprised.

Octavia peered over the Vestal's shoulder to read the scroll. "Ah, little Quintina," she mused. "I have seen her. A good candidate, to be sure. Her father has a good political and religious background, and her family has a history of serving the goddess."

"Yes," Pomponia's mouth felt dry, and she took a sip of her water. "Her distant aunt was the Vestal Tacita." She smirked. "She beat a Gaul to death with an iron stoker when he broke into the temple and tried to extinguish the sacred fire."

"I have heard the story many times," smiled Octavia. "A true Vestal and a true Roman. There is good blood in that girl."

"I know it," Pomponia said more throatily than she had intended. "I suppose that I shall have to meet with her."

* * *

A temple slave escorted Quintus and his wide-eyed daughter Quintina through the House of the Vestals, toward the office of the Vestalis Maxima.

The girl gripped her father's hand tightly as she absorbed the beauty of the home: colorful nature frescoes on the walls, intricate mosaics on the floors, colonnades with Ionic and Corinthian columns and strings of flowers wrapped around them, gold furnishings and painted statuary, and heavy curtains of red, green, and yellow. The smell of incense and fresh greenery. The sound of water from indoor fountains reverberating off the marble.

The new Vestalis Maxima sat at her large desk surrounded by blue frescoed walls upon which were painted all the gods and goddesses of the Roman pantheon. Her head was down as one hand busily scribbled something on a scroll and the other hand absently tucked a loose lock of hair behind her ear.

"Domina," said the slave, "Quintus Vedius Tacitus and his daughter Quintina are here."

Pomponia rose. She saw Quintus's eyes move over her, and it occurred to her that he rarely saw her dressed in anything other than a stola or formal attire. Their interactions were almost always at religious or semiformal social events. Today, however, no real formality was required, and she was dressed casually in a sleeveless long white tunica gathered under her breasts by a gold rope belt. Her brown hair was pinned up in a bun. She wore no veil.

"*Salve*, Quintus," she said as plainly as possible before smiling down at his daughter. "I am happy to meet you, Quintina. My name is Pomponia."

The girl bowed deeply. "High Priestess Pomponia," she said, "I wish to join the Vestal order. I love this house."

Quintus gave her arm a tug. "What did I tell you? Answer the questions put to you."

Pomponia moved from behind her desk to take Quintina's hand from her father. She could see the resemblance: the black hair and dark eyes, the strong features that seemed almost too adult for such a pretty child, as if she were older than her years. "Speak as freely as you like," she said to the girl, whose eyes widened even more. She had never seen anyone challenge her father's authority, never mind a woman. Even more shocking, her father conceded.

"I will show you one of my favorite things in this house," Pomponia said to Quintina. "Come." She looked at Quintus. "You may stay here or accompany us. It is your choice."

"I will come."

Pomponia led them through the house and along the peristyle to enter the courtyard, continuing toward one of the pools. It was surrounded by white rosebushes, and in its center stood a marble statue of Vesta tipping a bowl of flames into the water. Several blue birds cleaned their feathers with the water on the pool's edge.

It was the same scene depicted in the fresco on Caesar's wall, the one Pomponia had been admiring in the quiet alcove when Quintus had grasped her arm and kissed her. When he had spoken of love. That was almost two years ago.

"That is a pretty statue of Vesta," said Quintina.

"If such things please you," Quintus replied.

"They do, Father." The slightest hint of impertinence.

Pomponia suppressed a smile. The girl had a spark of her legendary aunt in her. No doubt she had a streak of her father's strong will as well, although with the right training that could be a good thing. But what of her mother?

For a moment, Pomponia wondered how Valeria would be coping with the possibility of her daughter joining the Vestal order. Then again, it didn't really matter.

The *patria potestas* gave Roman fathers ultimate control over their children. When a girl or woman married, control transferred to her husband.

There were exceptions, of course, where Roman women enjoyed legal and financial independence. Vestal priestesses were one such exception.

If Quintina was chosen to serve the goddess and the temple, Quintus would lose his power over her. If she chose to marry after her years of service, she would retain her legal independence and her wealth. The idea of her life being controlled by a husband would be as remote and distasteful to Quintina as it was to Pomponia.

"There is something here that may interest you even more," Pomponia said to Quintina. "Come."

The Vestal led Quintina and her father to the far end of the courtyard. There, in the shade of the peristyle, a life-size statue of a priestess was being cut from a massive marble block by dust-covered sculptors. Chisels, hammers, drills, and various scrapers and grinders lay scattered as the sculptors argued and shook their heads at what they perceived to be imperfections in their work.

The chief sculptor noticed the Vestal's approach. "Priestess," he said, "We are working diligently. You will be pleased with our finished work." He wiped dust out of his eyes.

"I know that, Agesander," Pomponia replied lightly. "Priestess Fabiana makes me sneak into the courtyard at night with her and inspect your progress by torchlight. Carry on."

The sculptor laughed and returned to the marble. Caesar may have commissioned these new statues, but it was Priestess Fabiana who had insisted that work be carried out in the courtyard rather than in the sculptor's shop. Pomponia knew why. Fabiana wanted to be there when the faces of priestesses she had known, the faces of her sisters, came to life again.

They kept walking along the peristyle until they came to one particular Vestal statue. The deep-brown eyes looked alive enough to blink. A gold necklace hung around the neck. "This is the priestess Tacita," Pomponia said to Quintina. "Your distant aunt."

The girl's face swelled with so much emotion that Pomponia herself could feel it. Without asking permission, Quintina picked a flower from the garden and placed it at the statue's feet.

Quintus's body tensed at his daughter's boldness. He had done his best over the years to suppress the girl's assuming nature, but now the priestess seemed to be encouraging it.

"Do you know the story of Tacita and the Gaul?" asked Pomponia.

"Oh yes," she said proudly. "Father says it is the greatest story in our family history. He tells it all the time."

It was the way Quintina looked up at her father. With such familiarity. A sudden image of Quintus formed in Pomponia's mind: he was in his home, chatting idly with Valeria and telling stories to his children. The children he had created with her in the dark of night and in the warmth of their bed. She could imagine him gripping Valeria's arm the same way he had once gripped her own.

It was a world and life she had never known, and it roused within her a mixture of emotions. Sadness. Curiosity. Envy. A longing to know Quintus in a way that was free of the protocol and custom that separated them. In the private, familiar way that Valeria knew him.

Quintina brought her back into the moment. "If I am accepted into the order will I still be able to see my father and mother?"

"Yes, of course. You will be able to visit your home quite often, and we have regular visiting days here for families."

"Do your parents visit you?"

"Sadly, no longer. They died when I was very young."

"How?"

"My mother died in childbirth with my brother Pomponius. My father was killed on campaign for Pompey the Great." Pomponia suddenly wondered whether Quintus remembered the purple flowers he had given her when they were children.

"How long have you been a Vestal?"

"I was chosen when I was seven years old, and I have been a Vestal for seventeen years, so . . ." Pomponia pretended to count on her fingers, "I have thirteen years of official service left."

Quintina giggled. "Do you want to get married when you're done or stay a priestess?"

Pomponia could feel Quintus's eyes on her. "The Fates have not spun that thread yet."

"How many priestesses live here?"

"There are six Vestal priestesses who are dedicated to tending the sacred flame in the temple and performing public rites and rituals," said Pomponia, "as well as three older Vestals who are retired but remain with the order. They often help us teach the novices, younger girls like you, how to perform their duties. If you are accepted, you will be one of several girls who are in training."

Quintina nodded, as if in approval. "Do the priestesses who train here go to other temples? What about the Temple of Vesta in Tivoli? Or the ones in Africa or the other provinces?"

"The Vestal order in Rome oversees as much as it can," said Pomponia. "Our priestesses are often sent to manage temples in other towns or regions, especially during times of change or crisis, but we try to make each temple as independent as possible."

"Because you already have enough to do, right?"

Pomponia laughed. "Yes, that's right." The girl had a streak of practicality that was all Quintus. "We have many important duties to attend to here. We must teach the novices, maintain the temple and supplies, collect the spring water, perform daily rites, manage the mill, attend all religious rituals and public events, safeguard important wills and documents, transcribe the pontifical books in the library, consult with Caesar and the Senate, visit with foreign dignitaries, report our accounting and—hmm, what have I forgotten?—oh yes, make sure the sacred fire doesn't go out!"

Quintina giggled as the Vestal looked over her shoulder at a smiling, sweet-faced young novice in a white tunica who was waiting patiently to speak.

"What is it, Sabina?" asked Pomponia.

"Priestess, can I show her inside the temple?"

"By all means. But find Nona and have her take you."

Quintus watched his daughter excitedly run off with the other girl. "She is too bold for a girl," he said. "She will be difficult to rule." He looked squarely at her, as if daring her to disagree.

His stare made Pomponia suddenly aware of her bare arms. She reached for a palla that lay on a chair in the peristyle, casually placing it over her head and wrapping it around her shoulders, as if she were chilled. "Some women wish to rule themselves," she said. "Is that really so hard for a man to understand?"

He took a step closer to her. "And what about you, Lady Pomponia? Do you rule yourself?"

Pomponia stepped back. She had felt in control since his arrival, but his sudden boldness and the familiar flutter in her stomach threatened to shatter the facade of her confidence.

He lowered his voice. "The Regia is empty after dark," he said. "If I asked you to meet me there alone tonight, would you?"

Her face flushed. "No."

Quintus offered her a patronizing smile. "Then you do not rule yourself at all, Priestess."

* * *

Her eyes were dilated, and her words were slurred. Her movements were slow, deliberate, clumsy. But at least she was quiet. At least her fury and her outbursts had subsided. At least she left him alone most of the time.

Quintus stood in the triclinium and looked at his wife, who reclined on a couch, draining the last of her wine. He knew the physician's tonic that he had stirred into her drink would soon usher her to sleep. It couldn't happen fast enough for him.

But for the moment, she was resisting it. "Did they cut her hair?" she asked him.

"Yes."

"Who cut it?"

"The Vestalis Maxima." He didn't tell her that Pomponia was now the chief Vestal. Valeria assumed it was still Fabiana. She hadn't been out of the house in weeks to learn otherwise, and there was no point in telling her. It would only mean a fight.

"Did she cry?"

"No."

"What did she do?"

"She was happy." He let out an irritated sigh. "She hung her hair on the Capillata tree herself."

"What else?"

"The Pontifex claimed her as a bride of Rome, and she said her vows. She was wearing a white tunica and had a veil on. When I saw her afterward, she looked . . . I don't know . . . like one of them."

Valeria tried to take another sip of wine but realized her cup was empty. She let it drop to the floor. "What else?"

"I don't know, Valeria," he barked. "Most of the captio rites happen inside the temple." He drained his own cup of wine in one swallow. "She'll be happier there."

"You couldn't care less about your daughter's happiness," slurred Valeria. "All you care about is your own advancement and having a good excuse to visit the House of the Vestals."

Quintus clenched his fist and rounded on her.

Valeria jabbed an angry finger at him. "You are sickeningly transparent, Quintus, but do you know what? I am thankful Quintina is at the temple. I am thankful that she will never have to submit to a husband like you. I am thankful . . . I am . . ."

Her head bobbed and then fell back onto the couch.

Quintus sat heavily on the couch beside her. Valeria was right. He was transparent. And if he didn't find a way to force Pomponia from his thoughts, it was only a matter of time until his feelings for her were seen by all.

He had already withdrawn from almost all of his religious functions to limit his public contact with her and had instead immersed himself in his civic and senatorial duties. That would have to continue. He couldn't risk having so many eyes on him when he was in her presence.

A female slave slipped quietly into the room. "Domine, should I take Lady Valeria to bed?"

"No," said Quintus. "Leave her here."

He glanced up at the slave, and she obediently nodded her head in understanding. "Of course, Domine. I will prepare myself and wait for you in your bedchamber."

There is always one way to forget, Quintus thought to himself.

CHAPTER XII

Militiae Species Amor Est
Love is a kind of war.

—OVID

ROME, 36-33 BCE
One year later

"Blessed Luna's tits," Livia swore under her breath. Her blood had come yet again. Every month, her cycle was as certain and predictable as the moon's.

She had been trying to conceive a child with Octavian for nearly three full years. After all, Caesar needed a son. His nephew Marcellus was already named his heir, but there was no way Livia would let that spoiled brat or Octavia keep that distinction. Yet it was getting harder to cling to hope. It used to be that her husband would ask every month, "Are you with child?" But no more. Now he didn't even bother to ask. Now he was beginning to realize that his wife's womb was as barren as salted Carthage.

The slave named Medousa handed her the menstrual wool to absorb her flow, and Livia pushed it between her legs. The cramps were coming, so she allowed the slave to wind a heated wrap around her middle before falling back on her bed with a pained groan.

"Medousa, tell me something."

"Yes, Domina?"

"Has Caesar been taking you more lately?"

"Yes, Domina."

"Oh. I thought as much."

Medousa placed a pillow under Livia's head. The two of them had developed a somewhat unique dynamic over the past couple of years, largely due to the fact that Medousa was still considered the property of the Vestalis Maxima Pomponia.

The ownership issue didn't really affect day-to-day life. Medousa was a slave in the house of Caesar and was expected to do anything asked of her, which included satisfying Caesar's sexual needs. Yet the special arrangement did mean that she often escaped the harsher treatment Livia doled out to other house slaves.

Medousa had discovered early on that Livia was the type of mistress who would beat her slaves halfway to Hades just for the exercise. Caesar, however, frowned on such behavior and often spoke publicly against the excessive abuse of slaves.

Nonetheless, Livia was known to shred a back or two when he was away.

Livia yanked a blanket over her legs. "When you are coupling with him," she asked, "what does he have you do? Is there anything . . . unusual? Anything that might surprise me to know about?"

Medousa sat on the edge of the bed. It was an informality that would have had any other slave whipped to the white of her spine.

"The first time he took me, he believed I was a virgin," she began. "He had a fantasy that I was Rhea Silvia and he was Mars. Lately, he has been having that fantasy again. I use a blood-soaked sponge and when he penetrates me, I act like it hurts and the blood comes. It seems to give him much pleasure, Domina."

Livia furrowed her brow, but she wasn't angry. She was thinking. "Is it just me, Medousa, or does Caesar at times look at his sister with desire?"

"I have not noticed that, Domina. But he does seem to be drawn to purity and virtue. I think that is why he asks Lady Octavia to dress the way she does. She has so many white stolas in her wardrobe that I sometimes think I'm back at the temple."

Livia snorted. The slave had a mouth on her, but at least it was a useful mouth. "Get your cloak, Medousa. I have an errand for you to run."

* * *

The last time Medousa had been to a slave market, she had been the merchandise. This time she was shopping for it. The memories came back all the same.

The bustle of bodies and the shouts of competing bids. The wooden cages with dirt-covered men, women, and children crouching inside. Some of them stared vacantly past the bars. These were the ones who had been bought and sold before. They knew what was happening. It was just life. All they could do was wait and see what master they'd be serving tonight.

Others wept, prayed, or trembled with fear. These were the ones who had been torn from their homes in other lands—the spoils of war or piracy—and taken to Rome to be sold as slaves. Families clung to each other as if their embrace could prevent the slave traders from tearing them apart and removing all hope that they would ever see each other again in this life.

They called out in a chorus of foreign tongues, but they all said the same thing: "Don't take my child!" "I want my mother!" "Stop! I am not a slave!" "Please have mercy!" "Gods, help me!"

In her mind, Medousa heard a voice from long ago. *I love you, Penelope. Mother loves you. Never forget. No matter what happens, never forget.*

The voice felt like a wound opening. She tried to picture her mother's face, but nothing formed except the vision of the Medusa pendant she always wore around her neck and a vague image of thick auburn hair.

She could still see her father's face, though. Dark, bearded, and strong. He had held himself with dignity and courage until he had seen his wife stripped naked on the auction block, and then he had raged against the chains that bound him like a wild animal in the arena.

Only Hera knew what had become of them.

"Medousa, is that you?"

The voice brought her back. She turned her head and found herself staring into the face of Quintus Vedius Tacitus. He wore a practical yet expensive short-sleeved tunica, belted at the waist, and held a much-used wax tablet in one hand and a stylus in the other. The slave at his side carried an armful of scrolls.

"Yes, it's me," she said flatly. "I didn't know you were in the slave business."

"I'm not. I'm here on official business," he pointed his chin at the scrolls his slave was holding. "Tax audits of slave traders."

"Oh." She stared at him frostily. "Is there anything else?"

He averted his eyes uncomfortably and then looked back at her. For a moment, Medousa thought he might offer an apology or at least some kind of acknowledgment of how his sacrilege had separated her from Pomponia. But of course he didn't. The beastly man had no capacity to think of anyone but himself.

He shifted uneasily on one foot, and Medousa grinned. She knew he wanted to ask about the high priestess, but she wouldn't give him the chance.

"If you'll excuse me," she said, and walked past him without looking back. She was on official business too.

Medousa craned her neck above the crowd until she finally saw what she was looking for: a large wooden sign that advertised *Virgo* and boasted a rough drawing of a naked woman. A raised platform had been erected under the sign, upon which stood a naked girl perhaps sixteen years old.

She tried to cross her arms to cover her bare breasts, but the slave trader poked her with a stick, and she lowered them to her sides. He barked something and pointed the stick at her again, and she turned around slowly to show her backside to the bidders.

"That's three thousand denarii," the slave trader shouted. "Do I hear three and a half thousand? It should be more—it should be five or six thousand at least! Look at this girl, such a beauty. And so docile! Just like a little lamb. Speaks Latin well enough. Guaranteed intact and fertile." He jabbed her with the stick, and she turned back around.

"Prove it," yelled a toothless man from the crowd. "Open her legs!"

The slave trader threw a rock and hit him on the head. "Get out of here you sack of shit, or I'll call the guards. Serious buyers only! Go to the Subura if you want a free look."

"Three and a half thousand denarii," shouted Medousa.

"Where is your man, honey?" asked the slave trader.

"Private buyer," she replied and held up the heavy purse Livia had given her.

"Three and a half thousand," he announced. "Four? Did I mention that this one can read a little?" But the crowd was already breaking up and moving on to cheaper fare. The slave trader shrugged his shoulders. Three and half thousand was still a half thousand more than he had expected. People just weren't spending these days. The increasingly strained alliance between Caesar and Antony, and the rumors that the granaries were less than full, were bad for business. People didn't spend money in uncertain times. He tossed the girl a stained tunica and she pulled it over her head.

Medousa set a few more coins onto the slave trader's rickety desk to expedite the transaction, and soon the slave girl was obediently trailing behind her along the cobblestone street to Caesar's house on the Palatine Hill.

By the time they arrived, night was falling and both of them were dripping with sweat. Medousa led the girl, who said her name was Maia, into the slaves' bathhouse, where Despina was already waiting, along with the beauty slave, who stood ready with her tray of grooming tools.

She cropped the girl's hair, removed her body hair, and scrubbed her clean in the water before dressing her in a white stola and veil.

"A man is going to penetrate you," Medousa said to the wide-eyed girl. A nod.

"It will be painful, but do not try to hide your pain. Let him see it. It will not last long, and afterward you will be cared for and fed. Do you have any questions?"

The girl shook her head just as Livia strode purposefully into the room. She looked the girl up and down as though she were a side of beef. Inspection was necessary, but not necessarily pleasant. "Intact?" she asked Medousa.

"Yes, Domina. The physician at the market confirmed it."

"Good." She lifted the slave's stola to look beneath it, dropped it, and then said, "Come with me."

With the girl in tow, Livia marched through the dimly lit house directly to her and Octavian's bedchamber, forcing her sober expression to transform into a flirtatious smile before opening the door a crack and peeking around the corner like a mischievous child playing a game.

"Hello, dear," said Octavian. He was lying on top of their luxurious four-post bed. The red silk canopy that was draped over it was blowing lightly in the breeze of an open window. When he noticed her expression, he set down the scroll he was reading and looked sideways at her impish grin. "What are you up to, you little minx? You look like Discordia about to strike."

"I have a gift for you, husband."

He folded his hands across his chest and clucked his tongue. "And what might that be?"

Livia opened the door wider and led the slave girl to the foot of the bed. "Husband, this gift is wrapped in pure white"—she lovingly smoothed the veil that fell down the girl's back—"and for a reason that you will soon discover."

"Oh?" Octavian tried to maintain a dispassionate expression, but Livia could see evidence of his arousal already forming beneath his tunica. "Tell me, wife, are you going to share this gift with me?"

"I think not," Livia said naughtily, "but I will share a cup of wine with my husband when he is finished with it." She put her hands on the slave girl's shoulders to urge her onto the bed and then glided giddily back to the door, winking at her husband as she departed. "Hail, Caesar," she said.

As the door closed behind her, Livia exhaled and leaned against it. Medousa was already waiting in the hall.

"It will be over in less time than it takes to boil an egg, Domina."

"When it's over, take the girl to the slave quarters for the night. Bring her back to the market first thing in the morning and sell her."

"She won't be worth as much now."

"I don't care about that," said Livia. "And next time, Medousa, pick one that isn't quite so pretty."

"Yes, Domina."

"Have some fresh linen ready," Livia ordered. "I want the sheets changed as soon as it's over. And bring a washing bowl for Caesar too."

"Yes, Domina."

"And then come back with some refreshments. Wine. Perhaps some pears or figs, and a little cold meat. I will eat with Caesar."

"All will be done, Domina."

Livia watched Medousa disappear down the hall. She pressed her ear to the door. A grunt. A cry of pain. *Less time than it takes to boil an egg.*

Livia knew that she had failed to fulfill her primary purpose as the wife of Caesar: to provide her powerful husband with a son and heir.

As a divorced woman with children from another man, neither could she exploit the univira virtue that Caesar loved to preach about. Although she had a good family name, her personal past lent little weight to his public persona as a man who upheld traditional Roman morals and sexual values.

Yet there were other ways to be useful to him. And as long as she kept bringing those ways to his bedside—dressed all in white and pure as Alps snow—her status as Caesar's wife would be secure.

* * *

"Aargh." Pomponia lifted her stola above her ankles as she navigated her way through a patch of sticky mud in the Vestal stable. She glared at several stable slaves who were hurrying toward her. "Why is this not cleaned?"

"Deepest apologies, High Priestess. It rained last night."

"It rains every night in October," she scolded, "hardly a supernatural event." She bit her lip. She was sounding more like Fabiana every day.

As she sat down on a bench, a female slave rushed toward her with a washing basin. She untied the priestess's sandals and placed her dirty feet in the warm water. With her feet soaking, Pomponia waved her hand in irritation at the slave.

"Move," she said, "I can't see."

She looked toward the riding arena, where Quintina was cantering a white horse in wide circles. The girl caught on quickly to everything, and learning to ride a horse was no exception.

Every Vestal was trained to tack and ride a horse in the event that a hasty exit from Rome—whether on account of fire, flood, or invasion—was required, and the Vestal order had its own stables not far from the temple for such training.

Riding for pleasure was also one of the many privileges that Vestal priestesses enjoyed. Tuccia could be found quite often at the stables. Pomponia, however, rarely had the time—or the inclination. She had always preferred scrolls to saddles.

The stable manager—a tall, muscly freedman named Laurentius—waved politely to Pomponia as he approached. Quintus was walking beside him, and the two men were chatting casually. Quintus's visits to watch his daughter ride had become a regular occurrence, and today was nothing unusual.

"High Priestess," he said, "Quintus Vedius Tacitus is here to see Miss Quintina."

"Thank you, Laurentius."

The stable manager left, and Quintus scraped the bottom of his sandal on the low rung of a fence, leaving a lump of mud on it. "You should beat your slaves," he growled.

"Perhaps I should let you do it," said Pomponia. "It might put you in a better mood."

Quintus stopped scraping his sandals and looked squarely at her. "This is my normal mood."

"I know." She rubbed her bare feet together in the water to scrape off the last of the dirt as Quintus sat down beside her, albeit at a respectable distance. He leaned forward with his hands on his knees.

It was the way Quintus always sat when he was beside her. Still awkward. Still uncertain, even though Quintina was nearing her fourth year of training with the Vestal order and he always scheduled his visits to the stables when he knew Pomponia would be present.

In fact, those visits had been growing more frequent these last months. They had also been growing more personal. Their shared interest in Quintina had cleared common ground upon which an uneasy but evolving friendship had, after so many years of knowing each other, finally taken root.

It was a different relationship than it had been during those years they had performed their religious duties together, always rigid and self-conscious in the public eye. Now, without the scrutiny of the whole of Rome watching his every interaction with Pomponia, Quintus could breathe a little easier. Of course, Quintus was still Quintus. Hard, critical, authoritarian. If he was learning to talk to Pomponia like a real person, it was by degrees.

"How is Priestess Fabiana?" he asked.

Pomponia shrugged. "Good days and bad. She is starting to forget things."

"And how is Perseus?"

"Perseus is a wretched little hellhound who digs up the flowers and chews my sandals. That dog must be a hundred years old by now. He is an immortal."

Quintus smiled widely.

Pomponia hated when he did that. His face opened up in that rare way, and for a passing moment the normally detached, choleric Quintus became accessible, even inviting. It always disarmed her, and she found it hard to pull her eyes away. It reminded her of that day, years ago. In Caesar's house, by the fresco in the alcove.

Pomponia, what do you think of me?

I think you're a savage in a good toga who has to control every situation and who delights in telling me what to do.

You have me there. Tell me that I'm the only man you'll ever love. Swear it on the Altar of Juno.

They had not spoken of that day since. Nor had they spoken of the day years ago when Quintus had first brought his daughter to visit the temple, the day he had abandoned all pretense by daring Pomponia to meet him in the Regia after nightfall.

They never spoke of these things, yet the memories were part of every conversation, every glance, and every interaction between them. From the words they chose to the way they sat next to each other, the tension was always there. The unspoken past was ever-present.

"Your wife and younger daughter, Tacita, are well, I trust," said Pomponia. She splashed her feet in the water to emphasize how carefree the question was.

Quintus's smile suddenly turned into a snigger. That was nothing new. One moment he would be pleasant enough, the next he would snap back into his usual sullen, fractious self. There was no predicting it.

Even at his most tolerant, he was always a breath away from flashing Pomponia a scolding glance or chastising her for some real or imagined misstep. She had learned to live with it. To ignore it.

He shook his head in irritation for a moment, and then turned to her. "Why must you ask questions you know the answers to?"

"Why must you be so changeable?"

He fumed quietly for a moment and then said, "My younger daughter is well enough. My wife is . . ." He shook his head again. "Irrelevant."

"I'm sure she would be delighted to hear so."

Fully expecting Quintus to stand up and storm off, Pomponia forced herself to casually take her feet out of the basin as if she didn't care one way or the other what he did. She reached for the towel beside her, but Quintus wrested it from her hand.

To her open-mouthed shock, he knelt on the ground before her. He spread the towel over his legs and then set Pomponia's bare feet on top, lifting the edges of the towel to softly, almost reverently, dry her feet.

The act was forbidden in a thousand ways.

"Quintus . . ." She told herself to pull her feet away from him, but for some reason they felt like they were too heavy to lift off his legs. The soles of her bare feet tingled with the warmth and sensation of his body beneath them. The sight and feel of his hands moving over the top of her feet quickened her breath.

"I saw Medousa in the market again," he said, as if nothing unusual was happening.

Pomponia caught her breath. "What was she doing?"

"Just buying more slaves for Caesar's house, I assume." He held the towel in one hand and moved it above her ankle to absorb the moisture there.

At the same time, his other hand caressed her lower leg, moving slowly upward, until his fingers slipped behind the bend in her knee to stroke the soft, sensitive skin.

"Quintus, stop."

He didn't stop, of course. He never did what she told him. But this time he wasn't being defiant. He was simply lost in the feel of her. He stopped stroking and gripped her leg more tightly.

"Caesar is sending me to Egypt," he said abruptly. "Queen Cleopatra has stopped paying her taxes to Rome. Worse, the grain shipments are getting smaller. Caesar suspects that Marc Antony is conspiring with Sextus Pompey to starve Rome and overthrow him. I am to meet with General Antony and assess the situation." He loosened his grip and again caressed her more gently. "A war is mounting between Caesar and Antony.

It will happen soon. General Agrippa is already planning his campaign."

"I knew it was bad," said Pomponia. "I didn't know it was that bad." She pressed her feet into his legs. He responded by wrapping his strong hands around her ankles. "When do you leave?" she asked breathily.

"Tomorrow."

"Tomorrow? Why didn't you tell me earlier?"

"I only found out this morning."

"How can he send you so soon? With no warning?"

"He is Caesar. He can do as he likes."

She pressed her lips together. "How long must you stay there?"

"Indefinitely."

Pomponia put her hands to her face. "Then you will be there when the war between Egypt and Rome begins?"

"Without doubt," he said, "but I have seen battle before."

"Not like this. Caesar will be relentless, and Antony will fight like a cornered animal."

"That is like any battle, Pomponia." He realized he had said her name without the honorific *Priestess*, but did not apologize. Instead, he got up and stood in front of her so that she had to look up to meet his eyes. "You will meet me at the Regia tonight after dark," he said. It wasn't a request. It was an order. "We will say our goodbyes then."

And then he was gone, picking his way through the mud toward the riding arena and the waving form of his daughter on horseback.

A female slave returned carrying Pomponia's washed and dried sandals. She knelt down to tie them, but Pomponia waved her away. "I'll do it myself."

She tied them quickly and then marched toward the stable house, where Laurentius was busily repairing some tack on an outdoor workbench.

"I must leave now," she said to the stable manager. "Quintina's guards will bring her home after her lesson. And Laurentius, send a few extra slaves from the stables to accompany them, would you? Make sure they're armed."

"Is anything wrong, Domina?"

"No, I am just feeling a bit jumpy today."

"Always wise to heed such feelings, High Priestess. It is how the gods speak to us. I will send my best men with her litter."

"Thank you."

Pomponia stepped into the lectica and let her body collapse back onto the cushions before the litter-bearers had even taken up their positions.

There was no way she would meet Quintus in the way he had said. His words and his presumptuousness were grossly insulting to her, and worse, they were a sacrilegious affront to the great goddess and the Vestal order itself.

If that weren't enough to condemn him—and it was—there was his barbaric lack of judgment and total disregard for the danger he was putting them both in. Her reluctance to see him flayed alive in the Forum was matched only by her reluctance to see herself buried alive in the Campus Sceleratus.

But now Quintus was leaving for Egypt, possibly to never return.

Keenly aware of each passing hour, she moved through the rest of her day's duties. She supervised the inventory of wood kindling and sacred wafers, and then inspected the mill. She wrote letters to other temples. She reviewed Caecilia's curricula for the novices, confirmed documents in the vaults, and spent some time in the archives. She checked on the construction happening in various areas of the House of the Vestals. She scheduled Tuccia, Caecilia, and Lucretia for upcoming rituals, festivals, and public events.

Yet no matter the task, she found her mind wandering back to the stables, and to Quintus. To the feel of his strong hands wrapped around her ankles. To the sound of his voice. To the thought that he would be walking out of her life soon and crossing the Mare Nostrum to whatever the Fates had in store.

It was one of those long days when her Vestal duties didn't bring her anywhere near the temple's fiery hearth. It was one of those days when she longed for simpler times, when she would spend quiet hours in the temple tending to Vesta's sacred fire with her own hands.

Life was simpler before Fabiana had retired. Life was simpler before Quintus too.

She told herself she would meet him tonight, although only to say goodbye. Only to say that, despite his vulgar insolence and her sacred vows, she hoped in her heart that he would be safe. She would pray daily and offer to the goddess to make it so.

Finally, sunset descended on Rome like a vibrant orange blanket putting the city to bed. Pomponia wandered through the still House of the Vestals. The other priestesses were either on watch in the temple or in their private quarters. Except for a few slaves whose work was never finished, she alone was awake. Or so she thought. Perseus came trotting down a corridor to greet her, his nails clicking on the marble floor and his tongue hanging out.

She bent down to scratch his ears. "I am afraid to go alone, Perseus," she whispered. "You can come with me."

Pomponia slipped out of the portico and onto the empty cobblestone street of the Via Sacra. She looked over her shoulder. The setting sun had cast a deep-orange glow onto the white marble of the circular Temple of Vesta. It looked even more beautiful than it usually did. She watched the smoke from the sacred hearth bloom out of the opening in the temple's domed bronze roof and spiral upward into the evening sky, up toward the goddess.

She could hear Caeso and Publius laughing and telling off-color jokes with other Forum guards on the other side of the Temple of Vesta, by the Temple of Castor and Pollux. The Forum Romanum was securely walled and closed to the public after dark, so their laxity was not a problem. In fact, it worked to her advantage as they could not see her from their position.

Pomponia hesitated for a moment, but then Perseus tugged on his leash, as if daring her to go through with it, and she walked toward the Regia with renewed purpose.

There was no doubt that the Regia, located only steps from the Temple of Vesta, would be empty. As the historic residence of the first kings of Rome, including Numa, and the current office of the Pontifex Maximus, it was only used during the day and, then, only when Lepidus was in Rome, which he currently wasn't.

As she approached the portico of the Regia, her eyes moved to the nearby Temple of the Comet Star. This was the temple that Octavian had dedicated to Julius Caesar several years earlier. It stood on the exact spot where the frenzied mob had erected a makeshift funeral pyre and burned the dictator with flames taken from the sacred fire of Vesta.

Pomponia remembered it well. As the crowd—roused to action by Antony's funeral speech—had pushed forward to carry Caesar's body off the Rostra, Quintus had appeared at her side. He had seen her through the chaotic streets of the Forum to the safety of the temple's steps. But Valeria was already there. She had gripped her husband's cloak in anger: *I knew you would be here!*

A pang of guilt stabbed at Pomponia. While she wasn't strictly violating her religious vows by meeting Quintus—they would only speak—their affection for each other meant that she was dishonoring the marriage vows he had exchanged with Valeria.

She wound Perseus's leash so tightly around her hand that it blanched and began to throb.

I am losing my way, she said to herself. *I am losing sight of who I am. I must commune with the goddess.*

She loosened the leash around her hand and turned to walk back to the House of the Vestals. At that moment, Quintus opened the doors to the Regia from within.

"Come," he said.

Pomponia looked around nervously. Other than the preoccupied temple guards and the few sanitation workers who swept and scrubbed the streets and collected trash by the light of their torches, she and Quintus seemed to be the only souls still awake.

She climbed the steps of the Regia and stepped inside. Quintus closed the heavy doors behind her, and she strained to see by the light of the single torch that was fixed to one of the blood-red walls.

By its flickering flame, a painted image of the warrior god Mars seemed to come to life, ready to kill and eager for the excitement of battle.

Pomponia had been in this somber space many times. It held a particularly imposing and sacred shrine to Mars on account of the ancient relics—a massive shield and spear—that lay heavily across the marble altar.

It was said that these had belonged to Mars himself and that the god had thrown them down from the heavens to protect the people of Rome. Past pontiffs and priests of Mars had said that the spear trembled and rattled on the altar, as if demanding to be picked up, whenever Rome was threatened.

Perseus whimpered and then sat obediently in front of the altar. At any other time, the sight of the little dog communing with the great god of war would have made Pomponia laugh out loud. But not now. Now, her heart was hammering in her chest, and her stomach fluttered with a strange mixture of apprehension and arousal.

All at once, Quintus came toward her. His strong arms enveloped her, drew her in until her face rested against his solid chest. Her body flooded with warmth, and she felt a strange hardness pressing into her midsection.

"That is my desire for you," he said, his voice softer than Pomponia had ever heard it. "I am not ashamed of it." He moved his head so that his face was pressed against the nape of her neck. "You belong to Rome now," he said into her hair. "But I swear on the Altar of Mars that you will belong to me one day." He pulled back and clutched her face in his hands. "Mars protect you while I cannot."

She put her hands on top of his and felt the blood on his palm drip down her cheek. He had offered his own blood to the war god. To protect her. "Vesta bring you home," she said.

And then he was out the door, and all she could hear was his receding footfalls and the scratching of brooms on cobblestone.

CHAPTER XIII

Auribus Teneo Lupum
I hold a wolf by the ears.

−TERENCE

EGYPT AND ROME, 32 BCE

One year later

Queen Cleopatra sat on the glassy blue edge of the pool in the palace courtyard and gazed thoughtfully into the turquoise water. The *weet weet weet* of a sandpiper echoed somewhere in the marshy waters of the expansive gardens, and she smiled languidly at the pleasant sound. She had reason to smile today.

She could imagine Octavia's face when her brother gave her the news: *Your husband Marc Antony has forsaken you. He has married the Egyptian queen.*

It had been a hard-won battle for Cleopatra. Antony had not been as pliable as she had expected. Despite his boyish and boorish nature, he had proven to be a Roman through and through. Every time he read a letter from his Roman wife Octavia, his sense of Roman pride and obligation had sent him scurrying across the sands, back home to her bed. And every time he did, his alliance with Octavian was renewed and strengthened.

Those damn letters. They had always found a way into Antony's hands, no matter how many guards Cleopatra had assigned to intercept them in the shipyards, in the desert, and in the palace itself. The queen suspected Octavian's man Quintus was responsible. What a cheerless puritan that man was.

Cleopatra hadn't written any letters to Antony. She had sent messengers to Rome instead. It was a much more personal and persuasive approach. She had chosen these messengers with care.

First, they were selected from among the most strikingly beautiful women in Egypt. They were then trained in the dramatic arts so their tears would appear genuine and their words sincere. They wept when they described how a heartbroken Cleopatra was only a breath away from opening her wrists and how their loving children, Alexander Helios and Cleopatra Selene, shed tears day and night for the return of their great father.

But their training went beyond their ability to act, for they all carried a very personal message to Antony, one directly from the lips of the queen. And when he was alone in his Roman bedchamber, they would kneel before him and deliver it with their own lips.

It had worked. Antony had returned to Egypt. And this time, Cleopatra was determined to make him stay for good. She had to. Her life, the life of her children, and her throne depended on it.

Her spies in Rome had told her all about Antony's wife, Octavia, who by all accounts was the ideal Roman matron. Obedient. Docile. Subordinate to her husband. Free of vice or ambition. Virtuous and proper in every way. Apparently, she dressed the part too. When she wasn't in a white stola, she was in a white tunica. Had she not been sullied by her husband, she could have been a Vestal Virgin.

Instead of trying to compete with Octavia's submissive and accommodating nature, Cleopatra did precisely the opposite. Where Octavia would have bent to Antony's wisdom, Cleopatra challenged it. Where Octavia would have soothed him, Cleopatra scolded him. Where Octavia would have quietly slipped away when he became drunk, Cleopatra poured more wine and played drinking games with him.

Instead of the dowdy Roman matron draped in layers of white fabric, Cleopatra chose vibrantly colored dresses that clung to her every curve. Her earrings grazed her bare shoulders, and her necklaces dipped down between her breasts, drawing Antony's eyes to the places she wanted him to focus on. Her exotic perfume filled his nostrils and quickened his breath.

When he finally took her, she didn't lie silently in virtuous submission to his desires as her spies had told her Octavia did. Rather, she cried out in shameless pleasure, struck him across the face, and climbed on top of his body. It had been a risky strategy, but it had worked like a charm.

Yet the most effective strategy she had employed was the one that worked on every man she had ever known, and doubly so on Roman men. She inflated his ego.

She told him, time and time again, how that upstart runt Octavian was no Caesar, but rather a mewling little weakling who was no match for Antony's strength and ability. She told him, again and again, how Octavian's child-general Agrippa was no match for Antony's military genius.

How dare those spoiled little boys tell the great Roman general Marc Antony what to do! How dare they send to Egypt and demand that he account for grain or coin!

It had lit a fire of indignation and a growing desire for violence in Antony's stomach.

She heard a shuffling behind her and turned her head to see Antony—completely naked but only partially drunk—strolling into the courtyard. He spotted her by the pool and hiccupped as he made his way toward her.

"Hello, my love," she greeted. "Come rest your head in your loving wife's lap." He obeyed, and she stroked his hair. "You should not walk naked through the palace," she said. "The servants may mistake you for Hercules and forget their duties."

"You have the mouth of a snake charmer, Cleopatra."

She scratched his scalp with her fingernails, and he moaned in pleasure. "A thought occurred to me today," she said, "a thought about Julius Caesar's will."

"What of it?"

"Caesar had great affection for you. He told me so on many occasions. He relied upon your military skill and your personal devotion to him. Is it not strange that he made Octavian his sole heir?"

"It is not so strange. Caesar was not one for sentimentality."

"That is nonsense," she gently challenged. "He regarded you as a son. By comparison, he barely knew the boy Octavian."

"Your point?"

She pursed her lips and slid her soft palms over his cheeks. "I have long suspected that Caesar's will was forged."

"Impossible. The will was kept in the Temple of Vesta. It was sacrosanct."

"Perhaps," she said, and then spoke on as though the thoughts were just now occurring to her, "But then again, Octavian and his sister are both friends with the Vestal Pomponia, are they not? Perhaps those friendships go back further than you know. There is no telling what could have happened to Caesar's will behind the closed doors of the temple, especially in the chaos that followed his assassination."

"I've known that priestess for years," said Antony. "There's no way. The will could not have been a forgery."

"As you say," Cleopatra replied lightly. She shifted her eyes to Charmion, who stood silently by the pool. The slave nodded discreetly in understanding and left.

A moment later, Charmion returned with a platter of delicacies and a fresh amphora of wine. Although Antony was in no condition to notice it, the wine was still swirling from the tincture of opium that had been added to it. He sat up and drained two cups, one right after the other.

Cleopatra waited patiently. And then she tried again.

"I remember how Caesar used to speak of you," she said, "with such fondness and acclaim. When I heard that Octavian was the heir in his will, I could not believe it. I said to myself, 'Cleopatra, some mischief has been done here. Some ambitious and unscrupulous person has forged the will.' The Caesar I knew and loved had planned to leave both his legacy and his fortune to his closest friend and ally, Marc Antony."

Antony blinked slowly and then squinted at her. "It is a bit odd," he said, "that I was left nothing at all."

"Octavian has no scruples."

"He has no balls either," said Antony. "He's just the sort of gutless weasel to get a woman to do his dirty work. And my wife . . . I mean my ex-wife . . . well, she always was his eager little handmaiden. If he asked her to get a forged will into the temple, she would've sucked off Jupiter to make it happen."

"Ah. Now Rome's great general thinks clearly."

Antony jumped to his feet, suddenly infused with violent energy. "I hold a wolf by the ears," he said. "I control Egypt's riches and its army. I control the granaries. I decide whether Octavian can pay his legions and whether

Rome has food on its table." He shook his head as the thoughts ran through it. "But at some point I must let go of the wolf. And when I do, it will bite."

Cleopatra knelt on the floor and wrapped her arms around his bare legs. "My love," she said. "We will kill it before it can bite us. And when the wolf that is Rome is dead, Egypt shall rule the world."

He squatted down and took her in his muscular arms. "You have it wrong," he said. "Antony and Cleopatra shall rule the world."

* * *

He had been gone for a year. Yet his letters faithfully arrived at least once a month, always carried by the same discreet Egyptian slave Quintus had bought in Alexandria, always addressed to the Vestalis Maxima and always secured with Caesar's seal. Quintus's duties in Egypt permitted him the use of Caesar's seal, and that small piece of stamped red wax was the greatest secret-keeper Pomponia could have asked for. After all, the punishment for breaking Caesar's seal wasn't just death—it was death by means of the most painful, gruesome ways Rome's executioners could dream up. And they were a very creative sort.

Pomponia sat at her desk and opened the scroll. Quintus always wrote to her on the finest Egyptian papyrus, and many of his letters were accompanied by small gifts. A pack of exotic spices. A tiny cat or doll made of reeds. Dried flowers or herbs. Small garnets, carnelians, or smoothed lapis lazuli.

Once he had even sent a dead scarab beetle. No doubt he had thought the Egyptian insect would interest her, but when the black creature had unexpectedly tumbled out of the scroll onto her lap, she had shrieked and knocked over a lit beeswax candle on her desk, nearly setting the letter on fire before she had even read it.

Now, she opened his scrolls more carefully.

My dearest love,
    These Egyptians are not right in the head. Their gods are beasts on top and men on the bottom. Yet their temples are as magnificent as any in Rome, may the gods forgive me for saying so. You would be

tempted to crucify their priests and priestesses, though, since I have discovered the trickery they use—a sort of temple magic—to compel devotion to their gods.

I have seen the colossal statue of Isis at the great temple. The goddess weeps real tears from her eyes, yet after a few minutes of devout prayer from the gathering, the flow of tears stop. The people are convinced that their faith has pleased the goddess. Yet soon enough, the tears start again, and the people are compelled to pray even more.

I am angered to say that at first I fell for the scam myself, but then I followed the priest into the sanctuary, where all was revealed. The statue has a hidden hole at the back of its head. The priest adds a magic substance to an amphora of water and then fills the statue's head with it. At first, the substance does nothing, but soon it solidifies to plug the passage of water for a short time. It would be ingenious were it not such a sacrilege. Nonetheless, I have sent you some of this substance—it comes from the inside of a certain leaf—so that you can see it for yourself.

It is similar showmanship at the Temple of Horus. When a pipe plays music, the hawk-headed god's arms open wide and a massive pair of feathered wings emerge from them. When the music stops, the wings fold back into the god's arms. The effect is masterful and truly a sight to behold. I have heard of other temples where the statues actually throw spears, but I have not seen this with my own eyes. I cannot decide whether the gods should curse or applaud such dupery.

Earlier this month, I had reason to visit the old Egyptian city of Giza. It is an ancient place with the most unbelievable monuments imaginable. There is a sprawling necropolis upon which sit three pyramid structures that are so large the visitor must lift and move his head to take it all in. The eye cannot see it all at once. No one seems to know what these pyramids were first used for. Some say they were the tombs of ancient pharaohs. Others say they match the positioning of the stars in the firmament above and therefore are a message to the gods. I have even heard it said that when the wind blows a certain way, the pyramids make a sound that speaks to the gods.

Near these pyramids is an enormous monolith of a Sphinx, which *is a monstrous creature with a human head and a lion's body. The local population calls this creature the Father of Dread. It is said that the Sphinx and the pyramids are over two thousand years old. Even the Black Stone is not believed to be so ancient! My slave Ankhu is very talented, and I had him paint the entire scene for you on the skin of a camel (a most obnoxious beast, by the way). Alas, it will not be dry when I send him off with this letter, so I shall send it next time.*

My beloved Pomponia, do not think that I enjoy such exotics. They only pass the time, and I only take them in so that I may later write of them to you. Most of my time is spent trying not to burst into flames from the Egyptian sun, wrenching the fabric of my tunica from the claws of the queen's wretched cats, or toiling over the abysmal state of the royal treasury. Insanos deos! How strange that these Egyptians excel in astronomy, mathematics, science, and engineering and yet cannot load a trunk with coin for Rome!

I awoke this morning and for a moment I thought I caught the scent of your hair. But then I realized it was only the scent of some lotus flowers through the open window of my bedchamber. The experience gave me pause, though, for the Egyptians believe that the strong fragrance of a flower means that a goddess is close by. It is no wonder I thought of you.

I sacrifice to Mars every week for your safety. I pray to Venus for your love.

Quintus

Pomponia finished the letter. And then she read it again. And again. In person, Quintus could be as ill-natured as the Minotaur. On papyrus, however, he could be as romantic and lyrical as Cupid in love.

Once she had all but committed his letter to memory, she rolled it up and dipped the edge of the scroll into the flame of the beeswax candle on her desk. As the papyrus burned, the words flew up to the goddess. Pomponia had no secrets from her.

She dropped the scroll's cinders into a silver bowl and then uncurled the blank papyrus Quintus had included with his letter, taking up her stylus to write.

Quintus,

How strange and wonderful the pyramids and the Sphinx must be. I doubt I shall ever stand before them, but your letters let me see them through your eyes, and that pleases me greatly. As for the temple magic practiced by the Egyptians—well, I suppose that is for the gods to judge. Although I must say that such antics smack of comedy more than piety.

You sound well, Quintus, although frustrated by the Egyptian queen. Fear not, you have good company in this regard. As I am sure Caesar has told you in his letters, Roman sentiment continues to mount against Cleopatra. The people are convinced that she has cast a spell on Antony and that is why he remains in Egypt. They have always loved the general, and even as their bellies growl, they make excuses for him, saying it is not he who blocks the grain, despite everything Caesar says to the contrary.

But to happier news. Your daughter Quintina continues to thrive at the Temple of Vesta. I often marvel that she is Vesta incarnate. Her face grows lovelier each week, and she masters any ritual or rite the first time she sees it. Her tutors are constantly amazed by the sharpness of her mind. I am happy to report that she has none of your surly or sullen nature—what a relief!—but is rather cheerful and inspiring at all times. She is a blessing to the temple and to me personally, Quintus. I have come to love her dearly, and I will take the liberty of saying that she loves me too.

Quintina tells me that she has written to you about the welfare of her younger sister, Tacita, and has requested guardianship of her until you return to Rome. I know you do not know your daughters that well, Quintus, and that you have been gone a long time, but I urge you to accept counsel from Quintina. She is a young woman of fourteen now, although her wisdom and judgment exceed her years.

The unpleasant truth is that the girls' mother has immersed herself in the cult of Bacchus. It is well known in our circle and in higher society that she engages in scandalous behavior with other Bacchants, including certain bodily rites that are not becoming to a woman of her class. Your younger daughter is still years from marriage, but her reputation must be upheld if she is to obtain a quality husband. That is all I will say on the matter as it is not my place. I only mention this so that you take the words of your eldest daughter seriously.

I make daily offerings to Vesta so that she may bring you home, and I thank you for your sacrifice to Mars. You need not burden Venus with too many prayers, for my affection is as it should be.

Pomponia

She set down the stylus and reread her words as the ink dried. Quintus openly spoke of his love for her in his letters, at times with a lovesick abandon that she would never have thought him capable of. Her replies to him were always more measured. The two of them had already had one close call, and if their relationship were suspected of being an intimate one, especially a physically intimate one, the punishment would be unthinkable for both of them.

Plus, she was the Vestalis Maxima, and despite her feelings for him, she had a duty to the goddess, to the Vestal order, and to all of Rome. No matter how her heart ached when she thought of him, that duty had to come first.

Anyway, it doesn't matter what I write, she thought as she rolled up the scroll, sealed it, and slipped it into a scroll box. *Quintus will read the words he wants to see. He knows the secret love I have for him.* She smiled despite herself at his characteristic presumptuousness and called for his Egyptian messenger slave.

* * *

It was the Vestalia, Vesta's annual public festival in June, and none of the priestesses had enjoyed a full night's sleep in over two months. The time leading up to the Vestalia was as busy as the festival itself.

One reason for this was the production of the *mola salsa* mixture and the sacred wafers: water had to be collected from the springs, flour had to be milled, salt had to be sanctified. And all had to be done according to the same strict and sacred rites the Vestals had honored for centuries.

Once finished, the sacred wafers would be distributed to altars, shrines, and other locations throughout the city of Rome. And considering that the city's population was over a million people, this was no small task.

In years past, people had come to the temple to request the wafers during religious festivals or times of trouble, but after the foot traffic in the Forum had become too congested during the Vestalia, Fabiana had arranged for citywide disbursements. It was just one of the ways the former Vestalis Maxima had updated the practices of the order to cope with the city's growing numbers.

While either loose mola salsa or sacred wafers could be used to purify sacrificial animals and offer into Vesta's fire, the wafers were often favored. The Roman people offered them into their household hearths as purified food for the goddess so that she would stay within their walls and make their home a sacred space. Yes, they would also offer other things to the fire—a bit of bread, fruit, oil, or wine—but the wafers were special, so the Vestals continued to make token amounts for the public.

Yet many people still made the trip to the Forum during the Vestalia. They did so to offer into the temple's exterior firebowls and to take embers from them home. It was also during the Vestalia that women—and only women—were allowed to enter the sanctum to see the sacred fire and make an offering directly to the goddess.

They came dressed in the finest of silks and the roughest of tunicas, leaving their sandals at the base of the temple's marble steps to enter the sanctum barefoot. They carried plates of food to offer the goddess. Some contained rich delicacies, others dry crusts of bread. They bowed their heads and walked across the white-and-black mosaic floor, saw the *aeterna flamma* burning in its hearth, and felt its heat on their faces. As the fire crackled and snapped, they set the plates of food on the floor along the curved inner wall of the temple. To the Vestals who stood watch over the fire, they gifted jewelry, sweet treats, decorative carvings, or fine fabrics.

As high priestess, Pomponia had spent most of the festive day inside the temple, standing beside the sacred hearth with Tuccia and accepting the prayers and offerings of Vesta's faithful.

Needing a breath of fresh air, she had Nona take her place. As she descended the temple's steps—always under the watchful eyes of her guards, Caeso and Publius—she was rejuvenated by the scent of the laurel and flower garlands that wound around the temple's columns and hung from its frieze. Around the sacred area of Vesta, musicians played lively pipes.

Priestess Caecilia stood beside one of the bronze firebowls outside the temple, blessing those who were eager to meet a Vestal Virgin face-to-face. Pomponia approached her for a quick word.

"Rome is getting too big," she said. "Next year, I'm going to propose that we keep the temple open for another day or two during the Vestalia. I've heard people say they can't make it inside."

"I think that is wise," said Caecilia. "A necessary change." She glanced at Fabiana seated on a cushioned chair several feet away. "Although you might face some opposition."

"I don't know. Fabiana seems to care little about custom these days. Just look at her! A holy day like this, and there she is with that foul-smelling creature soiling her stola. What precedent exists for that?"

They both smiled at the former chief Vestal, who sat on a high-backed chair before the temple, a royal-purple canopy stretched over her head. Curled on her lap was Perseus.

Caecilia laughed. "And yet it is you who takes that 'foul-smelling creature' for a walk every night in the Forum. Oh yes, Pomponia, we've all seen you sit on the steps of the Regia with him and look up at the stars."

The dog raised his head to regard every man, woman, and child who knelt before Fabiana in turn, each asking her blessing or praying to the goddess with her.

Pomponia knew—everyone knew—this might be the last Vestalia the ailing Fabiana would share with them. Fabiana seemed to know it too, which is why she had forced herself from her cool bedchamber to sit all day in the sun by the temple. Pomponia tried not to think that the appearance was Fabiana's way of saying goodbye to the people of Rome.

Pomponia rocked on her heels and looked around. Priestess Lucretia was moving among a crowd of men and boys who held out plates of food to her. Only women were permitted in the temple, but the Fates took many women in childbirth, which meant that some families no longer had a wife or mother who could make a temple offering to Vesta.

The men and boys in such families would therefore wait outside and ask a Vestal to make an offering for them. Such was Lucretia's duty today. She was fulfilling it tirelessly, even as the hot sun beat down on her white-veiled head.

In front of another bronze firebowl, Quintina stood on a step and leaned over into a large terracotta pot—it was nearly as big as she was—that contained an excess of the flour used to make the sacred wafers. She emerged with a ladleful of the mix and poured it into a chipped bowl held by a hungry-looking boy.

"Don't give all of this to the goddess," she told the boy. "Vesta is full. Eat it yourself."

"Yes, ma'am!" The boy ran off and the next person in line approached Quintina with his empty bowl.

Somewhere down the line, a bit of roughhousing between two or three men had started, causing a little girl to fall to the cobblestone. She stood up, and a woman wiped the blood from her knees.

A grim-looking centurion, one of many positioned around the temple to assist the regular guard, cast the men a warning glare and put his hand on his sword. "Get to the back of the line, you shit-eaters!" The men hung their heads like pouting children and did as they were told.

Pomponia regarded the bustling Forum beyond the Temple of Vesta. As was customary, garlands of bread and flowers hung from shops, basilicas, and the Rostra, as well as other buildings and temples. Similar garlands decorated private homes throughout Rome. Yet Pomponia had noticed that this year there were more flowers than bread.

A sudden swell of excited shouts and applause caught her attention, and she looked down the Via Sacra to see Caesar's grand litter slowly making its way through the throngs of people toward the temple. Runners sprinted ahead to clear the street of people or of anything the muscly, finely dressed lecticarii might trip on.

Coins flew out of the large lectica onto the cobblestone, and people scrambled to gather them up. Others waved in awe and lifted their children onto their shoulders to catch a glimpse of Caesar.

Concordia's mercy, thought Pomponia, *just when I thought I had Chaos in chains.*

The litter set down near the temple. As Caesar's lictors and soldiers surrounded it, Octavia stepped out of the lectica, followed by her brother. Some people clapped and called out, but others just stared, their eyes expressionless at best and accusatory at worst. Hunger had dulled their goodwill toward Caesar. He could throw all the coin he wanted to; there was less and less bread to buy with it.

Octavian greeted Pomponia first. He pointed his chin at two women fighting over a denarius in the street. "It is unfortunate they cannot eat silver," he said, seeming to read the Vestal's mind.

Octavia, dressed in a white stola, bowed her head to Pomponia. "I have come to make an offering to Vesta," she said. She held a simple terracotta plate upon which was some fruit and bread dipped in oil.

"The goddess will be pleased," said Pomponia.

A moment later, another figure emerged from the lectica: Caesar's wife, Livia. Unlike her modest sister-in-law, she wore a vibrant green dress with earrings that dripped down to her shoulders. Clutching a gold plate stacked with exotic meats, she stepped gingerly onto the cobblestone and bowed her head to the Vestal. "Priestess Pomponia," she said, "I hope our presence does not add to your labors today. We shall make our offerings and leave."

"Not at all," said Pomponia. "Make your offering to the goddess, and then we shall all have some sweet lemon water in the courtyard."

As the two women removed their sandals at the base of the temple's steps and moved through the open doors into the sanctum, Pomponia studied Livia. She had known many ambitious men and women in her time with the Vestal order, but there was something about Caesar's young wife that had always stood apart—something about her smile and the way every expression, every word, seemed strategically chosen for a reason that only she knew.

Livia was a river of ambition, yes, but there was something below the ambition: insecurity. It was the unseen but unstoppable undercurrent, and Pomponia sensed it would wash away anything that crossed its path.

After the two women had made their temple offerings, Pomponia escorted them and Caesar through the portico of the House of the Vestals and into the courtyard. The garden offered a semishaded refuge from the relentless sun and febrile heat, and she gestured to two canopied couches by one of the pools. She and Octavia sat on one, Octavian and Livia on the other.

"Lemon water," Pomponia said to a house slave. "Sweet. And with ice, if we still have it."

"At once, Domina."

"I cannot recall a time when the serious heat came so early," said Octavian.

"It makes the people petulant, Caesar," Pomponia noted. "It's been orderly today, but I can still feel it."

"Hot and hungry," said Octavian. "An unhealthy combination, especially when it comes to public order."

It was Octavia who said what everyone was thinking. "My husband is to blame for it."

"How are you coping, Octavia?" asked Pomponia.

"Good days and bad, my friend. Juno gives me strength."

"I am happy to hear so." Pomponia shook her head in frustration. "The day Julius Caesar was assassinated, Antony came here to hide. He stood right here, at this pool, and drank. It was here that I gave him Caesar's will . . . Oh, if only I could have known what he would become. I would have had Quintus open his throat at Vesta's feet. Forgive me, the heat inflames my anger too. It is hard to believe what Antony is doing to his wife and his own people."

"We have all said and thought much worse," said Octavian. The slave arrived with honey lemon water, mint leaves swirling in the tall glass jug and ice chips already floating in the full glasses. Octavian took a long draw of the cool liquid. "The problem is that Antony still has some support in the Senate and the common people do not believe he would act against them."

"If only there was a way to prove Antony's disloyalty," said Livia.

Octavian crunched an ice chip between his teeth and glanced at her. His wife was not yet as smooth as he or his sister.

Pomponia looked at Octavian. "What are you asking, Caesar?"

He met her eyes. "Antony's will is in the temple. I believe it will show that his allegiance and affection lie with his Egyptian wife and children, not with his Roman ones."

Octavia took the Vestal's hands. "The people need to know what is in his heart."

"And what good will that do?" asked Pomponia. "It will not change him. It will not make the taxes or the grain come."

"No," said Octavian, "but proving his loyalty lies with Cleopatra will give me the support I need in the Senate to declare war on her, kill Antony as a traitor, and take control of Egypt myself."

Pomponia paused. Here it was, finally—the price of friendship with Caesar. She chose each word carefully. "I have no allegiance to Antony. I have never had much use for the man. But you know that I cannot do what you ask. The temple is sacrosanct. Rome's most important men have entrusted the Vestal order with their wills for centuries, and Antony is still a general of Rome. The Senate and the religious collegia would be highly critical of the sacrilege and of me as Vestalis Maxima. They would be critical of you as well, Caesar, especially if the will contains nothing damning to Antony." She squeezed Octavia's hands. "I make this decision out of religious and legal duty. If I were at liberty to make it out of friendship, it would be a different decision."

"Of course," said Octavia. "Forgive us."

"Yes, forgive us," Octavian echoed. "The request was born of desperation. We shall find another way to do what must be done."

More lemon water and small talk followed until Livia exhaled heavily and stood up. "Husband," she said, "and sister, I fear that the heat is quite getting the better of me."

"We should go," said Octavian. "I apologize again for my misguided appeal, Priestess. It was not fair of me to put political pressure on our most sacred order."

"There is nothing to apologize for," said Pomponia. "You are Caesar, and you are doing the work of Caesar."

Livia bowed her head to the Vestal. "Thank you for taking the time to visit with us on this busy day. I wonder if you might come dine with Octavia and me at Caesar's house after the Vestalia? Our new cook prepares the most exquisite dormice you have ever tasted, does he not, Octavia? He is the mortal son of Edesia, I'm sure of it."

"Yes, I would like that," said Pomponia. "Our dormice taste like boiled leather. I've just bought a new cook from the country, though, so we have high hopes." She walked them out of the house to Caesar's litter, which awaited them on the street before the portico.

They exchanged partings. Livia stepped into the lectica, followed by Octavia, but Octavian paused. He looked as though he was going to say something of weight, but then offered Pomponia a light goodbye and stepped in after his wife and sister. As the high priestess waved and walked back toward the temple, he closed the red curtains of the lectica and sat back.

"I told you she wouldn't do it," he said to Livia.

"It was worth a try, husband."

"Perhaps." He didn't sound convinced.

Octavia wiped away a tear and then rested her head on her sister-in-law's shoulder. Livia felt her chest tighten in irritation—the woman had become insufferably whiny since Antony had married Cleopatra—but she suppressed her annoyance and stroked Octavia's hair tenderly. "There, there, dear sister," she said. "We shall find a way to make that barbarian husband of yours pay for his infidelity."

"We shall indeed," said Octavian. "One must admire Priestess Pomponia," he continued thoughtfully. "She is a duteous chief Vestal, yet clearly she favors us politically. That may still be useful."

Livia's chest tightened even more. *Mala Fortuna! The Vestal refuses you, yet your regard for her grows?* She licked her lips. She had fully expected the Vestalis Maxima to refuse Caesar's request for Antony's will and had privately hoped the refusal would have soured her husband's attitude toward the Vestal Virgins. To her dismay, it seemed to have had the opposite effect.

"Who is this Quintus the high priestess spoke of?" she asked innocently. "Is it the same Quintus you sent to Egypt? The one with the Bacchant wife?"

"Yes, the same," said Octavian.

"I did not know they were such good friends," said Livia. This was worth remembering.

But her husband didn't hear her. He was already distracted, sifting through a basket of scrolls and growling about overdue taxes, clogged public latrines, and an epidemic of sexual blisters in the brothels of the Subura. All Rome's problems seemed to rise up to Caesar.

"Apparently, I am to blame not only for their hunger pangs," he muttered, "but for the warts on their cocks as well."

"I see." Livia felt Octavia's head grow heavy as the slow, rhythmic movement of the litter rocked her to sleep. Instead of pushing her off, however, she made a cooing sound and continued to stroke her hair. Caesar was always impressed when his wife showed sisterly love toward Octavia.

Octavian busied himself with his scrolls until they arrived at the portico of his house. Still preoccupied by the business of Rome, he stepped out of the lectica and was giving orders to his secretary before Livia had even shaken Octavia awake.

"Oh, I'm sorry, Livia," said a blinking Octavia. "I think the heat got to me too."

They followed Octavian inside and then went their separate ways: Octavia to bed, Livia to the slaves' bathhouse, where Medousa was overseeing the preparation of Livia's latest gift to her husband—nine virgin girls, one for each night of the Vestalia.

Five of them sat submerged to their chins in a bath, doing their best to communicate with each other in various foreign tongues, while three others sat quietly as their long hair was cropped short. One stood in the center of the room, her arms and legs open, as the beauty slave removed her body hair.

"How are these ones, Medousa?" asked Livia.

"They are very good, Domina. Caesar will thank his wife."

"That's the idea."

Medousa hesitated and then risked it. "Did you see the Vestalis Maxima today?"

"Yes."

"How did she look?"

"She looked as she always looks," Livia grumbled. "Very white."

"Yes, Domina." Medousa cursed herself. It was pointless to ask her mistress anything.

Nonetheless, she felt a bittersweet swell of nostalgia as she imagined

Pomponia and the other Vestal priestesses tending to the sacred flame and navigating the crowds of faithful that descended upon the temple on this day, the first day of the Vestalia.

The Vestalia was always a busy time at the temple. And although only a slave, Medousa had been entrusted with many important duties. She had found great joy in serving the goddess in her own way, and even Fabiana, who had disliked Medousa from the start, always commended her on her conduct during the festival.

Things were different these days. She had spent the last few Vestalia festivals purchasing and preparing virgin girls to be deflowered by Caesar. It was an insult to the goddess. And every time a girl emerged from Caesar's bedchamber, disheveled and weeping, Medousa begged forgiveness from Vesta.

Livia put her hands on her hips and scrutinized the naked girl in the center of the room. Under her watchful eye, Medousa and another slave dressed the girl in a pure white stola and covered her short hair with a white veil. A tear rolled down the girl's cheek.

"Juno, give me strength!" groaned Livia. "I have had my fill of sobbing women today." She let her arms drop to her sides and then looked contemplatively at the other eight girls in the bathhouse. "If my husband keeps going through virgins at his current rate," she said, "we'll be staffing the temple with whores by the kalends."

* * *

My dearest Pomponia,

The Egyptian sun continues to persecute me. There are only two types of weather here: oppressive heat and oppressive heat in a sandstorm. Today is the latter. My eyes sting from the whipping of sand they took this morning, so if my letters are written sideways, you will know the reason.

In honor of the Vestalia last month, Queen Cleopatra permitted an altar fire dedicated to Vesta to burn at the Temple of Isis. Many Roman soldiers and officials came to pray, including myself. A few officials have their Roman wives here with them, and these women spent the day making offerings into the fire on behalf of the men. Some offered honey to the goddess, since that is what the Egyptians offer to their gods. They asked Vesta to bring home all the Roman men in Egypt. I found that I missed you very keenly when I heard these prayers.

While at the temple, I spoke privately with several of Marc Antony's soldiers. There is growing discord in the ranks, and many men are losing patience with their general. They say that Cleopatra is a fatale monstrum *who has cast a spell on Antony and who will be his undoing. They despise her. I have even heard some of them say that she poisons his mind with an exotic compound that makes him her creature.*

It is a strange thing to see them together. Were I not cursed with a cynical nature, I might say it is a true love match. Cleopatra is shrewd beyond measure, and Antony regards her judgment as highly as his own. Then again, Antony has a history of choosing women who think they are as capable as men. It is no wonder he has forsaken the Lady Octavia. She is a virtuous Roman matron who knows her place, and his soldiers have not looked kindly on his abandonment of her.

It is common knowledge among the people here that Antony and Caesar grow more openly hostile with each other every day. Antony sends little coin or support home, yet as far as I know, most of the grain does leave. For my part, I see Antony and Cleopatra sit on their golden thrones as though they are king and queen of the world. It baffles me, but Cleopatra has both the support and the love of her people. She tells them that Egypt is not merely Rome's breadbasket but a great independent nation with its own gods and history. What gall that painted harlot has!

I have found your news about my daughters' mother to be useful and will permit Quintina to manage her younger sister's guardianship.

My gift for you this month is a silver amulet of a shen ring. I acquired this from a priest of Isis. The circle symbolizes eternity. When I was told that, I thought of the love that I have for you and the eternal fire in your keep.

Quintus

Once she had reread his letter and burned it in the candle's flame, Pomponia picked up her stylus and chewed contemplatively on its end. There were still times she didn't know what to make of Quintus. He could be bitter as iron in one sentence—grumbling about how a woman should "know her place"—and then sweet as honeycomb in the next: *I thought of the love that I have for you.*

She looked at the silver amulet on her desk, warmed as she imagined him choosing it for her, and then put the point of her stylus on the papyrus.

Quintus,

The gift is beautiful, as always. But does Ankhu not weary from carrying so many letters between Rome and Alexandria, and so quickly? Either he is winged Mercury or he rides Pegasus over the sea. I do not complain. No woman in Rome is as happy as I to greet the messenger. You should know that Ankhu is reliable and pleasant, and your letters always arrive in perfect condition.

I am glad to know that Quintina will assume the care of her younger sister. She anticipated your approval and has already been making arrangements for Tacita to live with your brother and his wife. I am told they are fine people who are above reproach and hold true affection for their niece.

What a lovely image you have given me of Vesta's sacred fire burning in the Temple of Isis. There is a shrine to Isis in the Campus Martius, and there was talk of building a temple there which our order would manage, but Caesar has forbidden that now because of Egypt's hostility. I will nonetheless find a reason to visit the shrine, and when I do, I shall think of you baking unhappily in the Egyptian heat.

How I wish the situation between Antony and Caesar would resolve itself, one way or the other. Perhaps a battle is better than this infernal uncertainty and tension. It keeps both Rome and Egypt on the edge of a knife, and it keeps us apart.

I fear it has also put a strain on my relations with Caesar and his sister. It is almost unbelievable, but they asked me to give them Antony's will from the temple. Caesar believes its contents will justify a war against him. I had no choice but to refuse him, although it brought me no happiness to do so.

Of course, Caesar was as politic and gracious as ever in the face of my refusal. But only the goddess knows what he is thinking or what he will do. I fear he is the wolf in sheep's clothing that the Greek storyteller Aesop speaks of in his fables. I fear I hold that wolf by the ears. If I show any sign of weakness as Vestalis Maxima, he will enter the temple and tear the heart out of its sanctity.

Rome is also abuzz with talk about Cleopatra's power over Antony. I saw for myself many years ago, when Julius Caesar loved her, what influence the Egyptian queen can have over Roman men. Perhaps if Roman women were permitted to rule themselves as Cleopatra rules herself, the pharaoh's charm and resourcefulness would not hold such novel appeal to our men.

But enough talk of politics and philosophy. Let us instead pray to Vulcan that the smoke of these days soon clears and that the skillful god can forge a bridge of iron to bring you home.

Pomponia lifted the stylus off the papyrus and rolled the writing instrument between her fingers in thought. Her eyes again settled on the silver amulet on her desk. There was so much she wanted to say to Quintus, so many ways she wanted and yet still hesitated, still feared, to express her love for him.

She put the stylus to the papyrus and finished the letter with such raw honesty that tears welled in her eyes.

I miss you dearly, Quintus.

Pomponia

CHAPTER XIV

De Fumo in Flammam
Out of the smoke, into the fire.

–ROMAN PROVERB

ROME, FEBRUARY, 31 BCE

One year later

The newsreader stood on his platform in front of the Rostra, bellowing the latest developments from Egypt to those gathered around him in the Forum.

The moment he finished one announcement, and before he could even start with the next, the news began to move through the city as people ran up and down the cobblestone streets, spreading the official reports as quickly as they normally spread rumors. News—good and bad—traveled quickly in Rome.

"From the timeless sands of Egypt," the newsreader called out, "Queen Cleopatra's binding exotic spell on the once-great General Marc Antony holds fast. Caesar's spies tell us that the pharaoh is as decadent as she is cunning, having performed sexual favors for one hundred of Antony's soldiers!"

"Tell Caesar's spies to send grain," shouted an angry woman, "not this smutty gossip!"

A heated cheer of consensus.

The newsreader ignored her. Hecklers were nothing new.

"By order of the Senate and Caesar," he continued, "no vandalism of public buildings, disruption of public ceremony, interruption of religious ritual, or public acts of sexual indecency are permitted during the Lupercalia. Any such acts will be considered treason, and those found responsible will be committed to the Carcer for public flogging or execution." He ran a finger across his throat like a blade and opened his eyes wide for effect. "No exceptions!"

A low grumble.

"And lastly," he pointed into the Forum to nowhere in particular, "citizens are advised to avoid the brothels in the Subura district at least until the Veneralia," he dropped a hand to cup his genitals, "on account of severe venereal outbreak." He cast a warning glare into the crowd, handed the scroll to his secretary, and stepped off the speaker's platform.

Valeria watched the newsreader cross the cobblestone to a wine vendor in the Basilica Aemilia. She wrapped her woolen palla around her shoulders. It was a cool, wet day. Perhaps not the most enjoyable weather for the Lupercalia, but rain was always auspicious during this time. It symbolized a cleansing, a sort of purification, which promoted the health and fertility of Rome.

The Lupercalia—the festival of the wolf—honored the she-wolf, called the Lupa, who saved and then suckled Romulus and Remus, twin sons of the Vestal Rhea Silvia and the god Mars.

Valeria used to love the spirit and unique celebration of the festival. It used to give her hope, for it was believed that a woman who conceived during the Lupercalia would be sure to give birth to a strong son. She swallowed a rise of sadness at the memory of her little gray baby boy lying in his death basket.

She walked along the Via Sacra, paying little heed to the crush of people visiting the magnificent multicolored temples and basilicas, kneeling in prayer before the great statues of the gods, or stopping at some of the makeshift shrines and vendor carts that were permitted to line the streets of the Forum during the celebration.

Eventually, she made her way closer and then up a staircase to the Palatine Hill, much of which had been opened to the public on this day. She stopped briefly at a fountain for a drink of clear water, but a rough heavy-set woman shouldered her aside and thrust a pile of cups into the basin of clean water.

"Who do you think you are, missy," the woman cackled, "Queen Salacia? Drink up and move your fancy ass out of the way. Some of us have work to do."

In days past, Valeria might have hit her with the water ladle. These days, she just didn't care. She kept walking until she reached the sanctuary that was at the heart of the Lupercalia: the cave in which the she-wolf had suckled and nourished the twins, filling Romulus with the wolfish ferocity and fierce devotion it would take to found the great city of Rome.

Although the entrance to the cave was sealed for fear the grotto would collapse, the new Caesar had vowed to employ the best engineers in the world to fortify the cave and bring it to the magnificence that it deserved. Of course, the man had a civil war to win first. Such was the sadder aspect of the twins' legacy: brother versus brother. It had defined Rome since its earliest days.

The Pontifex Maximus Lepidus and two other priests were already standing before an altar to the Lupa and presiding over the public sacrifice—which consisted of two male goats and one dog—as a gathering of men, women, and children watched.

Valeria spotted a few of her fellow Bacchants leaning against a large column and talking a bit too loudly. She moved through the crowd to stand closer to them. The wine spilled over the rim of their cups and they laughed, seemingly oblivious to the ritual happening only steps away.

As the sacrificial dog collapsed in a pool of its own blood, the Pontifex Maximus bowed his head to a white-veiled figure who stepped forward toward the fire that burned within a large bronze bowl atop the altar. The Vestalis Maxima Pomponia held up a patera and sprinkled a few drops of milk into the fire before pouring the rest over the altar.

Valeria gave the Vestal the evil eye. She was so busy giving it, in fact, that she didn't notice the soldiers who had surrounded her and her rowdy companions. The soldiers grabbed the troublemakers by the scruff of their necks. Only one had the poor judgment to put up a fight, for which he quickly received a helmet to the face and a nose that fractured into a particularly gruesome arrangement.

Valeria made a run for it. She wound her way through and then out of the celebratory crowds on the Palatine and past the arcade of shops along the Circus Maximus until she found herself on an unknown but busy merchant street in the city. Panting, she risked a backward glance. The soldier was still in pursuit.

She ran faster, darting behind columns, between storefronts and vendor stands, and hiding behind a snorting barrel-chested donkey until the street before her cleared unexpectedly. She lifted her dress and scampered over the cobblestone, ignoring the mud and waste that stuck to the bottom of her sandals.

Finally, she saw a hiding spot of sorts—a public latrine. She slipped inside, lifted her dress above her waist, and quickly chose a toilet beside a seated mother and daughter who appeared to be having some kind of argument over the daughter's boyfriend while they relieved themselves. She was safe. Only the most zealous of soldiers would follow a simple rabble-rouser into the unpleasantness of the public toilets.

Unfortunately for Valeria, the soldier who had given chase suffered from just such a streak of zealousness. He barged into the latrine like the Cretan bull, indifferent to the profanity-laden shrieks of the mother and daughter, and hauled Valeria out over his shoulder as if she were a weightless Pasiphae.

"Put me down," she yelled. "I am a noblewoman!"

"You're a drunken woman, that's what you are," said the soldier, "and you're disrupting a public ritual. I have my orders."

He carried her to a metal-barred prison cart that stunk of vomit and tossed her inside. She tried to stand up but forgot that the bottoms of her sandals were coated in muck. She slipped and hit her head hard.

The soldier's voice was strangely muffled, and a ringing sounded in her ears before the world went silent and black.

Slowly her hearing returned. The clang of metal. A dry, hacking cough somewhere in the distance. The rattle of chains and the click of a steel lock. The sound of men's voices echoing in a confined space.

Her vision came next, blurry at first but then clear. The space around her was dim. Solid. The ceiling seemed too close, too heavy. Her head ached and her throat was raw.

"Have some water, Lady Valeria."

She pushed herself up to a sitting position and met eyes with Priestess Pomponia.

The Vestal handed her a cup of water. She accepted it and drank.

"You are in the Carcer," said Pomponia. "You have been arrested for public disorder. It isn't your first arrest for this, and you will likely be sentenced to death this time. The priests of the Lupercalia will see the disruption of their ritual as a bad omen and recommend execution."

Valeria said nothing.

"Your daughter Quintina is waiting outside in the litter. Would you like me to send her in?"

"No." Valeria shook her head. "I don't want her to see me like this." Her dress and hair were both covered in brown muck, and she could feel her bottom lip was swollen. "Does my husband love you?"

Strangely enough, the blunt question did not surprise Pomponia. "Yes," she said.

"Have you coupled with him?"

"No. I would never break my sacred vows to Vesta. He would never ask me to."

"But if he loves you . . ."

"Love is not forbidden to a Vestal," said Pomponia. "Coupling is."

Valeria pushed her messy hair off her face. "He never loved me," she said matter-of-factly. "Do you think he loves his daughters?"

"There is no doubt of it."

"How are they?" asked Valeria. "How are my girls?"

"They grow like roses in May," said Pomponia. "They are happy and cared for."

Valeria stretched her back and winced at the pain that shot down her spine. "I wasted too many years trying to make him love me," she said. "What a fool I was." She laughed. A bitter laugh. "I sound like an actor in a Greek tragedy. Self-awareness only comes at the end."

"It need not be the end, Valeria. I can pardon you, but you cannot stay in Rome. Your vices are well known, and you have become the subject of ridicule. I cannot allow your reputation to taint Quintina's service. Exile is the only option." Pomponia glanced around the small stone cell. "That has its benefits. You can have a new life, a fresh start. You will live comfortably, and I will permit letters between you and Quintina. Who knows what the Fates will spin for you? Perhaps one day you can be part of your daughters' lives again."

"Why would you do this for me?"

"Quintina is the brightest young priestess our order has seen in many years," said Pomponia. "I have gone through the archives and there hasn't been a girl with her capacity for ritual and understanding in generations. Perhaps it is in her blood from the great Vestal Tacita. Regardless, Mother Vesta chose you to bring her to us. You must hold yourself to a higher standard. You have your own duty to the goddess."

"Yes."

The Vestal stood. "I will make the arrangements. You will be released shortly. Go home and await news of your departure. You need to leave Rome soon, before Caesar hears of this and overrules my pardon."

Without another word, the Vestal walked out of the prison cell and disappeared down the dark corridor. A guard slammed the steel-barred prison door closed behind her.

"You have some fancy friends, lady," he said to his prisoner.

Valeria leaned back against the cold stone wall of the cell and closed her eyes. The next thing she knew, the steel-barred door was once again open, and the guard was shouting at her.

"Come on already," he said. "Wake up. It's time to be on your way now, fancy-ass."

And then the blue sky was overhead again. It was almost as though the last few hours—the most terrifying, emotional, and surreal hours of her life—had never happened. She descended the staircase from the prison, stepping between the dead bodies of two executed criminals—they would be left there for the rest of the day as a warning to others—and then, as she so often did, she found herself walking along the cobblestone streets of the Roman Forum.

She wanted to go home. She wanted to wrap herself in her bedsheets like a caterpillar in a cocoon and wait until the knock at the door came and a ship sailed her off to a new life in a new land. If she ever hoped to see her children again and regain their love, she had to get out of Rome.

But first, there was something she had to do.

The sounds and sights of the Lupercalia swirled around her as she made her way to the Temple of Vesta. Garlands of fresh greenery and flowers wound around its columns, base to capital, as they did every festival. Smoke from Vesta's eternal fire billowed out of the bronze roof, drifting up to the goddess. The flames that burned in the bronze firebowls outside the temple crackled and snapped.

Valeria walked past the temple and its guards—she was lucky they didn't stop her because of her bedraggled appearance—and continued along the exterior of the House of the Vestals until she reached the grove of trees at the rear of the Vestals' expansive house.

She approached one of the trees in the quiet orchard and bent down until she spotted what she was looking for in the grass at its base—a wide, flat piece of paving stone that was left over from previous work in the grove.

Kneeling, she picked at the stone until it came loose to reveal the black soil underneath. She dug deep into the soil with her fingers, finally reaching the tightly curled curse tablet she had placed there years earlier.

"What do you have there?"

Valeria jumped to her feet. It was the same soldier who had arrested her during the Lupercalia ritual. His streak of zealousness had extended to following her on foot, just to make sure she went straight home as the high priestess had instructed.

"It's nothing," Valeria stammered. "None of your concern."

"I'll be the judge of that." He yanked the tablet from her hands, pried the nail out with the blade of his dagger, and uncurled the lead sheet.

By this time, a small crowd had gathered. An elderly woman wrapped in a black palla pointed at the lead scroll in the soldier's hands. "That's a curse tablet!" she shouted. "Here in Vesta's grove! She put a curse on the priestesses!"

"No," exclaimed Valeria, "I was removing it! I was revoking it!"

"Read it out loud," someone yelled to the soldier.

As he read the words pressed into the lead, the soldier's face blanched and his hands began to tremble. "I call upon black and shaded Pluto. I call upon dark and hidden Proserpina. *Plutoni hoc nomen offero*: the *Virgo Vestalis* Pomponia, white-veiled harpy. I curse her food, her drink, her thoughts, her virginity. I curse her watch over the sacred fire and her service to the goddess. I divorce her as a bride of Rome and marry her to Pluto."

When the soldier looked up from the tablet, the crowd had grown from a few to a few dozen.

The old woman in the black palla pointed a crooked finger at Valeria. "You cursed the Vestalis Maxima! You have made the goddess forsake us! Rome starves and stands on the brink of war, and it is all because of you!"

The crowd surrounded Valeria like a pack of hungry wolves circling a wounded animal. When the first stone struck her, she didn't even feel the pain, such was the shock. But then more stones followed, as did the pain and panic. Bodies closed in on her from all sides. There was nowhere to run. *Who knows what the Fates will spin for you?* For the second time in one day, a ringing sounded in her ears and the world went silent and black.

The soldier drew his sword but didn't know where—or who—to strike. Should he stab the old woman? The patrician man in his expensive toga? The bejeweled matron? The plebeian boy? The merchant? The bearded Jew? He had just decided on the bearded Jew, when someone shouted, "She's dead!" and the crowd broke apart and scattered into the Forum.

As the soldier bent down to pick up the body of the woman—he couldn't just leave it in Vesta's grove, could he?—the old woman in the black palla knelt on the ground and began to scratch the words off the lead tablet with the sharp edge of a paving stone.

A younger woman who was similarly wrapped in a black palla knelt down beside her elder and poured a small vial of salt that hung from around her neck onto the lead tablet. Both women rubbed the salt into the lead with their hands while murmuring soft incantations to Proserpina, gently pleading with her to revoke the curse.

"Will that work?" the soldier asked them, the dead woman's body slung over one shoulder.

"It will remove the curse," said the younger woman, "but only the gods know when."

*　*　*

The more Livia stared at the coarse black hair of her younger son Drusus, the more she suspected he was the product of that hairy pig Diodorus.

"How old are your sons now, Domina?" asked Medousa.

"Oh, I'm not exactly sure, Medousa. The blockheaded fat one is ten or eleven and the little hairy one is seven or eight."

"How delightful, Domina."

Livia thought about whipping the slave for a moment, but couldn't be bothered. In the eight years she'd lived with Medousa, she had learned to let a lot go. Had she not, Medousa would have been lashed to shreds years ago, and her own hands would be raw from holding the whip.

The blockheaded Tiberius and the hairy Drusus ran up to her with mischief in their eyes. Tiberius opened his hand, and in the center of his palm, the black body of a spider—only two of its eight legs still intact—flopped around. "Look what I did, Mother," he said.

"What a prince you are," said Livia.

It was that moment that Octavian's daughter Julia wandered into the triclinium. She peered into Tiberius's palm, scowled, and pushed his chest so hard that he fell onto his bottom. "You are a cruel and petty boy, Tiberius," she said. "No wonder my father hates you so."

Tiberius picked himself off the floor and glared at Julia, his temper threatening to boil over. He lifted a fist as if to strike the little girl, but she laughed in his face. "As if you had the nerve," she said, smirking at him over her shoulder as she left the room to look for her cousin Marcellus.

Tiberius stood rigidly, his jaw tight with anger. Like his mother, he had despised his stepsister since the day he had first seen her pompous little face asleep in her cradle.

"Tiberius, go outside!" snapped Livia. "And take Drusus with you."

Grumbling, he grabbed his brother's arm and ran off, no doubt in search of more spiders to take out his frustrations on.

Livia cursed her ex-husband Tiberius for bringing the boys here, to Caesar's house. Normally, she visited them at their father's house. On those occasions Tiberius wanted the boys gone, Livia would arrange for them to be sent to her sister Claudia's house so that she could visit them there.

Not that she was particularly interested in visiting them at all. When it came to her sons, she was caught between Scylla and Charybdis. If she didn't see them, she came across to Caesar as a cold and uncaring mother. Yet if she did see them, Caesar was reminded of the fact that she had produced two sons for her former husband but none for him.

She reclined on a couch in the triclinium as Medousa brought a bowl of grapes, and a guest, into the richly frescoed room. "Domina, your sister, Lady Claudia, is here."

Claudia turned up her nose at the mud on the floor as she entered the triclinium, dressed as always in one of her trademark purple dresses. "I assume the darling demons are visiting?" she asked drily, resting on the couch beside her younger sister.

"That wretch Tiberius," fumed Livia. "He knows I hate it when he drops them off unannounced. He does it just to goad me, you know. It's his pathetic way of waving his cock before Caesar."

"It's still early," Claudia replied. "Perhaps he'll send a litter to retrieve them before Caesar returns."

"I doubt it. There is no Senate business today, so I expect Caesar home earlier than usual."

"Has he warmed up to the boys at all?" asked Claudia.

"He tolerates Drusus, but he despises Tiberius."

"Do you think he suspects?" Claudia lowered her voice. "That they may have different fathers, that is?"

"I think he does his best not to think about it at all," Livia replied, "and so do I. You've heard how he drones on and on about the virtues of the Roman matron and the importance of pure sexual morals. Never mind how many of his friends' wives he's screwed in the pantry during his dinner parties or how many virgin slave girls he's pierced, the man would choke on his moral standards if he knew how hard Diodorus used to drill it into me."

"Sexual hypocrisy is the luxury of manhood, dear sister."

Livia exhaled heavily and rolled onto her back, suddenly pensive. "Still . . . the boys are so different from each other, Claudia, it's hard not to wonder. They're both beasts, to be sure, but Drusus at least has some ambition. Unless Tiberius turns him into a drunk or a catamite, he might actually make something of himself."

"Hmm. Let's hope." Claudia placed a bunch of grapes in her palm, plucked a plump one, and popped it into her mouth. She spoke as she chewed. "I heard that the grain rations were increased for the Lupercalia."

"The Senate ordered the increase. Caesar didn't oppose it, but he wasn't happy about it. He said that a full stomach for one day means an empty stomach for two days."

"And he still refuses to take Antony's will from the Temple of Vesta?"

"As far as my husband is concerned, the sun shines out the asses of the Vestals."

Claudia chewed another grape. "And the virgins you bring him? Does he tire of that yet?"

"Does a fox tire of the hen house?"

"Hmm." Claudia spat a grape seed onto the floor. Truly, her sister would try the patience of Clementia. Here she was, the wife of Caesar, and already out of his bed. She couldn't let the situation deteriorate any more. After all, her own fortunes were tied to Livia's, and she quite enjoyed the adulation of being known as Caesar's sister-in-law. She rolled a grape between her fingers. "Seems to me, sister, that it's time your husband lost his idolatry of the Vestals."

"Nice thought, but I doubt that will happen. I thought he would be angry with the high priestess when she refused to give him Antony's will, but instead, his admiration for her only deepened. I couldn't believe it!"

"He admires their virtue," said Claudia. "The more virtuous the behavior, the more he reveres them. His reaction therefore wasn't surprising."

"Whatever you say."

"You're not listening to me, Livia." She leaned forward. "That means the opposite is also true. The less virtuous the behavior, the less he will revere them. Your husband must see that the Vestals are not the chaste guardians of the sacred flame that he thinks they are."

Livia sat up and faced her sister squarely. "I'm listening now, Claudia."

* * *

My beloved Pomponia,

Today I have seen three sights that I could never have imagined. The first concerns Marc Antony. This morning one of the greatest generals that Rome has ever known emerged from his dressing chamber wearing the cosmetics of a woman.

It is customary for men in Alexandria to wear black makeup around their eyes to protect them from the tyrannical Egyptian sun, and Antony has taken up the practice whenever he is to go outdoors. He wears kohl that covers his eyelids and makes his eyes look like those of a cat. I hope I do not sound womanish describing this to you. I am uncomfortable discussing it, but I wanted to tell you. He has also taken to drinking beer over wine, as the Egyptians do. I have tried the stuff but cannot stomach it.

The second thing concerns Caesarion, son of Julius Caesar and Cleopatra. You may still think of him as a young child of two or three years, the age he was when Cleopatra was in Rome, but time flies and he is now sixteen years old.

Although I have been in Alexandria for two years, today was the first time I saw Caesarion on Egyptian soil as Cleopatra only lets Romans who have sworn an oath to her and Antony be near him. The encounter was by accident. I was to travel in a litter with one of Antony's men, but there was some confusion and I stepped into a lectica within which sat the queen and Caesarion.

I must tell you, Pomponia, looking at the boy was no different than looking at Caesar. Although Caesar never acknowledged him and there has always been speculation the child was not his, I am convinced there can be no doubt of his parentage.

Antony's men tell me that Caesarion has the makings of a capable leader. He has his mother's undeniable intelligence and his father's even temperament. But alas, if Octavian Caesar ever comes to Egypt with sword in hand, the young Caesarion will not be long for this world. I cannot imagine the adopted son of the divine Julius would let the true blood son live.

The third thing I saw this day was the making of a mummy. One of the queen's favorite astrologers died, and Marius—one of Antony's soldiers I have become friends with—petitioned the priests to let us watch the process. Marius has become quite friendly with the locals and has adopted many Egyptian customs (other than wearing makeup, for which I am very grateful).

Now Pomponia, you may think that you have seen some disturbing things in your life, but nothing compares to mummification. While we Romans are reasonable in our knowledge that only the spirit travels to Elysium, the Egyptians believe that their physical bodies go to the afterlife. They therefore need to preserve the body to house the spirit.

I urge you to sit down while you read this process lest the description weaken your womanly constitution. After the priests have made their incantations to the gods, the embalmers remove the brain from the body, bit by bit, by means of a sharp hook inserted through the nose. If the brain is stubborn, an embalmer strikes the body on top of the skull to dislodge it. Once the brain is out, the embalmers pour liquid resin into the nose to fill the space where the brain was.

The body is then cut in a ritualistic fashion, and the stomach and other organs are removed and set in an urn. Only the heart is left in the body. The Egyptians believe that their spirit and all that they are resides in the heart. The embalmers then wrap the body in white gauze, using strange smelling unguents to hold the fabric in place, while the priests chant and place amulets along the body to ward off evil spirits.

The body is then put in a sarcophagus and buried deep in the earth with items it will need in the afterlife, such as food and couches.

This confused me above all for I had to wonder how the Egyptian afterlife could be so poorly stocked that the dead must bring their own sustenance and furniture. More strangely, no one left a coin with the body to pay the ferryman. The priests said they did not believe in such things, but Marius and I suspect they simply did not want to part with any money. I left a coin by the sarcophagus when no one was looking.

The Lupercalia will be over by the time this letter reaches you, but I trust it will arrive before the kalends of March and the renewal of Vesta's eternal flame in the temple. My greatest wish is to once again watch you perform a sacred ritual with my own eyes. For now, I shall light a candle on the kalends and make an offering to the goddess. I will tell her of my love for you, and surely she will light my path home very soon.

Quintus

PS: I have written to Valeria and divorced her. You have six years left in the Vestal order. When I return to Rome, I shall make arrangements for our future. We will wed and live in Tivoli.

Pomponia set the scroll on her desk and leaned back in her chair. She often felt dizzy after reading Quintus's letters. They were invariably full of contradictory emotions and messages: warmth and affection in one sentence, haughtiness and condescension in the next. This evening, the dizziness was stronger than usual.

She reread the postscript: *You have six years left in the Vestal order. When I return to Rome, I shall make arrangements for our future. We will wed and live in Tivoli.*

How typical. It was not a declaration of love or a humble marriage proposal but rather an order.

She loved Quintus. That much was undeniable. Yet she had given little serious thought as to whether she would leave the order at the end of her thirty years of service. It gave her joy to know that Quintus felt such love for her, yet as always, he assumed she was his to rule over as he pleased. Her wish to rule herself didn't just irritate him; it baffled him.

She read the postscript again before rolling the scroll back up and dipping the end into the flame of the beeswax candle on her desk. As the papyrus burned, the words flew up to the goddess and Pomponia wondered what she would make of them. What would Vesta want her to do? Become the bride of Quintus or remain a bride of Rome?

The idea of a private life with Quintus was compelling. They had shared brief intimate moments that had foreshadowed the pleasures he could give her.

Many times she had thought of the press of his full lips, the feel of his breath and strong arms, and the sound of his loving whisper in her ear. These moments had been shadows of a life that one day she might see clearly. For years she had imagined knowing him in a familiar way. The way that Valeria knew him.

Valeria. Quintina had written to Quintus about her mother's death, but clearly the letter had not yet arrived. Pomponia had to wonder how Quintus would react. He had never shown affection for her, and it was no surprise that he had chosen to divorce her now, when both of his daughters were out of her care. But would news of her death spark some kind of guilt or regret?

Pomponia's face reddened at the thought of Valeria: a highborn woman, the mother of a blessed priestess, and yet found with a curse tablet that threatened a Vestal's watch over the sacred fire. Had she not cared what misery and death such a curse could bring to Rome and its people?

It was Vesta's sacred fire that kept the barbarians out of Rome and Roman citizens out of slavery. It protected Roman wives and children from raping invaders and watched over Roman men on the battlefield. It blessed and sanctified the home. To cast such a curse was unforgivable, and Pomponia could spare no pity for the violent way Valeria had crossed Pluto's threshold.

As if giving sound to Pomponia's anger, distant shouts echoed from somewhere in the house. A swell of loud voices—strange at any time, never mind this late in the evening. She hastily burned Quintus's letter and went to investigate, running down the stairs and toward the atrium, where the ruckus was coming from.

The moment she turned the corner into the atrium, she was met by the unexpected face of a man. Lepidus.

He was accompanied by two soldiers who stood uncomfortably at his side. Their heads were bowed, and they avoided making eye contact with the two priestesses—Tuccia and Lucretia—who stood in front of them, their hands on their hips in angry indignation.

"Pontifex," said Pomponia. "Are you mad? What is the meaning of this trespass?"

Lepidus rubbed his temples and then shook his head. "I cannot believe it."

"What is it? What has happened?"

"Priestess Pomponia," said Lepidus, "it is my most grievous duty, but I must tell you that an accusation of incestum has been made against the Vestal order."

The blood drained from Pomponia's face. "Against which priestess?"

He paused and licked his lips before handing Pomponia a scroll. "Against Priestess Tuccia."

Tuccia put her hands to her face and slumped to the floor. "*Protege me, Dea!*" she breathed. Goddess, protect me!

Lepidus took a step toward Pomponia and lowered his voice. "I am sorry, it gives me no pleasure to say so, but she must come with us. She cannot remain near the sacred fire. It may be her impurity that has caused us to lose favor with the goddess. Caesar and Antony's alliance has fallen apart, and Egypt's power over the grain supply threatens the dole. We'll have open panic soon."

"Pontifex," Pomponia said sternly, holding up the scroll Lepidus had given her. "Unless this scroll contains the goddess's handwriting in solid gold condemning Tuccia, we can assume it is a false accusation. We remain in Vesta's favor."

"We cannot take the chance," Lepidus replied. "I am the Pontifex Maximus, Priestess. The decision lies with me. She must come with us."

"Pomponia, no!" cried Tuccia. "It is not so, I swear it is not true!"

Pomponia forced herself to think. What was the protocol for this?

"Stand up, Tuccia." It was Fabiana's voice. The elderly priestess walked past the soldiers and the Pontifex Maximus as if they weren't there and looked down at Tuccia. "Remember what you are and stand up at once."

Tuccia stood up. Her legs were shaking, but she faced Lepidus with sudden dignity.

"You will go with them," said Fabiana. She looked at Lepidus. "Take her to the house of the former Vestal Perpennia on the Esquiline Hill."

"Yes, Priestess."

"We will see what must be done and send word to you tomorrow," Fabiana said to Tuccia. "Mother Vesta goes with you."

Tuccia folded her trembling arms across her chest and followed the Pontifex Maximus and the soldiers out of the House of the Vestals. As she left, she crossed paths with Nona and Caecilia, who had just come from the temple to investigate why the Pontifex Maximus—with soldiers, no less—would possibly be attending the House of the Vestals at this hour. They watched Tuccia walk by them, but her eyes were fixed on the scarlet cloak of the soldier in front of her and she did not look at them.

The Vestals stood silently together, waiting for the initial wave of astonishment and disbelief to pass. Pomponia thought about chastising Nona and Caecilia for leaving the temple to the care of novices, even for a few moments and when it was under guard, but then she thought again. Right now, a show of unity was needed. Plus, she had never felt justified in correcting the elder Nona, not even now that she was the chief Vestal. She opened the scroll in her hand and read it.

"Tuccia is accused of incestum with someone named Gallus Gratius Januarius."

"I know him," said Lucretia. "He's a chariot racer for the Blues."

Pomponia felt her head throb. *A chariot racer.* That was a bad sign. Tuccia's love of the races was well known in Rome, and the pretty young priestess openly befriended popular charioteers. She kept reading the scroll. "Her accuser is Claudia Drusilla."

"Why does that name sound familiar?" asked Caecilia.

Nona clucked her tongue. "She is the sister of Caesar's wife," she said, "and a gossiping, maneuvering little trollop if there ever was one."

The younger Vestals raised their eyebrows at the pious senior priestess. Every now and then, when it really mattered, Nona could spit out a spark.

Lucretia wiped a tear from her cheek, and they all fell into a sober silence until a soft clicking on the marble floor made them all glance across the room.

Perseus trotted into the atrium and up to Fabiana, gave a bored yawn, and sat at her feet. The mighty hero, come to slay the beast and save them. Caecilia picked him up and placed him in Fabiana's arms.

"Let's go to the temple," Fabiana said to the priestesses. "I have a story to tell you."

CHAPTER XV

The Story of the Vestal Licinia

ROME, FEBRUARY, 31 BCE

The same night

The evening had cooled considerably as Fabiana led the other priestesses, all of them barefoot, up the marble steps of the white Temple of Vesta in the quiet Roman Forum.

As they moved through the bronze doors, the black, starry canopy of the night sky gave way to the soaring circular dome of the temple's sanctum. The eternal fire roared and crackled in its marble-and-bronze hearth, and the sacred smoke rose upward, billowing out of the oculus at the dome's apex and ascending to the goddess.

The temple was lit not just by the fire but by a number of oil lamps affixed to the marble columns that encircled the sanctum. They cast flickering shadows on the rounded walls. The white-and-black mosaic floor was cool below the Vestals' bare feet.

Pomponia dismissed the novices who were tending the hearth, and they left noiselessly, their eyes full of fear and confusion. Using a pair of iron tongs, she chose two pieces of kindling from an earthenware container and carefully placed them in the sacred fire. Lucretia roused the fire with an iron stoker and it roared up anew, fresh sparks flying out and snapping in the air.

Pomponia looked into the fire. Only yesterday, she and Tuccia had debated whether divine law would permit longer-burning coal to be used in the hearth instead of just wood. Nona had resisted the idea but, to their surprise, Fabiana had spoken in favor of it.

"*Tempora mutantur, nos et mutamur in illis,*" she had told them. Times change, and we change with them.

Fabiana had been a natural Vestalis Maxima. She had always been able to balance ancient custom with new ideas. She had always been able to withstand any crisis, political or religious, with grace and competence. Pomponia silently thanked the goddess that despite Fabiana's age, she was still strong enough to help navigate the wicked storm that had descended upon them.

The priestesses sat on simple wooden chairs beside the hearth. Fabiana stroked the old little dog that slept on her lap, and everyone sat quietly waiting for her to speak. When she finally did, her words mixed with the snapping fire and reverberated against the marble walls. Pomponia had the sense that the goddess herself was listening.

"When I was a novice Vestal of only eight years old," began Fabiana, "my favorite priestess was a young woman named Licinia. Everyone loved her. Her father owned a large apiary in the country, and he used to ship giant crates of candied honey to her for the Vestalia. She would hand these out to the novices and the children of Rome. Oh, I remember it well. The honey was sticky and so delicious. Sometimes you could taste just a little thyme or rosemary. Children would swarm the temple like bees during Vesta's festival and wait for hours for a single piece.

"Licinia was a bit of a trickster. This endeared her to the novices and the public but often found her out of favor with the Vestalis Maxima, who at that time was Tullia. You all know of Tullia. Her statue has stood in the peristyle for decades. Tullia was a diligent chief Vestal and a true servant of the goddess. She felt her most important duty was to uphold the dignity of our order, and she could be quite severe when faced with any deviation from sacred custom, no matter how small.

"Licinia was of the wealthy and noble family Licinius, which in those days was much richer and grander than it is today. The Licinii owned some of the finest land in Italy, and Licinia added to her own wealth by purchasing an expansive villa at Frascati and another on Capri. I remember she

once took all the novices to her house in Frascati and we had the most delicious sweetened ice you could imagine.

"In those days, Cisalpine Gaul was a torment. There were some good-
sized Roman settlements there, but these were always under attack. The
worst of the barbarians was a tribe called the Cimbri, who threatened to
invade Italy itself. Now, you all know your history—the consul Gaius
Marius and his legate Sulla ultimately defeated the Cimbri and stopped
the invasion—but for a while, victory was not assured. It was a frightening time, with the constant worry of invasion, and the high priestess Tullia
was forever offering to Vesta for Rome's safety.

"Even though the war was won in the end, there were some early losses.
One of the worst military defeats happened to the legions of Gnaeus Carbo.
Were I not on consecrated ground right now, I would spit on the floor at
his name. Carbo was an incompetent fool who marched nearly one thousand Roman soldiers straight to their deaths at the hands of barbarians.

"Upon his return to Rome, Carbo was expelled from the army and
reviled for his spectacular stupidity and loss. It was expected he would
commit suicide, but he retreated from public life for a few months and
went to holiday at a friend's villa on Capri. This friend was named Calidus, and his villa was adjacent to Licinia's.

"I never saw Licinia's villa on Capri, but everyone said it was much
nicer than the one owned by Calidus. It was on the coast and grew the
finest grapes. It had a huge olive press, and Licinia often had the oil sent to
the temple for use in sacred rites. There were rumors that the Sirens rested
on rocks that could be seen from Licinia's shore, and that on the hottest of
summer nights they could be heard singing of the fall of Troy. This would
cause the house slaves to rush around and close all the windows in fear.

"Ah, where was I? . . . Oh yes, now I remember. When Carbo returned
to Rome, he wasn't alone. His friend Calidus was with him. They went
straight to the Senate and asked for the floor. Of course they were at first
denied, but Carbo's family was still important in Rome, so he had standing. He assured the senators that Rome's very existence hinged on what
he and Calidus had to say, and such were their dramatics and portents of
doom that they were heard.

"Carbo told the Senate that the battle he lost was not his fault. Rather, it was the fault of an unchaste Vestal—Licinia. She had been seen consorting with one of his legionary soldiers, a man named Marcus Sergius Rufus. With shaking hands and moist eyes, Carbo swore that the priestess's incestum had caused Vesta to turn her back on Rome.

"He cried that her betrayal had broken the Pax Deorum and angered the gods, and warned that his military loss would be only the beginning if the priestess was not made to atone for her broken vows. For without the protection of Vesta, the invasion of Rome and the enslavement of her people would surely follow.

"Of course, no one believed him. They had known Licinia since she was a novice of only six years old. Yet Carbo said that he had quality witnesses and Calidus, a wealthy landowner, was one of them. Calidus testified that on more than one occasion he had visited the Vestal's villa at Capri on neighborly business and had seen her in the embrace of the same legionary soldier, Rufus. The two men also had a Greek priest provide a Sibylline prophecy that supported their accusation.

"At last the rotten seed sprouted, and some people began to wonder. It was true that Licinia was a favorite of this particular soldier's legion, and had been since she was a child. Many of the soldiers gifted her with spoils from their campaigns in exchange for the goddess's blessing. Yet other legions did the same with their favorite Vestals. Such had been the custom for as long as anyone could remember.

"However, the timing of the accusation was fatalistic. It came just before another defeat by the Cimbri in Gaul, and the threat of invasion seemed imminent. A wave of panic began to spread throughout Rome. The people needed a sacrifice. And that sacrifice was Licinia.

"I remember the men bursting into the sanctity of our home in the middle of the night . . ." At the memory of it, Fabiana's voice cracked and trailed off. She wiped away a tear with her palla and scratched Perseus's ear.

"The Pontifex Maximus was with them. Tullia threw a statuette at him. I remember because I thought the Pontifex would be angry, but he wasn't. He apologized and told her that Licinia had to come with them. Licinia came out of her room to see what all the noise was about. She was holding a cup of water, and when they told her what was happening, she dropped it onto the floor and it shattered. I was such a child. I remember thinking, *They're going to make me clean that up.*

"Poor Licinia, that lovely young woman . . . They took her to the ancient Temple of Jupiter, when it still stood on the Capitoline, before fire destroyed it and it was rebuilt. That temple had several underground chambers, and it was there, in those dark caverns, that she was scourged. They had to bring in a man from Judea to do it. No Roman man would do it, not even those who condemned her.

"The high priestess Tullia had all of us, even some of the novices, wait outside the Temple of Jupiter. We had an oil lamp lit with the living flame, and we all prayed over it. I saw Licinia when they brought her out. Her white dress was torn to strips, and rivers of red blood ran down her legs. She could not walk but was dragged along by two priests.

"They had a cart and horses ready to take her to the Campus Sceleratus. She looked at us—oh, I will never forget her face—as they put fabric around her mouth to stifle her sobs. They bound her wrists and put her in a box. That was the last time I saw her. The high priestess and Priestess Flavia refused to ride in their carriage and instead climbed up into the cart with the box. Flavia sat on her knees and put her mouth to the box. She must have been speaking to Licinia through it.

"Then the cart left, and we all stood there for a long while, just watching it disappear down the street. Cassia, do you remember what you said? You said—" Fabiana caught herself. "Oh, what am I thinking? Priestess Cassia is dead, of course." She stroked Perseus as the Vestals exchanged heartsick glances.

Pomponia took one of Fabiana's hands and held it tightly. "Tell us the rest. What of the soldier?"

Fabiana nodded sadly. "Rufus had been a legionary soldier for fifteen years. He was a large man, even for a legionary. His wife had died in childbirth, and his son lived with Rufus's sister and her family. He was a proud man too. When the Pontifex Maximus asked if he wanted to beg the goddess's forgiveness for his crime, he asked the Pontifex if he wanted to beg his wife's forgiveness for having such a small cock.

"They stripped him and tied him to a post in front of the Rostra. He was flogged more times than I could count. I saw a large mass of skin on his back peel away, like plaster coming off a wall. He called out his dead wife's name, and then never made another sound. His murder was as revolting to the goddess as Licinia's was.

"When Tullia and Flavia returned from the Campus Sceleratus, we were all still in the temple praying for Licinia. Flavia went to her bedchamber, but Tullia came into the sanctum. She stood by the fire"—Fabiana pointed her finger—"right there, by that chip in the hearth. I can still see her standing there. She said nothing, but she began to weep. We were all shocked. We had never seen the high priestess cry, not even when her sister had died earlier that year.

"She wept like a child. She was inconsolable. The more she cried, the more we knew that whatever she had seen at the Evil Field was beyond horror, beyond sorrow. A year passed before she could talk about it. She told us how Licinia had cried out to the goddess for protection, but how she had regained her dignity and climbed down into the black pit as bravely as Perseus had faced Medusa. She told us that she had sent the sacred flame down into the pit with her."

Lucretia brushed tears from her face. "What of her accusers?"

"Ah, of course," said Fabiana. "Those men—demonic larvae both. Carbo was no longer considered a disgraced general, but the savior of Rome. The tide of the war eventually turned in Rome's favor, and many said it was Carbo's discovery of the Vestal's incestum that had saved the city and its people.

"Calidus also had reason to be pleased. Licinia's properties were sold off, and he was able to acquire her villa on Capri for a song." Fabiana snorted. "At the time of Licinia's murder, there was a shipment of olive oil already on its way to the temple. Would you believe that demon tried to charge Rome for it, claiming it was his property?"

Fabiana sighed. Her shoulders dropped as if releasing some of the tension and bitterness she had been holding inside. "But Veritas always swims out of her dark well and into the light of day. You see, Rufus had a loving son. He did not believe the accusation against his father, and it wasn't long before Rome realized what it had done. And the horror of the truth was even worse than the lie had been.

"The younger Rufus presented evidence that proved the innocence of his father and of the Vestal. It started with the discovery of several letters written by Calidus to Licinia in which he offered to buy her villa at Capri. He wanted to add her property onto his own. She declined the offer, but he kept sending letters, each one more aggressive than the last.

"And then there was the Greek priest who had presented the Sibylline prophecy. It turned out the man was not a priest after all but rather the Greek freedman of a true priest. The man knew just enough to sound believable. He cracked like a nut during his interrogation.

"But the spark that truly set fire to the men's funeral pyre was the return to Rome of a man called Laenas. He was a respected centurion in Carbo's legions. During the battle that had disgraced Carbo, Laenas was one of the few officers who had maintained his men's respect. There were many accounts of his bravery and how he risked his life to save even the lowest of the men under his command. At the time the accusations were made, he was fighting with Sulla's legions in Gaul.

"When word of what had happened reached him, Laenas returned to Rome like a thunderbolt thrown by Jupiter, furious and at lightning speed. What he said shook Rome. He said that he had once overheard a drunken Carbo telling a now-dead soldier that, if he lost the battle, he would blame it on the broken vows of a Vestal, even if he had to screw the priestess himself.

"So, for the second time in one year, I watched a man scourged in the Forum. Flavia chose to stay and tend the sacred flame in the temple, but Tullia insisted the rest of us go to witness it, even the youngest novices. I remember it vividly. Tullia set her chair an arm's length away from the post they tied Carbo to. When they flogged him, the blood spattered her stola. She never took her eyes off him the whole time.

"When he was near dead, Tullia called out for the flogging to stop. For a moment we thought she would grant mercy. Instead, she ordered that he be taken to the top of the Tarpeian Rock and flung from the cliff to his death. It was done. So much for Carbo.

"But Calidus escaped the executioner's lash. The man was as rich as

Midas, and he bribed his way out of the Carcer, although he probably wished he hadn't. The younger Rufus knew he would try it. He and some men followed Calidus into the countryside on horseback. They captured him and crucified him along the Via Appia. The story came back that it had taken two full days for Calidus to perish and that Rufus and his men drank and celebrated the entire time. They left his body hanging for the crows.

"For months, people came to kneel before the temple to beg forgiveness, not just of the goddess, but of the priestesses too. The Pontifex asked Tullia to make a public statement of forgiveness from the Rostra, but she refused.

"Flavia left the order less than a month after her thirty years of service were completed. She married an ex-consul about a year later, and if I remember right, they had a daughter who later married a young kin of Sulla. She bought a country house outside Pompeii and swore to never return to Rome, not even for her daughter's wedding. Everyone had to go to Pompeii for the ceremony."

Fabiana sighed heavily and put her hands on the arms of her chair. "Lucretia, help me up."

"Yes, Fabiana." The younger Vestal lifted Perseus off Fabiana's lap and set the little dog on the floor as she helped Fabiana to her feet.

"I'm tired," said the old priestess. "I leave the matter with you, Pomponia. But I will say this: the black pit in the Campus Sceleratus is filled with enough of our bones. And although we serve the goddess, you cannot rely on her intervention. Tuccia's life depends on you." Tapping her leg to call Perseus behind her, Fabiana shuffled out of the temple.

The Vestals sat in silence for a long time, the only sound the crackling of the sacred fire in the temple's hearth. Finally, Pomponia spoke.

"Our beloved sister Tuccia has been disparaged by a scheming little shrew," she said. "But Pluto will have to go through us to get to her. Let me think on this tonight. We will speak in the morning."

She stood and took a handful of loose salted flour from a terracotta bowl, sprinkling it into the sacred fire in a V pattern. The flame surged upward as Vesta accepted the offering.

Leaving Nona and Caecilia behind to tend to the hearth, she led the other priestesses out of the temple and back to the House of the Vestals, where they each returned to the privacy of their own quarters and their own thoughts.

Only Pomponia did not return to her bedchamber. She continued along the peristyle and then slipped into the private walled garden space that was designated for the use of the Vestalis Maxima only. She did not use this space very often. To her, it still felt like Fabiana's personal retreat.

An altar of red marble with thick white veins stood against one wall. On its surface, a firebowl burned with Vesta's flame. Beside that were a number of earthenware bowls and some cereal grains, fresh laurel, fragrant pinecones, and several pieces of sweet fruit.

Pomponia selected a ripe apricot and placed it in a small earthenware bowl. She placed a pinecone next to it, sprinkled it with a handful of grain, and then arranged a blanket of laurel leaves on top. She sealed the bowl and then, a prayer to Vesta on her lips, placed it in the low flames of the bronze firebowl.

Once the earthenware bowl was charred, she wrapped it in her palla to protect her hands from the heat and carried it to the heavy wooden door opposite the altar. She unlocked the door and pushed it open to step directly outdoors into Vesta's grove.

As her eyes again adjusted to the darkness of the night, she walked through the treed space until she reached one tree in particular. The tree under which Valeria had buried the curse tablet. Pomponia knelt down and lifted up the old paving stone at the base of the tree. Not caring that the grass and dirt were staining her white tunica, she dug a hole in the soil with her bare hands, going deeper and deeper, until her fingertips were raw.

"I make this offering, Mother Vesta, so that you may forgive me for my desires. Do not let my sister Tuccia, your immaculate priestess, be a sacrifice for my faults. I make this offering so that you will remove the curse that another has put on your temple and your house."

Pomponia lowered the earthenware bowl of burnt offerings into the hole and then refilled it with black dirt, placing the paving stone on top. She sat back on her heels and tried not to think about how much it resembled a tombstone.

She pushed herself to her feet and wandered back into the house.

Exhausted but knowing there was no way she could fall asleep, she climbed the stairs to the second floor and continued to her office, slumping into the chair behind her desk. She brushed the black dirt off her hands, onto the floor.

Outside the open window of her office, she could hear the sweeping of a broom on the cobblestone as the street cleaners moved through the Forum, doing their work by torchlight in the still of night.

The sound always made her think of Quintus and the night before he had left for Egypt.

The night he had held his bloody palm to her cheek and sworn on the Altar of Mars that they would be together, and she had stood inside the Regia as he departed, listening to the sound of his receding footfalls and the scratching of brooms on the cobblestone.

The memory of it, and her longing to once again see his face, caught as a sob in her throat. She looked at the silver bowl of ashes on her desk, and then her eyes moved over some of the gifts he had sent her in the two years he had been gone: a small painting of the pyramids and the Sphinx, a shen ring, some gemstones, a jar of exotic plant extract used for temple magic.

And then Pomponia, holy priestess of Vesta, had a most unholy idea.

CHAPTER XVI

Mus Uni Non Fidit Antro
A mouse does not rely on just one hole.

−PLAUTUS

ROME, FEBRUARY−MARCH, 31 BCE

The next day

It was a clear, warm day for February, but Gallus Gratius Januarius had no way of knowing that. He sat hunched in the corner of a cold black hole in the stone-walled Carcer, twelve feet below the living world.

Gallus wasn't a man who was accustomed to such soundless solitude. His world was a loud one, full of hooves thundering on sand, chariots roaring down the track, and the frenzied cheers of tens of thousands of spectators.

The soldiers had arrived at his house in the middle of the night. The pounding on the door had sounded like a battering ram. Gallus had quickly donned a tunica and stood in front of his wife, who held their infant son to her breast in fear as his house slave opened the door. He could still vividly see the look of shock on her face as the accusation was read: a charge of incestum committed with the Vestal Virgin Tuccia.

He covered his face with his hands. *This can't be happening*, he thought. Despite the ghost stories of Vestals being buried alive, there had only been a handful of accusations of incestum throughout the long history of their order, and even those were surrounded in uncertainty.

Even if a Vestal were so inclined, she'd have a hard time finding a partner in crime. There were plenty of women to be had. No point losing the skin on your back and the head on your shoulders for one that Rome and the gods had deemed off-limits.

Gallus chewed at his fingers. Claudia Drusilla. Who in Hades was she? A woman he had wronged in some way? Perhaps a misguided or obsessive fan of a competing chariot team? Outside of the racing track, he had no enemies he knew of. He owed no debts.

He scratched anxiously at his head as a memory came to him. *No . . . Could that be it?* He picked at an insect that had attached itself to his scalp and cursed himself.

At the end of the last games, Priestess Tuccia had been asked to present the victory palm to the winning charioteer. That had been Gallus, of course. The Vestal's love of the races and of a particular horse on his team—Ajax—was common knowledge, and she had even visited the stables on occasion to fawn over him.

As she had presented Gallus with the victory palm, he had surprised her with the gift of Ajax's golden bridle. The crowd had gone wild. Now, Gallus wondered whether the innocent gesture had been seen by some as a sign of a greater guilt.

A scraping noise sounded above him, and he sensed that the barred grating at the hole's entrance had been slid open. A moment later, a dark figure landed heavily at his feet and the grating scraped closed again.

The man groaned once and then fell silent. By the scarce light of the single torch that burned in the hole, Gallus could see a dark pool of blood spreading out from the man's skull. A white bone protruded from one leg. Gallus pushed himself up and stepped away. He leaned against the stone wall and waited, like an animal locked in the pit of the arena, to see what his fate would be.

He had no way of knowing that the Fates were spinning their thread at that very moment.

* * *

The Forum Boarium ran along the banks of the Tiber. On any ordinary day, the forum's cattle market was a bustling mass of people and stock animals. It was Rome's main riverside hub of trading and commercial activity, where boats loaded and unloaded inventory, where blacksmiths noisily hammered at hipposandals, and where farriers broke their backs fastening shoes to the hooves of high-strung horses and muscular working oxen. Every day, wooden carts packed with hay, straw, feed, or manure rambled and rattled down the cobblestone and a dirty child could be seen running to catch an escaped goat, pig, or chicken.

But not today. Today, the Forum Boarium was closed for business. It was still packed with people, however—people who had come to witness one of the most inconceivable spectacles anyone could have imagined would happen during their lifetime. A Vestal Virgin, accused of incestum, was going to call upon the goddess to decide her fate by either proving her innocence or confirming her guilt.

The agitated crowd stood near a round temple beside the Tiber, their nervous excitement held at bay by a long line of no-nonsense soldiers whose polished armor reflected the light of the sun and whose hands rested menacingly on their swords.

The temple honored Hercules, who had driven cattle through the area during one of his labors. More importantly, it was also near the spot where the river god Tiberinus had gently guided the twins Romulus and Remus to shore to be found by the she-wolf.

Although the eternal flame did not burn within the temple, the Vestals still used its circular sanctum to consecrate water from the Tiber. As the god who had saved the twins—and rescued their priestess mother from captivity, later marrying her—Father Tiber was for good reason specially honored by the Vestals during the Tibernalia.

Considering what she had in mind, Pomponia hoped the river god would be as beneficent to the Vestal Tuccia as he had been to the Vestal Rhea Silvia. As the Vestals' horse-drawn carriage entered the Forum Boarium, she moved the curtain aside to peer outside.

Standing closer to the temple was a throng of senators, various magistrates, and officials, all of whom looked visibly anxious. The city newsreader was also there with his secretary. The senators were speaking with the Flamines Maiores, the High Priests of Jupiter and Mars, as the augurs looked on with sober concern. The priests of Pluto were also present, their black robes and somber chants, which sounded like low music behind the din of conversation, adding an even greater sense of dread to the occasion.

When the Vestals' horse-drawn carriage approached the round temple and stopped before it, the Pontifex Maximus Lepidus covered his head with his pontifical robe and raised his arms to quell the chatter and command attention.

An apprehensive silence descended over the Forum Boarium as High Priestess Pomponia stepped down from the carriage, followed by the elder Priestess Nona and then Priestess Tuccia.

All three were dressed in the white stolas and veils of the Vestals. The black-haired novice Quintina, wearing a long, white tunica dress and simple veil, stepped down from the carriage after them and quickly dropped to her knees to straighten the bottoms of their stolas. She then reached back into the carriage, first pulling out a round wooden sieve, which she presented to the Vestalis Maxima, and then an earthenware amphora, which she gave to the Vestal Nona.

Pomponia faced the crowd, casting the same superior but indignant look to everyone, whether respected priest or state official, wealthy citizen or common slave. "We, the faithful priestesses of Vesta Mater," she began, "who keep the eternal flame in the temple, who offer our youth to the goddess and to Rome, come before you today to answer a sacrilegious charge of obscene incestum against the virtuous Priestess Tuccia."

After she was certain that all eyes were on her, Pomponia held out the sieve with extended arms. As she did, Nona poured the water from the amphora into it. The water ran straight through to create a large puddle on the ground.

Pomponia took two steps to stand beside Tuccia. "Only the goddess can judge the purity of her priestesses," she said, and then passed the sieve to Tuccia.

Tuccia held the sieve above her head. "O holy Vesta," she called out. "If I have always tended your sacred fire with pure hands, make it now so that with this sieve I shall be able to draw water from the Tiber and bring it to the temple. Let the water remain in the sieve as my vows remain unbroken."

At that, Tuccia walked toward and then past the temple to where a few stone steps led to the banks of the Tiber. She walked down the steps as the

Pontifex Maximus and the high priests of Jupiter and Mars followed her, everyone else jostling to see what they could.

The newsreader muttered to his secretary, who feverishly transcribed his account of what was happening. Regardless of how this ended, he knew he would be shouting out the news for days in the Forum.

Pomponia remained beside Nona and Quintina in front of the temple. Her face wore an expression of cool certainty, but her heart hammered against her chest in doubt and fear.

Tuccia stopped at the bottom of the steps on top of a white marble platform that extended into the river and allowed the Vestals to collect flowing water from the Tiber. A gold plaque had been affixed to its center. It read: *On this holy spot, the Vestals collect the sacred water of Father Tiber.*

She gently immersed the sieve in the river, left it submerged for a moment, and then lifted it out. Though they could not believe their eyes, the Pontifex and the priests nodded in confirmation: it was indeed full of water. It did not drain through but remained in the sieve, splashing against its high wooden rim even as Tuccia walked back up the steps.

Still holding the sieve, she walked back to the temple to stand before the mesmerized crowd. Not a drop had drained.

The Pontifex Maximus stood beside her and looked into the sieve. Cupping his hands, he filled them with water and took a sip. The crowd drew in a collective gasp of amazement.

"Mother Vesta," said Tuccia, "your priestess is as pure and faithful as always." She passed the sieve to the Pontifex Maximus. Almost immediately, water began to drip through it. A moment later, the pool of water in the sieve gushed out the bottom to drench the chief priest's sandals.

The Pontifex Maximus raised the sieve over his head, even as the last of the water dripped down onto him. "*Jure divino!*" he shouted. "By divine law, our priestess is innocent!"

The crowd erupted into a chorus of cheers, applause, and prayers that all flowed into one jubilant song. Lepidus pointed to a centurion. "Go immediately to the Carcer and free Gallus Gratius Januarius."

Pomponia felt pressure on her hand. Tuccia was clutching it. Her eyes were wet, and her chest was heaving with deep breaths. She had the face of one who had been too close to death, one who had already stepped into Charon's boat but at the last moment had been pulled out by an unseen hand.

As she gripped Pomponia's hand in relief, Tuccia's eyes grew questioning. She had followed Pomponia's hasty and cryptic instructions without thinking. There had been no other choice than to put her life and her trust in the hands of her friend, the Vestalis Maxima.

Gently fill the sieve with water from the river and then bring it back. Walk quickly. The goddess will not permit it to drain and you will be proved innocent. Don't think about it, just do it.

But how? Had Vesta truly intervened? That was doubtful. Yet it was unthinkable that Pomponia would have practiced deception in the name of the goddess.

Pomponia saw the questions on Tuccia's face and squeezed her hand. "*E duobus malis minus eligendum est,*" she whispered, as they stepped up into the carriage with Nona and Quintina.

Of two evils, you must always choose the lesser.

* * *

After the *miraculum* of Vesta's show of divinity by the banks of the Tiber, the renewal of the eternal flame of Vesta on the kalends of March had been a more meaningful ritual than it had been in years.

Despite its hunger pangs and the ongoing hostilities between Caesar in Italy and Antony in Egypt, all of Rome had embraced the ceremony with particular zeal. As the sacred flame had been reignited, the people's faith in the gods, the Vestal order, and the greatness of Rome had been renewed. Hope had been renewed.

Following the renewal ceremony, as was customary, two Vestals remained in the temple while others left to participate in dedications or celebrations elsewhere in Rome. This year, Lucretia and Caecilia remained, while Fabiana had surprised Pomponia by saying she wanted to go. The former Vestalis Maxima hadn't seemed well enough to Pomponia, but it was pointless to argue.

Along with Fabiana, Pomponia made sure that Tuccia and Nona were the Vestals who accompanied her to these other events. As the three priestesses who had stood by the Tiber together only a week earlier, she wanted a show of solidarity. The more they could be seen in public, proud and confident, the sooner the incestum ordeal could be wiped from the public's memory.

The chariot races in the Circus Maximus provided the perfect opportunity for such a display. Tuccia was determined to act like nothing had happened and to cheer on her beloved Blues as she had done since she was a young girl. In fact, she had gone a step further by inviting the wife of Gallus Gratius Januarius, who was currently in the lead chariot, to sit beside her on Caesar's balcony.

As Tuccia and Gallus's wife shouted and waved long blue ribbons, Pomponia chatted comfortably with Medousa. Despite Pomponia's refusal to give him Antony's will from the temple, Octavian had remained as friendly and accommodating as ever and continued to bring Medousa to events that he knew the Vestalis Maxima would be attending.

Yet the day had its tensions. The largest of these was named Claudia Drusilla.

She sat beside her sister Livia, struggling to reclaim her status by socializing with an assortment of senators, priests, noblemen and noblewomen, and of course, the Vestals themselves. Dressed in gowns of purple and blue, and dripping with gold and gemstones, the two sisters made a stark contrast to the white-veiled priestesses who sat a few rows ahead of them.

Following Tuccia's astonishing show of innocence, Claudia had issued a public apology to her and to the Vestal order. She had retracted the accusation, claiming that it was only her profound love for the Roman people and her sorrow over so many empty stomachs that had compelled her to see guilt in the innocent interactions between the charioteer and the priestess and to worry that a breach in the Pax Deorum had caused Vesta to forsake Rome.

Along with the apology, she had donated a mountain of grain from her hoarded personal stores to some of Rome's poorest districts, all in the name of Vesta. The quick gestures of contrition, along with her status as Caesar's sister-in-law, seemed to have saved her skin.

Of course, none of the priestesses believed the remorse was genuine.

Even if it had been, it would change nothing. The damage was done, and forgiveness from the Vestal order would never come.

Claudia was beginning to suspect as much. She leaned over to whisper to her sister but had to raise her voice to be heard over a swell of ear-splitting screams from the frenzied spectators.

"How much grain must I part with before I am back in their good graces?" she asked.

"You could transform into holy Ceres and hand them Egypt on a silver platter, and they still wouldn't forgive you," said Livia. "They are not change-able." Frustrated, she fidgeted with a gold-and-ruby bracelet on her wrist as she watched the chariots peal violently around the circular track. "Medea's hot cunt, what a mess the whole thing is! The incestum charge was sup-posed to make Caesar see the Vestals as impure, but now he sees their purity as *divine* and sanctioned by the goddess. Worse, he now openly asks me to send virgins to his bedchamber and grows sullen if I don't send one nightly. The gods know when he'll get between my legs again."

"And what of war with Antony? Will Caesar declare it?"

"He cannot. There are still senators who refuse to believe that Antony is stopping the grain."

"But Agrippa destroyed Sextus Pompey years ago," said Claudia. "So who else could be responsible but Marc Antony?"

Livia looked at her sister and shrugged. "Antony has men in Rome, and they spread the rumor that Caesar has been sinking shiploads of the stuff at sea and blaming it on Antony." She folded her arms across her chest. "I wish Antony were dead. I would be first woman of Rome if he were dead. No more holding back, waiting to see what he does, and no more playing second woman to that sniveling prude Octavia."

"Hmm." Claudia drummed her fingers on the wooden arm of her chair. "You need Antony's will from the temple."

"Caesar will never forcibly take it," said Livia. "Not after that divine spectacle by the Tiber. It would be political suicide to violate Vesta's temple now." Exhaling an irritated sigh, she straightened her back and craned her neck to look around. "Where is that ugly slave with the wine? I don't know why we bother bringing slaves to the Circus. They pretend to be busy when really they've sneaked off to watch the races. We'll see if they think it's worth it when their backs are bleeding tonight. Never mind, I'll find the wine myself—that is, providing the damn augurs haven't already drunk it all."

Livia stood up and left her seat. A moment later, someone else took it. The former Vestalis Maxima Fabiana.

Claudia smiled awkwardly. "Priestess, it is good to see you looking so well." When Fabiana said nothing, Claudia cleared her throat and folded her hands on her lap. She would not let this frail old woman rattle her, former chief Vestal or not. "I hope you have accepted my apology."

Fabiana reached out to pat the back of Claudia's hand reassuringly. She leaned in to speak softly. "An honorable woman would take her own life."

Claudia felt her mouth drop open.

But then Fabiana looked up with a pleasant smile. "Oh, here is your sister." With the help of her slaves, the elderly Vestal stood up to give Livia back her seat. "Lady Livia, how alike you and your sister are. Like Helen and Clytemnestra. Now if you will excuse me, I think I will return home to rest."

"Do take care, Priestess," said Livia. When the Vestal had moved on, she sat beside Claudia and handed her a cup of wine. "It took me for-ever to find the wine slave," she grumbled, "hiding behind a column and watching the races, just as I thought."

"Hmm." Claudia took a sip of her wine. And then another. But no matter how much wine she drank, her mouth still felt dry.

CHAPTER XVII

Aequitas Enim Lucet Ipsa per Se
Justice shines by her own light.

—CICERO

EGYPT AND ROME, APRIL, 31 BCE

Later the same year

Sunrise was still a few hours away, but Quintus didn't care. He had spent over two years in this beast-worshiping desert wasteland where women ruled men and men wore makeup. It was time to go home. Home to her. To Pomponia. But first, there was one last Egyptian wonder to visit, one that he knew would hold special fascination for Pomponia as chief priestess of the sacred fire.

The monumental Lighthouse of Alexandria dominated the small island of Pharos in the Alexandrian harbor and stretched hundreds of feet into the sky. There was not a taller structure known anywhere in the world. It was anchored to the earth by a broad stone platform, on top of which the lighthouse stood and reached higher into the heavens than anything made by mortal hands should.

The massive white stone structure was adorned and capped with statues of ocean gods. Each time his Egyptian slave Ankhu had set sail from Alexandria to bring a message to Pomponia, Quintus had stood in the shipyard and looked out at the lighthouse in silent prayer to Neptune and Triton, but especially to Triton, messenger of the sea, in the hopes that he would blow his horn and calm the waters enough for the ship to travel with speed.

During the day, the lighthouse used mirrors to reflect sunlight and serve as a beacon for ships at sea. It was rumored that these mirrors could generate such intense beams of light that enemy ships could be set on fire long before they reached the shores. *Egyptian delusions of grandeur*, thought Quintus. *How typical.*

A fire also burned day and night at the top of the lighthouse. During the day, it created black smoke that was released through the lighthouse's apex to form a thick column that could further help ships navigate safely to port. It reminded Quintus of the plume of smoke that billowed from the Temple of Vesta.

At night, and throughout the dark hours until dawn, this fire burned more fiercely, producing a vibrant orange flame that could be seen from great distances by ships trying to navigate the sea and enter the port. It was this fire that Quintus wanted to see up close. After all, was it not a type of eternal fire? And would that not be of interest to a Vestal priestess? He felt a smile spread across his face as he imagined Pomponia's fascinated expression as he told her all about it—but then he forced himself to stop smiling. *Stop being so damn womanish*, he told himself.

It had been a moonless but starry night, and the stars were still bright in these quiet hours before dawn. Quintus and Ankhu had climbed the winding stairs of the lighthouse all the way to an observation deck hundreds of feet above the ground. There, they had stopped to wait for Marius, who had bribed some person or another to gain them access to the very top of the lighthouse.

Quintus leaned over the edge of the observation deck and gazed upon the sleeping city of Alexandria. The Royal Library was clearly visible, some of its windows flickering with light. No doubt those annoying Egyptian academics and philosophers were already busying themselves debating the mysteries of the gods and creating more scrolls to join the hundreds of thousands that were said to fill the bibliotheca.

He turned his head to look down at the shipyard in the Alexandrian port. It was mostly quiet and still at this hour, although there were a few early risers working by torchlight to load crates, freight, and trading goods into ships for whatever voyage awaited them.

In just a few hours, he would be on one of those boats on his way home to Pomponia. He allowed himself a smile as the raucous cries of sea birds, the splashing of black waves against the rocks, and the roaring of the great fire above him sounded in his ears.

Quintus faced Ankhu. They had climbed what seemed like a thousand stairs, and even though Quintus could feel the sweat soak through his tunica, the Egyptian looked as composed as ever with his clean-shaven head, black-lined eyes, and white linen skirt. "You remembered your supplies, correct?" he asked. "I want you to paint the fire and the view from the top when we get up there. I want the priestess to see it."

"Yes, Domine."

"Good." Quintus reached into his goatskin sack and pulled out a scroll, handing it to Ankhu.

"What is this, Domine?" Ankhu uncurled the scroll and gasped.

"It's your manumission," said Quintus. "I've freed you."

"Domine," the slave stammered. "By all the gods of Rome and Egypt, I—I thank you. I cannot express my—"

"Oh, stop sputtering, you fool. I don't have time to sell you for any profit, so I might as well set you free. Finish your paintings, and then you can do as you like. You can come to Rome and work for me or stay in this sandblown version of Hades, it's no concern of mine."

"Yes, Domine! Of course, Domine."

Quintus spat on the ground at the sight of tears running down the former slave's face and then waved as he spotted his friend Marius emerging from the lighthouse to join them on the observation deck.

"*Salve*, Quintus," panted Marius. "I have a big heart because you are leaving Egypt this morning, but it is not big enough to forgive you for making me climb these stairs before I've had my breakfast. I'm winded." He struggled to catch his breath. "You said you were departing early, but I didn't think you meant before Ra rose in the sky."

"You and your damned Egyptian gods," said Quintus.

"The Egyptian gods rule this land," Marius grinned back. "It is only prudent to honor them. Now, my friend, let's keep moving. If I stop for too long, I won't be able to get going again."

The three men—two Romans and a freed Egyptian slave—labored up the last stairway to the top of the lighthouse. As they ascended into the uppermost chamber, they felt an unexpected swell of heat on their faces from the fire that burned in the middle of the circular space. The snapping and crackling of its flames were surprisingly loud and echoed in the round chamber.

Yet most dazzling and unexpected to Quintus was the way the vibrant orange flames reflected off the multitude of mirrors that encircled the chamber. The effect was spectacular and like nothing he had ever seen before. He raised his eyebrows and nodded to Ankhu. Yes. It was worth climbing the thousand stairs. This would *definitely* impress Pomponia.

Quintus appreciated the fire for a few long moments, and then took several cautious steps over the mirrored floor to peer out one of the wide slotted openings through which the fiery orange beacon was made visible to ships at sea. With the heat of the fire on the back of his head and the cool ocean air on his face, he again felt a rise of excitement in his gut. He was going home.

He turned to say something to Ankhu, but furrowed his brow as he caught an expression of shock on the former slave's face. A moment later, Quintus's insides burned with a searing heat that he could not have imagined possible. He clutched the solid instrument that had impaled him—a red-hot iron stoker from the fire—and tried to pull it out of his body, but then the pain crippled him entirely, and he collapsed onto the mirrored floor.

His vision was blurred to the point of near blindness, but he felt movement. Someone was lifting his body. Was it Marius? Ankhu? An intense feeling of falling, fast, washed over him.

Or perhaps it wasn't falling. He couldn't be sure. He was suddenly very disoriented. No, he wasn't falling. He was moving forward. He could feel watery movement below him. *Oh good, I'm already on the boat*, he thought, *the Egyptian boat to Italy.* But then he realized his mistake.

This was Charon's boat. The silent black-cloaked figure stood at the prow, pushing his pole in the black river to move the boat forward. Someone else was in the boat too. A woman stood above him, locks of her chestnut hair visible under her white veil. She placed a gold coin in the ferryman's hand and then looked down at Quintus. The boat moved forward. Fast. And the faster it went, the clearer he could see where they were going.

He could see the shores of Italy, the towering cypress trees that lined the road to Rome, the cobblestone of the Via Sacra, and the smoke billowing out the dome of the white circular temple in the Forum. He could see her white dress, her smile as she met him, her body as they made love, and her small hand in his as they walked through the green fields of their villa in Tivoli.

He could see the orange glow of the hearth fire that burned in their home, and he watched it until the light in his eyes went out.

*   *   *

Pomponia was working at her desk when a slave escorted the messenger Ankhu into her office. She dismissed the slave and rose to greet Ankhu as she always did, holding out her hand for Quintus's letter.

"Please sit down, Priestess," he said. His face was drawn. His normally impeccable dress was rumpled, and a few days' growth of beard was evident.

She sat down, suddenly unable to take a deep breath. Ankhu's voice sounded muffled and distant, like she was hearing him speak through a thick wall.

Quintus was dead, stabbed in the Lighthouse of Alexandria by one of Marc Antony's men. His body had been thrown from the top of the tower to fall from the sky like a seabird struck by an arrow. Murdered on the very morning he was to return home. Ankhu had been marked for death as well and had only escaped by killing the assassin himself and then running for his life.

The Egyptian allowed her a moment to absorb the shock of his words. He had to make sure she understood what he was telling her. She said nothing, but gave a slight nod of her head.

He pressed on, gently. "My master gave me strict instructions to follow in the event of his death in Egypt," he said. "I was able to retrieve his body, and I followed his instructions with all diligence. First, I was to cremate his body and return his remains to you." He placed a round funerary urn on Pomponia's desk.

The Vestal stared at the urn but still said nothing.

"Also," continued Ankhu, "I am to present you with this ring, which you are instructed to wear as the wife of Quintus Vedius Tacitus." He set

Quintus's silver intaglio ring, the one with the carnelian sealstone of Vesta, on her desk.

This the Vestal picked up. Her hands were trembling.

Ankhu folded his hands together. Of course, he had always suspected that the relationship between the Vestal and Quintus was an intimate one. He had learned enough of Roman law and religion to know that it was a forbidden one too—but his duty was to his master, not to the foreign gods of Rome.

"Finally, I am to paint images of the fire atop the Alexandrian lighthouse, as well as the view. I have not had occasion to complete this task, but I will do so."

For several long moments, the Vestal said nothing. Finally, she reached for a purse on her desk, removed several coins, and placed them in Ankhu's hand, her own hands still shaking. "Is there anything else I should know?" Her voice was breathless.

Ankhu lowered his head. "My master had freed me shortly before his death. The manumission paper was lost when I jumped into the water."

She nodded. "You shall have your freedom, Ankhu. You have earned it. Come back in a few days."

Ankhu bowed deeply and then slipped out of her office, leaving Pomponia to stare at the intaglio ring in her hand. *I am to present you with this ring, which you are instructed to wear as the wife of Quintus Vedius Tacitus.*

Typical Quintus. She slid the ring onto one of the gold chains he had sent her from Egypt and then fastened it around her neck. One way or another, she always ended up obeying him.

As the initial shock subsided, Pomponia felt grief swell inside her, and she knew the tears would soon come. They would be as insistent and unstoppable as the floodwaters of the Nile, that great deluge Quintus had described in his letters. Compelling her breaths to remain steady, she removed the lid from the urn.

On top of the mix of gray ash and bone sat a lock of Quintus's dark hair. She suspected that was Ankhu's idea. It seemed too sentimental a gesture for Quintus to think of.

She removed the lock of hair and placed it in her desk drawer and then poured the ashes from the silver bowl on her desk into the urn with Quintus's remains. His body and his words together. She would take them to the temple and put them in the *favissa*, the sacred depository under the sanctum's floor where ashes from the eternal fire were kept.

The goddess would not mind. After all, she had answered her priestess's prayers by bringing Quintus back home. It just wasn't in the way that Pomponia had expected. But then, the gods had their own way of doing things.

She had a sudden vision of Quintus in the Regia, the last time they had seen each other: his bloodied palm pressed against her cheek, his face close to hers and his deep voice slipping into her ears.

Mars protect you while I cannot.

Vesta bring you home.

Her grief flooded over the banks now. Her throat tightened and tears welled in her eyes, even as she heard the muted sound of voices in the corridor outside drawing closer to her office. How would she explain such uncontrolled sorrow to the other priestesses?

But then the goddess gave her a way. Quintina swung open her office door and ran inside, her cheeks wet with tears.

"You must come at once, Pomponia," she said. "Fabiana is dead."

CHAPTER XVIII

Multa Ceciderunt Ut Altius Surgerent
Many things have fallen only to rise higher.

−SENECA

The next day

The former high priestess Fabiana lay in state in the courtyard of the House of the Vestals. Her body had been washed and prepared by the priestesses and then dressed in the formal white stola, headband, and veil of a Vestalis Maxima. A gold coin had been placed in her mouth, a sacred wafer in her right hand.

Countless friends, family, aristocrats, senators, magistrates, and religious colleagues had come to pay their respects. Every person present had known Fabiana, either personally or by reputation, for his or her entire life. Indeed, almost every person alive in Rome knew of her. She had served with the Vestal order for an unprecedented number of years.

Octavian had already announced plans to commission a new mausoleum for the Vestal order in Fabiana's name and it was he, standing alongside the pontiffs Lepidus and Pomponia, who would be delivering the eulogy from the Rostra later that day. Another high-profile death, another opportunity for self-promotion.

After the service, Fabiana's body would be placed on its funeral pyre and set alight. Wine would be used to douse the embers, and her ashes would be collected by her family and the pontiffs. Fabiana had requested that they be put in the temple's favissa. Pomponia knew she would never deposit ash from the sacred fire there again without thinking of Quintus and Fabiana.

Word of Quintus's death had not yet reached Octavian, although it would within a day or two. Octavian would be offended—*How dare Antony order the killing of Caesar's delegate!*—but otherwise, he wouldn't care. Quintus's death was hardly important enough to start a war over. There would be no speech from the Rostra for Quintus.

Quintina and her sister were similarly unaware of Quintus's death. For now, that was good. The delay gave Pomponia time to manage her own shock and sorrow, and it would help Quintina portion the grief of suffering two losses so close together.

The little dog Perseus scratched at Pomponia's leg, and she bent down to pick him up. He smelled better than usual. One of the house slaves had bathed and perfumed him. *Small mercies*, thought Pomponia.

Despite the people and activity in the courtyard, the space seemed strangely empty to Pomponia. The two people she had made such important memories with here were now gone, and their absence was painfully palpable. All the things that were so familiar—the statues in the peristyle, the pools, the statue of Vesta in the water, the trees and white roses—all seemed so foreign, somehow changed, in a world where Quintus and Fabiana no longer existed.

But then the familiar form of Medousa arrived, trailing respectfully behind the stately Caesar and his sparkling wife Livia, and Pomponia felt more grounded.

Livia spoke first, rushing ahead to wrap her arms around Pomponia as if they had been the best of friends for all their lives. "Oh, Priestess Pomponia," she said, "I was heartbroken to learn that our great priestess has crossed the black river. What a loss this must be to you. Vesta and Juno give you strength."

"Thank you, Lady Livia."

Octavian took Pomponia's hand. "Rome has lost a powerful guardian," he said. "And you and I have lost a beloved friend. I mourn with you."

"I know you do, Caesar. Thank you both." She gestured to Fabiana's body. "You may say goodbye if you wish," she said.

"We shall."

"If you do not mind," said Pomponia, "I would like to borrow Medousa for a moment."

Livia blinked to squeeze a strategic tear from her eye and then touched Pomponia's arm with affected sincerity. "Of course," she said. "I know she is a comfort to you. We will leave you to grieve in private." She took Octavian's hand and they made their way across the courtyard to Fabiana's body and the somber gathering that surrounded it.

When they were out of earshot, Medousa let out an exasperated sigh. "That woman's tears are pure poison. I'm surprised they don't burn through her cheeks." She glared at Livia across the courtyard. "And who wears *pink* to a funeral?"

"Come with me, Medousa." Pomponia led her through the peristyle and into the house, taking tired steps up the marble-inlaid stairs and into the privacy of her office. She closed the door, sat on a couch against a blue frescoed wall, and began to cry.

"I am sorry about Fabiana," said Medousa. She sat down beside Pomponia and gently brushed the hair off the Vestal's drawn face.

"I do not weep only for Fabiana."

"For who else then?"

"Quintus Vedius Tacitus."

Medousa sat straight up. "Why would you weep for him, Priestess?"

"He is dead. Killed in Alexandria by one of Antony's men."

"I have heard nothing of this . . ."

"Caesar doesn't know yet. No one knows—not even Quintina. The news will arrive in a day or two."

"Then, Domina," said Medousa, "how is that you know this information so soon?" She shook her head. "Although I think I already know the answer."

Pomponia stood up quickly and faced Medousa. "I do not answer to a slave," she said, a burst of anger suddenly mixing with the sadness.

Medousa stood up and embraced her. "Forgive me." She forced the words out of her mouth. "If there was affection between you, I am sorry he is dead."

"He is *murdered*, and it is Marc Antony who did it." Pomponia wiped the tears from her eyes and walked to her desk, where she removed a cylindrical silver scroll box from a drawer. She allowed her eyes to rest on the lock of Quintus's hair that lay within the open drawer before closing it with renewed purpose and holding the scroll box out to Medousa. "Give this to Caesar as soon as you can be alone with him."

Medousa wrapped the scroll box in her palla. "What are you doing, Domina?"

"I'm letting go of a wolf, Medousa. One that I hope will tear open Antony's throat."

* * *

"How goes the war against Antony and Cleopatra, sister? Has your husband won yet?" Claudia reclined on the couch next to Livia in Caesar's brightly frescoed triclinium.

"Oh, General Agrippa just won some big naval battle by Actium," said Livia. "Octavian says it is the beginning of the end for Antony and Cleopatra. He doesn't think they can hold out more than another couple of months at the most." She looked into her wine cup. "Medousa! Bring more wine. And something to eat."

The auburn-haired slave appeared with a tray of food and drink and set it down before Livia and Claudia. She had no sooner taken a step back than Livia's sons, Tiberius and Drusus, snatched pieces of glazed baked bird and melons off the tray with grimy hands and raced into the courtyard, nearly knocking over the cups of wine she had just poured for the two sisters.

Medousa mopped up the spill. "Is that all, Domina?"

"Yes. You can go." Livia let her head hang over the edge of the scarlet-colored couch and smiled widely at her sister. "Thanks be to Fortuna, it looks like I will soon be first woman of Rome *and* Egypt, Claudia."

"Your husband was right all along," said Claudia. "Antony's will was his death warrant. It's nailed to the doors of the Senate, you know. The newsreader reads it three times a day in front of the Rostra. It's read at every gate into the city too. Everyone in Rome could recite it word-for-word from memory by now. But I don't understand, Livia. How did Caesar get it? I thought the Vestal had refused to give it to him."

"She didn't give it to him," Livia replied. "Not exactly. She gave him a copy of it. She transcribed the whole thing herself. The official line is that Caesar's soldiers found the copy at Antony's house in Capua, and because it was so seditious, the high priestess permitted Caesar to take the authentic will from the temple." Livia shook her head. "Honestly, what was Antony thinking? I thought he was just playing at being mad, but no, the man has truly lost all sense. In his will, he renounces Rome and embraces Egypt, divorces Octavia and marries Cleopatra, and disowns his Roman children so that he can leave the eastern provinces to his Egyptian children by her. The document was a checklist of reasons for Rome to declare war on Egypt. The Senate and the people want Antony's head on a spike."

"No doubt your husband will give it to them, sister. It's been a remarkable turn of events," said Claudia, frowning at a wine stain on her costly purple dress. "I never imagined the people could have such hatred for the general they once loved so."

"Hate comes easy when you're hungry." Livia bit into a baked baby pheasant. "Or so I hear." She wiped her mouth with the back of her hand. "But the worst part of the will by far—at least as far as my husband is concerned—was Antony's declaration that Caesarion is the true heir of Julius Caesar. The boy is doomed. Caesar will never let him live."

"Your status and fortune rise as never before," said Claudia. "Rome now loves your husband, Caesar, with as much passion as they hate Antony." She slurped glaze off her fingers. "I hope you are mindful to share your fortune with those who have helped you acquire it."

Livia stopped chewing. "Speak plainly, sister."

"I want an estate in Capua." Claudia's thoughts turned to Fabiana, to the way the old Vestal had patted the back of her hand. She needed to get out of Rome. Soon.

"Claudia, Rome is at war," said Livia. "Caesar is off wading through Greece and Egypt with his armies. The treasury is as empty as the grain bins. I cannot now be seen granting an extravagant estate in Capua to my sister. The people would rise up, and my husband would be livid with me. Have patience."

"Patience is not one of my virtues, Livia."

"Then you must learn to acquire it. As I have."

"I'll learn patience when you learn gratitude." Claudia threw the meat in her hand onto a tray. "If it weren't for me, you wouldn't just be out of Caesar's bed, you'd be out of his house too. You'd be begging for scraps at your blockheaded ex-husband's door or whoring yourself out to that hairy Greek pig you love to hate."

"Sister, calm down."

Claudia sat up and thumped her chest. "You have me to thank for your good luck, sister, not Fortuna. I was the one who helped you convince Caesar that his wife Scribonia was unfaithful so that he would divorce her. I was the one who figured out a way for you to be useful to Caesar. I was the one who risked everything to accuse the Vestal."

"It was worth a try," said Livia. She took another bite of baked pheasant.

"You owe me," said Claudia. "I was the one who advised you to bribe Antony's man in Egypt and have him kill that Quintus Vedius Tacitus fellow. That is the only reason the high priestess revealed what was in Antony's will."

"I can see how you'd like to take credit for that, Claudia," said Livia, "but she didn't do it for a man. The woman is sexless. It was a quid pro quo between her and Caesar. She gave him Antony's will, and he agreed that any future accusations of incestum against a Vestal would be dealt with under a fairer process by the Pontifex Maximus and the *quaestio*. She probably thinks it's better than relying on miracles. Personally, I'd rather leave my fate to the gods than to men."

"Sister," said Claudia. "I have taken great risks for you, and it has made me enemies. Those Vestals are a vengeful nest of vipers. I want an estate outside of Rome. It is for my safety."

Livia looked unmoved.

Claudia took a deep, calming breath. "It will make you look good in front of Caesar," she said. "He will think you are sending me away from Rome out of respect for the Vestals. The people and the Senate will see it that way too."

Livia raised her eyebrows in thought. "Ah yes, you have a point there. I will find you a fine villa in Capua. Do not misunderstand my words, sister, but it would be best if you left Rome as soon as possible. Perhaps you may return in two or three years, after the wounds of the incestum accusation have healed. I will miss you terribly, of course."

Satisfied, Claudia settled back onto the couch as Medousa returned with fresh wine and delicacies. The two sisters met eyes but remained silent as the slave busied herself. It was only when Medousa had left the room that Claudia spoke again.

"Take one last word of advice from your older sister," she said. "You are a fool to keep that slave around. I swear by the secret-keeper Jana, she keeps snakes under that white veil of hers. And each one slithers to the temple after dark to hiss into the ear of Priestess Pomponia."

* * *

The vomit basin by Medousa's bed was full yet again. The slave Despina hastily replaced it with an empty one, only to have Medousa lean over and heave more of her curdled stomach contents into it.

Despina looked into the basin and furrowed her brow. She looked at a subordinate slave. "Go fetch the physician. There's blood in it now, and the retching is getting worse. It should be easing up by now."

"She doesn't need a physician, Despina." Livia strolled casually into the room, talking through a mouthful of fresh fig. "She just needs to rest. The physician will only afflict her with a cure that is worse than the ill." She wrinkled her nose. "Leeches, bleedings . . . Why should we put poor Medousa through such torment?"

Despina turned back to the retching auburn-haired slave and wiped her forehead with a cloth. "Tell me again, Medousa, what did you eat?"

"She ate what the rest of you ate," snapped Livia, "bread, wine, and figs from the garden."

Medousa rolled onto her back, and the sight of her blanched, sunken face gave Despina a start. The whites of her eyes were yellow, and the bedsheets were soaked through from her profuse, foul-smelling perspiration.

"I had some fish from the kitchen," Medousa moaned, "but only one or two bites." She had no sooner spoken than she vomited again and then passed out from exhaustion.

Despina stared into the basin. "It had to be the fish. Only rancid meat could do this. But she said that she only had a bite or two . . ."

Livia shrugged. "You know what they say, Despina. Fish and company go bad after three days." She turned to the other slave in the room. "Go to the kitchen and make sure Cook throws out the fish. You'll be scrubbing the floors for a week if he serves it for dinner."

"Yes, Domina."

Medousa made a whimpering sound and regained consciousness, her eyes wide open and already in search of the vomit basin.

Despina held it to her mouth and Medousa ejected into it again. Brown sputum, bright-red blood, and yellow bile. Medousa sighed, rolled onto her back, and fell into a still sleep.

Thank Juno, thought Despina. *She needs a few moments of relief.*

But then Medousa's fingers began to twitch in the most disturbing way, followed by her arms and legs. A moment later, her entire body erupted into a violent seizure that made her bounce up and down on the bed. The Medusa pendant around her neck clinked with the fierce movement, and her eyes rolled back in her head.

The spasm stopped as suddenly as it had started. Medousa's body lay unmoving. A strange exhalation escaped her lips.

Despina placed her ear on Medousa's chest and floated her hand over her mouth, feeling for breath.

"She's gone."

Livia tossed a half-eaten fig into the vomit basin.

"Now aren't you glad we didn't send for a physician?" she asked. "It's a priest that we need."

CHAPTER XIX

Damnatio Memoriae
Damnation of memory.

—LATIN PHRASE

EGYPT, AUGUST 30 BCE

Later the same year

Cleopatra VII Philopator, queen and pharaoh of Egypt, peered out a high window of her heavily fortified palace. She felt another thud of panic against her ribs. Panic had become a chronic feeling in the last few days.

Caesar's forces had surrounded the Royal Palace in Alexandria. They struck battering rams against the reinforced doors. They tried to scale the side of the palace to enter through windows. They hacked at the walls with axes.

And they were making progress.

She turned from the window to address Charmion and Iras.

"It is time," she said. "Tell Apollonius to send Caesarion away now. Through the tunnels."

Iras nodded. "It shall be done, Majesty." She hurried away.

Charmion put her hand on Cleopatra's back. "Are you sure you don't want to know where they will take him?"

"No," said Cleopatra. "It is for his own safety. If I am tortured by Caesar . . ." She put her face in her hands.

"Caesar would never violate the queen of Egypt."

"Caesar would *gut* the queen of Egypt with his own hands to find Caesarion," spat Cleopatra, "and then lick the blood off his fingers."

A moment later, Iras returned and offered the queen a nod. Caesarion was safe. Behind the slave, however, stood a Roman centurion. He wore the same heavy armor and blood-red cloak they all did, but he held his red-crested helmet in his hands. Cleopatra smirked. A rare show of Roman humility.

"Majesty," said Iras, "this man has a message from Caesar."

Cleopatra stood as straight as she could. "What is it, boy?"

The centurion looked her in the eye. So much for Roman humility.

"Caesar says that if you give him General Antony, he will spare you and your children. He gives his personal assurance that you will keep your throne, although a Roman presence will remain in Alexandria to ensure you do your duty to Rome. Caesar wishes no further disruption in Egypt. You have until morning to comply."

Without waiting to be dismissed by the queen, the centurion turned on his heel and left.

Cleopatra collapsed onto the green-leaf mosaic of the marble floor. Charmion knelt beside her. "See? He wants Antony, not you."

"No," said Iras. "Caesar will never let her live. He just doesn't want the Egyptian people seeing him hack their queen to death in the sand." She also knelt on the floor beside Cleopatra. "Majesty, he knows you want to live. He knows you want your children to live. He gives false hope so that you will give him Antony and do his job for him."

The queen took Iras's face in her hands. "But what if it isn't false hope, Iras? What if it is true? What if I can save the lives of my children? What if I can keep my throne, even if it is just as Caesar's puppet? Is that not better than death?"

Charmion nodded and looked at Iras. "Caesar hates Antony. If he can kill him, he will be the top man in Rome, and that is all he cares about. He has nothing to lose by keeping Cleopatra alive, especially if he leaves a detachment here. It is in his best interests to have her remain a figurehead on the throne. The Egyptian people support her reign. It ensures stability and avoids more bloodshed."

Iras shook her head. "You know what he has said about her," she countered. "That she practices the black arts and can cast spells on Roman men. That she wants to rule Egypt and Rome, to enslave the Roman people and watch them starve. That is what his people believe of the queen. He cannot leave her on the throne, or he will be seen as weak." She stroked

Cleopatra's hair. "And then there is Caesarion. Majesty, you know he will never let him live. Caesarion is the true blood son of Julius Caesar, while he is only the adopted son. Think on it. You know I speak the truth."

Cleopatra sprawled herself on the floor and fell into an open sob. "I know it, Iras," she wept, "but still I want to live. I want my children to live. If there is any chance . . ."

"Then we shall try," said Iras. She met eyes with Charmion. "Send word to Antony that the queen has committed suicide," she said. "He will follow her."

"He will want to see her," Charmion replied.

"Tell him it is forbidden. The queen's body cannot be seen by anyone but the priests."

Charmion stood and was about to leave, but Cleopatra gripped her ankle. "Wait," she said, "do not send word."

"Majesty, I know you love him, but—"

"Do not send word," Cleopatra repeated. "He will not believe it. Deliver the message yourself."

Charmion nodded gravely. "Yes, Majesty." She left the queen's chambers without looking back.

*　*　*

General Marc Antony was in his secret strategy room—his *war room*, he called it. He sat on the high square base of a massive statue: a red, bronze, and gold lion with its front foot resting regally on a turquoise globe, the kingly master of the world. He wore an Egyptian tunica with Roman sandals.

A giant map of Italy, Greece, Egypt, and Africa hung on the wall, and he was staring vacantly at it. The back of his heels thumped rhythmically against the statue's base.

"General Antony," said Charmion. "The goddess Isis sends word. Cleopatra is with her."

Antony looked at her sideways. "What are you talking about, woman?" But then the light of realization shone in his eyes. He swallowed hard. "Take me to her."

"It is not permitted. Only the priests can see the queen's body."

"I don't give a shit about the priests," he said. "Take me to her."

"They have already taken her away," said Charmion. "I do not know where. The location must be kept secret so that Caesar does not find her. Her body must be prepared for the afterlife. It must be done properly, you see."

Antony's body jerked forward and he slid off the base of the statue, slowly lowering himself to the floor in shock. Charmion took a step toward him, and he reached out to wrap his arms around her legs. His shoulders twitched with heavy, loud sobs, and he buried his face in the fabric of her dress, clutching it so tightly that she had to pry his hands off to prevent him from pulling it off her body.

The slave bent down and withdrew the dagger out of the gold sheath that hung from the fallen general's left side. She gripped the blade so hard that her blood ran down it, and then held it in front of his face.

"The queen of Egypt orders you to follow her," she said. "Now."

Antony ripped the dagger from her hands and scrambled to his knees. "*Futuo*, you spiteful gods," he seethed, and in one fast, hard motion thrust the blade upward into his chest to pierce his heart.

Except that the blade didn't pierce his heart. Blood pooled on the floor and spurted from his nose, but he didn't die. Instead, he rolled in agony on the orange-and-brown tiles, his grunts and groans of pain mixing with gasped sobs of despair.

At that moment, the door flew open and Cleopatra rushed inside the war room, Iras close behind her.

"Antony, no!" shrieked the queen. "I was frightened, I changed my . . ." She took a few faltering steps and then sank to her knees at the sight of his writhing, bloody body on the floor. She crawled to his side, nuzzling her nose into his hair.

Antony's legs twitched and straightened as he struggled to sit up and look at her. *Alive?* His blood-soaked, shaking hands reached up to wrap around her neck. "You conniving Egyptian whore!"

"My love," she cried. "I am sorry. I am—"

His hands tightened around her neck and, with breathless alarm, she tried to pry off his fingers. Charmion dropped to her knees to help her queen wrench Antony's death grip from her throat, both of them slipping on the blood-covered floor. But his grip was too tight.

Desperate, Iras lunged for Antony's dagger on the bloody floor and swiped the blade across the general's throat. As his body slumped to the side, Cleopatra broke free and fell back.

A shout—in Latin—echoed off the walls.

"*Cleopatra Regina!*" barked the same centurion she had spoken to earlier. "Stand up and step away from the general. You are now under the authority of Caesar and the laws of Rome."

The queen turned her head to see what appeared to be an entire legion of Roman soldiers filling the war room. They had entered the palace. It was indeed over. Caesar had won.

She stood up slowly to avoid slipping in blood, her eyes fixed on Antony. Her husband. His eyes stared blankly at death, and his mouth hung open. His body had stopped moving. He was dead.

He died hating me, thought the queen. *He will not look for me in the afterlife.*

Abandoning all pretenses, the centurion grabbed the queen's arm and pulled her back toward her chambers as Charmion and Iras followed. He tossed Cleopatra into the room. Her advisers scrambled to her side and walked her to a couch. She sat down, dazed.

"You will await Caesar's orders." The centurion slammed the doors.

On the other side of the queen's doors, the trembling women heard the deep voices of more Roman soldiers. They were talking and laughing. It was a happy day for them. They would soon be going home to their families as victors. No doubt they were already eyeing the riches in the Royal Palace, waiting for Caesar's permission to fill their sacks and helmets with Egyptian gold, gems, and ancient treasures.

Caesar. He would arrive any moment to see Antony's body for himself. And to speak with the queen.

Cleopatra looked down at her dress. It was covered in streaks of red and the bottom was heavy, soaked with Antony's blood. "Caesar cannot see me like this," she said to Iras and Charmion.

Her slaves moved with wordless haste to undress and wash her. They outfitted the queen of Egypt in her finest gown, draping gold around her neck and winding it up her arms, darkening the black outline of her eyes and deepening the red of her lips.

Cleopatra reclined on the couch in her chambers, arranged in a way that conveyed both regality and her own brand of inviting femininity, the kind that had worked so well in the past with Roman men. Iras and Charmion stood behind her. Although the slaves dripped with perspiration, they appeared as composed as ever.

And then all three of them waited.

Finally, the doors opened, and Octavian strode into Cleopatra's chambers, wearing a formed, embossed-leather cuirass around his torso and a heavy red cloak. His expression was cool and confident, even casual—as if conquering a nation and taking its queen captive was an everyday occurrence for him.

He stood in front of Cleopatra and offered a tight, officious smile. "I have confirmed that Antony is dead," he said. "Rome is grateful for your cooperation."

Cleopatra returned his smile. "Rome is grateful? And what of Caesar?"

"Caesar and Rome are one," said Octavian.

The queen allowed her smile to broaden and then sat up straighter on the couch. Her fingers moved over the bare skin of her neck. "Then come sit with me, Caesar," she invited. "Rome and Egypt have much to discuss."

Octavian's smile faded. As far as he was concerned, there was nothing to discuss. And even if there were, it was not the conquered queen's place to say so. Whatever had worked on Julius Caesar and Marc Antony would not work on him. "You will be advised of what is required of you," he said.

As he turned to leave, Cleopatra sat up straight. "My children."

Octavian faced her again. "Your children by Antony will not be harmed. I can assure you of that."

"And Caesarion?"

"My little brother," mused Octavian. "What would he have to fear from me?"

Cleopatra's hatred for him swelled and swirled in the pit of her stomach, mixing with the acidic anxiety that was already there.

"I have other business to attend to right now," said Octavian, "but we shall speak again soon." His eyes moved over her neck until they lingered on the trace of a bloody fingerprint. He cast the queen a knowing glance. "Rest now, Cleopatra."

He left her chambers, and the guards closed the doors behind him, locking them from the outside and falling into muffled chatter.

Cleopatra fought to regain control of her breath. She spoke as levelly as she could. "What will happen now?" she asked her advisers.

Iras sat beside her. "You will be taken to Rome and marched before the Roman people in Caesar's triumph."

"And then?"

"Then you will be publicly executed. Perhaps strangled, but most likely beheaded."

Cleopatra looked at Charmion, waiting for her opposing opinion. The queen had spent her entire life depending on the alternating advice her two wisest advisers were known for, an insightful process of back-and-forth strategizing.

Charmion only nodded. "It will be so," she said.

The queen's face contorted into a fearful sob. "And what of the children?"

Again, it was Iras who spoke. "He will likely let your children by Antony live. It will be seen by his people as an act of mercy and respect for the children of a once-great Roman."

"And Caesarion?"

"Caesarion will only live if Caesar cannot find him. But he will tear Egypt apart until he does find him."

Charmion nodded in sober agreement.

"Isis holds out her hand to me," said Cleopatra. "It is over." She stood and walked slowly through her chambers, past a colonnade of palm-tree columns to lie down on her bed.

The exhaustion of the past weeks, the guilty horror of Antony's death, the threat to Caesarion, and the hopeless finality of her situation all combined to rock the queen into a sudden, strange sleep.

* * *

She awoke with a start. The same impudent Roman centurion as before was in her chambers. He stood above her holding a platter of food and drink in his hands. He was in the midst of a heated argument with the unyielding Charmion.

He set the tray on the bed when he saw Cleopatra open her eyes. "You haven't had anything since yesterday," he said. "You need to eat and drink."

Cleopatra ignored him. "Is it tomorrow?" she asked Charmion.

"Yes, Majesty."

"What has happened? Where are my children?"

"They brought Alexander Helios and Cleopatra Selene to the doors early this morning," said Charmion. "We could not wake you, Majesty. But your children live and are unharmed. Iras and I both saw them."

Cleopatra looked at the two women. She wanted more. She wanted news of Caesarion.

"No other news," said Iras.

The centurion pushed the tray closer to her. "Eat."

"I am not hungry," said Cleopatra.

The centurion brought his lips close to her ear. "You will eat this bread," he said, "or Caesar will eat your children." He smiled at her, studying her face.

For a fleeting moment, she thought he would risk an insolent kiss. What better bragging rights to spread among his fellow soldiers than a stolen kiss from the queen of Egypt? But then he seemed to think twice and merely lowered his head with mock respect and stood back, waiting for her to eat.

"Why should Caesar care if I eat?" she muttered.

"You need your strength," said Charmion. She glared at the Roman soldier. "He cannot march you to your execution in his triumph if you've already starved yourself to death."

"Caesar only has your health and well-being in mind," the centurion said unconvincingly.

Cleopatra slid off the bed. As she rose, Charmion and Iras instinctively fussed over their mistress's dress and hair, making sure they were arranged properly. The queen positioned herself in front of the Roman soldier and studied him as he had studied her.

"Tell Caesar I will do all that he asks," she said. "I am his Egyptian prize, and I will shine as he wishes me to. But first I wish to anoint Antony's body in the mausoleum."

"I will inform Caesar," he said. "I am certain that can be arranged."

Not caring that his heavy cloak brushed indecorously against the great queen of Egypt, the centurion turned and left Cleopatra's chambers, slamming the doors behind him.

Iras was the first to speak. "Majesty, it should be the priests and embalmers who anoint Antony's body," she said cautiously. "The linseed oil can heat and char the skin if not properly applied, and—"

"I know that, you foolish woman," snapped Cleopatra. She spoke urgently, under her breath. "Do you not remember what is in the mausoleum? You put it there yourself, Iras."

The gravity of the queen's meaning descended upon her. "Of course, Majesty."

Moments later, the doors to the queen's chambers opened once again. The centurion stood outside and cocked his head at Cleopatra. "I am to take you to the mausoleum," he said. "Caesar trusts you will perform as promised afterward."

Perform. The word struck Cleopatra. *I will indeed perform for Caesar,* she thought, *but I will not be triumphed over.* She smiled at the Roman soldier. "The queen will do all that Caesar requires."

The centurion and what seemed like a full cohort of Roman soldiers escorted Cleopatra and her two advisers out of the palace, where the glaring light of day pierced their eyes.

They walked along a sand-covered limestone path under the searing heat of the Egyptian summer sun until they reached the seven-meter-high door of the mausoleum. The door was built of pure granite, and it took a small army of Roman soldiers to open it. After all, it was meant to be closed once and never reopened.

Rays of light illuminated the interior of the luxurious gilded tomb, and Cleopatra strode inside without waiting for permission from her Roman captors.

She brought her hand to her mouth. The body of Marc Antony lay naked on a wide table. His flesh gleamed with the oil that had already been applied by the embalmers.

Although Cleopatra had known his body would be here, she didn't know that Caesar had permitted and already arranged for Antony to receive the full Egyptian funerary rites he had dictated in his will. The sight of his body being prepared for the afterlife refreshed the sorrow of his death.

She walked slowly to his body as the door of the tomb closed, sealing the mausoleum from the outside world of sunshine and sound.

The oil on Antony's bare chest, arms, and legs reflected the flickering light of the oil lamps affixed to the walls of the tomb. She touched his skin. It felt as warm in death as it did in life. But he did not move. He did not rouse and reach for her in the way he always did when she touched him.

She leaned over to kiss his mouth. "I am coming, my love," she whispered. Cleopatra looked over her shoulder at Charmion and Iras, who stood trembling but dutiful behind her. They would follow their queen into death. "I am ready," she said to them. "We must move quickly."

Charmion nodded and moved to open a wardrobe decorated with lapis lazuli, removing a jeweled diadem and a gold-and-green robe. She placed the crown on Cleopatra's head, while Iras dressed the queen in her royal attire.

Cleopatra sat on a golden couch as Iras retrieved a large pottery bowl within which lay a coiled cobra. The skin on its long body twitched when the perforated lid was removed, but it seemed otherwise unperturbed, even when Iras wrapped her hand around it and gingerly pulled it out. It yawned and moved lazily through her fingers.

"Give it to me," said Cleopatra. "It must bite me first."

The queen held the cobra in her hands. The creature was waking up now and becoming more interested in its surroundings. It glided through Cleopatra's fingers and encircled her left wrist and forearm.

A sound at the door of the tomb. The soldiers were returning. They would not risk leaving the queen—their master's Egyptian prize—unattended for too long.

Cleopatra pinched the cobra's face and it bit her on the wrist, its curved fangs sinking into a blue vein so quickly that she didn't even see it happen. The bite was hot and sharp, but otherwise, she felt nothing. She dropped the cobra onto her lap.

A moment later, it began. A sudden shortness of breath. The queen inhaled deeply, yet her lungs still felt empty. She tried to draw in another breath, hungry for the feeling of full lungs, but she could not. She held out her hands, and Charmion and Iras took them, interlocking their fingers with hers.

Cleopatra lay back on the golden couch as her breaths became shallow and then stopped.

Iras put her face to the queen's lips.

"It is done," she said to Charmion. "Isis took her quickly."

More sounds from the door. Any moment, it would open and the light of day and realization would fill the tomb.

Iras picked up the cobra and pinched its mouth as Cleopatra had done. It struck her in the crook of her elbow.

Wordlessly, she passed the snake to Charmion, who hesitated for a split second before seeing a slant of daylight pierce the darkness. She coaxed the cobra to strike her.

It bit her on the back of her hand, but its fangs lodged in her skin, and she had to pry its head off her. She dropped it onto the floor, and it slithered away, looking for a quiet spot to sleep, indifferent to the drama unfolding around it.

Sunlight blazed into the tomb as more than a dozen Roman soldiers rushed in. The same centurion who had brought Cleopatra and her advisers into the mausoleum was the first to see the sight: Cleopatra lying dead on a golden couch, dressed in royal attire, with her advisers Iras and Charmion lying at her feet.

"Pluto's withered cock!" he shouted. He took off his helmet and threw it hard against the wall of the tomb and then kicked over a large amphora. It fell, broke, and spilled oil over the floor. Taking an angry step closer, he saw that Charmion still clung to the last of life.

"Are you happy now, Charmion?" he asked bitterly.

"Happier than you, Roman," she said. "I fulfilled my duty." She rested her head on Iras's stomach and joined her friend and her queen.

The centurion ignored the parting gibe, but just when he thought the situation couldn't get any worse, there was a swell of shouts and marching footsteps behind him. Caesar was coming. He muttered another obscene curse to the gods of the underworld and reluctantly turned toward the approaching Caesar—now the sole and undisputed leader of the Roman world—to explain why he had failed in his duty.

"Caesar," he began, "we only left her for a matter of minutes, as instructed. We did not—"

Octavian held up his hand for silence. He walked slowly, dreadfully, to Cleopatra's body and stared at it for a long while. *You lying Egyptian bitch*, he thought.

General Agrippa appeared at his shoulder. "Ah," he said, as he assessed the situation. He knew exactly what Caesar was thinking: his triumph just wouldn't have the same flair to it. "It is a lost opportunity," he admitted, "but I have news that will lift your spirits, Caesar."

"Oh? What's that?"

"We found the boy Caesarion. I decapitated him myself."

"Thank Jupiter and all the gods. What did you do with his body?"

"Buried it in the desert. As much as anything can be buried in sand, that is."

Octavian gripped Agrippa's shoulder. "Good work," he said. And then more seriously. "Tell me, was it true what they say? Did he really look like Caesar?"

"Nothing like," said Agrippa. *Honesty will not serve me here*, he thought.

Octavian winked at him. "I thought not." He smiled to himself, a self-assured smile, and then gestured to the dead queen on the golden couch. "Maecenas advises that our men go through the Royal Library and destroy anything Cleopatra wrote," he said. "I'm told there's an entire wing of her books on mathematics, astronomy, philosophy, and the gods know what else. Burn them. She was no queen and no scholar. She was a sorceress and a whore."

"Yes, Caesar." The general summoned a handful of soldiers to follow him and set out for the Royal Library.

Caesar called over his shoulder. "Leave me." His soldiers quietly filed out of the mausoleum, the disgraced centurion being the last out.

Octavian fixed his eyes on the body of Cleopatra and shook his head in restrained rage.

Thank the gods, he thought, *that Roman women are not capable of such trickery.*

CHAPTER XX

Ecce Caesar Nunc Triumphat
Behold Caesar, who now triumphs.

−SUETONIUS, AS SUNG DURING THE TRIUMPH OF JULIUS CAESAR

ROME, 29 BCE

One year later

Pomponia had been thinking about Vercingetorix the Gaul all morning. She had been reflecting on Julius Caesar's triumph so many years ago, when the King of the Gauls had been paraded around the entire oval of the Circus Maximus and then along the cobblestone streets of the Forum before a jeering Roman mob.

He had been sworn and spat at by men and women, and had food and filth thrown at him by children. He had been dragged to the Rostra and forced to wait for the moment a triumphant Caesar of Rome would give the word. "Kill!"

Now it was the new Caesar's turn. As the chief Vestal looked around, she imagined that Octavian's triumph was everything he could have hoped for. Loud, colorful, spectacular, and indulgent in every way. There was just one thing missing—well, two things, actually: Antony and Cleopatra. They were already dead. And even Caesar didn't have the power to make someone die twice.

Pomponia sat on the Rostra near Livia, Octavia, Julia, and Marcellus. Caesar, dressed in a purple toga and wearing a gilded crown of laurels, stood an arm's length away. Dressed like the statue of Jupiter on the Capitoline, all he was missing was the lightning bolt. General Agrippa stood behind him. Caesar held up an arm to acknowledge the Roman mob that spilled into every street, colonnade, and portico in the Forum, and that sat perched on top of basilicas and monuments.

Red banners with the gold letters *SPQR* flapped regally in the wind, and horns sounded, although they were drowned out by the crowd's victory cheers.

A parade of spoils from the palaces and temples of faraway Egypt rolled through the streets, and people swarmed to catch a glimpse. There were giant painted statues of foreign gods with the heads of animals: a falcon, a jackal, a ram. A particularly strange one—with the head of a black scarab beetle and the body of a man—received more than its share of jeers and finger-pointing.

But then along came a procession of mummies propped up in jeweled sarcophagi and the beetle-headed god was forgotten.

Another round of cheers went up as the mummies gave way to a golden couch upon which reclined an effigy of Cleopatra. It had been outfitted with the queen's jeweled diadem and gold robe. Its arms were crossed over its chest, showing the Egyptian pharaoh in death.

Following close behind the effigy of the dead queen were her two living children by Marc Antony: Alexander Helios and Cleopatra Selene. They walked slowly with their heads down. What was there for them to see? Ahead of them was the effigy of their dead mother. Around them were the faces of their conquerors.

Yet Caesar had kept his word and allowed them to live. In fact, he had placed them under the care of his sister Octavia, who continued to bear the dictates of the Fates and her powerful brother with regal composure. Pomponia had never known anyone who accepted her duty and fate so willingly.

Octavian raised an arm again, and the crowd roared even louder. Octavian. Then Caesar. Now *Augustus*.

Following his defeat of Antony and Cleopatra, the Senate had bestowed upon him the lofty name of Augustus. It meant "the great one" and was a step up from the banal *princeps*, or "first man," title he tended to use. Pomponia smiled to herself. The man sprouted more names than the Hydra sprouted heads.

The month of Sextilius had also been renamed: it was now known as August in honor of Rome's savior, and it was only fitting that it followed the month of July which had been named after his divine father. The son follows the father.

"Citizens," shouted Caesar. "I now give Rome a gift. The death of Antony and Cleopatra!"

At that, the main attraction rolled before the Rostra. It was a massive prison cart decorated to resemble the Royal Palace in Alexandria.

Inside the cart, was a man dressed in the style of an Egyptian male, complete with garish makeup on his face, and a woman dressed as the queen of Egypt, complete with diadem and royal robes: Antony and Cleopatra—or more accurately, two slaves whose greatest misfortune in life had been the striking resemblance they bore to the Egyptian queen and her Roman lover. They sat facing each other, fastened to golden thrones—the very thrones Antony and Cleopatra had ruled from in Alexandria.

Caesar nodded to the executioners, and the performance that everyone had come to see began.

Four men dressed as snake charmers carried heavy baskets to the prison cart. They tipped the baskets through the bars—careful to stand back as far as possible—as hundreds of snakes spilled into the bottom of the cart.

The mob of people moved, weaved, and climbed over whatever or whomever they could to get a better view.

Tied to the thrones inside the cart, the man and woman began to buck in their seats and scream as snakes of every shape, size, and color swarmed around their tethered feet. To add to the drama, the snake charmers used long sticks with hooks on the end to grab snakes from the bottom of the cart and place them on the bodies of the couple—their laps, heads, and shoulders—even shoving them under their clothing.

Pomponia grimaced and looked away. Her thoughts were wandering. They moved from Vercingetorix to the Carcer, from the Carcer to Quintus.

Pomponia turned her head and smiled amiably at Livia. Caesar's wife wore a green dress with a teal veil, her hair sparkling with gemstones and her teeth bared in a wide smile as she beamed at her powerful husband and basked in her newfound status as first woman of Rome.

The Vestal spoke quietly. "Tell me, Lady Livia, how does your sister like her new villa in Capua?"

"She likes it very well, High Priestess. Perhaps too well, since she has not replied to the last three letters I sent. I think country life has gotten to her."

"Maybe she ate some bad fish," said Pomponia.

Livia felt a sudden hot flush in her cheeks but resisted the urge to make eye contact with the Vestal.

"It is such an important day for your great husband," Pomponia continued. "And for you as well."

"The gods bless us."

"Not all the gods."

"Oh?"

"Vesta does not bless you," said Pomponia. "Neither does Juno. The divine sisters have not blessed your home by giving you children with Caesar. They have not blessed your bed. I am told that common slave girls and the wives of other men spend more time in it with your husband than you do, regardless of how energetically you perform when you do get an invitation."

Livia bristled. "Priestess . . . such matters are private."

"There is no need for privacy between friends," said Pomponia. "That is why I have taken it upon myself to know all of your secrets. Although not all are so innocuous. I could have you fed to the lions in the arena for some of them. Your husband could easily find another slave trader to staff his bedchamber."

"Caesar would never—"

"Oh, hush now, Livia," Pomponia said. "Caesar would push you off the Tarpeian Rock himself if he learned you had slandered the Vestal order. He reveres the goddess. Our order is a political asset to him. He has made it so. You and your childless belly are becoming a liability."

"Caesar knows my worth." The words came out weaker than she would have preferred, and Livia exhaled out her nose. She hadn't expected this. Her blood quickened with anger. No matter how many stinking beasts she sacrificed to Fortuna, no matter how many backs she managed to clamber over, there was always someone in her way. Unfortunately, the Vestal had the high ground. Yet again, she found herself caught between Scylla and Charybdis with no escape, no option. Not yet. Not with a barren belly. "How might I strengthen our friendship, Priestess?"

"By becoming a friend of the Vestal order," said Pomponia. "You've tried to reduce us because of your own insecurities. Now, I want you to do the opposite. I want you to offer your patronage and elevate us, even more than your husband does."

"I would be happy to do so."

"Good." Pomponia lifted a disapproving eyebrow at Livia's garishly colored dress. "You may begin by wearing a white stola for all public occasions. And less makeup. You're pretty enough, nay?"

She reached her hands behind Livia's neck to secure Medousa's pendant around it. "You may also wear this, if it pleases you. I have had emeralds set into the Gorgon's eyes, just for you. The Egyptians believe the gemstones bring fertility, you know."

Taking a break from the adoring mob, Caesar turned to smile at his wife sitting alongside the Vestal. The two women seemed to be getting along very well. The high priestess was even giving Livia a gift. Wonderful. He nodded at Livia in approval, and she smiled back at him.

Pomponia carried on. "You will mint Vesta on your coinage and adopt the modest dress of a Vestal in your statuary. You will extol our order at all public sacrifices and festivals, and you will make regular donations in the amount that I specify. I shall spend part of your first donation by commissioning a statue of Tuccia for the gardens outside the Circus Maximus."

Pomponia accepted a glass of cool cucumber water from a passing slave, took a sip, and then continued. "I must admit, it will be amusing to watch the public ridicule your attempts at purity. After all, the rumors of your purchases at the slave market are already the tastiest topic at every dinner party in Rome."

She swirled an ice chip in her glass until it made a clinking sound. "And then there's your own matrimonial history. A divorced woman with children by another man. Or rather by two other men. There is no question your elder son is the legacy of that square-headed Tiberius, but Drusus . . ." Pomponia shook her head and bit her lip in mock concern for

Livia's welfare. "Caesar would recoil at how often Diodorus used you. And he'd do much worse if he knew you'd birthed a Greek bastard."

Livia's nostrils flared and she opened her mouth, but Pomponia spoke first. "Oh, look, Livia. The general is making a run for it. Let's see how it all ends."

As the crowd roared anew, the slave who was playing the part of Marc Antony dramatically broke free of his restraints and tried to climb the wooden bars of the prison cart to escape the sea of snakes at his feet. He slid down the bars at every try.

And then in an act of pure desperation, he tipped over the throne upon which was tied the slave Cleopatra and scrambled on top of it.

The slave woman's face was buried in the moving sea of snakes. It moved and bobbed for a while, but then she succumbed to either suffocation or the venom of countless snake bites.

The mob loved every moment of it.

Pomponia stared at the unmoving body of the slave Cleopatra. She grew pensive and sincere. "Do you know what is strange, Lady Livia?"

"What is that, Priestess?"

"I believe that you and I had more in common with Cleopatra than we think. I met her, you know. The last time was on the day I became a full Vestal."

"Oh? What was she like?"

Pomponia thought about this. "Overconfident."

When Livia didn't reply, Pomponia sat back in her chair. *Well, that's done*, she thought. *I now hold a she-wolf by the ears.*

The Vestal took another sip of the cucumber water, hoping it would help her face cool from the quiet confrontation. Livia had retreated, but she wouldn't wait long to advance again. They both knew it.

Pomponia pushed the thought from her mind and forced herself to enjoy Caesar's victory show. Had she not played a small part in making it happen?

In the prison cart before the Rostra, the slave Antony was still balanced on the overturned throne of his queen. No matter how many snakes coiled and glided their way up to him, he managed to either avoid them or toss them off. If this went on much longer, the crowd would grow bored.

Caesar gave a quick nod of his head to a centurion who stood beside the cart. The soldier unsheathed the dagger that hung at his side, thrust his arm through the bars and stabbed the slave in the chest. The slave bellowed a cry of pain but then toppled over to land in the moving nest of snakes below him.

The show was over. But Caesar's triumph would go on.

More importantly to Pomponia, so too would the triumph of the Vestal order. She had seen it through the fall of the Republic and the rise of the Empire. Not since the time of Romulus and Numa had a leader of Rome been as dedicated to the Vestal order as Caesar Augustus, Rome's first emperor.

Following the military defeat of Antony and Cleopatra, and the now-legendary story of Tuccia's miracle, the people's devotion to Vesta was also stronger than ever. Rome was at peace.

Of course, the goddess's living flame had always burned in the temple and in the homes and hearts of those in Rome. But now that flame, the *viva flamma*, was spreading.

It was burning in lands beyond Italy: in Macedonia, Greece, Gaul, Africa, Asia, Syria, and Egypt. Pomponia knew it would continue to spread to Judea, Britannia, Arabia, Germania, and even to lands that had not yet been discovered, new lands the geographers said existed beyond the Ocean of Atlas. After all, the very nature of fire was to spread.

CHAPTER XXI

Triginta Anni
Thirty years

Four years later

She wasn't fated to walk through the green fields of Tivoli with Medousa after all. Neither would she walk through them with Quintus. But she was walking through them just the same with her memories of them both. That was something.

Pomponia sat down on a marble bench and enjoyed the view of the beautiful Temple of Vesta in Tivoli. Surrounded by gardens, lush, rolling green hills and vividly colored flowers, and boasting a fine vineyard for libations to the goddess, the circular temple perched on the edge of a grassy cliff to overlook the roaring falls of the Aniene River.

A Vestal priestess named Cassia approached and sat beside her. Pomponia liked Cassia. She reminded her of Tuccia.

"Any decisions, Pomponia?" Cassia asked.

"I am staying with the order," said Pomponia. "Although I think I will stay here in Tivoli for a while longer. I'm finding it harder and harder to leave my quiet villa for the noise of the city. The temple here is lovely, and the Aniene falls are an excellent source of sacred water that I'd like to start sending to Rome." She picked a long piece of grass and twirled it around her finger. "I can be useful here, especially if Quintina stays with me. Tuccia has Nona and more than enough priestesses and novices in Rome."

Cassia wrapped an arm around Pomponia. "I am not surprised," she said, "but I am happy to hear the words anyway. This will be big news for our little town. May I tell Cossinia and the other priestesses?"

"Of course."

Cassia made her way back to the temple. As Pomponia watched her go, she touched the Vesta intaglio ring that hung from a chain around her neck.

Her love and her loss of Quintus didn't blind her to the truth. The marriage between the two of them would have been an unhappy one. Not at first, but eventually. He could not have changed his sullen disposition, and she could not have tolerated it.

It was better that she remained a bride of Rome. She could be Quintus's bride in the afterlife. Perhaps Pluto could make sure he was a pleasant husband to her.

She stood and walked to the edge of the falls. The rush and spray of the water was invigorating, and yet thoughts of the past—of Medousa, of Quintus—always made her melancholy.

It was fitting that she should find herself at the Temple of Vesta in Tivoli. It was a newer temple, newer than the old one in the Roman Forum at least, and it was the first temple that Fabiana had ordered to be built after being appointed Vestalis Maxima.

The sound of a dog barking in the distance slipped into Pomponia's ear, and for a moment her heart longed to see the little dog Perseus scampering toward her, his nails clicking on the marble floor and his tongue hanging out.

She had buried his thin white body in the flowers at the base of Fabiana's statue. How could she so dearly miss something that had tormented her so?

She heard conversation and turned toward the garden beside the white marble temple, where Quintina was leaning against the trunk of a tall cypress tree. She was talking to a young priest from the Temple of Mars in Tivoli. *What was his name? Oh yes, Septimus.*

He said something to Quintina that Pomponia could not hear, but it made the young priestess put her hands on her hips in indignation and march away from him, straight up the marble steps and through the doorway of the temple.

Septimus watched her walk away with a grin of self-satisfaction on his face. Yet instead of leaving once Quintina had disappeared into the sanctum, he stood where he was and continued to stare at the closed bronze doors of the temple.

The sight made Pomponia think on the words of Horace, one of Caesar's favorite poets: *Mutate nomine, de te fabula narratur.* Change the name, and the story is about you.

But then the poetic sentiment faded. She heard Medousa's voice—churlish, cautionary—bringing her back to reality with one of the slave's more pointed sayings: *Nec amor nec tussis celatur.* Love, like a cough, cannot be hidden.

She walked to the temple and spoke to Septimus from the top step, her eyebrows raised. "I've heard the skin on a man's back comes off like plaster from a wall."

"Yes, Priestess." He nodded deferentially and left.

And then Pomponia pulled open the doors and stepped into the sanctum to join her sister Vestals around the eternal fire.

EPILOGUE

Ducunt Volentem Fata, Nolentem Trahunt
Fate leads the willing and drags the unwilling.

—SENECA

SYRIA, 24 BCE

One year later

She still wore the same purple dress she had been wearing that night. The night the men had burst through the doors of her villa and dragged her by the hair over the floor, and outside into the stinking cart. The night the grimy, toothless slave women in the cart had mocked her as she shrieked her protests to her captors. *I am not a slave, you fools! Return me to my home at once! I am family to Caesar!*

It hadn't taken long for her demands to turn to pleas. *Please! I am rich, I can pay you anything! My sister is a powerful woman! She will pay a fortune for my freedom!*

At one time, her dress had been the finest that money could buy. Now it was rags. Now she had to knot it in places to hold it together.

Sitting cross-legged on the ground, she bit into a crust of bread that was so hard it made her gums bleed. Her next bite was more cautious, but her mouth was too sore to chew. She tossed the bread aside with a thump.

She felt a sudden tug at her ankle and flinched in pain. The skin under the iron manacle was rubbed raw. Her captor—a fat, filthy, foul-mouthed man named Hostus—tugged the chain harder, and she stood up. If she didn't stand, he would just drag her. He liked to do that. She scowled at his odious bare chest with its tufts of black hair. Rain or shine, the madman never wore a tunica but scurried about with only a sagging loincloth, ratty sandals, and a whip.

Hostus handed the chain to another man. This one was well dressed and composed, but not Roman. She knew the style—yes, Egyptian. He placed a gold coin in the slave owner's greasy palm and took hold of her chain. She followed obediently behind him.

Not that it mattered anymore, not that she really cared after all these years, but she found herself wondering where she was. The convoy of slave carts had been traveling for weeks. All she knew was that the sand stung her eyes and the landscape was more barren than any place she had ever seen.

Yet here in the middle of the barren desert, in the middle of nowhere, there stood a rickety arena held together by splintered wood and worn ropes. Through the uproar of cheers and jeers, through the ruckus of shouts and sobs, through the crack of the whip against flesh, she heard a sound she had heard many times in Rome: the roar of a hungry lion.

She dropped to her knees, wrapped her fingers around the chain, and pulled. "No!"

But her raspy voice was lost in the blowing sands as the Egyptian dragged her toward the arena.

AFTERWORD

In 1989, when I was twenty years old, I visited the Roman Forum for the first time. The experience sparked a lifelong fascination in ancient Roman history and religion, particularly Vesta. I have been back to Rome several times since, including during the writing of this book series. I never want to lose that fascination, and I sincerely hope that I have passed it on to you, even in a small way.

In *Brides of Rome*, book one in the Vesta Shadows series, my goal was to bring the beautiful Vestal order and religion to life in an engaging, informative, and respectful way. I wanted to position the Vestals within the larger world of ancient Rome, particularly during the Augustan Age as this time was so important to the order. To do that, and to dramatize Vestal rituals and beliefs, I used everything from ancient references and coins to modern excavations.

Yet this novel is historical fiction. I have taken well-known figures, events, reports, and conditions from a variety of academic and artistic sources, and I have blended them with my own interpretations and, since history is full of holes, educated guesses. To create an original story for a mainstream readership, I have adjusted or simplified complex ideas, timelines, and genealogies, and occasionally adapted the writings of ancient authors such as Pliny, Tacitus, Livy, Dio, Ovid, Plutarch, Gellius, Suetonius, etc.

Unlike historical figures such as Julius Caesar, Octavian, and Livia—about whom we can glean a lot from various ancient sources, including their own words—we know little to nothing about the personalities, motivations, affections, struggles, or personal lives of most historical Vestals. Yet I've used what is available, along with some artistic license, to bring Pomponia to life. Her full name in the book, Pomponia Occia, is a composite of two real Vestals: Occia, the Vestalis Maxima who served during the late Republic and early Roman Empire, and Pomponia, who served later in the empire.

I've done a similar thing with other Vestal characters, again those women we just don't know that much about. The second names of Nona Fonteia and Caecilia Scantia are the names of real Vestals who lived around this time. As for Tuccia and the sieve, the account is true, although it happened earlier than in the book. The actual manner in which she performed her miracle remains a mystery. It is also true that a Vestal named Licinia was condemned to death circa 113 BCE, but I drew elements in the fabricated charges against her from other cases.

The same holds true for other characters and circumstances. There is no note I could find of Livia having a sister, but Roman naming practices, which changed so much over the years, makes *Claudia* possible. Livia did publicly align herself with the Vestals, and her statuary shows her dressed similarly, modest stola and all. No doubt this was for the mutual benefit of the Vestal order and her political image, as she was in fact married previously with two sons by her first husband. It was also rumored that Livia poisoned her adversaries and supplied her husband with virgins to deflower.

As for Octavian, the Vestal Virgins did intercede on behalf of his "divine father," Julius Caesar, during the proscriptions of Sulla. Octavian was given the honorific Augustus, although this happened a couple of years later than in the book. The emperor Caesar Augustus was a powerful benefactor of the Vestals. Vesta and her priestesses are featured in two of the greatest monuments of his age: the literary epic *The Aeneid* and the marble Ara Pacis Augustae. He also mentions them in his autobiography the *Res Gestae Divi Augusti*, a Latin copy of which today beautifully adorns the outside of the Ara Pacis museum in the Eternal City.

Octavian did in fact enter Vesta's sanctuary to take Antony's will, possibly without too much opposition from the Vestals, and the will was damning to Antony. That event is something I drew on when creating the dynamic between Octavian and Pomponia. The idea of Pomponia providing Caesar with a copy, thereby assuring him the risky act would be worth it, is my imagining. To Octavian's dismay, Antony and Cleopatra did commit suicide before he could execute them in his triumph.

It's important to know that there was never just one "Ancient Rome." Like any nation or culture, it was always changing. The Roman Forum is a perfect example. New monuments and structures were continually being added or improved, while others were removed, whether intentionally or through disaster. The Temple of Vesta and the House of the Vestals are no exception. I've spent hours wandering what remains of those, and I've taken elements from them in their grandest forms to use in this book series.

While there are countless resources and books on ancient Rome, there are several specific and wonderful books that I have found relevant in different ways: *Rome's Vestal Virgins* by Robin Lorsch Wildfang; *Excavations in the Area Sacra of Vesta (1987–1996)*: edited by Russell T. Scott; *Mythology* by Edith Hamilton; *Augustus* by Pat Southern; and *Cleopatra* by Stacy Schiff. Any deviations from fact in this story are mine, for artistic reasons, and not theirs. As mentioned earlier, I have also drawn from Suetonius's irresistible *The Lives of the Twelve Caesars*.

Classical historians, archaeologists, and avid readers of historical fiction will know where I have taken creative liberties. If that's you, I hope you have found a fresh perspective in this novel and enjoyed revisiting a world we both love. If you are new to the world of ancient Rome, I hope you have enjoyed learning about this important time, as well as the remarkable people, places, and events that have fascinated so many of us for so long.

I also hope you will go on to read the second book in this series, the even bolder sequel, *To Be Wolves: A Novel of the Vestal Virgins*.

If you want to learn more about the Vesta religion and its priesthood, I invite you to visit VestaShadows.com for additional resources, including a gallery of images from my personal collection plus blogs, videos, and more.

Thank you for reading and all the best.

DRAMATIS PERSONAE

Agrippa Marcus Vipsanius Agrippa, general and friend of Octavian

Alexander Helios Son of Cleopatra and Marc Antony

Ankhu Egyptian messenger slave owned by Quintus

Apollonius Adviser to and slave of Cleopatra

Brutus Senator and assassin of Julius Caesar

Caecilia Scantia Vestal priestess

Caesarion Son of Cleopatra and Julius Caesar

Caeso Guard of the Vestal Pomponia

Calidus Wealthy landowner who conspired against Licinia

Calpurnia Wife of Julius Caesar

Cassia The name of a deceased Vestal priestess; also the name of a Vestal serving in Tivoli

Cassius Senator and assassin of Julius Caesar

Charmion Adviser to and slave of Cleopatra

Cicero Marcus Tullius Cicero, Roman orator and statesman

Claudia Drusilla Sister of Livia Drusilla

Cleopatra VII Philopator Queen of Egypt

Cleopatra Selene Daughter of Cleopatra and Antony

Cossinia Vestal priestess serving in Tivoli

Despina Chief slave in the house of Octavian and Livia

Diodorus Greek friend of Livia's first husband, Tiberius

Drusus Younger son of Livia Drusilla with her first husband Tiberius

Fabiana *Vestalis Maxima*, or high priestess of the Vestal order

Flamma Famed gladiator

Flavia Vestal priestess

Gallus Gratius Januarius Chariot racer

Gnaeus Carbo Roman general whose legions were defeated by the Cimbri and who conspired against Licinia

Iras Adviser to and slave of Cleopatra

Julia Caesaris filia Daughter of Octavian

Julius Caesar Gaius Julius Caesar, Roman general and dictator

Laenas Centurion in Carbo's legions

Lepidus *Pontifex Maximus*, or chief priest of Rome

Licinia Vestal priestess

Livia Drusilla Roman noblewoman

Lucretia Manlia Vestal priestess

Maecenas Gaius Maecenas, close political adviser to Octavian

Marc Antony Roman general, second to Julius Caesar

Marcellus Octavian's nephew; Octavia's son from her first marriage

Marius Friend of Quintus in Alexandria

Medousa Greek slave of the Vestal Pomponia

Nona Fonteia Vestal priestess

Octavian Great-nephew and adoptive son of Julius Caesar, becomes Rome's first emperor

Octavia Sister of Octavian

Perseus Fabiana's dog (named after the hero who slew Medusa)

Pomponia Occia Vestal priestess

Publius Guard of the Vestal Pomponia

Quintina Vedia Elder daughter of Quintus and Valeria

Quintus Vedius Tacitus Priest of Mars, former soldier under Julius Caesar

Rufus Marcus Sergius Rufus, a soldier accused of being with Licinia; also the name of his son

Sabina Novice Vestal

Scribonia Roman noblewoman, mother of Julia

Sextus Pompey Son of Pompey the Great

Septimus Young priest of Mars in Tivoli

Tacita Vedia Younger daughter of Quintus and Valeria

Taurus Senator and wealthy patron of the amphitheater

Tiberius Claudius Nero First husband of Livia Drusilla; also the name of their son

Tuccia Vestal priestess

Tullia Vestal priestess

Valeria Wife of Quintus Vedius Tacitus

ROMAN GODS, GODDESSES & MYTHICAL FIGURES

Aeneas A Trojan hero who fled the burning city and became the ancestor of Rome's founder, Romulus

Apollo The god of the sun and the arts

Athena The Greek goddess of wisdom; the Greek equivalent of Minerva

Atlas Titan who held the heavens on his shoulders

Bacchus The god of wine

Basilisk A snakelike monster

Cerberus The three-headed hound of Hades that guards the entrance to the underworld

Ceres The goddess of grain

Charon The ferryman of Hades; carries souls across the River Styx

Charybdis A sea monster in Homer's *Odyssey*; counterpart of Scylla

Clementia The goddess of clemency and leniency

Clytemnestra The sister of Helen of Troy

Concordia The goddess of harmony and agreement

Cyclops A one-eyed monster from Homer's *Odyssey*

Diana The goddess of the hunt

Dis Pater A god of the underworld

Discordia The goddess of discord

Edesia The goddess of feasts

Europa A woman who fell in love with Zeus, who came to her in the form of a bull

Fates Three goddesses who determine human destiny

Fortuna The goddess of fortune and luck

Gorgons Three sisters with snakes for hair; their gaze turned all who met it into stone

Hades The underworld; also the Greek name for Pluto

Harpy A terrifying mythical creature that is half bird and half woman

Helen of Troy A beautiful woman whose supposed abduction by the prince of Troy angered her husband, a Greek king, and started the Trojan War; credited with being "the face that launched a thousand ships"

Hera The Greek equivalent of Juno

Hercules A legendary hero famous for his strength

Isis An Egyptian goddess

Janus The two-faced god of beginnings and endings

Juno The wife of Jupiter; goddess of marriage

Jupiter The king of the gods; god of thunder and the sky

Laocoön A Trojan priest who tried in vain to warn his people about the dangers of the Trojan horse

Luna The goddess of the moon

Lupa The she-wolf that nursed Romulus and his brother Remus

Mars The god of war

Medea The enchantress who helped Jason and the Argonauts find the Golden Fleece

Medusa A snake-haired Gorgon; looking at her face turned people to stone

Mercury The messenger god

Midas A legendary king with the power to turn whatever he touched to gold

Minerva The goddess of wisdom

Minotaur A monster with the head of a bull and body of a man

Nemean lion A giant lion with an impenetrable hide; killed by Hercules as one of his twelve labors

Neptune The god of the sea

Pegasus A white, winged horse belonging to Zeus

Perseus The legendary hero who slew the Gorgon Medusa

Pluto The god of Hades, the underworld

Proserpina The queen of the underworld

Remus One of the sons of Rhea Silvia; brother of Romulus

Rhea Silvia A Vestal Virgin; mother, by Mars, of the twins Romulus and Remus

Romulus The legendary founder of Rome

Scylla A sea monster in Homer's *Odyssey*; counterpart of Charybdis

Spes The goddess of hope

Tiberinus The god of the Tiber River, often called Father Tiber

Trojan horse A massive wooden horse presented as a gift to the besieged city of Troy by the attacking Greeks; hiding inside the horse, however, were Greek soldiers who, once the gift had passed through the gates, exited and destroyed the city

Venus The goddess of love

Veritas The goddess of truth

Vesta The goddess of the hearth and home

Vulcan The god of fire; blacksmith of the gods

Zeus The Greek equivalent of Jupiter

GLOSSARY OF LATIN
AND IMPORTANT TERMS AND PLACES

Aedes Vestae The sacred building that housed the sacred flame; that is, the Temple of Vesta

aeterna flamma The "eternal flame" of Vesta

Aquila The Eagle of Rome

atrium The central open hall or court of a Roman home, around which were arranged on all sides the house's various rooms

Attat! Latin expression of surprise, fear, etc.

augur Priest who interprets the will of the gods via the flight of birds

ave A word of greeting or farewell. When addressing more than one person the form *avete* was used.

Black Stone The Black Stone, or *Lapis Niger* in Latin, was a mysterious and revered stone block in the Roman Forum, a monument thought to date back to the earliest period of Roman history.

Bona Dea The "Good Goddess," whose rites were overseen by the Vestal Virgins

Campus Martius The Field of Mars

Campus Sceleratus The "Evil Field," where Vestals were buried alive

Capillata tree An ancient tree so-named because Vestals would hang their cut hair from it—*capillata* means "hairy, or having long hair" in Latin

captio The "seizure" ceremony, where a girl is taken as a Vestal

Caput Mundi "Capital of the world," meaning Rome

Carcer The notorious structure where prisoners were incarcerated

catamite A pubescent or adolescent boy kept by a man for sexual purposes

causarius A soldier discharged after being wounded in battle

chaste tree A small tree native to the Mediterranean that was considered sacred to the virginal goddess Vesta. Its fruit has long been believed to quell sexual desire.

Circus Maximus A large stadium in Rome that was used for chariot races, public games, mock battles, and gladiatorial combat

Curia The Senate house of Rome, located in the Roman Forum

divi filius Son of the Divine Julius Caesar (i.e. Octavian)

Divus Julius The Divine Julius Caesar

Domina The deferential name a slave would use with his or her female owner

Domine The deferential name a slave would use with his or her male owner

domus A Roman home

dormouse A special type of mouse eaten as a delicacy

Elysian Fields The afterlife: a beautiful space, for the good

Equus October The "October Horse" was an annual sacrifice to Mars on the ides of October

fatale monstrum A "deadly monster"

favissa Underground temple depositories where sacred items no longer in use were placed. The favissa of the Temple of Vesta was where ashes from the sacred fire were stored.

fibula A brooch or pin used to fasten clothing or a cloak: on Vestals, it secured the suffibulum

Flamen Dialis The high priest of Jupiter

Flamen Martialis The high priest of Mars

Fordicidia An annual fertility festival held in mid-April

forum a public square or commercial marketplace that often included important judicial, political, historical and/or religious structures

Forum Boarium Rome's cattle and animal forum near the Tiber River

Forum of Julius Caesar A forum built by Julius Caesar near the Forum Romanum; also known as Caesar's Forum

Forum Romanum The Roman Forum was a rectangular forum in the heart of Rome which contained many official and religious buildings, as well as monuments

Futuo! Literally, "I fuck"; used here as a vulgar expression

gladius A type of short sword; the primary sword of Roman foot soldiers

Gratias vobis ago, divine Jane, divina Vesta. A thank-you to the gods Janus and Vesta, this phrase was used at the end of a ritual or ceremony

haruspex [*pl.* haruspices] A person who reads the entrails of sacrificed animals

ides The middle of the month, which was considered to be the fifteenth day for "full" months and the thirteenth day for the shorter, or "hollow," ones

ignis inexstinctus The "inextinguishable fire" of Vesta

imperator The title given to a citizen, such as a magistrate or general, who held *imperium* (great governmental or military authority); later, this term became nearly synonymous with *emperor*

impluvium A shallow sunken pool in the atrium of a Roman house, where rainwater collected

incestum The legal charge against a Vestal who was suspected of having broken her vow of chastity

infula The ceremonial woolen headband worn by Vestals

Insanos deos! "Insane gods!"—an exclamation of dismay, disbelief, or bewilderment

insula [*pl.* insulae] A Roman apartment block

Ista quidem vis est! "Why, this is violence!"—the phrase Julius Caesar is said to have cried out when he was attacked and assassinated.

Iuppiter Jupiter, Father Jove, or Sky Father

jure divino An expression meaning "by divine law"

kalends The first day of the month

Lacus Curtius A deep and mysterious pit, chasm, or pool in the Roman Forum

lanista The manager, trainer, or owner of a gladiator or gladiatorial school

lararium A household shrine to the gods and ancestors

lectica A covered or enclosed couch-like mode of transport used by the upper classes and carried on the shoulders of slaves

lecticarius [*pl.* lecticarii] A man, typically a slave, who helped carry a *lectica*; a litter-bearer

Liberalia The annual celebration of Liber, god of wine, fertility, and freedom

lictor An officer who accompanied magistrates or important officials

litter A *lectica*; also used for a horse-drawn carriage that transported important people

Lupercalia An annual fertility festival honoring Lupa, the she-wolf that suckled Romulus and Remus

lustratio [*pl.* lustrationes] A ceremonial purification

lyre A stringed musical instrument not unlike a harp

Mala Fortuna! An exclamation meaning "Evil Fortuna!" or "Bad luck!"

manumission Release from slavery; the termination of a slave's servitude, at which point a slave becomes a freedman or freedwoman

Mare Nostrum The Roman name for the Mediterranean Sea

Mea dea! An exclamation meaning "My goddess!"

Mehercule! An exclamation meaning "By Hercules!"

mola salsa A ritual salted-flour mixture prepared by Vestals

palla A woman's shawl that was worn when out of the house and which could be pulled over her head

patera A shallow bowl that held libations

patria potestas The legal power that a man held over his household, including his wife and children

Pax Deorum The peaceful accord between humanity and the gods, which was ensured only by proper religious observance

penus The hidden innermost chamber in the Temple of Vesta, where sacred objects and important items were kept

Pontifex Maximus The chief priest of Rome

quaestio A secular tribunal

quaestor A public official; a position that could lead to a political career

Regia The building that served as the office of the Pontifex Maximus and which had been the home of the early kings

retiarius A type of gladiator that fought with a net and trident

Rex Sacrorum A high-ranking priest

Rostra A large, decorated speaker's platform in the Roman Forum

rudis A wooden sword given to a gladiator upon manumission

salve A word of greeting; when addressing more than one person, the form *salvete* was used.

scutum A type of Roman shield

secutor A type of gladiator that carried a shield and a short sword or dagger and was trained to fight a *retiarius*

seni crines A braided hairstyle worn by brides and Vestal Virgins

simpulum A long-handled ladle-like vessel that held libations

spina A low barrier wall that ran down the center of a circus. The Circus Maximus had a decorated spina with conical posts at each end, around which the horses and chariots turned

SPQR An initialism of the phrase *Senatus Populusque Romanus*—"the Senate and People of Rome"

stola A type of dress worn by married Roman women and Vestals

stultus A fool

suffibulum A short ceremonial veil worn by Vestal Virgins

tablinum The office of a Roman house, where business might be conducted

Tabularium A public office building in the Roman Forum

Tarpeian Rock A tall cliff overlooking the Forum that was used as an execution site: criminals were thrown from it

Tiberinalia The annual festival honoring Father Tiber, the god of the Tiber River

toga The traditional garment of adult male Roman citizens. The color of the toga's stripe or border denoted a man's status; for example, a reddish-purple stripe was reserved for high-status men, while a toga of solid purple could be worn only by the emperor. A dark-colored toga was worn for funerals and during periods of mourning.

toga virilis The common white or off-white woolen toga of adult male citizens

triclinium The dining room of a Roman house, furnished with couches for reclining on while eating and socializing

tunica A garment worn alone or under a toga or stola

Veneralia An annual religious festival to celebrate Venus

Vesta Aeterna "Eternal Vesta"

Vesta Felix Vesta, who brings good luck or fortune

Vesta Mater "Mother Vesta"

Vesta, permitte hanc actionem. An appeal meaning "Vesta, permit this action."

Vesta te purificat. "Vesta purifies you."

Vestalia An annual religious festival to celebrate Vesta

Vestalis Maxima The head, or high priestess, of the Vestal order

Vestam laudo. "I praise Vesta."

Virgo Vestalis A Vestal Virgin; one of six temple priestesses tasked with keeping the sacred flame of the goddess Vesta burning

vittae A type of ribbon or band worn in the hair; on Vestals, loops hung down over the shoulders

viva flamma The "living flame" of Vesta

Ancient Roman coin showing Vesta with sacrificial implements at sacred hearth.

Ancient Roman men's seal ring, with an image of Vesta (as worn by Quintus).

The Vestal Tuccia Carrying the Sieve by Hector Leroux.

Ancient Roman coin showing the Temple of Vesta and a voting urn. The *AC* stands for *absolve/condemn*—this depicts a case where a Vestal Virgin was accused of incestum and a vote was taken to determine her innocence or guilt.